BEATRIX

LECTOR HOUSE PUBLIC DOMAIN WORKS

BEATRIX

HONORE DE BALZAC,
KATHARINE PRESCOTT WORMELEY

ISBN: 978-93-90294-97-8

Published: -

LECTOR HOUSE LLP
E-MAIL: lectorpublishing@gmail.com

BEATRIX

BY

HONORE DE BALZAC

TRANSLATED BY
KATHARINE PRESCOTT WORMELEY

NOTE

It is somewhat remarkable that Balzac, dealing as he did with traits of character and the minute and daily circumstances of life, has never been accused of representing actual persons in the two or three thousand portraits which he painted of human nature.

In "The Great Man of the Provinces in Paris" some likenesses were imagined: Jules Janin in Etienne Lousteau, Armand Carrel in Michel Chrestien, and, possibly, Berryer in Daniel d'Arthez. But in the present volume, "Beatrix," he used the characteristics of certain persons, which were recognized and admitted at the time of publication. Mademoiselle des Touches (Camille Maupin) is George Sand in character, and the personal description of her, though applied by some to the famous Mademoiselle Georges, is easily recognized from Couture's drawing. Beatrix, Conti, and Claude Vignon are sketches of the Comtesse d'Agoult, Liszt, and the well-known critic Gustave Planche.

The opening scene of this volume, representing the manners and customs of the old Breton family, a social state existing no longer except in history, and the transition period of the vieille roche as it passed into the customs and ideas of the present century, is one of Balzac's remarkable and most famous pictures in the "Comedy of Human Life."

K.P.W.

CONTENTS

BEATRIX

CHAPTER I.

A BRETON TOWN AND MANSION

France, especially in Brittany, still possesses certain towns completely outside of the movement which gives to the nineteenth century its peculiar characteristics. For lack of quick and regular communication with Paris, scarcely connected by wretched roads with the sub-prefecture, or the chief city of their own province, these towns regard the new civilization as a spectacle to be gazed at; it amazes them, but they never applaud it; and, whether they fear or scoff at it, they continue faithful to the old manners and customs which have come down to them. Whoso would travel as a moral archaeologist, observing men instead of stones, would find images of the time of Louis XV. in many a village of Provence, of the time of Louis XIV. in the depths of Pitou, and of still more ancient times in the towns of Brittany. Most of these towns have fallen from states of splendor never mentioned by historians, who are always more concerned with facts and dates than with the truer history of manners and customs. The tradition of this splendor still lives in the memory of the people,—as in Brittany, where the native character allows no forgetfulness of things which concern its own land. Many of these towns were once the capitals of a little feudal State,—a county or duchy conquered by the crown or divided among many heirs, if the male line failed. Disinherited from active life, these heads became arms; and arms deprived of nourishment, wither and barely vegetate.

For the last thirty years, however, these pictures of ancient times are beginning to fade and disappear. Modern industry, working for the masses, goes on destroying the creations of ancient art, the works of which were once as personal to the consumer as to the artisan. Nowadays we have *products*, we no longer have *works*. Public buildings, monuments of the past, count for much in the phenomena of retrospection; but the monuments of modern industry are freestone quarries, saltpetre mines, cotton factories. A few more years and even these old cities will be transformed and seen no more except in the pages of this iconography.

One of the towns in which may be found the most correct likeness of the feudal ages is Guerande. The name alone awakens a thousand memories in the minds of painters, artists, thinkers who have visited the slopes on which this splendid jewel of feudality lies proudly posed to command the flux and reflux of the tides and the dunes,—the summit, as it were, of a triangle, at the corners of which are two other jewels not less curious: Croisic, and the village of Batz. There are no towns after Guerande except Vitre in the centre of Brittany, and Avignon in the south of France, which preserve so intact, to the very middle of our epoch, the type and form of the middle ages.

Guerande is still encircled with its doughty walls, its moats are full of water, its battlements entire, its loopholes unencumbered with vegetation; even ivy has never cast its mantle over the towers, square or round. The town has three gates, where may be seen the rings of the portcullises; it is entered by a drawbridge of iron-clamped wood, no longer raised but which could be raised at will. The mayoralty was blamed for having, in 1820, planted poplars along the banks of the moat to shade the promenade. It excused itself on the ground that the long and beautiful esplanade of the fortifications facing the dunes had been converted one hundred years earlier into a mall where the inhabitants took their pleasure beneath the elms.

The houses of the old town have suffered no change; and they have neither increased nor diminished. None have suffered upon their frontage from the hammer of the architect, the brush of the plasterer, nor have they staggered under the weight of added stories. All retain their primitive characteristics. Some rest on wooden columns which form arcades under which foot-passengers circulate, the floor planks bending beneath them, but never breaking. The houses of the merchants are small and low; their fronts are veneered with slate. Wood, now decaying, counts for much in the carved material of the window-casings and the pillars, above which grotesque faces look down, while shapes of fantastic beasts climb up the angles, animated by that great thought of Art, which in those old days gave life to inanimate nature. These relics, resisting change, present to the eye of painters those dusky tones and half-blurred features in which the artistic brush delights.

The streets are what they were four hundred years ago, — with one exception; population no longer swarms there; the social movement is now so dead that a traveller wishing to examine the town (as beautiful as a suit of antique armor) may walk alone, not without sadness, through a deserted street, where the mullioned windows are plastered up to avoid the window-tax. This street ends at a postern, flanked with a wall of masonry, beyond which rises a bouquet of trees planted by the hands of Breton nature, one of the most luxuriant and fertile vegetations in France. A painter, a poet would sit there silently, to taste the quietude which reigns beneath the well-preserved arch of the postern, where no voice comes from the life of the peaceful city, and where the landscape is seen in its rich magnificence through the loop-holes of the casemates once occupied by halberdiers and archers, which are not unlike the sashes of some belvedere arranged for a point of view.

It is impossible to walk about the place without thinking at every step of the habits and usages of long-past times; the very stones tell of them; the ideas of the middle ages are still there with all their ancient superstitions. If, by chance, a gendarme passes you, with his silver-laced hat, his presence is an anachronism against which your sense of fitness protests; but nothing is so rare as to meet a being or an object of the present time. There is even very little of the clothing of the day; and that little the inhabitants adapt in a way to their immutable customs, their unchangeable physiognomies. The public square is filled with Breton costumes, which artists flock to draw; these stand out in wonderful relief upon the scene around them. The whiteness of the linen worn by the *paludiers* (the name given to men who gather salt in the salt-marshes) contrasts vigorously with the blues and browns of the peasantry and the original and sacredly preserved jewelry of the women. These two classes, and that of the sailors in their jerkins and varnished leather caps are as distinct from one another as the castes of India, and still recognize the distance that parts them from the bourgeoisie, the nobility, and the clergy. All lines are clearly marked; there the revolutionary level found the masses too rugged and too hard to plane; its instrument would have been notched, if not broken. The character of immutability which science gives to zoological species is found in Breton human nature. Even now, after the Revolution of 1830, Guerande is still a town apart, essentially Breton, fervently Catholic, silent, self-contained, — a place where modern ideas have little access.

Its geographical position explains this phenomenon. The pretty town overlooks a salt-marsh, the product of which is called throughout Brittany the Guerande salt, to which many Bretons attribute the excellence of their butter and their sardines. It is connected with the rest of France by two roads only: that coming from Savenay, the arrondissement to which it belongs, which stops at Saint-Nazaire; and a second road, leading from Vannes, which connects it with the Morbihan. The arrondissement road establishes communication by land, and from Saint-Nazaire by water, with Nantes. The land road is used only by government; the more rapid and more frequented way being by water from Saint-Nazaire. Now, between this village and Guerande is a distance of eighteen miles, which the mail-coach does not serve, and for good reason; not three coach passengers a year would pass over it.

These, and other obstacles, little fitted to encourage travellers, still exist. In the first place, government is slow in its proceedings; and next, the inhabitants of the region put up readily enough with difficulties which separate them from the rest of France. Guerande, therefore, being at the extreme end of the continent, leads nowhere, and no one comes there. Glad to be ignored, she thinks and cares about herself only. The immense product of her salt-marshes, which pays a tax of not less than a million to the Treasury, is chiefly managed at Croisic, a peninsular village which communicates with Guerande over quicksands, which efface during the night the tracks made by day, and also by boats which cross the arm of the sea that makes the port of Croisic.

This fascinating little town is therefore the Herculaneum of feudality, less its winding sheet of lava. It is afoot, but not living; it has no other ground of existence except that it has not been demolished. If you reach Guerande from Croisic, after crossing a dreary landscape of salt-marshes, you will experience a strong sensation at sight of that vast fortification, which is still as good as ever. If you come to it by Saint-Nazaire, the picturesqueness of its position and the naive grace of its environs will please you no less. The country immediately surrounding it is ravishing; the hedges are full of flowers, honeysuckles, roses, box, and many enchanting plants. It is like an English garden, designed by some great architect. This rich, coy nature, so untrodden, with all the grace of a bunch of violets or a lily of the valley in the glade of a forest, is framed by an African desert banked by the ocean, — a desert without a tree, an herb, a bird; where, on sunny days, the laboring *paludiers*, clothed in white and scattered among those melancholy swamps where the salt is made, remind us of Arabs in their burrows.

Thus Guerande bears no resemblance to any other place in France. The town produces somewhat the same effect upon the mind as a sleeping-draught upon the body. It is silent as Venice. There is no other public conveyance than the springless wagon of a carrier who carries travellers, merchandise, and occasionally letters from Saint-Nazaire to Guerande and *vice versa*. Bernus, the carrier, was, in 1829, the factotum of this large community. He went and came when he pleased; all the country knew him; and he did the errands of all. The arrival of a carriage in Guerande, that of a lady or some invalid going to Croisic for sea-bathing (thought to have greater virtue among those rocks than at Boulogne or Dieppe) is still an immense event. The peasants come in on horseback, most of them with commodities for barter in sacks. They are induced to do so (and so are the *paludiers*) by the necessity of purchasing the jewels distinctive of their caste which are given to all Breton brides, and the white linen, or cloth for their clothing.

For a circuit ten miles round, Guerande is always GUERANDE,—the illustrious town where the famous treaty was signed in 1365, the key of the coast, which may boast, not less than the village of Batz, of a splendor now lost in the night of time. The jewels, linen, cloth, ribbon, and hats are made elsewhere, but to those who buy them they are from Guerande and nowhere else. All artists, and even certain bourgeois, who come to Guerande feel, as they do at Venice, a desire (soon forgotten) to end their days amid its peace and silence, walking in fine weather along the beautiful mall which surrounds the town from gate to gate on the side toward the sea. Sometimes the image of this town arises in the temple of memory; she enters, crowned with her towers, clasped with her girdle; her flower-strewn robe floats onward, the golden mantle of her dunes enfolds her, the fragrant breath of her briony paths, filled with the flowers of each passing season, exhales at every step; she fills your mind, she calls to you like some enchanting woman whom you have met in other climes and whose presence still lingers in a fold of your heart.

Near the church of Guerande stands a mansion which is to the town what the town is to the region, an exact image of the past, the symbol of a grand thing destroyed,—a poem, in short. This mansion belongs to the noblest family of the province; to the du Guaisnics, who, in the times of the du Guesclins, were as superior to the latter in antiquity and fortune as the Trojans were to the Romans. The Guaisqlains (the name is also spelled in the olden time du Glaicquin), from which comes du Guesclin, issued from the du Guaisnics.

Old as the granite of Brittany, the Guaisnics are neither Frenchmen nor Gauls,—they are Bretons; or, to be more exact, they are Celts. Formerly, they must have been Druids, gathering mistletoe in the sacred forests and sacrificing men upon their dolmens. Useless to say what they were! To-day this race, equal to the Rohans without having deigned to make themselves princes, a race which was powerful before the ancestors of Hugues Capet were ever heard of, this family, pure of all alloy, possesses two thousand francs a year, its mansion in Guerande, and the little castle of Guaisnic. All the lands belonging to the barony of Guaisnic, the first in Brittany, are pledged to farmers, and bring in sixty thousand francs a year, in spite of ignorant culture. The du Gaisnics remain the owners of these lands although they receive none of the revenues, for the reason that for the last two hundred years they have been unable to pay off the money advanced upon them. They are in the position of the crown of France towards its *engagistes* (tenants of crown-lands) before the year 1789. Where and when could the barons obtain the million their farmers have advanced to them? Before 1789 the tenure of the fiefs subject to the castle of Guaisnic was still worth fifty thousand francs a year; but a vote of the National Assembly suppressed the seigneurs' dues levied on inheritance.

In such a situation this family — of absolutely no account in France, and which would be a subject of laughter in Paris, were it known there — is to Guerande the whole of Brittany. In Guerande the Baron du Guaisnic is one of the great barons of France, a man above whom there is but one man, — the King of France, once elected ruler. To-day the name of du Guaisnic, full of Breton significances (the roots of which will be found explained in "The Chouans") has been subjected to the same alteration which disfigures that of du Guaisqlain. The tax-gatherer now writes the name, as do the rest of the world, du Guenic.

At the end of a silent, damp, and gloomy lane may be seen the arch of a door, or rather gate, high enough and wide enough to admit a man on horseback, — a circumstance which proves of itself that when this building was erected carriages did not exist. The arch, supported by two jambs, is of granite. The gate, of oak, rugged as the bark of the tree itself, is studded with enormous nails placed in geometric figures. The arch is semicircular. On it are carved the arms of the Guaisnics as clean-cut and clear as though the sculptor had just laid down his chisel. This escutcheon would delight a lover of the heraldic art by a simplicity which proves the pride and the antiquity of the family. It is as it was in the days when the crusaders of the Christian world invented these symbols by which to recognize each other; the Guaisnics have never had it quartered; it is always itself, like that of the house of France, which connoisseurs find inescutcheoned in the shields of many of the old families. Here it is, such as you may see it still at Guerande: Gules, a hand proper gonfaloned ermine, with a sword argent in pale, and the terrible motto, FAC. Is not that a grand and noble thing? The circlet of a baronial coronet surmounts this simple escutcheon, the vertical lines of which, used in carving to represent gules, are clear as ever. The artist has given I know not what proud, chivalrous turn to the hand. With what vigor it holds the sword which served but recently the present family!

If you go to Guerande after reading this history you cannot fail to quiver when you see that blazon. Yes, the most confirmed republican would be moved by the fidelity, the nobleness, the grandeur hidden in the depths of that dark lane. The du Guaisnics did well yesterday, and they are ready to do well to-morrow. To DO is the motto of chivalry. "You did well in the battle" was the praise of the Connetable *par excellence,* the great du Guesclin who drove the English for a time from France. The depth of this carving, which has been protected from the weather by the projecting edges of the arch, is in keeping with the moral depth of the motto in the soul of this family. To those who know the Guaisnics this fact is touching.

The gate when open gives a vista into a somewhat vast court-yard, on the right of which are the stables, on the left the kitchen and offices. The house is build of freestone from cellar to garret. The facade on the court-yard has a portico with a double range of steps, the wall of which is covered with vestiges of carvings now effaced by time, but in which the eye of an antiquary can still make out in the centre of the principal mass the Hand bearing the sword. The granite steps are now disjointed, grasses have forced their way with little flowers and mosses through the fissures between the stones which centuries have displaced without however lessening their solidity. The door of the house must have had a charming character. As far as the relics of the old designs allow us to judge, it was done by an artist of the great Venetian school of the thirteenth century. Here is a mixture, still visible, of the Byzantine and the Saracenic. It is crowned with a circular pediment, now wreathed with vegetation, — a bouquet, rose, brown, yellow, or blue, according to the season. The door, of oak, nail-studded, gives entrance to a noble hall, at the end of which is another door, opening upon another portico which leads to the garden.

This hall is marvellously well preserved. The panelled wainscot, about three feet high, is of chestnut. A magnificent Spanish leather with figures in relief, the gilding now peeled off or reddened, covers the walls. The ceiling is of wooden boards artistically joined and painted and gilded. The gold is scarcely noticeable; it is in the same condition as that of the Cordova leather, but a few red flowers and the green foliage can be distinguished. Perhaps a thorough cleaning might bring out paintings like those discovered on the plank ceilings of Tristan's house at Tours. If so, it would prove that those planks were placed or restored in the reign of Louis XI. The chimney-piece is enormous, of carved stone, and within it are gigantic andirons in wrought-iron of precious workmanship. It could hold a cart-load of wood. The furniture of this hall is wholly of oak, each article bearing upon it the arms of the family. Three English guns equally suitable for chase or war, three sabres, two game-bags, the utensils of a huntsman and a fisherman hang from nails upon the wall.

On one side is a dining-room, which connects with the kitchen by a door cut through a corner tower. This tower corresponds in the design of the facade toward the court-yard with another tower at the opposite corner, in which is a spiral staircase leading to the two upper stories.

The dining-room is hung with tapestries of the fourteenth century; the style and the orthography of the inscription on the banderols beneath each figure prove their age, but being, as they are, in the naive language of the *fabliaux*, it is impossible to transcribe them here. These tapestries, well preserved in those parts where light has scarcely penetrated, are framed in bands of oak now black as ebony. The ceiling has projecting rafters enriched with foliage which is varied for each rafter; the space between them is filled with planks painted blue, on which twine garlands of golden flowers. Two old buffers face each other; on their shelves, rubbed with Breton persistency by Mariotte the cook, can be seen, as in the days when kings were as poor in 1200 as the du Guaisnics are in 1830, four old goblets, an ancient embossed soup-tureen, and two salt-cellars, all of silver; also many pewter plates and many pitchers of gray and blue pottery, bearing arabesque designs and the arms of the du Guaisnics, covered by hinged pewter lids. The chimney-piece is modernized. Its condition proves that the family has lived in this room for the last century. It is of carved stone in the style of the Louis XV. period, and is ornamented with a mirror, let in to the back with gilt beaded moulding. This anachronism, to which the family is indifferent, would grieve a poet. On the mantel-shelf, covered with red velvet, is a tall clock of tortoise-shell inlaid with brass, flanked on each side with a silver candelabrum of singular design. A large square table, with solid legs, fills the centre of this room; the chairs are of turned wood covered with tapestry. On a round table supported by a single leg made in the shape of a vine-shoot, which stands before a window looking into the garden, is a lamp of an odd kind. This lamp has a common glass globe, about the size of an ostrich egg, which is fastened into a candle-stick by a glass tube. Through a hole at the top of the globe issues a wick which passes through a sort of reed of brass, drawing the nut-oil held in the globe through its own length coiled like a tape-worm in a surgeon's phial. The windows which look into the garden, like those that look upon the court-yard, are mullioned in stone with hexagonal leaded panes, and are draped by curtains, with heavy valances and stout cords, of an ancient stuff of crimson silk with gold reflections, called in former days either brocatelle or small brocade.

On each of the two upper stories of the house there are but two rooms. The first is the bedroom of the head of the family, the second is that of the children. Guests were lodged in chambers beneath the roof. The servants slept above the kitchens and stables. The pointed roof, protected with lead at its angles and edges, has a noble pointed window on each side, one looking down upon the court-yard, the other on the garden. These windows, rising almost to the level of the roof, have slender, delicate casings, the carvings of which have crumbled under the salty vapors of the atmosphere. Above the arch of each window with its crossbars of stone, still grinds, as it turns, the vane of a noble.

Let us not forget a precious detail, full of naivete, which will be of value in the eyes of an archaeologist. The tower in which the spiral staircase goes up is placed at the corner of a great gable wall in which there is no window. The staircase comes down to a little arched door, opening upon a gravelled yard which separates the house from the stables. This tower is repeated on the garden side by another of five sides, ending in a cupola in which is a bell-turret, instead of being roofed, like the sister-tower, with a pepper-pot. This is how those charming architects varied the symmetry of their sky-lines. These towers are connected on the level of the first floor by a stone gallery, supported by what we must call brackets, each ending in a grotesque human head. This gallery has a balustrade of exquisite workmanship. From the gable above depends a stone dais like those that crown the statues of saints at the portal of churches. Can you not see a woman walking in the morning along this balcony and gazing over Guerande at the sunshine, where it gilds the sands and shimmers on the breast of Ocean? Do you not admire that gable wall flanked at its angles with those varied towers? The opposite gable of the Guaisnic mansion adjoins the next house. The harmony so carefully sought by the architects of those days is maintained in the facade looking on the court-yard by the tower which communicates between the dining-room and the kitchen, and is the same as the staircase tower, except that it stops at the first upper story and its summit is a small open dome, beneath which stands a now blackened statue of Saint Calyste.

The garden is magnificent for so old a place. It covers half an acre of ground, its walls are all espaliered, and the space within is divided into squares for vegetables, bordered with cordons of fruit-trees, which the man-of-all-work, named Gasselin, takes care of in the intervals of grooming the horses. At the farther end of the garden is a grotto with a seat in it; in the middle, a sun-dial; the paths are gravelled. The facade on the garden side has no towers corresponding to those on the court-yard; but a slender spiral column rises from the ground to the roof, which must in former days have borne the banner of the family, for at its summit may still be seen an iron socket, from which a few weak plants are straggling. This detail, in harmony with the vestiges of sculpture, proves to a practised eye that the mansion was built by a Venetian architect. The graceful staff is like a signature revealing Venice, chivalry, and the exquisite delicacy of the thirteenth century. If any doubts remained on this point, a feature of the ornamentation would dissipate them. The trefoils of the hotel du Guaisnic have four leaves instead of three. This difference plainly indicates the Venetian school depraved by its commerce with the East, where the semi-Saracenic architects, careless of the great Catholic thought, give four leaves to clover, while Christian art is faithful to the Trinity. In this respect Venetian art becomes heretical.

If this ancient dwelling attracts your imagination, you may perhaps ask yourself why such miracles of art are not renewed in the present day. Because to-day mansions are sold, pulled down, and the ground they stood on turned into streets. No one can be sure that the next generation will possess the paternal dwelling; homes are no more than inns; whereas in former times when a dwelling was built men worked, or thought they worked, for a family in perpetuity. Hence the grandeur of these houses. Faith in self, as well as faith in God, did prodigies.

As for the arrangement of the upper rooms they may be imagined after this description of the ground-floor, and after reading an account of the manners, customs, and physiognomy of the family. For the last fifty years the du Guaisnics have received their friends in the two rooms just described, in which, as in the court-yard and the external accessories of the building, the spirit, grace, and candor of the old and noble Brittany still survives. Without the topography and description of the town, and without this minute depicting of the house, the surprising figures of the family might be less understood. Therefore the frames have preceded the portraits. Every one is aware that things influence beings. There are public buildings whose effect is visible upon the persons living in their neighborhood. It would be difficult indeed to be irreligious in the shadow of a cathedral like that of Bourges. When the soul is everywhere reminded of its destiny by surrounding images, it is less easy to fail of it. Such was the thought of our immediate grandfathers, abandoned by a generation which was soon to have no signs and no distinctions, and whose manners and morals were to change every decade. If you do not now expect to find the Baron du Guaisnic sword in hand, all here written would be falsehood.

CHAPTER II.

THE BARON, HIS WIFE, AND SISTER

Early in the month of May, in the year 1836, the period when this scene opens, the family of Guenic (we follow henceforth the modern spelling) consisted of Monsieur and Madame du Guenic, Mademoiselle du Guenic the baron's elder sister, and an only son, aged twenty-one, named, after an ancient family usage, Gaudebert-Calyste-Louis. The father's name was Gaudebert-Calyste-Charles. Only the last name was ever varied. Saint Gaudebert and Saint Calyste were forever bound to protect the Guenics.

The Baron du Guenic had started from Guerande the moment that La Vendee and Brittany took arms; he fought through the war with Charette, with Cathelineau, La Rochejaquelein, d'Elbee, Bonchamps, and the Prince de Loudon. Before starting he had, with a prudence unique in revolutionary annals, sold his whole property of every kind to his elder and only sister, Mademoiselle Zephirine du Guenic. After the death of all those heroes of the West, the baron, preserved by a miracle from ending as they did, refused to submit to Napoleon. He fought on till 1802, when being at last defeated and almost captured, he returned to Guerande, and from Guerande went to Croisic, whence he crossed to Ireland, faithful to the ancient Breton hatred for England.

The people of Guerande feigned utter ignorance of the baron's existence. In the whole course of twenty years not a single indiscreet word was ever uttered. Mademoiselle du Guenic received the rents and sent them to her brother by fishermen. Monsieur du Guenic returned to Guerande in 1813, as quietly and simply as if he had merely passed a season at Nantes. During his stay in Dublin the old Breton, despite his fifty years, had fallen in love with a charming Irish woman, daughter of one of the noblest and poorest families of that unhappy kingdom. Fanny O'Brien was then twenty-one years old. The Baron du Guenic came over to France to obtain the documents necessary for his marriage, returned to Ireland, and, after about ten months (at the beginning of 1814), brought his wife to Guerande, where she gave him Calyste on the very day that Louis XVIII. landed at Calais,—a circumstance which explains the young man's final name of Louis.

The old and loyal Breton was now a man of seventy-three; but his long-continued guerilla warfare with the Republic, his exile, the perils of his five crossings through a turbulent sea in open boats, had weighed upon his head, and he looked a hundred; therefore, at no period had the chief of the house of Guenic been more in keeping with the worn-out grandeur of their dwelling, built in the days when a court reigned at Guerande.

Monsieur du Guenic was a tall, straight, wiry, lean old man. His oval face was lined with innumerable wrinkles, which formed a net-work over his cheek-bones and above his eyebrows, giving to his face a resemblance to those choice old men whom Van Ostade, Rembrandt, Mieris, and Gerard Dow so loved to paint, in pictures which need a microscope to be fully appreciated. His countenance might be said to be sunken out of sight beneath those innumerable wrinkles, produced by a life in the open air and by the habit of watching his country in the full light of the sun from the rising of that luminary to the sinking of it. Nevertheless, to an observer enough remained of the imperishable forms of the human face which appealed to the soul, even though the eye could see no more than a lifeless head. The firm outline of the face, the shape of the brow, the solemnity of the lines, the rigidity of the nose, the form of the bony structure which wounds alone had slightly altered,—all were signs of intrepidity without calculation, faith without reserve, obedience without discussion, fidelity without compromise, love without inconstancy. In him, the Breton granite was made man.

The baron had no longer any teeth. His lips, once red, now violet, and backed by hard gums only (with which he ate the bread his wife took care to soften by folding it daily in a damp napkin), drew inward to the mouth with a sort of grin, which gave him an expression both threatening and proud. His chin seemed to seek his nose; but in that nose, humped in the middle, lay the signs of his energy and his Breton resistance. His skin, marbled with red blotches appearing through his wrinkles, showed a powerfully sanguine temperament, fitted to resist fatigue and to preserve him, as no doubt it did, from apoplexy. The head was crowned with abundant hair, as white as silver, which fell in curls upon his shoulders. The face, extinguished, as we have said, in part, lived through the glitter of the black eyes in their brown orbits, casting thence the last flames of a generous and loyal soul. The eyebrows and lashes had disappeared; the skin, grown hard, could not unwrinkle. The difficulty of shaving had obliged the old man to let his beard grow, and the cut of it was fan-shaped. An artist would have admired beyond all else in this old lion of Brittany with his powerful shoulders and vigorous chest, the splendid hands of the soldier,—hands like those du Guesclin must have had, large, broad, hairy; hands that once had clasped the sword never, like Joan of Arc, to relinquish it until the royal standard floated in the cathedral of Rheims; hands that were often bloody from the thorns and furze of the Bocage; hands which had pulled an oar in the Marais to surprise the Blues, or in the offing to signal Georges; the hands of a guerilla, a cannoneer, a common solder, a leader; hands still white though the Bourbons of the Elder branch were again in exile. Looking at those hands attentively, one might have seen some recent marks attesting the fact that the Baron had recently joined MADAME in La Vendee. To-day that fact may be admitted. These hands were a living commentary on the noble motto to which no Guenic had proved recreant: *Fac!*

His forehead attracted attention by the golden tones of the temples, contrasting with the brown tints of the hard and narrow brow, which the falling off of the hair had somewhat broadened, giving still more majesty to that noble ruin. The countenance—a little material, perhaps, but how could it be otherwise?—presented, like all the Breton faces grouped about the baron, a certain savagery, a stolid calm which resembled the impassibility of the Huguenots; something, one might say, stupid, due perhaps to the utter repose which follows extreme fatigue, in which the animal nature alone is visible. Thought was rare. It seemed to be an effort; its seat was in the heart more than in the head; it led to acts rather than ideas. But, examining that grand old man with sustained observation, one could penetrate the mystery of this strange contradiction to the spirit of the century. He had faiths, sentiments, inborn so to speak, which allowed him to dispense with thought. His duty, life had taught him. Institutions and religion thought for him. He reserved his mind, he and his kind, for action, not dissipating it on useless things which occupied the minds of other persons. He drew his thought from his heart like his sword from its scabbard, holding it aloft in his ermined hand, as on his scutcheon, shining with sincerity. That secret once penetrated, all is clear. We can comprehend the depth of convictions that are not thoughts, but living principles,—clear, distinct, downright, and as immaculate as the ermine itself. We understand that sale made to his sister before the war; which provided for all, and faced all, death, confiscation, exile. The beauty of the character of these two old people (for the sister lived only for and by the brother) cannot be understood to its full extent by the right of the selfish morals, the uncertain aims, and the inconstancy of this our epoch. An archangel, charged with the duty of penetrating to the inmost recesses of their hearts could not have found one thought of personal interest. In 1814, when the rector of Guerande suggested to the baron that he should go to Paris and claim his recompense from the triumphant Bourbons, the old sister, so saving and miserly for the household, cried out:—

"Oh, fy! does my brother need to hold out his hand like a beggar?"

"It would be thought I served a king from interest," said the old man. "Besides, it is for him to remember. Poor king! he must be weary indeed of those who harass him. If he gave them all France in bits, they still would ask."

This loyal servant, who had spent his life and means on Louis XVIII., received the rank of colonel, the cross of Saint-Louis, and a stipend of two thousand francs a year.

"The king did remember!" he said when the news reached him.

No one undeceived him. The gift was really made by the Duc de Feltre. But, as an act of gratitude to the king, the baron sustained a siege at Guerande against the forces of General Travot. He refused to surrender the fortress, and when it was absolutely necessary to evacuate it he escaped into the woods with a band of Chouans, who continued armed until the second restoration of the Bourbons. Guerande still treasures the memory of that siege.

We must admit that the Baron du Guenic was illiterate as a peasant. He could read, write, and do some little ciphering; he knew the military art and heraldry, but, excepting always his prayer-book, he had not read three volumes in the course of his life. His clothing, which is not an insignificant point, was invariably the same; it consisted of stout shoes, ribbed stockings, breeches of greenish velveteen, a cloth waistcoat, and a loose coat with a collar, from which hung the cross of Saint-Louis. A noble serenity now reigned upon that face where, for the last year or so, sleep, the forerunner of death, seemed to be preparing him for rest eternal. This constant somnolence, becoming daily more and more frequent, did not alarm either his wife, his blind sister, or his friends, whose medical knowledge was of the slightest. To them these solemn pauses of a life without reproach, but very weary, were naturally explained: the baron had done his duty, that was all.

In this ancient mansion the absorbing interests were the fortunes of the dispossessed Elder branch. The future of the exiled Bourbons, that of the Catholic religion, the influence of political innovations on Brittany were the exclusive topics of conversation in the baron's family. There was but one personal interest mingled with these most absorbing ones: the attachment of all for the only son, for Calyste, the heir, the sole hope of the great name of the du Guenics.

The old Vendean, the old Chouan, had, some years previously, a return of his own youth in order to train his son to those manly exercises which were proper for a gentleman liable to be summoned at any moment to take arms. No sooner was Calyste sixteen years of age than his father accompanied him to the marshes and the forest, teaching him through the pleasures of the chase the rudiments of war, preaching by example, indifferent to fatigue, firm in his saddle, sure of his shot whatever the game might be,—deer, hare, or a bird on the wing,—intrepid in face of obstacles, bidding his son follow him into danger as though he had ten other sons to take Calyste's place.

So, when the Duchesse de Berry landed in France to conquer back the kingdom for her son, the father judged it right to take his boy to join her, and put in practice the motto of their ancestors. The baron started in the dead of night, saying no word to his wife, who might perhaps have weakened him; taking his son under fire as if to a fete, and Gasselin, his only vassal, who followed him joyfully. The three men of the family were absent for three months without sending news of their whereabouts to the baroness, who never read the "Quotidienne" without trembling from line to line, nor to his old blind sister, heroically erect, whose nerve never faltered for an instance as she heard that paper read. The three guns hanging to the walls had therefore seen service recently. The baron, who considered the enterprise useless, left the region before the affair of La Penissiere, or the house of Guenic would probably have ended in that hecatomb.

When, on a stormy night after parting from MADAME, the father, son, and servant returned to the house in Guerande, they took their friends and the baroness and old Mademoiselle du Guenic by surprise, although the latter, by the exercise of senses with which the blind are gifted, recognized the steps of the three men in the little lane leading to the house. The baron looked round upon the circle of his anxious friends, who were seated beside the little table lighted by the antique lamp, and said in a tremulous voice, while Gasselin replaced the three guns and the sabres in their places, these words of feudal simplicity:—

"The barons did not all do their duty."

Then, having kissed his wife and sister, he sat down in his old arm-chair and ordered supper to be brought for his son, for Gasselin, and for himself. Gasselin had thrown himself before Calyste on one occasion, to protect him, and received the cut of a sabre on his shoulder; but so simple a matter did it seem that even the women scarcely thanked him. The baron and his guests uttered neither curses nor complaints of their conquerors. Such silence is a trait of Breton character. In forty years no one ever heard a word of contumely from the baron's lips about his adversaries. It was for them to do their duty as he did his. This utter silence is the surest indication of an unalterable will.

This last effort, the flash of an energy now waning, had caused the present weakness and somnolence of the old man. The fresh defeat and exile of the Bourbons, as miraculously driven out as miraculously re-established, were to him a source of bitter sadness.

About six o'clock on the evening of the day on which this history begins, the baron, who, according to ancient custom, had finished dining by four o'clock, fell asleep as usual while his wife was reading to him the "Quotidienne." His head rested against the back of the arm-chair which stood beside the fireplace on the garden side.

Near this gnarled trunk of an ancient tree, and in front of the fireplace, the baroness, seated on one of the antique chairs, presented the type of those adorable women who exist in England, Scotland, or Ireland only. There alone are born those milk-white creatures with golden hair the curls of which are wound by the hands of angels, for the light of heaven seems to ripple in their silken spirals swaying to the breeze. Fanny O'Brien was one of those sylphs, — strong in tenderness, invincible under misfortune, soft as the music of her voice, pure as the azure of her eyes, of a delicate, refined beauty, blessed with a skin that was silken to the touch and caressing to the eye, which neither painter's brush nor written word can picture. Beautiful still at forty-two years of age, many a man would have thought it happiness to marry her as she looked at the splendors of that autumn coloring, redundant in flowers and fruit, refreshed and refreshing with the dews of heaven.

The baroness held the paper in the dimpled hand, the fingers of which curved slightly backward, their nails cut square like those of an antique statue. Half lying, without ill-grace or affectation, in her chair, her feet stretched out to warm them, she was dressed in a gown of black velvet, for the weather was now becoming chilly. The corsage, rising to the throat, moulded the splendid contour of the shoulders and the rich bosom which the suckling of her son had not deformed. Her hair was worn in *ringlets*, after the English fashion, down her cheeks; the rest was simply twisted to the crown of her head and held there with a tortoise-shell comb. The color, not undecided in tone as other blond hair, sparkled to the light like a filagree of burnished gold. The baroness always braided the short locks curling on the nape of her neck — which are a sign of race. This tiny braid, concealed in the mass of hair always carefully put up, allowed the eye to follow with delight the undulating line by which her neck was set upon her shoulders. This little detail will show the care which she gave to her person; it was her pride to rejoice the eyes of the old baron. What a charming, delicate attention! When you see a woman displaying in her own home the coquetry which most women spend on a single sentiment, believe me, that woman is as noble a mother as she is a wife; she is the joy and the flower of the home; she knows her obligations as a woman; in her soul, in her tenderness, you will find her outward graces; she is doing good in secret; she worships, she adores without a calculation of return; she loves her fellows, as she loves God,—for their own sakes. And so one might fancy that the Virgin of paradise, under whose care she lived, had rewarded the chaste girlhood and the sacred life of the old man's wife by surrounding her with a sort of halo which preserved her beauty from the wrongs of time. The alterations of that beauty Plato would have glorified as the coming of new graces. Her skin, so milk-white once, had taken the warm and pearly tones which painters adore. Her broad and finely modelled brow caught lovingly the light which played on its polished surface. Her eyes, of a turquoise blue, shone with unequalled sweetness; the soft lashes, and the slightly sunken temples inspired the spectator with I know not what mute melancholy. The nose, which was aquiline and thin, recalled the royal origin of the high-born woman. The pure lips, finely cut, wore happy smiles, brought there by loving-kindness inexhaustible. Her teeth were small and white; she had gained of late a slight embonpoint, but her delicate hips and slender waist were none the worse for it. The autumn of her beauty presented a few perennial flowers of her springtide among the richer blooms of summer. Her arms became more nobly rounded, her lustrous skin took a finer grain; the outlines of her form gained plenitude. Lastly and best of all, her open countenance, serene and slightly rosy, the purity of her blue eyes, that a look too eager might have wounded, expressed illimitable sympathy, the tenderness of angels.

At the other chimney-corner, in an arm-chair, the octogenarian sister, like in all points save clothes to her brother, sat listening to the reading of the newspaper and knitting stockings, a work for which sight is needless. Both eyes had cataracts; but she obstinately refused to submit to an operation, in spite of the entreaties of her sister-in-law. The secret reason of that obstinacy was known to herself only; she declared it was want of courage; but the truth was that she would not let her brother spend twenty-five louis for her benefit. That sum would have been so much the less for the good of the household.

These two old persons brought out in fine relief the beauty of the baroness. Mademoiselle Zephirine, being deprived of sight, was not aware of the changes which eighty years had wrought in her features. Her pale, hollow face, to which the fixedness of the white and sightless eyes gave almost the appearance of death, and three or four solitary and projecting teeth made menacing, was framed by a little hood of brown printed cotton, quilted like a petticoat, trimmed with a cotton ruche, and tied beneath the chin by strings which were always a little rusty. She wore a *cotillon*, or short skirt of coarse cloth, over a quilted petticoat (a positive mattress, in which were secreted double louis-d'ors), and pockets sewn to a belt which she unfastened every night and put on every morning like a garment. Her body was encased in the *casaquin* of Brittany, a species of spencer made of the same cloth as the *cotillon*, adorned with a collarette of many pleats, the washing of which caused the only dispute she ever had with her sister-in-law,—her habit being to change it only once a week. From the large wadded sleeves of the *casaquin* issued two withered but still vigorous arms, at the ends of which flourished her hands, their brownish-red color making the white arms look like poplar-wood. These hands, hooked or contracted from the habit of knitting, might be called a stocking-machine incessantly at work; the phenomenon would have been had they stopped. From time to time Mademoiselle du Guenic took a long knitting needle which she kept in the bosom of her gown, and passed it between her hood and her hair to poke or scratch her white locks. A stranger would have laughed to see the careless manner in which she thrust back the needle without the slightest fear of wounding herself. She was straight as a steeple. Her erect and imposing carriage might pass for one of those coquetries of old age which prove that pride is a necessary passion of life. Her smile was gay. She, too, had done her duty.

As soon as the baroness saw that her husband was asleep she stopped reading. A ray of sunshine, stretching from one window to the other, divided by a golden band the atmosphere of that old room and burnished the now black furniture. The light touched the carvings of the ceiling, danced on the time-worn chests, spread its shining cloth on the old oak table, enlivening the still, brown room, as Fanny's voice cast into the heart of her octogenarian blind sister a music as luminous and as cheerful as that ray of sunlight. Soon the ray took on the ruddy colors which, by insensible gradations, sank into the melancholy tones of twilight. The baroness also sank into a deep meditation, one of those total silences which her sister-in-law had noticed for the last two weeks, trying to explain them to herself, but making no inquiry. The old woman studied the causes of this unusual pre-occupation, as blind persons, on whose soul sound lingers like a divining echo, read books in which the pages are black and the letters white. Mademoiselle Zephirine, to whom the dark hour now meant nothing, continued to knit, and the silence at last became so deep that the clicking of her knitting-needles was plainly heard.

"You have dropped the paper, sister, but you are not asleep," said the old woman, slyly.

At this moment Mariotte came in to light the lamp, which she placed on a square table in front of the fire; then she fetched her distaff, her ball of thread, and a small stool, on which she seated herself in the recess of a window and began as usual to spin. Gasselin was still busy about the offices; he looked to the horses of the baron and Calyste, saw that the stable was in order for the night, and gave the two fine hunting-dogs their daily meal. The joyful barking of the animals was the last noise that awakened the echoes slumbering among the darksome walls of the ancient house. The two dogs and the two horses were the only remaining vestiges of the splendors of its chivalry. An imaginative man seated on the steps of the portico and letting himself fall into the poesy of the still living images of that dwelling, might have quivered as he heard the baying of the hounds and the trampling of the neighing horses.

Gasselin was one of those short, thick, squat little Bretons, with black hair and sun-browned faces, silent, slow, and obstinate as mules, but always following steadily the path marked out for them. He was forty-two years old, and had been twenty-five years in the household. Mademoiselle had hired him when he was fifteen, on hearing of the marriage and probable return of the baron. This retainer considered himself as part of the family; he had played with Calyste, he loved the horses and dogs of the house, and talked to them and petted them as though they were his own. He wore a blue linen jacket with little pockets flapping about his hips, waistcoat and trousers of the same material at all seasons, blue stockings, and stout hob-nailed shoes. When it was cold or rainy he put on a goat's-skin, after the fashion of his country.

Mariotte, who was also over forty, was as a woman what Gasselin was as a man. No team could be better matched,—same complexion, same figure, same little eyes that were lively and black. It is difficult to understand why Gasselin and Mariotte had never married; possibly it might have seemed immoral, they were so like brother and sister. Mariotte's wages were ninety francs a year; Gasselin's, three hundred. But thousands of francs offered to them elsewhere would not have induced either to leave the Guenic household. Both were under the orders of Mademoiselle, who, from the time of the war in La Vendee to the period of her brother's return, had ruled the house. When she learned that the baron was about to bring home a mistress, she had been moved to great emotion, believing that she must yield the sceptre of the household and abdicate in favor of the Baronne du Guenic, whose subject she was now compelled to be.

Mademoiselle Zephirine was therefore agreeably surprised to find in Fanny O'Brien a young woman born to the highest rank, to whom the petty cares of a poor household were extremely distasteful,—one who, like other fine souls, would far have preferred to eat plain bread rather than the choicest food if she had to prepare it for herself; a woman capable of accomplishing all the duties, even the most painful, of humanity, strong under necessary privations, but without courage for commonplace avocations. When the baron begged his sister in his wife's name to continue in charge of the household, the old maid kissed the baroness like a sister; she made a daughter of her, she adored her, overjoyed to be left in control of the household, which she managed rigorously on a system of almost inconceivable economy, which was never relaxed except for some great occasion, such as the lying-in of her sister, and her nourishment, and all that concerned Calyste, the worshipped son of the whole household.

Though the two servants were accustomed to this stern regime, and no orders need ever have been given to them, for the interests of their masters were greater in their minds than their own,—*were* their own in fact,—Mademoiselle Zephirine insisted on looking after everything. Her attention being never distracted, she knew, without going up to verify her knowledge, how large was the heap of nuts in the barn; and how many oats remained in the bin without plunging her sinewy arm into the depths of it. She carried at the end of a string fastened to the belt of her *casaquin*, a boatswain's whistle, with which she was wont to summon Mariotte by one, and Gasselin by two notes.

Gasselin's greatest happiness was to cultivate the garden and produce fine fruits and vegetables. He had so little work to do that without this occupation he would certainly have felt lost. After he had groomed his horses in the morning, he polished the floors and cleaned the rooms on the ground-floor, then he went to his garden, where weed or damaging insect was never seen. Sometimes Gasselin was observed motionless, bare-headed, under a burning sun, watching for a field-mouse or the terrible grub of the cockchafer; then, as soon as it was caught, he would rush with the joy of a child to show his masters the noxious beast that had occupied his mind for a week. He took pleasure in going to Croisic on fast-days, to purchase a fish to be had for less money there than at Guerande.

Thus no household was ever more truly one, more united in interests, more bound together than this noble family sacredly devoted to its duty. Masters and servants seemed made for one another. For twenty-five years there had been neither trouble nor discord. The only griefs were the petty ailments of the little boy, the only terrors were caused by the events of 1814 and those of 1830. If the same things were invariably done at the same hours, if the food was subjected to the regularity of times and seasons, this monotony, like that of Nature varied only by alterations of cloud and rain and sunshine, was sustained by the affection existing in the hearts of all,—the more fruitful, the more beneficent because it emanated from natural causes.

CHAPTER III.

THREE BRETON SILHOUETTES

When night had fairly fallen, Gasselin came into the hall and asked his master respectfully if he had further need of him.

"You can go out, or go to bed, after prayers," replied the baron, waking up, "unless Madame or my sister—"

The two ladies here made a sign of consent. Gasselin then knelt down, seeing that his masters rose to kneel upon their chairs; Mariotte also knelt before her stool. Mademoiselle du Guenic then said the prayer aloud. After it was over, some one rapped at the door on the lane. Gasselin went to open it.

"I dare say it is Monsieur le cure; he usually comes first," said Mariotte.

Every one now recognized the rector's foot on the resounding steps of the portico. He bowed respectfully to the three occupants of the room, and addressed them in phrases of that unctuous civility which priests are accustomed to use. To the rather absent-minded greeting of the mistress of the house, he replied by an ecclesiastically inquisitive look.

"Are you anxious or ill, Madame la baronne?" he asked.

"Thank you, no," she replied.

Monsieur Grimont, a man of fifty, of middle height, lost in his cassock, from which issued two stout shoes with silver buckles, exhibited above his hands a plump visage, and a generally white skin though yellow in spots. His hands were dimpled. His abbatial face had something of the Dutch burgomaster in the placidity of its complexion and its flesh tones, and of the Breton peasant in the straight black hair and the vivacity of the brown eyes, which preserved, nevertheless, a priestly decorum. His gaiety, that of a man whose conscience was calm and pure, admitted a joke. His manner had nothing uneasy or dogged about it, like that of many poor rectors whose existence or whose power is contested by their parishioners, and who instead of being, as Napoleon sublimely said, the moral leaders of the population and the natural justices of peace, are treated as enemies. Observing Monsieur Grimont as he marched through Guerande, the most irreligious of travellers would have recognized the sovereign of that Catholic town; but this same sovereign lowered his spiritual superiority before the feudal supremacy of the du Guenics. In their salon he was as a chaplain in his seigneur's house. In church, when he gave the benediction, his hand was always first stretched out toward the chapel belonging to the Guenics, where their mailed hand and their device were carved upon the key-stone of the arch.

"I thought that Mademoiselle de Pen-Hoel had already arrived," said the rector, sitting down, and taking the hand of the baroness to kiss it. "She is getting unpunctual. Can it be that the fashion of dissipation is contagious? I see that Monsieur le chevalier is again at Les Touches this evening."

"Don't say anything about those visits before Mademoiselle de Pen-Hoel," cried the old maid, eagerly.

"Ah! mademoiselle," remarked Mariotte, "you can't prevent the town from gossiping."

"What do they say?" asked the baroness.

"The young girls and the old women all say that he is in love with Mademoiselle des Touches."

"A lad of Calyste's make is playing his proper part in making the women love him," said the baron.

"Here comes Mademoiselle de Pen-Hoel," said Mariotte.

The gravel in the court-yard crackled under the discreet footsteps of the coming lady, who was accompanied by a page supplied with a lantern. Seeing this lad, Mariotte removed her stool to the great hall for the purpose of talking with him by the gleam of his rush-light, which was burned at the cost of his rich and miserly mistress, thus economizing those of her own masters.

This elderly demoiselle was a thin, dried-up old maid, yellow as the parchment of a Parliament record, wrinkled as a lake ruffled by the wind, with gray eyes, large prominent teeth, and the hands of a man. She was rather short, a little crooked, possibly hump-backed; but no one had ever been inquisitive enough to ascertain the nature of her perfections or her imperfections. Dressed in the same style as Mademoiselle du Guenic, she stirred an enormous quantity of petticoats and linen whenever she wanted to find one or other of the two apertures of her gown through which she reached her pockets. The strangest jingling of keys and money then echoed among her garments. She always wore, dangling from one side, the bunch of keys of a good housekeeper, and from the other her silver snuff-box, thimble, knitting-needles, and other implements that were also resonant. Instead of Mademoiselle Zephirine's wadded hood, she wore a green bonnet, in which she may have visited her melons, for it had passed, like them, from green to yellowish; as for its shape, our present fashions are just now bringing it back to Paris, after twenty years absence, under the name of Bibi. This bonnet was constructed under her own eye and by the hands of her nieces, out of green Florence silk bought at Guerande, and an old bonnet-shape, renewed every five years at Nantes,—for Mademoiselle de Pen-Hoel allowed her bonnets the longevity of a legislature. Her nieces also made her gowns, cut by an immutable pattern. The old lady still used the cane with the short hook that all women carried in the early days of Marie-Antoinette. She belonged to the very highest nobility of Brittany. Her arms bore the ermine of its ancient dukes. In her and in her sister the illustrious Breton house of the Pen-Hoels ended. Her younger sister had married a Kergarouet, who, in spite of the deep disapproval of the whole region, added the name of Pen-Hoel to his own and called himself the Vicomte de Kergarouet-Pen-Hoel.

"Heaven has punished him," said the old lady; "he has nothing but daughters, and the Kergarouet-Pen-Hoel name will be wiped out."

Mademoiselle de Pen-Hoel possessed about seven thousand francs a year from the rental of lands. She had come into her property at thirty-six years of age, and managed it herself, inspecting it on horseback, and displaying on all points the firmness of character which is noticeable in most deformed persons. Her avarice was admired by the whole country round, never meeting with the slightest disapproval. She kept one woman-servant and the page. Her yearly expenses, not including taxes, did not amount to over a thousand francs. Consequently, she was the object of the cajoleries of the Kergarouet-Pen-Hoels, who passed the winters at Nantes, and the summers at their estate on the banks of the Loire below l'Indret. She was supposed to be ready to leave her fortune and her savings to whichever of her nieces pleased her best. Every three months one or other of the four demoiselles de Kergarouet-Pen-Hoel, (the youngest of whom was twelve, and the eldest twenty years of age) came to spend a few days with her.

A friend of Zephirine du Guenic, Jacqueline de Pen-Hoel, brought up to adore the Breton grandeur of the du Guenics, had formed, ever since the birth of Calyste, the plan of transmitting her property to the chevalier by marrying him to whichever of her nieces the Vicomtesse de Kergarouet-Pen-Hoel, their mother, would bestow upon him. She dreamed of buying back some of the best of the Guenic property from the farmer *engagistes*. When avarice has an object it ceases to be a vice; it becomes a means of virtue; its privations are a perpetual offering; it has the grandeur of an intention beneath its meannesses. Perhaps Zephirine was in the secret of Jacqueline's intention. Perhaps even the baroness, whose whole soul was occupied by love for her son and tenderness for his father, may have guessed it as she saw with what wily perseverance Mademoiselle de Pen-Hoel brought with her her favorite niece, Charlotte de Kergarouet, now sixteen years of age. The rector, Monsieur Grimont, was certainly in her confidence; it was he who helped the old maid to invest her savings.

But Mademoiselle de Pen-Hoel might have had three hundred thousand francs in gold, she might have had ten times the landed property she actually possessed, and the du Guenics would never have allowed themselves to pay her the slightest attention that the old woman could construe as looking to her fortune. From a feeling of truly Breton pride, Jacqueline de Pen-Hoel, glad of the supremacy accorded to her old friend Zephirine and the du Guenics, always showed herself honored by her relations with Madame du Guenic and her sister-in-law. She even went so far as to conceal the sort of sacrifice to which she consented every evening in allowing her page to burn in the Guenic hall that singular gingerbread-colored candle called an *oribus* which is still used in certain parts of western France.

Thus this rich old maid was nobility, pride, and grandeur personified. At the moment when you are reading this portrait of her, the Abbe Grimont has just indiscreetly revealed that on the evening when the old baron, the young chevalier, and Gasselin secretly departed to join MADAME (to the terror of the baroness and the great joy of all Bretons) Mademoiselle de Pen-Hoel had given the baron ten thousand francs in gold,—an immense sacrifice, to which the abbe added another ten thousand, a tithe collected by him,—charging the old hero to offer the whole, in the name of the Pen-Hoels and of the parish of Guerande, to the mother of Henri V.

Mademoiselle de Pen-Hoel treated Calyste as if she felt that her intentions gave her certain rights over him; her plans seemed to authorize a supervision. Not that her ideas were strict in the matter of gallantry, for she had, in fact, the usual indulgence of the old women of the old school, but she held in horror the modern ways of revolutionary morals. Calyste, who might have gained in her estimation by a few adventures with Breton girls, would have lost it considerably had she seen him entangled in what she called innovations. She might have disinterred a little gold to pay for the results of a love-affair, but if Calyste had driven a tilbury or talked of a visit to Paris she would have thought him dissipated, and declared him a spendthrift. Impossible to say what she might not have done had she found him reading novels or an impious newspaper. To her, novel ideas meant the overthrow of succession of crops, ruin under the name of improvements and methods; in short, mortgaged lands as the inevitable result of experiments. To her, prudence was the true method of making your fortune; good management consisted in filling your granaries with wheat, rye, and flax, and waiting for a rise at the risk of being called a monopolist, and clinging to those grain-sacks obstinately. By singular chance she had often made lucky sales which confirmed her principles. She was thought to be maliciously clever, but in fact she was not quick-witted; on the other hand, being as methodical as a Dutchman, prudent as a cat, and persistent as a priest, those qualities in a region of routine like Brittany were, practically, the equivalent of intellect.

"Will Monsieur du Halga join us this evening?" asked Mademoiselle de Pen-Hoel, taking off her knitted mittens after the usual exchange of greetings.

"Yes, mademoiselle; I met him taking his dog to walk on the mall," replied the rector.

"Ha! then our *mouche* will be lively to-night. Last evening we were only four."

At the word *mouche* the rector rose and took from a drawer in one of the tall chests a small round basket made of fine osier, a pile of ivory counters yellow as a Turkish pipe after twenty years' usage, and a pack of cards as greasy as those of the custom-house officers at Saint-Nazaire, who change them only once in two weeks. These the abbe brought to the table, arranging the proper number of counters before each player, and putting the basket in the centre of the table beside the lamp, with infantine eagerness, and the manner of a man accustomed to perform this little service.

A knock at the outer gate given firmly in military fashion echoed through the stillness of the ancient mansion. Mademoiselle de Pen-Hoel's page went gravely to open the door, and presently the long, lean, methodically-clothed person of the Chevalier du Halga, former flag-captain to Admiral de Kergarouet, defined itself in black on the penumbra of the portico.

"Welcome, chevalier!" cried Mademoiselle de Pen-Hoel.

"The altar is raised," said the abbe.

The chevalier was a man in poor health, who wore flannel for his rheumatism, a black-silk skull-cap to protect his head from fog, and a spencer to guard his precious chest from the sudden gusts which freshen the atmosphere of Guerande. He always went armed with a gold-headed cane to drive away the dogs who paid untimely court to a favorite little bitch who usually accompanied him. This man, fussy as a fine lady, worried by the slightest *contretemps*, speaking low to spare his voice, had been in his early days one of the most intrepid and most competent officers of the old navy. He had won the confidence of de Suffren in the Indian Ocean, and the friendship of the Comte de Portenduere. His splendid conduct while flag-captain to Admiral Kergarouet was written in visible letters on his scarred face. To see him now no one would have imagined the voice that ruled the storm, the eye that compassed the sea, the courage, indomitable, of the Breton sailor.

The chevalier never smoked, never swore; he was gentle and tranquil as a girl, as much concerned about his little dog Thisbe and her caprices as though he were an elderly dowager. In this way he gave a high idea of his departed gallantry, but he never so much as alluded to the deeds of surpassing bravery which had astonished the doughty old admiral, Comte d'Estaing. Though his manner was that of an invalid, and he walked as if stepping on eggs and complained about the sharpness of the wind or the heat of the sun, or the dampness of the misty atmosphere, he exhibited a set of the whitest teeth in the reddest of gums, — a fact reassuring as to his maladies, which were, however, rather expensive, consisting as they did of four daily meals of monastic amplitude. His bodily frame, like that of the baron, was bony, and indestructibly strong, and covered with a parchment glued to his bones as the skin of an Arab horse on the muscles which shine in the sun. His skin retained the tawny color it received in India, whence, however, he did not bring back either facts or ideas. He had emigrated with the rest of his friends, lost his property, and was now ending his days with the cross of Saint-Louis and a pension of two thousand francs, as the legal reward of his services, paid from the fund of the Invalides de la Marine. The slight hypochondria which made him invent his imaginary ills is easily explained by his actual suffering during the emigration. He served in the Russian navy until the day when the Emperor Alexander ordered him to be employed against France; he then resigned and went to live at Odessa, near the Duc de Richelieu, with whom he returned to France. It was the duke who obtained for this glorious relic of the old Breton navy the pension which enabled him to live. On the death of Louis XVIII. he returned to Guerande, and became, after a while, mayor of the city.

The rector, the chevalier, and Mademoiselle de Pen-Hoel had regularly passed their evenings for the last fifteen years at the hotel de Guenic, where the other noble personages of the neighborhood also came. It will be readily understood that the du Guenics were at the head of the faubourg Saint-Germain of the old Breton province, where no member of the new administration sent down by the government was ever allowed to penetrate. For the last six years the rector coughed when he came to the crucial words, *Domine, salvum fac regem.* Politics were still at that point in Guerande.

CHAPTER IV.

A NORMAL EVENING

Mouche is a game played with five cards dealt to each player, and one turned over. The turned-over card is trumps. At each round the player is at liberty to run his chances or to abstain from playing his card. If he abstains he loses nothing but his own stake, for as long as there are no forfeits in the basket each player puts in a trifling sum. If he plays and wins a trick he is paid *pro rata* to the stake; that is, if there are five sous in the basket, he wins one sou. The player who fails to win a trick is made *mouche*; he has to pay the whole stake, which swells the basket for the next game. Those who decline to play throw down their cards during the game; but their play is held to be null. The players can exchange their cards with the remainder of the pack, as in ecarte, but only by order of sequence, so that the first and second players may, and sometimes do, absorb the remainder of the pack between them. The turned-over trump card belongs to the dealer, who is always the last; he has the right to exchange it for any card in his own hand. One powerful card is of more importance than all the rest; it is called Mistigris. Mistigris is the knave of clubs.

This game, simple as it is, is not lacking in interest. The cupidity natural to mankind develops in it; so does diplomatic wiliness; also play of countenance. At the hotel du Guenic, each of the players took twenty counters, representing five sous; which made the sum total of the stake for each game five farthings, a large amount in the eyes of this company. Supposing some extraordinary luck, fifty sous might be won,—more capital than any person in Guerande spent in the course of any one day. Consequently Mademoiselle de Pen-Hoel put into this game (the innocence of which is only surpassed in the nomenclature of the Academy by that of La Bataille) a passion corresponding to that of the hunters after big game. Mademoiselle Zephirine, who went shares in the game with the baroness, attached no less importance to it. To put up one farthing for the chance of winning five, game after game, was to this confirmed hoarder a mighty financial operation, into which she put as much mental action as the most eager speculator at the Bourse expends during the rise and fall of consols.

By a certain diplomatic convention, dating from September, 1825, when Mademoiselle de Pen-Hoel lost thirty-five sous, the game was to cease as soon as a person losing ten sous should express the wish to retire. Politeness did not allow the rest to give the retiring player the pain of seeing the game go on without him. But, as all passions have their Jesuitism, the chevalier and the baron, those wily politicians, had found a means of eluding this charter. When all the players but one were anxious to continue an exciting game, the daring sailor, du Halga, one of those rich fellows prodigal of costs they do not pay, would offer ten counters to Mademoiselle Zephirine or Mademoiselle Jacqueline, when either of them, or both of them, had lost their five sous, on condition of reimbursement in case they won. An old bachelor could allow himself such gallantries to the sex. The baron also offered ten counters to the old maids, but under the honest pretext of continuing the game. The miserly maidens accepted, not, however, without some pressing, as is the use and wont of maidens. But, before giving way to this vast prodigality the baron and the chevalier were required to have won; otherwise the offer would have been taken as an insult.

Mouche became a brilliant affair when a Demoiselle de Kergarouet was in transit with her aunt. We use the single name, for the Kergarouets had never been able to induce any one to call them Kergarouet-Pen-Hoel,—not even their servants, although the latter had strict orders so to do. At these times the aunt held out to the niece as a signal treat the *mouche* at the du Guenics. The girl was ordered to look amiable, an easy thing to do in the presence of the beautiful Calyste, whom the four Kergarouet young ladies all adored. Brought up in the midst of modern civilization, these young persons cared little for five sous a game, and on such occasions the stakes went higher. Those were evenings of great emotion to the old blind sister. The baroness would give her sundry hints by pressing her foot a certain number of times, according to the size of the stake it was safe to play. To play or not to play, if the basket were full, involved an inward struggle, where cupidity fought with fear. If Charlotte de Kergarouet, who was usually called giddy, was lucky in her bold throws, her aunt on their return home (if she had not won herself), would be cold and disapproving, and lecture the girl: she had too much decision in her character; a young person should never assert herself in presence of her betters; her manner of taking the basket and beginning to play was really insolent; the proper behavior of a young girl demanded much more reserve and greater modesty; etc.

It can easily be imagined that these games, carried on nightly for twenty years, were interrupted now and then by narratives of events in the town, or by discussions on public events. Sometimes the players would sit for half an hour, their cards held fan-shape on their stomachs, engaged in talking. If, as a result of these inattentions, a counter was missing from the basket, every one eagerly declared that he or she had put in their proper number. Usually the chevalier made up the deficiency, being accused by the rest of thinking so much of his buzzing ears, his chilly chest, and other symptoms of invalidism that he must have forgotten his stake. But no sooner did he supply the missing counter than Zephirine and Jacqueline were seized with remorse; they imagined that, possibly, they themselves had forgotten their stake; they believed—they doubted—but, after all, the chevalier was rich enough to bear such a trifling misfortune. These dignified and noble personages had the delightful pettiness of suspecting each other. Mademoiselle de Pen-Hoel would almost invariably accuse the rector of cheating when he won the basket.

"It is singular," he would reply, "that I never cheat except when I win the trick."

Often the baron would forget where he was when the talk fell on the misfortunes of the royal house. Sometimes the evening ended in a manner that was quite unexpected to the players, who all counted on a certain gain. After a certain number of games and when the hour grew late, these excellent people would be forced to separate without either loss or gain, but not without emotion. On these sad evenings complaints were made of *mouche* itself; it was dull, it was long; the players accused their *mouche* as Negroes stone the moon in the water when the weather is bad. On one occasion, after an arrival of the Vicomte and Vicomtesse de Kergarouet, there was talk of whist and boston being games of more interest than *mouche*. The baroness, who was bored by *mouche*, encouraged the innovation, and all the company—but not without reluctance—adopted it. But it proved impossible to make them really understand the new games, which, on the departure of the Kergarouets, were voted head-splitters, algebraic problems, and intolerably difficult to play. All preferred their *mouche*, their dear, agreeable *mouche*. *Mouche* accordingly triumphed over modern games, as all ancient things have ever triumphed in Brittany over novelties.

While the rector was dealing the cards the baroness was asking the Chevalier du Halga the same questions which she had asked him the evening before about his health. The chevalier made it a point of honor to have new ailments. Inquiries might be alike, but the nautical hero had singular advantages in the way of replies. To-day it chanced that his ribs troubled him. But here's a remarkable thing! never did the worthy chevalier complain of his wounds. The ills that were really the matter with him he expected, he knew them and he bore them; but his fancied ailments, his headaches, the gnawings in his stomach, the buzzing in his ears, and a thousand other fads and symptoms made him horribly uneasy; he posed as incurable,—and not without reason, for doctors up to the present time have found no remedy for diseases that don't exist.

"Yesterday the trouble was, I believe, in your legs," said the rector.

"It moves about," replied the chevalier.

"Legs to ribs?" asked Mademoiselle Zephirine.

"Without stopping on the way?" said Mademoiselle de Pen-Hoel, smiling.

The chevalier bowed gravely, making a negative gesture which was not a little droll, and proved to an observer that in his youth the sailor had been witty and loving and beloved. Perhaps his fossil life at Guerande hid many memories. When he stood, solemnly planted on his two heron-legs in the sunshine on the mall, gazing at the sea or watching the gambols of his little dog, perhaps he was living again in some terrestrial paradise of a past that was rich in recollections.

"So the old Duc de Lenoncourt is dead," said the baron, remembering the paragraph of the "Quotidienne," where his wife had stopped reading. "Well, the first gentleman of the Bedchamber followed his master soon. I shall go next."

"My dear, my dear!" said his wife, gently tapping the bony calloused hand of her husband.

"Let him say what he likes, sister," said Zephirine; "as long as I am above ground he can't be under it; I am the elder."

A gay smile played on the old woman's lips. Whenever the baron made reflections of that kind, the players and the visitors present looked at each other with emotion, distressed by the sadness of the king of Guerande; and after they had left the house they would say, as they walked home: "Monsieur du Guenic was sad to-night. Did you notice how he slept?" And the next day the whole town would talk of the matter. "The Baron du Guenic fails," was a phrase that opened the conversation in many houses.

"How is Thisbe?" asked Mademoiselle de Pen-Hoel of the chevalier, as soon as the cards were dealt.

"The poor little thing is like her master," replied the chevalier; "she has some nervous trouble, she goes on three legs constantly. See, like this."

In raising and crooking his arm to imitate the dog, the chevalier exposed his hand to his cunning neighbor, who wanted to see if he had Mistigris or the trump,—a first wile to which he succumbed.

"Oh!" said the baroness, "the end of Monsieur le cure's nose is turning white; he has Mistigris."

The pleasure of having Mistigris was so great to the rector—as it was to the other players—that the poor priest could not conceal it. In all human faces there is a spot where the secret emotions of the heart betray themselves; and these companions, accustomed for years to observe each other, had ended by finding out that spot on the rector's face: when he had Mistigris the tip of his nose grew pale.

"You had company to-day," said the chevalier to Mademoiselle de Pen-Hoel.

"Yes, a cousin of my brother-in-law. He surprised me by announcing the marriage of the Comtesse de Kergarouet, a Demoiselle de Fontaine."

"The daughter of 'Grand-Jacques,'" cried the chevalier, who had lived with the admiral during his stay in Paris.

"The countess is his heir; she has married an old ambassador. My visitor told me the strangest things about our neighbor, Mademoiselle des Touches,—so strange that I can't believe them. If they were true, Calyste would never be so constantly with her; he has too much good sense not to perceive such monstrosities—"

"Monstrosities?" said the baron, waked up by the word.

The baroness and the rector exchanged looks. The cards were dealt; Mademoiselle de Pen-Hoel had Mistigris! Impossible to continue the conversation! But she was glad to hide her joy under the excitement caused by her last word.

"Your play, monsieur le baron," she said, with an air of importance.

"My nephew is not one of those youths who like monstrosities," remarked Zephirine, taking out her knitting-needle and scratching her head.

"Mistigris!" cried Mademoiselle de Pen-Hoel, making no reply to her friend.

The rector, who appeared to be well-informed in the matter of Calyste and Mademoiselle des Touches, did not enter the lists.

"What does she do that is so extraordinary, Mademoiselle des Touches?" asked the baron.

"She smokes," replied Mademoiselle de Pen-Hoel.

"That's very wholesome," said the chevalier.

"About her property?" asked the baron.

"Her property?" continued the old maid. "Oh, she is running through it."

"The game is mine!" said the baroness. "See, I have king, queen, knave of trumps, Mistigris, and a king. We win the basket, sister."

This victory, gained at one stroke, without playing a card, horrified Mademoiselle de Pen-Hoel, who ceased to concern herself about Calyste and Mademoiselle des Touches. By nine o'clock no one remained in the salon but the baroness and the rector. The four old people had gone to their beds. The chevalier, according to his usual custom, accompanied Mademoiselle de Pen-Hoel to her house in the Place de Guerande, making remarks as they went along on the cleverness of the last play, on the joy with which Mademoiselle Zephirine engulfed her gains in those capacious pockets of hers,—for the old blind woman no longer repressed upon her face the visible signs of her feelings. Madame du Guenic's evident preoccupation was the chief topic of conversation, however. The chevalier had remarked the abstraction of the beautiful Irish woman. When they reached Mademoiselle de Pen-Hoel's door-step, and her page had gone in, the old lady answered, confidentially, the remarks of the chevalier on the strangely abstracted air of the baroness:—

"I know the cause. Calyste is lost unless we marry him promptly. He loves Mademoiselle des Touches, an actress!"

"In that case, send for Charlotte."

"I have sent; my sister will receive my letter to-morrow," replied Mademoiselle de Pen-Hoel, bowing to the chevalier.

Imagine from this sketch of a normal evening the hubbub excited in Guerande homes by the arrival, the stay, the departure, or even the mere passage through the town, of a stranger.

When no sounds echoed from the baron's chamber nor from that of his sister, the baroness looked at the rector, who was playing pensively with the counters.

"I see that you begin to share my anxiety about Calyste," she said to him.

"Did you notice Mademoiselle de Pen-Hoel's displeased looks to-night?" asked the rector.

"Yes," replied the baroness.

"She has, as I know, the best intentions about our dear Calyste; she loves him as though he were her son, his conduct in Vendee beside his father, the praises that MADAME bestowed upon his devotion, have only increased her affection for him. She intends to execute a deed of gift by which she gives her whole property at her death to whichever of her nieces Calyste marries. I know that you have another and much richer marriage in Ireland for your dear Calyste, but it is well to have two strings to your bow. In case your family will not take charge of Calyste's establishment, Mademoiselle de Pen-Hoel's fortune is not to be despised. You can always find a match of seven thousand francs a year for the dear boy, but it is not often that you could come across the savings of forty years and landed property as well managed, built up, and kept in repair as that of Mademoiselle de Pen-Hoel. That ungodly woman, Mademoiselle des Touches, has come here to ruin many excellent things. Her life is now known."

"And what is it?" asked the mother.

"Oh! that of a trollop," replied the rector,—"a woman of questionable morals, a writer for the stage; frequenting theatres and actors; squandering her fortune among pamphleteers, painters, musicians, a devilish society, in short. She writes books herself, and has taken a false name by which she is better known, they tell me, than by her own. She seems to be a sort of circus woman who never enters a church except to look at the pictures. She has spent quite a fortune in decorating Les Touches in a most improper fashion, making it a Mohammedan paradise where the houris are not women. There is more wine drunk there, they say, during the few weeks of her stay than the whole year round in Guerande. The Demoiselles Bougniol let their lodgings last year to men with beards, who were suspected of being Blues; they sang wicked songs which made those virtuous women blush and weep, and spent their time mostly at Les Touches. And this is the woman our dear Calyste adores! If that creature wanted to-night one of the infamous books in which the atheists of the present day scoff at holy things, Calyste would saddle his horse himself and gallop to Nantes for it. I am not sure that he would do as much for the Church. Moreover, this Breton woman is not a royalist! If Calyste were again called upon to strike a blow for the cause, and Mademoiselle des Touches—the Sieur Camille Maupin, that is her other name, as I have just remembered—if she wanted to keep him with her the chevalier would let his old father go to the field without him."

"Oh, no!" said the baroness.

"I should not like to put him to the proof; you would suffer too much," replied the rector. "All Guerande is turned upside down about Calyste's passion for this amphibious creature, who is neither man nor woman, who smokes like an hussar, writes like a journalist, and has at this very moment in her house the most venomous of all writers,—so the postmaster says, and he's a *juste-milieu* man who reads the papers. They are even talking about her at Nantes. This morning the Kergarouet cousin who wants to marry Charlotte to a man with sixty thousand francs a year, went to see Mademoiselle de Pen-Hoel, and filled her mind with tales about Mademoiselle des Touches which lasted seven hours. It is now striking a quarter to ten, and Calyste is not home; he is at Les Touches,—perhaps he won't come in all night."

The baroness listened to the rector, who was substituting monologue for dialogue unconsciously as he looked at this lamb of his fold, on whose face could be read her anxiety. She colored and trembled. When the worthy man saw the tears in the beautiful eyes of the mother, he was moved to compassion.

"I will see Mademoiselle de Pen-Hoel to-morrow," he said. "Don't be too uneasy. The harm may not be as great as they say it is. I will find out the truth. Mademoiselle Jacqueline has confidence in me. Besides, Calyste is our child, our pupil,—he will never let the devil inveigle him; neither will he trouble the peace of his family or destroy the plans we have made for his future. Therefore, don't weep; all is not lost, madame; one fault is not vice."

"You are only informing me of details," said the baroness. "Was not I the first to notice the change in my Calyste? A mother keenly feels the shock of finding herself second in the heart of her son. She cannot be deceived. This crisis in a man's life is one of the trials of motherhood. I have prepared myself for it, but I did not think it would come so soon. I hoped, at least, that Calyste would take into his heart some noble and beautiful being,—not a stage-player, a masquerader, a theatre woman, an author whose business it is to feign sentiments, a creature who will deceive him and make him unhappy! She has had adventures—"

"With several men," said the rector. "And yet this impious creature was born in Brittany! She dishonors her land. I shall preach a sermon upon her next Sunday."

"Don't do that!" cried the baroness. "The peasants and the *paludiers* would be capable of rushing to Les Touches. Calyste is worthy of his name; he is Breton; some dreadful thing might happen to him, for he would surely defend her as he would the Blessed Virgin."

"It is now ten o'clock; I must bid you good-night," said the abbe, lighting the wick of his lantern, the glass of which was clear and the metal shining, which testified to the care his housekeeper bestowed on the household property. "Who could ever have told me, madame," he added, "that a young man brought up by you, trained by me to Christian ideas, a fervent Catholic, a child who has lived as a lamb without spot, would plunge into such mire?"

"But is it certain?" said the mother. "How could any woman help loving Calyste?"

"What other proof is needed than her staying on at Les Touches. In all the twenty-four years since she came of age she has never stayed there so long as now; her visits to these parts, happily for us, were few and short."

"A woman over forty years old!" exclaimed the baroness. "I have heard say in Ireland that a woman of this description is the most dangerous mistress a young man can have."

"As to that, I have no knowledge," replied the rector, "and I shall die in my ignorance."

"And I, too, alas!" said the baroness, naively. "I wish now that I had loved with love, so as to understand and counsel and comfort Calyste."

The rector did not cross the clean little court-yard alone; the baroness accompanied him to the gate, hoping to hear Calyste's step coming through the town. But she heard nothing except the heavy tread of the rector's cautious feet, which grew fainter in the distance, and finally ceased when the closing of the door of the parsonage echoed behind him.

CHAPTER V.

CALYSTE

The poor mother returned to the salon deeply distressed at finding that the whole town was aware of what she had thought was known to her alone. She sat down, trimmed the wick of the lamp by cutting it with a pair of old scissors, took up once more the worsted-work she was doing, and awaited Calyste. The baroness fondly hoped to induce her son by this means to come home earlier and spend less time with Mademoiselle des Touches. Such calculations of maternal jealousy were wasted. Day after day, Calyste's visits to Les Touches became more frequent, and every night he came in later. The night before the day of which we speak it was midnight when he returned.

The baroness, lost in maternal meditation, was setting her stitches with the rapidity of one absorbed in thought while engaged in manual labor. Whoever had seen her bending to the light of the lamp beneath the quadruply centennial hangings of that ancient room would have admired the sublimity of the picture. Fanny's skin was so transparent that it was possible to read the thoughts that crossed her brow beneath it. Piqued with a curiosity that often comes to a pure woman, she asked herself what devilish secrets these daughters of Baal possessed to so charm men as to make them forgetful of mother, family, country, and self-interests. Sometimes she longed to meet this woman and judge her soberly for herself. Her mind measured to its full extent the evils which the innovative spirit of the age—described to her as so dangerous for young souls by the rector—would have upon her only child, until then so guileless; as pure as an innocent girl, and beautiful with the same fresh beauty.

Calyste, that splendid offspring of the oldest Breton race and the noblest Irish blood, had been nurtured by his mother with the utmost care. Until the moment when the baroness made over the training of him to the rector of Guerande, she was certain that no impure word, no evil thought had sullied the ears or entered the mind of her precious son. After nursing him at her bosom, giving him her own life twice, as it were, after guiding his footsteps as a little child, the mother had put him with all his virgin innocence into the hands of the pastor, who, out of true reverence for the family, had promised to give him a thorough and Christian education. Calyste thenceforth received the instruction which the abbe himself had received at the Seminary. The baroness taught him English, and a teacher of mathematics was found, not without difficulty, among the employes at Saint-Nazaire. Calyste was therefore necessarily ignorant of modern literature, and the advance and present progress of the sciences. His education had been limited to geography and the circumspect history of a young ladies' boarding-school, the Latin and Greek of seminaries, the literature of the dead languages, and to a very restricted choice of French writers. When, at sixteen, he began what the Abbe Grimont called his philosophy, he was neither more nor less than what he was when Fanny placed him in the abbe's hands. The Church had proved as maternal as the mother. Without being over-pious or ridiculous, the idolized young lad was a fervent Catholic.

For this son, so noble, so innocent, the baroness desired to provide a happy life in obscurity. She expected to inherit some property, two or three thousand pounds sterling, from an aunt. This sum, joined to the small present fortune of the Guenics, might enable her to find a wife for Calyste, who would bring him twelve or even fifteen thousand francs a year. Charlotte de Kergarouet, with her aunt's fortune, a rich Irish girl, or any other good heiress would have suited the baroness, who seemed indifferent as to choice. She was ignorant of love, having never known it, and, like all the other persons grouped about her, she saw nothing in marriage but a means of fortune. Passion was an unknown thing to these Catholic souls, these old people exclusively concerned about salvation, God, the king, and their property. No one should be surprised, therefore, at the foreboding thoughts which accompanied the wounded feelings of the mother, who lived as much for the future interests of her son as by her love for him. If the young household would only listen to wisdom, she thought, the coming generation of the du Guenics, by enduring privations, and saving, as people do save in the provinces, would be able to buy back their estates and recover, in the end, the lustre of wealth. The baroness prayed for a long age that she might see the dawn of this prosperous era. Mademoiselle du Guenic had understood and fully adopted this hope which Mademoiselle des Touches now threatened to overthrow.

The baroness heard midnight strike, with tears; her mind conceived of many horrors during the next hour, for the clock struck one, and Calyste was still not at home.

"Will he stay there?" she thought. "It would be the first time. Poor child!"

At that moment Calyste's step resounded in the lane. The poor mother, in whose heart rejoicing drove out anxiety, flew from the house to the gate and opened it for her boy.

"Oh!" cried Calyste, in a grieved voice, "my darling mother, why did you sit up for me? I have a pass-key and the tinder-box."

"You know very well, my child, that I cannot sleep when you are out," she said, kissing him.

When the baroness reached the salon, she looked at her son to discover, if possible, from the expression of his face the events of the evening. But he caused her, as usual, an emotion that frequency never weakened, — an emotion which all loving mothers feel at sight of a human masterpiece made by them; this sentiment blues their sight and supersedes all others for the moment.

Except for the black eyes, full of energy and the heat of the sun, which he derived from his father, Calyste in other respects resembled his mother; he had her beautiful golden hair, her lovable mouth, the same curving fingers, the same soft, delicate, and purely white skin. Though slightly resembling a girl disguised as a man, his physical strength was Herculean. His muscles had the suppleness and vigor of steel springs, and the singularity of his black eyes and fair complexion was by no means without charm. His beard had not yet sprouted; this delay, it is said, is a promise of longevity. The chevalier was dressed in a short coat of black velvet like that of his mother's gown, trimmed with silver buttons, a blue foulard necktie, trousers of gray jean, and a becoming pair of gaiters. His white brow bore the signs of great fatigue, caused, to an observer's eye, by the weight of painful thoughts; but his mother, incapable of supposing that troubles could wring his heart, attributed his evident weariness to passing excitement. Calyste was as handsome as a Greek god, and handsome without conceit; in the first place, he had his mother's beauty constantly before him, and next, he cared very little for personal advantages which he found useless.

"Those beautiful pure cheeks," thought his mother, "where the rich young blood is flowing, belong to another woman! she is the mistress of that innocent brow! Ah! passion will lead to many evils; it will tarnish the look of those eyes, moist as the eyes of an infant!"

This bitter thought wrung Fanny's heart and destroyed her pleasure.

It may seem strange to those who calculate expenses that in a family of six persons compelled to live on three thousand francs a year the son should have a coat and the mother a gown of velvet; but Fanny O'Brien had aunts and rich relations in London who recalled themselves to her remembrance by many presents. Several of her sisters, married to great wealth, took enough interest in Calyste to wish to find him an heiress, knowing that he, like Fanny their exiled favorite, was noble and handsome.

"You stayed at Les Touches longer than you did last night, my dear one," said the mother at last, in an agitated tone.

"Yes, dear mother," he answered, offering no explanation.

The curtness of this answer brought clouds to his mother's brow, and she resolved to postpone the explanation till the morrow. When mothers admit the anxieties which were now torturing the baroness, they tremble before their sons; they feel instinctively the effect of the great emancipation that comes with love; they perceive what that sentiment is about to take from them; but they have, at the same time, a sense of joy in knowing that their sons are happy; conflicting feelings battle in their hearts. Though the result may be the development of their sons into superior men, true mothers do not like this forced abdication; they would rather keep their children small and still requiring protection. Perhaps that is the secret of their predilection for feeble, deformed, or weak-minded offspring.

"You are tired, dear child; go to bed," she said, repressing her tears.

A mother who does not know all that her son is doing thinks the worst; that is, if a mother loves as much and is as much beloved as Fanny. But perhaps all other mothers would have trembled now as she did. The patient care of twenty years might be rendered worthless. This human masterpiece of virtuous and noble and religious education, Calyste, might be destroyed; the happiness of his life, so long and carefully prepared for, might be forever ruined by this woman.

The next day Calyste slept till mid-day, for his mother would not have him wakened. Mariotte served the spoiled child's breakfast in his bed. The inflexible and semi-conventual rules which regulated the hours for meals yielded to the caprices of the chevalier. If it became desirable to extract from Mademoiselle du Guenic her array of keys in order to obtain some necessary article of food outside of the meal hours, there was no other means of doing it than to make the pretext of its serving some fancy of Calyste.

About one o'clock the baron, his wife, and Mademoiselle were seated in the salon, for they dined at three o'clock. The baroness was again reading the "Quotidienne" to her husband, who was always more awake before the dinner hour. As she finished a paragraph she heard the steps of her son on the upper floor, and she dropped the paper, saying: —

"Calyste must be going to dine again at Les Touches; he has dressed himself."

"He amuses himself, the dear boy," said the old sister, taking a silver whistle from her pocket and whistling once.

Mariotte came through the tower and appeared at the door of communication which was hidden by a silken curtain like the other doors of the room.

"What is it?" she said; "anything wanted?"

"The chevalier dines at Les Touches; don't cook the fish."

"But we are not sure as yet," said the baroness.

"You seem annoyed, sister; I know it by the tone of your voice."

"Monsieur Grimont has heard some very grave charges against Mademoiselle des Touches, who for the last year has so changed our dear Calyste."

"Changed him, how?" asked the baron.

"He reads all sorts of books."

"Ah! ah!" exclaimed the baron, "so that's why he has given up hunting and riding."

"Her morals are very reprehensible, and she has taken a man's name," added Madame du Guenic.

"A war name, I suppose," said the old man. "I was called 'l'Intime,' the Comte de Fontaine 'Grand-Jacques,' the Marquis de Montauran the 'Gars.' I was the friend of Ferdinand, who never submitted, any more than I did. Ah! those were the good times; people shot each other, but what of that? we amused ourselves all the same, here and there."

This war memory, pushing aside paternal anxiety, saddened Fanny for a moment. The rector's revelations, the want of confidence shown to her by Calyste, had kept her from sleeping.

"Suppose Monsieur le chevalier does love Mademoiselle des Touches, where's the harm?" said Mariotte. "She has thirty thousand francs a year and she is very handsome."

"What is that you say, Mariotte?" exclaimed the old baron. "A Guenic marry a des Touches! The des Touches were not even grooms in the days when du Guesclin considered our alliance a signal honor."

"A woman who takes a man's name,—Camille Maupin!" said the baroness.

"The Maupins are an old family," said the baron; "they bear: gules, three—" He stopped. "But she cannot be a Maupin and a des Touches both," he added.

"She is called Maupin on the stage."

"A des Touches could hardly be an actress," said the old man. "Really, Fanny, if I did not know you, I should think you were out of your head."

"She writes plays, and books," continued the baroness.

"Books?" said the baron, looking at his wife with an air of as much surprise as though she were telling of a miracle. "I have heard that Mademoiselle Scudery and Madame de Sevigne wrote books, but it was not the best thing they did."

"Are you going to dine at Les Touches, monsieur?" said Mariotte, when Calyste entered.

"Probably," replied the young man.

Mariotte was not inquisitive; she was part of the family; and she left the room without waiting to hear what the baroness would say to her son.

"Are you going again to Les Touches, my Calyste?" The baroness emphasized the *my*. "Les Touches is not a respectable or decent house. Its mistress leads an irregular life; she will corrupt our Calyste. Already Camille Maupin has made him read many books; he has had adventures—You knew all that, my naughty child, and you never said one word to your best friends!"

"The chevalier is discreet," said his father,—"a virtue of the olden time."

"Too discreet," said the jealous mother, observing the red flush on her son's forehead.

"My dear mother," said Calyste, kneeling down beside the baroness, "I didn't think it necessary to publish my defeat. Mademoiselle des Touches, or, if you choose to call her so, Camille Maupin, rejected my love more than eighteen months ago, during her last stay at Les Touches. She laughed at me, gently; saying she might very well be my mother; that a woman of forty committed a sort of crime against nature in loving a minor, and that she herself was incapable of such depravity. She made a thousand little jokes, which hurt me—for she is witty as an angel; but when she saw me weep hot tears she tried to comfort me, and offered me her friendship in the noblest manner. She has more heart than even talent; she is as generous as you are yourself. I am now her child. On her return here lately, hearing from her that she loves another, I have resigned myself. Do not repeat the calumnies that have been said of her. Camille is an artist, she has genius, she leads one of those exceptional existences which cannot be judged like ordinary lives."

"My child," said the religious Fanny, "nothing can excuse a woman for not conducting herself as the Church requires. She fails in her duty to God and to society by abjuring the gentle tenets of her sex. A woman commits a sin in even going to a theatre; but to write the impieties that actors repeat, to roam about the world, first with an enemy to the Pope, and then with a musician, ah! Calyste, you can never persuade me that such acts are deeds of faith, hope, or charity. Her fortune was given her by God to do good, and what good does she do with hers?"

Calyste sprang up suddenly, and looked at his mother.

"Mother," he said, "Camille is my friend; I cannot hear her spoken of in this way; I would give my very life for her."

"Your life!" said the baroness, looking at her son, with startled eyes. "Your life is our life, the life of all of us."

"My nephew has just said many things I do not understand," said the old woman, turning toward him.

"Where did he learn them?" said the mother; "at Les Touches."

"Yes, my darling mother; she found me ignorant as a carp, and she has taught me."

"You knew the essential things when you learned the duties taught us by religion," replied the baroness. "Ah! this woman is fated to destroy your noble and sacred beliefs."

The old maid rose, and solemnly stretched forth her hands toward her brother, who was dozing in his chair.

"Calyste," she said, in a voice that came from her heart, "your father has never opened books, he speaks Breton, he fought for God and for the king. Educated people did the evil, educated noblemen deserted their land,—be educated if you choose!"

So saying, she sat down and began to knit with a rapidity which betrayed her inward emotion.

"My angel," said the mother, weeping, "I foresee some evil coming down upon you in that house."

"Who is making Fanny weep?" cried the old man, waking with a start at the sound of his wife's voice. He looked round upon his sister, his son, and the baroness. "What is the matter?" he asked.

"Nothing, my friend," replied his wife.

"Mamma," said Calyste, whispering in his mother's ear, "it is impossible for me to explain myself just now; but to-night you and I will talk of this. When you know all, you will bless Mademoiselle des Touches."

"Mothers do not like to curse," replied the baroness. "I could not curse a woman who truly loved my Calyste."

The young man bade adieu to his father and went out. The baron and his wife rose to see him pass through the court-yard, open the gate, and disappear. The baroness did not again take up the newspaper; she was too agitated. In this tranquil, untroubled life such a discussion was the equivalent of a quarrel in other homes. Though somewhat calmed, her motherly uneasiness was not dispersed. Whither would such a friendship, which might claim the life of Calyste and destroy it, lead her boy? Bless Mademoiselle des Touches? how could that be? These questions were as momentous to her simple soul as the fury of revolutions to a statesman. Camille Maupin was Revolution itself in that calm and placid home.

"I fear that woman will ruin him," she said, picking up the paper.

"My dear Fanny," said the old baron, with a jaunty air, "you are too much of an angel to understand these things. Mademoiselle des Touches is, they say, as black as a crow, as strong as a Turk, and forty years old. Our dear Calyste was certain to fall in love with her. Of course he will tell certain honorable little lies to conceal his happiness. Let him alone to amuse himself with his first illusions."

"If it had been any other woman—" began the baroness.

"But, my dear Fanny, if the woman were a saint she would not accept your son." The baroness again picked up the paper. "I will go and see her myself," added the baron, "and tell you all about her."

This speech has no savor at the present moment. But after reading the biography of Camille Maupin you can then imagine the old baron entering the lists against that illustrious woman.

CHAPTER VI.
BIOGRAPHY OF CAMILLE MAUPIN

The town of Guerande, which for two months past had seen Calyste, its flower and pride, going, morning or evening, often morning and evening, to Les Touches, concluded that Mademoiselle Felicite des Touches was passionately in love with the beautiful youth, and that she practised upon him all kinds of sorceries. More than one young girl and wife asked herself by what right an old woman exercised so absolute an empire over that angel. When Calyste passed along the Grand Rue to the Croisic gate many a regretful eye was fastened on him.

It now became necessary to explain the rumors which hovered about the person whom Calyste was on his way to see. These rumors, swelled by Breton gossip, envenomed by public ignorance, had reached the rector. The receiver of taxes, the *juge de paix*, the head of the Saint-Nazaire custom-house and other lettered persons had not reassured the abbe by relating to him the strange and fantastic life of the female writer who concealed herself under the masculine name of Camille Maupin. She did not as yet eat little children, nor kill her slaves like Cleopatra, nor throw men into the river as the heroine of the Tour de Nesle was falsely accused of doing; but to the Abbe Grimont this monstrous creature, a cross between a siren and an atheist, was an immoral combination of woman and philosopher who violated every social law invented to restrain or utilize the infirmities of womankind.

Just as Clara Gazul is the female pseudonym of a distinguished male writer, George Sand the masculine pseudonym of a woman of genius, so Camille Maupin was the mask behind which was long hidden a charming young woman, very well-born, a Breton, named Felicite des Touches, the person who was now causing such lively anxiety to the Baronne du Guenic and the excellent rector of Guerande. The Breton des Touches family has no connection with the family of the same name in Touraine, to which belongs the ambassador of the Regent, even more famous to-day for his writings than for his diplomatic talents.

Camille Maupin, one of the few celebrated women of the nineteenth century, was long supposed to be a man, on account of the virility of her first writings. All the world now knows the two volumes of plays, not intended for representation on the stage, written after the manner of Shakespeare or Lopez de Vega, published in 1822, which made a sort of literary revolution when the great question of the classics and the romanticists palpitated on all sides,—in the newspapers, at the clubs, at the Academy, everywhere. Since then, Camille Maupin has written several plays and a novel, which have not belied the success obtained by her first publication—now, perhaps, too much forgotten. To explain by what net-work of circumstances the masculine incarnation of a young girl was brought about, why Felicite des Touches became a man and an author, and why, more fortunate than Madame de Stael, she kept her freedom and was thus more excusable for her celebrity, would be to satisfy many curiosities and do justice to one of those abnormal beings who rise in humanity like monuments, and whose fame is promoted by its rarity,—for in twenty centuries we can count, at most, twenty famous women. Therefore, although in these pages she stands as a secondary character, in consideration of the fact that she plays a great part in the literary history of our epoch, and that her influence over Calyste was great, no one, we think, will regret being made to pause before that figure rather longer than modern art permits.

Mademoiselle Felicite des Touches became an orphan in 1793. Her property escaped confiscation by reason of the deaths of her father and brother. The first was killed on the 10th of August, at the threshold of the palace, among the defenders of the king, near whose person his rank as major of the guards of the gate had placed him. Her brother, one of the body-guard, was massacred at Les Carmes. Mademoiselle des Touches was two years old when her mother died, killed by grief, a few days after this second catastrophe. When dying, Madame des Touches confided her daughter to her sister, a nun of Chelles. Madame de Faucombe, the nun, prudently took the orphan to Faucombe, a good-sized estate near Nantes, belonging to Madame des Touches, and there she settled with the little girl and three sisters of her convent. The populace of Nantes, during the last days of the Terror, tore down the chateau, seized the nuns and Mademoiselle des Touches, and threw them into prison on a false charge of receiving emissaries of Pitt and Coburg. The 9th Thermidor released them. Felicite's aunt died of fear. Two of the sisters left France, and the third confided the little girl to her nearest relation, Monsieur de Faucombe, her maternal great-uncle, who lived in Nantes.

Monsieur de Faucombe, an old man sixty years of age, had married a young woman to whom he left the management of his affairs. He busied himself in archaeology,—a passion, or to speak more correctly, one of those manias which enable old men to fancy themselves still living. The education of his ward was therefore left to chance. Little cared-for by her uncle's wife, a young woman given over to the social pleasures of the imperial epoch, Felicite brought herself up as a boy. She kept company with Monsieur de Faucombe in his library; where she read everything it pleased her to read. She thus obtained a knowledge of life in theory, and had no innocence of mind, though virgin personally. Her intellect floated on the impurities of knowledge while her heart was pure. Her learning became extraordinary, the result of a passion for reading, sustained by a powerful memory. At eighteen years of age she was as well-informed on all topics as a young man entering a literary career has need to be in our day. Her prodigious reading controlled her passions far more than conventual life would have done; for there the imaginations of young girls run riot. A brain crammed with knowledge that was neither digested nor classed governed the heart and soul of the child. This depravity of the intellect, without action upon the chastity of the body, would have amazed philosophers and observers, had any one in Nantes even suspected the powers of Mademoiselle des Touches.

The result of all this was in a contrary direction to the cause. Felicite had no inclinations toward evil; she conceived everything by thought, but abstained from deed. Old Faucombe was enchanted with her, and she helped him in his work,—writing three of his books, which the worthy old gentleman believed were his own; for his spiritual paternity was blind. Such mental labor, not agreeing with the developments of girlhood, had its effect. Felicite fell ill; her blood was overheated, and her chest seemed threatened with inflammation. The doctors ordered horseback exercise and the amusements of society. Mademoiselle des Touches became, in consequence, an admirable horsewoman, and recovered her health in a few months.

At the age of eighteen she appeared in the world, where she produced so great a sensation that no one in Nantes called her anything else than "the beautiful Mademoiselle des Touches." Led to enter society by one of the imperishable sentiments in the heart of a woman, however superior she may be, the worship she inspired found her cold and unresponsive. Hurt by her aunt and her cousins, who ridiculed her studies and teased her about her unwillingness for society, which they attributed to a lack of the power of pleasing, Felicite resolved on making herself coquettish, gay, volatile,—a woman, in short. But she expected in return an exchange of ideas, seductions, and pleasures in harmony with the elevation of her own mind and the extent of its knowledge. Instead of that, she was filled with disgust for the commonplaces of conversation, the silliness of gallantry; and more especially was she shocked by the supremacy of military men, to whom society made obeisance at that period. She had, not unnaturally, neglected the minor accomplishments. Finding herself inferior to the pretty dolls who played on the piano and made themselves agreeable by singing ballads, she determined to be a musician. Retiring into her former solitude she set to work resolvedly, under the direction of the best master in the town. She was rich, and she sent for Steibelt when the time came to perfect herself. The astonished town still talks of this princely conduct. The stay of that master cost her twelve thousand francs. Later, when she went to Paris, she studied harmony and thorough-bass, and composed the music of two operas which have had great success, though the public has never been admitted to the secret of their authorship. Ostensibly these operas are by Conti, one of the most eminent musicians of our day; but this circumstance belongs to the history of her heart, and will be mentioned later on.

The mediocrity of the society of a provincial town wearied her so excessively, her imagination was so filled with grandiose ideas that although she returned to the salons to eclipse other women once more by her beauty, and enjoy her new triumph as a musician, she again deserted them; and having proved her power to her cousins, and driven two lovers to despair, she returned to her books, her piano, the works of Beethoven, and her old friend Faucombe. In 1812, when she was twenty-one years of age, the old archaeologist handed over to her his guardianship accounts. From that year, she took control of her fortune, which consisted of fifteen thousand francs a year, derived from Les Touches, the property of her father; twelve thousand a year from Faucombe (which, however, she increased one-third on renewing the leases); and a capital of three hundred thousand francs laid by during her minority by her guardians.

Felicite acquired from her experience of provincial life, an understanding of money, and that strong tendency to administrative wisdom which enables the provinces to hold their own under the ascensional movement of capital towards Paris. She drew her three hundred thousand francs from the house of business where her guardian had placed them, and invested them on the Grand-livre at the very moment of the disasters of the retreat from Moscow. In this way, she increased her income by thirty thousand francs. All expenses paid, she found herself with fifty thousand francs a year to invest. At twenty-one years of age a girl with such force of will is the equal of a man of thirty. Her mind had taken a wide range; habits of criticism enabled her to judge soberly of men, and art, and things, and public questions. Henceforth she resolved to leave Nantes; but old Faucombe falling ill with his last illness, she, who had been both wife and daughter to him, remained to nurse him, with the devotion of an angel, for eighteen months, closing his eyes at the moment when Napoleon was struggling with all Europe on the corpse of France. Her removal to Paris was therefore still further postponed until the close of that crisis.

As a Royalist, she hastened to be present at the return of the Bourbons to Paris. There the Grandlieus, to whom she was related, received her as their guest; but the catastrophes of March 20 intervened, and her future was vague and uncertain. She was thus enabled to see with her own eyes that last image of the Empire, and behold the Grand Army when it came to the Champ de Mars, as to a Roman circus, to salute its Caesar before it went to its death at Waterloo. The great and noble soul of Felicite was stirred by that magic spectacle. The political commotions, the glamour of that theatrical play of three months which history has called the Hundred Days, occupied her mind and preserved her from all personal emotions in the midst of a convulsion which dispersed the royalist society among whom she had intended to reside. The Grandlieus followed the Bourbons to Ghent, leaving their house to Mademoiselle des Touches. Felicite, who did not choose to take a subordinate position, purchased for one hundred and thirty thousand francs one of the finest houses in the rue Mont Blanc, where she installed herself on the return of the Bourbons in 1815. The garden of this house is to-day worth two millions.

Accustomed to control her own life, Felicite soon familiarized herself with the ways of thought and action which are held to be exclusively the province of man. In 1816 she was twenty-five years old. She knew nothing of marriage; her conception of it was wholly that of thought; she judged it in its causes instead of its effect, and saw only its objectionable side. Her superior mind refused to make the abdication by which a married woman begins that life; she keenly felt the value of independence, and was conscious of disgust for the duties of maternity.

It is necessary to give these details to explain the anomalies presented by the life of Camille Maupin. She had known neither father nor mother; she had been her own mistress from childhood; her guardian was an old archaeologist. Chance had flung her into the regions of knowledge and of imagination, into the world of literature, instead of holding her within the rigid circle defined by the futile education given to women, and by maternal instructions as to dress, hypocritical propriety, and the hunting graces of their sex. Thus, long before she became celebrated, a glance might have told an observer that she had never played with dolls.

Toward the close of the year 1817 Felicite des Touches began to perceive, not the fading of her beauty, but the beginning of a certain lassitude of body. She saw that a change would presently take place in her person as the result of her obstinate celibacy. She wanted to retain her youth and beauty, to which at that time she clung. Science warned her of the sentence pronounced by Nature upon all her creations, which perish as much by the misconception of her laws as by the abuse of them. The macerated face of her aunt returned to her memory and made her shudder. Placed between marriage and love, her desire was to keep her freedom; but she was now no longer indifferent to homage and the admiration that surrounded her. She was, at the moment when this history begins, almost exactly what she was in 1817. Eighteen years had passed over her head and respected it. At forty she might have been thought no more than twenty-five.

Therefore to describe her in 1836 is to picture her as she was in 1817. Women who know the conditions of temperament and happiness in which a woman should live to resist the ravages of time will understand how and why Felicite des Touches enjoyed this great privilege as they study a portrait for which were reserved the brightest tints of Nature's palette, and the richest setting.

Brittany presents a curious problem to be solved in the predominance of dark hair, brown eyes, and swarthy complexions in a region so near England that the atmospheric effects are almost identical. Does this problem belong to the great question of races? to hitherto unobserved physical influences? Science may some day find the reason of this peculiarity, which ceases in the adjoining province of Normandy. Waiting its solution, this odd fact is there before our eyes; fair complexions are rare in Brittany, where the women's eyes are as black and lively as those of Southern women; but instead of possessing the tall figures and swaying lines of Italy and Spain, they are usually short, close-knit, well set-up and firm, except in the higher classes which are crossed by their alliances.

Mademoiselle des Touches, a true Breton, is of medium height, though she looks taller than she really is. This effect is produced by the character of her face, which gives height to her form. She has that skin, olive by day and dazzling by candlelight, which distinguishes a beautiful Italian; you might, if you pleased, call it animated ivory. The light glides along a skin of that texture as on a polished surface; it shines; a violent emotion is necessary to bring the faintest color to the centre of the cheeks, where it goes away almost immediately. This peculiarity gives to her face the calm impassibility of the savage. The face, more long than oval, resembles that of some beautiful Isis in the Egyptian bas-reliefs; it has the purity of the heads of sphinxes, polished by the fire of the desert, kissed by a Coptic sun. The tones of the skin are in harmony with the faultless modelling of the head. The black and abundant hair descends in heavy masses beside the throat, like the coif of the statues at Memphis, and carries out magnificently the general severity of form. The forehead is full, broad, and swelling about the temples, illuminated by surfaces which catch the light, and modelled like the brow of the hunting Diana, a powerful and determined brow, silent and self-contained. The arch of the eyebrows, vigorously drawn, surmounts a pair of eyes whose flame scintillates at times like that of a fixed star. The white of the eye is neither bluish, nor strewn with scarlet threads, nor is it purely white; it has the texture of horn, but the tone is warm. The pupil is surrounded by an orange circle; it is of bronze set in gold, but vivid gold and animated bronze. This pupil has depth; it is not underlaid, as in certain eyes, by a species of foil, which sends back the light and makes such eyes resemble those of cats or tigers; it has not that terrible inflexibility which makes a sensitive person shudder; but this depth has in it something of the infinite, just as the external radiance of the eyes suggests the absolute. The glance of an observer may be lost in that soul, which gathers itself up and retires with as much rapidity as it gushed for a second into those velvet eyes. In moments of passion the eyes of Camille Maupin are sublime; the gold of her glance illuminates them and they flame. But in repose they are dull; the torpor of meditation often lends them an appearance of stupidity[1]; in like manner, when the glow of the soul is absent the lines of the face are sad.

The lashes of the eyelids are short, but thick and black as the tip of an ermine's tail; the eyelids are brown and strewn with red fibrils, which give them grace and strength,—two qualities which are seldom united in a woman. The circle round the eyes shows not the slightest blemish nor the smallest wrinkle. There, again, we find the granite of an Egyptian statue softened by the ages. But the line of the cheekbones, though soft, is more pronounced than in other women and completes the character of strength which the face expresses. The nose, thin and straight, parts into two oblique nostrils, passionately dilated at times, and showing the transparent pink of their delicate lining. This nose is an admirable continuation of the forehead, with which it blends in a most delicious line. It is perfectly white from its spring to its tip, and the tip is endowed with a sort of mobility which does marvels if Camille is indignant, or angry, or rebellious. There, above all, as Talma once remarked, is seen depicted the anger or the irony of great minds. The immobility of the human nostril indicates a certain narrowness of soul; never did the nose of a miser oscillate; it contracts like the lips; he locks up his face as he does his money.

Camille's mouth, arching at the corners, is of a vivid red; blood abounds there, and supplies the living, thinking oxide which gives such seduction to the lips, reassuring the lover whom the gravity of that majestic face may have dismayed. The upper lip is thin, the furrow which unites it with the nose comes low, giving it a centre curve which emphasizes its natural disdain. Camille has little to do to express anger. This beautiful lip is supported by the strong red breadth of its lower mate, adorable in kindness, swelling with love, a lip like the outer petal of a pomegranate such as Phidias might have carved, and the color of which it has. The chin is firm and rather full; but it expresses resolution and fitly ends this profile, royal if not divine. It is necessary to add that the upper lip beneath the nose is lightly shaded by a charming down. Nature would have made a blunder had she

---

[1] George Sand says of herself, in "L'Histoire de Ma Vie," published long after the above was written: "The habit of meditation gave me l'air bete (a stupid air). I say the word frankly, for all my life I have been told this, and therefore it must be true."—TR.

not cast that tender mist upon the face. The ears are delicately convoluted,—a sign of secret refinement. The bust is large, the waist slim and sufficiently rounded. The hips are not prominent, but very graceful; the line of the thighs is magnificent, recalling Bacchus rather than the Venus Callipyge. There we may see the shadowy line of demarcation which separates nearly every woman of genius from her sex; there such women are found to have a certain vague similitude to man; they have neither the suppleness nor the soft abandonment of those whom Nature destines for maternity; their gait is not broken by faltering motions. This observation may be called bi-lateral; it has its counterpart in men, whose thighs are those of women when they are sly, cunning, false, and cowardly. Camille's neck, instead of curving inward at the nape, curves out in a line that unites the head to the shoulders without sinuosity, a most signal characteristic of force. The neck itself presents at certain moments an athletic magnificence. The spring of the arms from the shoulders, superb in outline, seems to belong to a colossal woman. The arms are vigorously modelled, ending in wrists of English delicacy and charming hands, plump, dimpled, and adorned with rosy, almond-shaped nails; these hands are of a whiteness which reveals that the body, so round, so firm, so well set-up, is of another complexion altogether than the face. The firm, cold carriage of the head is corrected by the mobility of the lips, their changing expression, and the artistic play of the nostrils.

And yet, in spite of all these promises—hidden, perhaps, from the profane—the calm of that countenance has something, I know not what, that is vexatious. More sad, more serious than gracious, that face is marked by the melancholy of constant meditation. For this reason Mademoiselle des Touches listens more than she talks. She startles by her silence and by that deep-reaching glance of intense fixity. No educated person could see her without thinking of Cleopatra, that dark little woman who almost changed the face of the world. But in Camille the natural animal is so complete, so self-sufficing, of a nature so leonine, that a man, however little of a Turk he may be, regrets the presence of so great a mind in such a body, and could wish that she were wholly woman. He fears to find the strange distortion of an abnormal soul. Do not cold analysis and matter-of-fact theory point to passions in such a woman? Does she judge, and not feel? Or, phenomenon more terrible, does she not feel and judge at one and the same time? Able for all things through her brain, ought her course to be circumscribed by the limitations of other women? Has that intellectual strength weakened her heart? Has she no charm? Can she descend to those tender nothings by which a woman occupies, and soothes and interests the man she loves? Will she not cast aside a sentiment when it no longer responds to some vision of infinitude which she grasps and contemplates in her soul? Who can scale the heights to which her eyes have risen? Yes, a man fears to find in such a woman something unattainable, unpossessable, unconquerable. The woman of strong mind should remain a symbol; as a reality she must be feared. Camille Maupin is in some ways the living image of Schiller's Isis, seated in the darkness of the temple, at whose feet her priests find the dead bodies of the daring men who have consulted her.

The adventures of her life declared to be true by the world, and which Camille has never disavowed, enforce the questions suggested by her personal appearance. Perhaps she likes those calumnies.

The nature of her beauty has not been without its influence on her fame; it has served it, just as her fortune and position have maintained her in society. If a sculptor desires to make a statue of Brittany let him take Mademoiselle des Touches for his model. That full-blooded, powerful temperament is the only nature capable of repelling the action of time. The constant nourishment of the pulp, so to speak, of that polished skin is an arm given to women by Nature to resist the invasion of wrinkles; in Camille's case it was aided by the calm impassibility of her features.

In 1817 this charming young woman opened her house to artists, authors of renown, learned and scientific men, and publicists,—a society toward which her tastes led her. Her salon resembled that of Baron Gerard, where men of rank mingled with men of distinction of all kinds, and the elite of Parisian women came. The parentage of Mademoiselle des Touches, and her fortune, increased by that of her aunt the nun, protected her in the attempt, always very difficult in Paris, to create a society. Her worldly independence was one reason of her success. Various ambitious mothers indulged in the hope of inducing her to marry their sons, whose fortunes were out of proportion to the age of their escutcheons. Several peers of France, allured by the prospect of eighty thousand francs a year and a house magnificently appointed, took their womenkind, even the most fastidious and intractable, to visit her. The diplomatic world, always in search of amusements of the intellect, came there and found enjoyment. Thus Mademoiselle des Touches, surrounded by so many forms of individual interests, was able to study the different comedies which passion, covetousness, and ambition make the generality of men perform,—even those who are highest in the social scale. She saw, early in life, the world as it is; and she was fortunate enough not to fall early into absorbing love, which warps the mind and faculties of a woman and prevents her from judging soberly.

Ordinarily a woman feels, enjoys, and judges, successively; hence three distinct ages, the last of which coincides with the mournful period of old age. In Mademoiselle des Touches this order was reversed. Her youth was wrapped in the snows of knowledge and the ice of reflection. This transposition is, in truth, an additional explanation of the strangeness of her life and the nature of her talent. She observed men at an age when most women can only see one man; she despised what other women admired; she detected falsehood in the flatteries they accept as truths; she laughed at things that made them serious. This contradiction of her life with that of others lasted long; but it came to a terrible end; she was destined to find in her soul a first love, young and fresh, at an age when women are summoned by Nature to renounce all love.

Meantime, a first affair in which she was involved has always remained a secret from the world. Felicite, like other women, was induced to believe that beauty of body was that of soul. She fell in love with a face, and learned, to her cost, the folly of a man of gallantry, who saw nothing in her but a mere woman. It was some time before she recovered from the disgust she felt at this episode. Her distress was perceived by a friend, a man, who consoled her without personal after-thought, or, at any rate, he concealed any such motive if he had it. In him Felicite believed she found the heart and mind which were lacking to her former lover. He did, in truth, possess one of the most original minds of our age. He, too, wrote under a pseudonym, and his first publications were those of an adorer of Italy. Travel was the one form of education which Felicite lacked. A man of genius, a poet and a critic, he took Felicite to Italy in order to make known to her that country of all Art. This celebrated man, who is nameless, may be regarded as the master and maker of "Camille Maupin." He bought into order and shape the vast amount of knowledge already acquired by Felicite; increased it by study of the masterpieces with which Italy teems; gave her the frankness, freedom, and grace, epigrammatic, and intense, which is the character of his own talent (always rather fanciful as to form) which Camille Maupin modified by delicacy of sentiment and the softer terms of thought that are natural to a woman. He also roused in her a taste for German and English literature and made her learn both languages while travelling. In Rome, in 1820, Felicite was deserted for an Italian. Without that misery she might never have been celebrated. Napoleon called misfortune the midwife of genius. This event filled Mademoiselle des Touches, and forever, with that contempt for men which later was to make her so strong. Felicite died, Camille Maupin was born.

She returned to Paris with Conti, the great musician, for whom she wrote the librettos of two operas. But she had no more illusions, and she became, at heart, unknown to the world, a sort of female Don Juan, without debts and without conquests. Encouraged by success, she published the two volumes of plays which at once placed the name of Camille Maupin in the list of illustrious anonymas. Next, she related her betrayed and deluded love in a short novel, one of the masterpieces of that period. This book, of a dangerous example, was classed with "Adolphe," a dreadful lamentation, the counterpart of which is found in Camille's work. The true secret of her literary metamorphosis and pseudonym has never been fully understood. Some delicate minds have thought it lay in a feminine desire to escape fame and remain obscure, while offering a man's name and work to criticism.

In spite of any such desire, if she had it, her celebrity increased daily, partly through the influence of her salon, partly from her own wit, the correctness of her judgments, and the solid worth of her acquirements. She became an authority; her sayings were quoted; she could no longer lay aside at will the functions with which Parisian society invested her. She came to be an acknowledged exception. The world bowed before the genius and position of this strange woman; it recognized and sanctioned her independence; women admired her mind, men her beauty. Her conduct was regulated by all social conventions. Her friendships seemed purely platonic. There was, moreover, nothing of the female author about her. Mademoiselle des Touches is charming as a woman of the world, — languid when she pleases, indolent, coquettish, concerned about her toilet, pleased with the airy nothings so seductive to women and to poets. She understands very well that after Madame de Stael there is no place in this century for a Sappho, and that Ninon could not exist in Paris without *grands seigneurs* and a voluptuous court. She is the Ninon of the intellect; she adores Art and artists; she goes from the poet to the musician, from the sculptor to the prose-writer. Her heart is noble, endowed

with a generosity that makes her a dupe; so filled is she with pity for sorrow,—
filled also with contempt for the prosperous. She has lived since 1830, the centre
of a choice circle, surrounded by tried friends who love her tenderly and esteem
each other. Far from the noisy fuss of Madame de Stael, far from political strifes,
she jokes about Camille Maupin, that junior of George Sand (whom she calls her
brother Cain), whose recent fame has now eclipsed her own. Mademoiselle des
Touches admires her fortunate rival with angelic composure, feeling no jealousy
and no secret vexation.

Until the period when this history begins, she had led as happy a life as a
woman strong enough to protect herself can be supposed to live. From 1817 to
1834 she had come some five or six times to Les Touches. Her first stay was after
her first disillusion in 1818. The house was uninhabitable, and she sent her man of
business to Guerande and took a lodging for herself in the village. At that time she
had no suspicion of her coming fame; she was sad, she saw no one; she wanted, as
it were, to contemplate herself after her great disaster. She wrote to Paris to have
the furniture necessary for a residence at Les Touches sent down to her. It came
by a vessel to Nantes, thence by small boats to Croisic, from which little place it
was transported, not without difficulty, over the sands to Les Touches. Workmen
came down from Paris, and before long she occupied Les Touches, which pleased
her immensely. She wanted to meditate over the events of her life, like a cloistered
nun.

At the beginning of the winter she returned to Paris. The little town of Guerande was by this time roused to diabolical curiosity; its whole talk was of the Asi-
atic luxury displayed at Les Touches. Her man of business gave orders after her
departure that visitors should be admitted to view the house. They flocked from
the village of Batz, from Croisic, and from Savenay, as well as from Guerande.
This public curiosity brought in an enormous sum to the family of the porter and
gardener, not less, in two years, than seventeen francs.

After this, Mademoiselle des Touches did not revisit Les Touches for two
years, not until her return from Italy. On that occasion she came by way of Croisic
and was accompanied by Conti. It was some time before Guerande became aware
of her presence. Her subsequent apparitions at Les Touches excited comparatively
little interest. Her Parisian fame did not precede her; her man of business alone
knew the secret of her writings and of her connection with the celebrity of Camille Maupin. But at the period of which we are now writing the contagion of the
new ideas had made some progress in Guerande, and several persons knew of the
dual form of Mademoiselle des Touches' existence. Letters came to the post-office,
directed to Camille Maupin at Les Touches. In short, the veil was rent away. In
a region so essentially Catholic, archaic, and full of prejudice, the singular life of
this illustrious woman would of course cause rumors, some of which, as we have
seen, had reached the ears of the Abbe Grimont and alarmed him; such a life could
never be comprehended in Guerande; in fact, to every mind, it seemed unnatural
and improper.

Felicite, during her present stay, was not alone in Les Touches. She had a
guest. That guest was Claude Vignon, a scornful and powerful writer who, though

doing criticism only, has found means to give the public and literature the impression of a certain superiority. Mademoiselle des Touches had received this writer for the last seven years, as she had so many other authors, journalists, artists, and men of the world. She knew his nerveless nature, his laziness, his utter penury, his indifference and disgust for all things, and yet by the way she was now conducting herself she seemed inclined to marry him. She explained her conduct, incomprehensible to her friends, in various ways,—by ambition, by the dread she felt of a lonely old age; she wanted to confide her future to a superior man, to whom her fortune would be a stepping-stone, and thus increase her own importance in the literary world.

With these apparent intentions she had brought Claude Vignon from Paris to Les Touches, as an eagle bears away a kid in its talons,—to study him, and decide upon some positive course. But, in truth, she was misleading both Calyste and Claude; she was not even thinking of marriage; her heart was in the throes of the most violent convulsion that could agitate a soul as strong as hers. She found herself the dupe of her own mind; too late she saw life lighted by the sun of love, shining as love shines in a heart of twenty.

Let us now see Camille's convent where this was happening.

CHAPTER VII.

LES TOUCHES

A few hundred yards from Guerande the soil of Brittany comes to an end; the salt-marshes and the sandy dunes begin. We descend into a desert of sand, which the sea has left for a margin between herself and earth, by a rugged road through a ravine that has never seen a carriage. This desert contains waste tracts, ponds of unequal size, round the shores of which the salt is made on muddy banks, and a little arm of the sea which separates the mainland from the island of Croisic. Geographically, Croisic is really a peninsula; but as it holds to Brittany only by the beaches which connect it with the village of Batz (barren quicksands very difficult to cross), it may be more correct to call it an island.

At the point where the road from Croisic to Guerande turns off from the main road of *terra firma*, stands a country-house, surrounded by a large garden, remarkable for its trimmed and twisted pine-trees, some being trained to the shape of sun-shades, others, stripped of their branches, showing their reddened trunks in spots where the bark has peeled. These trees, victims of hurricanes, growing against wind and tide (for them the saying is literally true), prepare the mind for the strange and depressing sight of the marshes and dunes, which resemble a stiffened ocean. The house, fairly well built of a species of slaty stone with granite courses, has no architecture; it presents to the eye a plain wall with windows at regular intervals. These windows have small leaded panes on the ground-floor and large panes on the upper floor. Above are the attics, which stretch the whole length of an enormously high pointed roof, with two gables and two large dormer windows on each side of it. Under the triangular point of each gable a circular window opens its cyclopic eye, westerly to the sea, easterly on Guerande. One facade of the house looks on the road to Guerande, the other on the desert at the end of which is Croisic; beyond that little town is the open sea. A brook escapes through an opening in the park wall which skirts the road to Croisic, crosses the road, and is lost in the sands beyond it.

The grayish tones of the house harmonize admirably with the scene it overlooks. The park is an oasis in the surrounding desert, at the entrance of which the traveller comes upon a mud-hut, where the custom-house officials lie in wait for him. This house without land (for the bulk of the estate is really in Guerande) derives an income from the marshes and a few outlying farms of over ten thousand francs a year. Such is the fief of Les Touches, from which the Revolution lopped its feudal rights. The *paludiers*, however, continue to call it "the chateau," and they would still say "seigneur" if the fief were not now in the female line. When Felicite set about restoring Les Touches, she was careful, artist that she is, not to change the desolate exterior which gives the look of a prison to the isolated structure. The sole change was at the gate, which she enlivened by two brick columns supporting an arch, beneath which carriages pass into the court-yard where she planted trees.

The arrangement of the ground-floor is that of nearly all country houses built a hundred years ago. It was, evidently, erected on the ruins of some old castle formerly perched there. A large panelled entrance-hall has been turned by Felicite into a billiard-room; from it opens an immense salon with six windows, and the dining-room. The kitchen communicates with the dining-room through an office. Camille has displayed a noble simplicity in the arrangement of this floor, carefully avoiding all splendid decoration. The salon, painted gray, is furnished in old mahogany with green silk coverings. The furniture of the dining-room comprises four great buffets, also of mahogany, chairs covered with horsehair, and superb engravings by Audran in mahogany frames. The old staircase, of wood with heavy balusters, is covered all over with a green carpet.

On the floor above are two suites of rooms separated by the staircase. Mademoiselle des Touches has taken for herself the one that looks toward the sea and the marshes, and arranged it with a small salon, a large chamber, and two cabinets, one for a dressing-room, the other for a study and writing-room. The other suite, she has made into two separate apartments for guests, each with a bedroom, an antechamber, and a cabinet. The servants have rooms in the attic. The rooms for guests are furnished with what is strictly necessary, and no more. A certain fantastic luxury has been reserved for her own apartment. In that sombre and melancholy habitation, looking out upon the sombre and melancholy landscape, she wanted the most fantastic creations of art that she could find. The little salon is hung with Gobelin tapestry, framed in marvellously carved oak. The windows are draped with the heavy silken hangings of a past age, a brocade shot with crimson and gold against green and yellow, gathered into mighty pleats and trimmed with fringes and cords and tassels worthy of a church. This salon contains a chest or cabinet worth in these days seven or eight thousand francs, a carved ebony table, a secretary with many drawers, inlaid with arabesques of ivory and bought in Venice, with other noble Gothic furniture. Here too are pictures and articles of choice workmanship bought in 1818, at a time when no one suspected the ultimate value of such treasures. Her bedroom is of the period of Louis XV. and strictly exact to it. Here we see the carved wooden bedstead painted white, with the arched headboard surmounted by Cupids scattering flowers, and the canopy above it adorned with plumes; the hangings of blue silk; the Pompadour dressing-table with its laces and mirror; together with bits of furniture of singular shape, — a "duchesse," a chaise-longue, a stiff little sofa, — with window-curtains of silk, like that of the furniture, lined with pink satin, and caught back with silken ropes, and a carpet of Savonnerie; in short, we find here all those elegant, rich, sumptuous, and dainty things in the midst of which the women of the eighteenth century lived and made love.

The study, entirely of the present day, presents, in contrast with the Louis XV. gallantries, a charming collection of mahogany furniture; it resembles a boudoir;

the bookshelves are full, but the fascinating trivialities of a woman's existence encumber it; in the midst of which an inquisitive eye perceives with uneasy surprise pistols, a narghile, a riding-whip, a hammock, a rifle, a man's blouse, tobacco, pipes, a knapsack,—a bizarre combination which paints Felicite.

Every great soul, entering that room, would be struck with the peculiar beauty of the landscape which spreads its broad savanna beyond the park, the last vegetation on the continent. The melancholy squares of water, divided by little paths of white salt crust, along which the salt-makers pass (dressed in white) to rake up and gather the salt into *mulons*; a space which the saline exhalations prevent all birds from crossing, stifling thus the efforts of botanic nature; those sands where the eye is soothed only by one little hardy persistent plant bearing rosy flowers and the Chartreux pansy; that lake of salt water, the sandy dunes, the view of Croisic, a miniature town afloat like Venice on the sea; and, finally the mighty ocean tossing its foaming fringe upon the granite rocks as if the better to bring out their weird formations—that sight uplifts the mind although it saddens it; an effect produced at last by all that is sublime, creating a regretful yearning for things unknown and yet perceived by the soul on far-off heights. These wild and savage harmonies are for great spirits and great sorrows only.

This desert scene, where at times the sun rays, reflected by the water, by the sands, whitened the village of Batz and rippled on the roofs of Croisic with pitiless brilliancy, filled Camille's dreaming mind for days together. She seldom looked to the cool, refreshing scenes, the groves, the flowery meadows around Guerande. Her soul was struggling to endure a horrible inward anguish.

No sooner did Calyste see the vanes of the two gables shooting up beyond the furze of the roadside and the distorted heads of the pines, than the air seemed lighter; Guerande was a prison to him; his life was at Les Touches. Who will not understand the attraction it presented to a youth in his position. A love like that of Cherubin, had flung him at the feet of a person who was a great and grand thing to him before he thought of her as a woman, and it had survived the repeated and inexplicable refusals of Felicite. This sentiment, which was more the need of loving than love itself, had not escaped the terrible power of Camille for analysis; hence, possibly, her rejection,—a generosity unperceived, of course, by Calyste.

At Les Touches were displayed to the ravished eyes of the ignorant young countryman, the riches of a new world; he heard, as it were, another language, hitherto unknown to him and sonorous. He listened to the poetic sounds of the finest music, that surpassing music of the nineteenth century, in which melody and harmony blend or struggle on equal terms,—a music in which song and instrumentation have reached a hitherto unknown perfection. He saw before his eyes the works of modern painters, those of the French school, to-day the heir of Italy, Spain, and Flanders, in which talent has become so common that hearts, weary of talent, are calling aloud for genius. He read there those works of imagination, those amazing creations of modern literature which produced their full effect upon his unused heart. In short, the great Nineteenth Century appeared to him, in all its collective magnificence, its criticising spirit, its desires for renovation in all directions, and its vast efforts, nearly all of them on the scale of the giant who cradled the infancy of the century in his banners and sang to it hymns with the lullaby of cannon.

Initiated by Felicite into the grandeur of all these things, which may, perhaps, escape the eyes of those who work them, Calyste gratified at Les Touches the taste for the glorious, powerful at his age, and that artless admiration, the first love of adolescence, which is always irritated by criticism. It is so natural that flame should rise! He listened to that charming Parisian raillery, that graceful satire which revealed to him French wit and the qualities of the French mind, and awakened in him a thousand ideas, which might have slumbered forever in the soft torpor of his family life. For him, Mademoiselle des Touches was the mother of his intellect. She was so kind to him; a woman is always adorable to a man in whom she inspires love, even when she seems not to share it.

At the present time Felicite was giving him music-lessons. To him the grand apartments on the lower floor, and her private rooms above, so coquettish, so artistic, were vivified, were animated by a light, a spirit, a supernatural atmosphere, strange and undefinable. The modern world with its poesy was sharply contrasted with the dull and patriarchal world of Guerande, in the two systems brought face to face before him. On one side all the thousand developments of Art, on the other the sameness of uncivilized Brittany. No one will therefore ask why the poor lad, bored like his mother with the pleasures of *mouche*, quivered as he approached the house, and rang the bell, and crossed the court-yard. Such emotions, we may remark, do not assail a mature man, trained to the ups and downs of life, whom nothing surprises, being prepared for all.

As the door opened, Calyste, hearing the sound of the piano, supposed that Camille was in the salon; but when he entered the billiard-hall he no longer heard it. Camille, he thought, must be playing on a small upright piano brought by Conti from England and placed by her in her own little salon. He began to run up the stairs, where the thick carpet smothered the sound of his steps; but he went more slowly as he neared the top, perceiving something unusual and extraordinary about the music. Felicite was playing for herself only; she was communing with her own being.

Instead of entering the room, the young man sat down upon a Gothic seat covered with green velvet, which stood on the landing beneath a window artistically framed in carved woods stained and varnished. Nothing was ever more mysteriously melancholy than Camille's improvisation; it seemed like the cry of a soul *de profundis* to God—from the depths of a grave! The heart of the young lover recognized the cry of despairing love, the prayer of a hidden plaint, the groan of repressed affliction. Camille had varied, modified, and lengthened the introduction to the cavatina: "Mercy for thee, mercy for me!" which is nearly the whole of the fourth act of "Robert le Diable." She now suddenly sang the words in a heart-rending manner, and then as suddenly interrupted herself. Calyste entered, and saw the reason. Poor Camille Maupin! poor Felicite! She turned to him a face bathed with tears, took out her handkerchief and dried them, and said, simply, without affectation, "Good-morning." She was beautiful as she sat there in her morning gown. On her head was one of those red chenille nets, much worn in those days, through which the coils of her black hair shone, escaping here and there. A short upper garment made like a Greek peplum gave to view a pair of cambric trousers with embroidered frills, and the prettiest of Turkish slippers, red and gold.

"What is the matter?" cried Calyste.

"He has not returned," she replied, going to a window and looking out upon the sands, the sea and the marshes.

This answer explained all. Camille was awaiting Claude Vignon.

"You are anxious about him?" asked Calyste.

"Yes," she answered, with a sadness the lad was too ignorant to analyze.

He started to leave the room.

"Where are you going?" she asked.

"To find him," he replied.

"Dear child!" she said, taking his hand and drawing him toward her with one of those moist glances which are to a youthful soul the best of recompenses. "You are distracted! Where could you find him on that wide shore?"

"I will find him."

"Your mother would be in mortal terror. Stay. Besides, I choose it," she said, making him sit down upon the sofa. "Don't pity me. The tears you see are the tears a woman likes to shed. We have a faculty that is not in man,—that of abandoning ourselves to our nervous nature and driving our feelings to an extreme. By imagining certain situations and encouraging the imagination we end in tears, and sometimes in serious states of illness or disorder. The fancies of women are not the action of the mind; they are of the heart. You have come just in time; solitude is bad for me. I am not the dupe of his professed desire to go to Croisic and see the rocks and the dunes and the salt-marshes without me. He meant to leave us alone together; he is jealous, or, rather, he pretends jealousy, and you are young, you are handsome."

"Why not have told me this before? What must I do? must I stay away?" asked Calyste, with difficulty restraining his tears, one of which rolled down his cheek and touched Felicite deeply.

"You are an angel!" she cried. Then she gaily sang the "Stay! stay!" of Matilde in "Guillaume Tell," taking all gravity from that magnificent answer of the princess to her subject. "He only wants to make me think he loves me better than he really does," she said. "He knows how much I desire his happiness," she went on, looking attentively at Calyste. "Perhaps he feels humiliated to be inferior to me there. Perhaps he has suspicions about you and means to surprise us. But even if his only crime is to take his pleasure without me, and not to associate me with the ideas this new place gives him, is not that enough? Ah! I am no more loved by that great brain than I was by the musician, by the poet, by the soldier! Sterne is right; names signify much; mine is a bitter sarcasm. I shall die without finding in any man the love which fills my heart, the poesy that I have in my soul—"

She stopped, her arms pendant, her head lying back on the cushions, her eyes, stupid with thought, fixed on a pattern of the carpet. The pain of great minds has something grandiose and imposing about it; it reveals a vast extent of soul which the thought of the spectator extends still further. Such souls share the privileges of royalty whose affections belong to a people and so affect a world.

"Why did you reject my—" said Calyste; but he could not end his sentence. Camille's beautiful hand laid upon his eloquently interrupted him.

"Nature changed her laws in granting me a dozen years of youth beyond my due," she said. "I rejected your love from egotism. Sooner or later the difference in our ages must have parted us. I am thirteen years older than *he*, and even that is too much."

"You will be beautiful at sixty," cried Calyste, heroically.

"God grant it," she answered, smiling. "Besides, dear child, I *want* to love. In spite of his cold heart, his lack of imagination, his cowardly indifference, and the envy which consumes him, I believe there is greatness behind those tatters; I hope to galvanize that heart, to save him from himself, to attach him to me. Alas! alas! I have a clear-seeing mind, but a blind heart."

She was terrible in her knowledge of herself. She suffered and analyzed her feelings as Cuvier and Dupuytren explained to friends the fatal advance of their disease and the progress that death was making in their bodies. Camille Maupin knew the passion within her as those men of science knew their own anatomy.

"I have brought him here to judge him, and he is already bored," she continued. "He pines for Paris, I tell him; the nostalgia of criticism is on him; he has no author to pluck, no system to undermine, no poet to drive to despair, and he dares not commit some debauch in this house which might lift for a moment the burden of his ennui. Alas! my love is not real enough, perhaps, to soothe his brain; I don't intoxicate him! Make him drunk at dinner to-night and I shall know if I am right. I will say I am ill, and stay in my own room."

Calyste turned scarlet from his neck to his forehead; even his ears were on fire.

"Oh! forgive me," she cried. "How can I heedlessly deprave your girlish innocence! Forgive me, Calyste—" She paused. "There are some superb, consistent natures who say at a certain age: 'If I had my life to live over again, I would do the same things.' I who do not think myself weak, I say, 'I would be a woman like your mother, Calyste.' To have a Calyste, oh! what happiness! I could be a humble and submissive woman—And yet, I have done no harm except to myself. But alas! dear child, a woman cannot stand alone in society except it be in what is called a primitive state. Affections which are not in harmony with social or with natural laws, affections that are not obligatory, in short, escape us. Suffering for suffering, as well be useful where we can. What care I for those children of my cousin Faucombe? I have not seen them these twenty years, and they are married to merchants. You are my son, who have never cost me the miseries of motherhood; I shall leave you my fortune and make you happy—at least, so far as money can do so, dear treasure of beauty and grace that nothing should ever change or blast."

"You would not take my love," said Calyste, "and I shall return your fortune to your heirs."

"Child!" answered Camille, in a guttural voice, letting the tears roll down her cheeks. "Will nothing save me from myself?" she added, presently.

"You said you had a history to tell me, and a letter to—" said the generous youth, wishing to divert her thoughts from her grief; but she did not let him finish.

"You are right to remind me of that. I will be an honest woman before all else. I will sacrifice no one—Yes, it was too late, yesterday, but to-day we have time," she said, in a cheerful tone. "I will keep my promise; and while I tell you that history I will sit by the window and watch the road to the marshes."

Calyste arranged a great Gothic chair for her near the window, and opened one of the sashes. Camille Maupin, who shared the oriental taste of her illustrious sister-author, took a magnificent Persian narghile, given to her by an ambassador. She filled the nipple with patchouli, cleaned the *bochettino*, perfumed the goose-quill, which she attached to the mouthpiece and used only once, set fire to the yellow leaves, placing the vase with its long neck enamelled in blue and gold at some distance from her, and rang the bell for tea.

"Will you have cigarettes?—Ah! I am always forgetting that you do not smoke. Purity such as yours is so rare! The hand of Eve herself, fresh from the hand of her Maker, is alone innocent enough to stroke your cheek."

Calyste colored; sitting down on a stool at Camille's feet, he did not see the deep emotion that seemed for a moment to overcome her.

CHAPTER VIII.
LA MARQUISE BEATRIX

"I promised you this tale of the past, and here it is," said Camille. "The person from whom I received that letter yesterday, and who may be here to-morrow, is the Marquise de Rochefide. The old marquis (whose family is not as old as yours), after marrying his eldest daughter to a Portuguese grandee, was anxious to find an alliance among the higher nobility for his son, in order to obtain for him the peerage he had never been able to get for himself. The Comtesse de Montcornet told him of a young lady in the department of the Orne, a Mademoiselle Beatrix-Maximilienne-Rose de Casteran, the youngest daughter of the Marquis de Casteran, who wished to marry his two daughters without dowries in order to reserve his whole fortune for the Comte de Casteran, his son. The Casterans are, it seems, of the bluest blood. Beatrix, born and brought up at the chateau de Casteran, was twenty years old at the time of her marriage in 1828. She was remarkable for what you provincials call originality, which is simply independence of ideas, enthusiasm, a feeling for the beautiful, and a certain impulse and ardor toward the things of Art. You may believe a poor woman who has allowed herself to be drawn along the same lines, there is nothing more dangerous for a woman. If she follows them, they lead her where you see me, and where the marquise came, — to the verge of abysses. Men alone have the staff on which to lean as they skirt those precipices, — a force which is lacking to most women, but which, if we do possess it, makes abnormal beings of us. Her old grandmother, the dowager de Casteran, was well pleased to see her marry a man to whom she was superior in every way. The Rochefides were equally satisfied with the Casterans, who connected them with the Verneuils, the d'Esgrignons, the Troisvilles, and gave them a peerage for their son in that last big batch of peers made by Charles X., but revoked by the revolution of July. The first days of marriage are perilous for little minds as well as for great loves. Rochefide, being a fool, mistook his wife's ignorance for coldness; he classed her among frigid, lymphatic women, and made that an excuse to return to his bachelor life, relying on the coldness of the marquise, her pride, and the thousand barriers that the life of a great lady sets up about a woman in Paris. You'll know what I mean when you go there. People said to Rochefide: 'You are very lucky to possess a cold wife who will never have any but head passions. She will always be content if she can shine; her fancies are purely artistic, her desires will be satisfied if she can make a salon, and collect about her distinguished minds; her debauches will be in music and her orgies literary.' Rochefide, however, is not an ordinary fool; he has as much conceit and vanity as a clever man, which gives him a mean and squinting jealousy, brutal when it comes to the surface, lurking and cowardly for six months, and murderous the seventh. He thought he was deceiving his wife, and yet he feared her,—two causes for tyranny when the day came on which the marquise let him see that she was charitably assuming indifference to his unfaithfulness. I analyze all this in order to explain her conduct. Beatrix had the keenest admiration for me; there is but one step, however, from admiration to jealousy. I have one of the most remarkable salons in Paris; she wished to make herself another; and in order to do so she attempted to draw away my circle. I don't know how to keep those who wish to leave me. She obtained the superficial people who are friends with every one from mere want of occupation, and whose object is to get out of a salon as soon as they have entered it; but she did not have time to make herself a real society. In those days I thought her consumed with a desire for celebrity of one kind or another. Nevertheless, she has really much grandeur of soul, a regal pride, distinct ideas, and a marvellous facility for apprehending and understanding all things; she can talk metaphysics and music, theology and painting. You will see her, as a mature woman, what the rest of us saw her as a bride. And yet there is something of affectation about her in all this. She has too much the air of knowing abstruse things,—Chinese, Hebrew, hieroglyphics perhaps, or the papyrus that they wrapped round mummies. Personally, Beatrix is one of those blondes beside whom Eve the fair would seem a Negress. She is slender and straight and white as a church taper; her face is long and pointed; the skin is capricious, to-day like cambric, to-morrow darkened with little speckles beneath its surface, as if her blood had left a deposit of dust there during the night. Her forehead is magnificent, though rather daring. The pupils of her eyes are pale sea-green, floating on their white balls under thin lashes and lazy eyelids. Her eyes have dark rings around them often; her nose, which describes one-quarter of a circle, is pinched about the nostrils; very shrewd and clever, but supercilious. She has an Austrian mouth; the upper lip has more character than the lower, which drops disdainfully. Her pale cheeks have no color unless some very keen emotion moves her. Her chin is rather fat; mine is not thin, and perhaps I do wrong to tell you that women with fat chins are exacting in love. She has one of the most exquisite waists I ever saw; the shoulders are beautiful, but the bust has not developed as well, and the arms are thin. She has, however, an easy carriage and manner, which redeems all such defects and sets her beauties in full relief. Nature has given her that princess air which can never be acquired; it becomes her, and reveals at sudden moments the woman of high birth. Without being faultlessly beautiful, or prettily pretty, she produces, when she chooses, ineffaceable impressions. She has only to put on a gown of cherry velvet with clouds of lace, and wreathe with roses that angelic hair of hers, which resembles floods of light, and she becomes divine. If, on some excuse or other, she could wear the costume of the time when women had long, pointed bodices, rising, slim and slender, from voluminous brocaded skirts with folds so heavy that they stood alone, and could hide her arms in those wadded sleeves with ruffles, from which the hand comes out like a pistil from a calyx, and could fling back the curls of her head into the jewelled knot behind her head, Beatrix would hold her own victoriously with ideal beauties like *that*—"

And Felicite showed Calyste a fine copy of a picture by Mieris, in which was a woman robed in white satin, standing with a paper in her hand, and singing with a Brabancon seigneur, while a Negro beside them poured golden Spanish wine into a goblet, and the old housekeeper in the background arranged some biscuits.

"Fair women, blonds," said Camille, "have the advantage over us poor brown things of a precious diversity; there are a hundred ways for a blonde to charm, and only one for a brunette. Besides, blondes are more womanly; we are too like men, we French brunettes—Well, well!" she cried, "pray don't fall in love with Beatrix from the portrait I am making of her, like that prince, I forget his name, in the Arabian Nights. You would be too late, my dear boy."

These words were said pointedly. The admiration depicted on the young man's face was more for the picture than for the painter whose *faire* was failing of its purpose. As she spoke, Felicite was employing all the resources of her eloquent physiognomy.

"Blond as she is, however," she went on, "Beatrix has not the grace of her color; her lines are severe; she is elegant, but hard; her face has a harsh contour, though at times it reveals a soul with Southern passions; an angel flashes out and then expires. Her eyes are thirsty. She looks best when seen full face; the profile has an air of being squeezed between two doors. You will see if I am mistaken. I will tell you now what made us intimate friends. For three years, from 1828 to 1831, Beatrix, while enjoying the last fetes of the Restoration, making the round of the salons, going to court, taking part in the fancy-balls of the Elysee-Bourbon, was all the while judging men, and things, events, and life itself, from the height of her own thought. Her mind was busy. These first years of the bewilderment the world caused her prevented her heart from waking up. From 1830 to 1831 she spent the time of the revolutionary disturbance at her husband's country-place, where she was bored like a saint in paradise. On her return to Paris she became convinced, perhaps justly, that the revolution of July, in the minds of some persons purely political, would prove to be a moral revolution. The social class to which she belonged, not being able, during its unhoped-for triumph in the fifteen years of the Restoration to reconstruct itself, was about to go to pieces, bit by bit, under the battering-ram of the bourgeoisie. She heard the famous words of Monsieur Laine: 'Kings are departing!' This conviction, I believe was not without its influence on her conduct. She took an intellectual part in the new doctrines, which swarmed, during the three years succeeding July, 1830, like gnats in the sunshine, and turned some female heads. But, like all nobles, Beatrix, while thinking these novel ideals superb, wanted always to protect the nobility. Finding before long that there was no place in this new regime for individual superiority, seeing that the higher nobility were beginning once more the mute opposition it had formerly made to Napoleon,—which was, in truth, its wisest course under an empire of deeds and facts, but which in an epoch of moral causes was equivalent to abdication,—she chose personal happiness rather than such eclipse. About the time we were all beginning to breathe again, Beatrix met at my house a man with whom I had expected to end my days,—Gennaro Conti, the great composer, a man of Neapolitan origin, though born in Marseilles. Conti has a brilliant mind; as a composer he has talent, though he will never attain to the first rank. Without Rossini, without Meyerbeer, he might perhaps have been taken for a man of genius. He has one advantage over those men,—he is in vocal music what Paganini is on the violin, Liszt on the piano, Taglioni in the ballet, and what the famous Garat was; at any rate he recalls that great singer to those who knew him. His is not a voice, my friend, it is a soul. When its song replies to certain ideas, certain states of feeling difficult to describe in which a woman sometimes finds herself, that woman is lost. The marquise conceived the maddest passion for him, and took him from me. The act was provincial, I allow, but it was all fair play. She won my esteem and friendship by the way she behaved to me. She thought me a woman who was likely to defend her own; she did not know that to me the most ridiculous thing in the world is such a struggle. She came to see me. That woman, proud as she is, was so in love that she told me her secret and made me the arbiter of her destiny. She was really adorable, and she kept her place as woman and as marquise in my eyes. I must tell you, dear friend, that while women are sometimes bad, they have hidden grandeurs in their souls that men can never appreciate. Well, as I seem to be making my last will and testament like a woman on the verge of old age, I shall tell you that I was ever faithful to Conti, and should have been till death, and yet I *know him*. His nature is charming, apparently, and detestable beneath its surface. He is a charlatan in matters of the heart. There are some men, like Nathan, of whom I have already spoken to you, who are charlatans externally, and yet honest. Such men lie to themselves. Mounted on their stilts, they think they are on their feet, and perform their jugglery with a sort of innocence; their humbuggery is in their blood; they are born comedians, braggarts; extravagant in form as a Chinese vase; perhaps they even laugh at themselves. Their personality is generous; like Murat's kingly garments, it attracts danger. But Conti's duplicity will be known only to the women who love him. In his art he has that deep Italian jealousy which led the Carlone to murder Piola, and stuck a stiletto into Paesiello. That terrible envy lurks beneath the warmest comradeship. Conti has not the courage of his vice; he smiles at Meyerbeer and flatters him, when he fain would tear him to bits. He knows his weakness, and cultivates an appearance of sincerity; his vanity still further leads him to play at sentiments which are far indeed from his real heart. He represents himself as an artist who receives his inspirations from heaven; Art is something saintly and sacred to him; he is fanatic; he is sublime in his contempt for worldliness; his eloquence seems to come from the deepest convictions. He is a seer, a demon, a god, an angel. Calyste, although I warn you about him, you will be his dupe. That Southern nature, that impassioned artist is cold as a well-rope. Listen to him: the artist is a missionary. Art is a religion, which has its priests and ought to have its martyrs. Once started on that theme, Gennaro reaches the most dishevelled pathos that any German professor of philosophy ever spluttered to his audience. You admire his convictions, but he hasn't any. Bearing his hearers to heaven on a song which seems a mysterious fluid shedding love, he casts an ecstatic glance upon them; he is examining their enthusiasm; he is asking himself: 'Am I really a god to them?' and he is also thinking: 'I ate too much macaroni to-day.' He is insatiable of applause, and he wins it. He delights, he is beloved; he is admired whensoever he will. He owes his success more to his voice than to his talent as a composer, though he would rather be a man of genius like Rossini than a performer like Rubini. I had committed the folly of attaching myself to him, and I was determined and resigned to deck this idol to the end. Conti, like a great many artists, is dainty in all his ways; he likes his ease, his enjoyments; he is always carefully, even elegantly dressed. I do respect his courage; he is brave; bravery, they say, is the only virtue into which hypocrisy cannot enter. While we were travelling I saw his courage tested; he risked the life he loved; and yet, strange contradiction! I have seen him, in Paris, commit what I call the cowardice of thought. My friend, all this was known to me. I said to the poor marquise: 'You don't know into what a gulf you are plunging. You are the Perseus of a poor Andromeda; you release me from my rock. If he loves you, so much the better! but I doubt it; he loves no one but himself.' Gennaro was transported to the seventh heaven of pride. I was not a marquise, I was not born a Casteran, and he forgot me in a day. I then gave myself the savage pleasure of probing that nature to the bottom. Certain of the result, I wanted to see the twistings and turnings Conti would perform. My dear child, I saw in one week actual horrors of sham sentiment, infamous buffooneries of feeling. I will not tell you about them; you shall see the man here in a day or two. He now knows that I know him, and he hates me accordingly. If he could stab me with safety to himself I shouldn't be alive two seconds. I have never said one word of all this to Beatrix. The last and constant insult Geranno offers me is to suppose that I am capable of communicating my sad knowledge of him to her; but he has no belief in the good feeling of any human being. Even now he is playing a part with me; he is posing as a man who is wretched at having left me. You will find what I may call the most penetrating cordiality about him; he is winning; he is chivalrous. To him, all women are madonnas. One must live with him long before we get behind the veil of this false chivalry and learn the invisible signs of his humbug. His tone of conviction about himself might almost deceive the Deity. You will be entrapped, my dear child, by his catlike manners, and you will never believe in the profound and rapid arithmetic of his inmost thought. But enough; let us leave him. I pushed indifference so far as to receive them together in my house. This circumstance kept that most perspicacious of all societies, the great world of Paris, ignorant of the affair. Though intoxicated with pride, Gennaro was compelled to dissimulate; and he did it admirably. But violent passions will have their freedom at any cost. Before the end of the year, Beatrix whispered in my ear one evening: 'My dear Felicite, I start to-morrow for Italy with Conti.' I was not surprised; she regarded herself as united for life to Gennaro, and she suffered from the restraints imposed upon her; she escaped one evil by rushing into a greater. Conti was wild with happiness,—the happiness of vanity alone. 'That's what it is to love truly,' he said to me. 'How many women are there who would sacrifice their lives, their fortune, their reputation?'—'Yes, she loves you,' I replied, 'but you do not love her.' He was furious, and made me a scene; he stormed, he declaimed, he depicted his love, declaring that he had never supposed it possible to love as much. I remained impassible, and lent him money for his journey, which, being unexpected, found him unprepared. Beatrix left a letter for her husband and started the next day for Italy. There she has remained two years; she has written to me several times, and her letters are enchanting. The poor child attaches herself to me as the only woman who will comprehend her. She says she adores me. Want of money has compelled Gennaro to accept an offer to write a French opera; he does not find in Italy the pecuniary gains which composers obtain in Paris. Here's the letter I received yesterday from Beatrix. Take it and read it; you can now understand it,— that is, if it is possible, at your age, to analyze the things of the heart."

So saying, she held out the letter to him.

At this moment Claude Vignon entered the room. At his unexpected apparition Calyste and Felicite were both silent for a moment,—she from surprise, he from a vague uneasiness. The vast forehead, broad and high, of the new-comer, who was bald at the age of thirty-seven, now seemed darkened by annoyance. His firm, judicial mouth expressed a habit of chilling sarcasm. Claude Vignon is imposing, in spite of the precocious deteriorations of a face once magnificent, and now grown haggard. Between the ages of eighteen and twenty-five he strongly resembled the divine Raffaelle. But his nose, that feature of the human face that changes most, is growing to a point; the countenance is sinking into mysterious depressions, the outlines are thickening; leaden tones predominate in the complexion, giving tokens of weariness, although the fatigues of this young man are not apparent; perhaps some bitter solitude has aged him, or the abuse of his gift of comprehension. He scrutinizes the thought of every one, yet without definite aim or system. The pickaxe of his criticism demolishes, it never constructs. Thus his lassitude is that of a mechanic, not of an architect. The eyes, of a pale blue, once brilliant, are clouded now by some hidden pain, or dulled by gloomy sadness. Excesses have laid dark tints above the eyelids; the temples have lost their freshness. The chin, of incomparable distinction, is getting doubled, but without dignity. His voice, never sonorous, is weakening; without being either hoarse or extinct, it touches the confines of hoarseness and extinction. The impassibility of that fine head, the fixity of that glance, cover irresolution and weakness, which the keenly intelligent and sarcastic smile belies. The weakness lies wholly in action, not in thought; there are traces of an encyclopedic comprehension on that brow, and in the habitual movement of a face that is childlike and splendid both. The man is tall, slightly bent already, like all those who bear the weight of a world of thought. Such long, tall bodies are never remarkable for continuous effort or creative activity. Charlemagne, Belisarious, and Constantine are noted exceptions to this rule.

Certainly Claude Vignon presents a variety of mysteries to be solved. In the first place, he is very simple and very wily. Though he falls into excesses with the readiness of a courtesan, his powers of thought remain untouched. Yet his intellect, which is competent to criticise art, science, literature, and politics, is incompetent to guide his external life. Claude contemplates himself within the domain of his intellectual kingdom, and abandons his outer man with Diogenic indifference. Satisfied to penetrate all, to comprehend all by thought, he despises materialities; and yet, if it becomes a question of creating, doubt assails him; he sees obstacles, he is not inspired by beauties, and while he is debating means, he sits with his arms pendant, accomplishing nothing. He is the Turk of the intellect made somnolent by meditation. Criticism is his opium; his harem of books to read disgusts him with real work. Indifferent to small things as well as great things, he is sometimes compelled, by the very weight of his head, to fall into a debauch, and abdicate for a few hours the fatal power of omnipotent analysis. He is far too preoccupied with the wrong side of genius, and Camille Maupin's desire to put him back on the right side is easily conceivable. The task was an attractive one. Claude Vignon thinks himself a great politician as well as a great writer; but this unpublished Machiavelli laughs within himself at all ambitions; he knows what he can do; he has instinctively taken the measure of his future on his faculties; he sees his greatness, but he also sees obstacles, grows alarmed or disgusted, lets the time roll by, and does not go to work. Like Etienne Lousteau the feuilletonist, like Nathan the dramatic author, like Blondet, another journalist, he came from the ranks of the bourgeoisie, to which we owe the greater number of our writers.

"Which way did you come?" asked Mademoiselle des Touches, coloring with either pleasure or surprise.'

"By the door," replied Claude Vignon, dryly.

"Oh," she cried, shrugging her shoulders, "I am aware that you are not a man to climb in by a window."

"Scaling a window is a badge of honor for a beloved woman."

"Enough!" said Felicite.

"Am I in the way?" asked Claude.

"Monsieur," said Calyste, artlessly, "this letter—"

"Pray keep it; I ask no questions; at our age we understand such affairs," he answered, interrupting Calyste with a sardonic air.

"But, monsieur," began Calyste, much provoked.

"Calm yourself, young man; I have the utmost indulgence for sentiments."

"My dear Calyste," said Camille, wishing to speak.

"'Dear'?" said Vignon, interrupting her.

"Claude is joking," said Camille, continuing her remarks to Calyste. "He is wrong to do it with you, who know nothing of Parisian ways."

"I did not know that I was joking," said Claude Vignon, very gravely.

"Which way did you come?" asked Felicite again. "I have been watching the road to Croisic for the last two hours."

"Not all the time," replied Vignon.

"You are too bad to jest in this way."

"Am I jesting?"

Calyste rose.

"Why should you go so soon? You are certainly at your ease here," said Vignon.

"Quite the contrary," replied the angry young Breton, to whom Camille Maupin stretched out a hand, which he took and kissed, dropping a tear upon it, after which he took his leave.

"I should like to be that little young man," said the critic, sitting down, and taking one end of the hookah. "How he will love!"

"Too much; for then he will not be loved in return," replied Mademoiselle des Touches. "Madame de Rochefide is coming here," she added.

"You don't say so!" exclaimed Claude. "With Conti?"

"She will stay here alone, but he accompanies her."

"Have they quarrelled?"

"No."

"Play me a sonata of Beethoven's; I know nothing of the music he wrote for the piano."

Claude began to fill the tube of the hookah with Turkish tobacco, all the while examining Camille much more attentively than she observed. A dreadful thought oppressed him; he fancied he was being used for a blind by this woman. The situation was a novel one.

Calyste went home thinking no longer of Beatrix de Rochefide and her letter; he was furious against Claude Vignon for what he considered the utmost indelicacy, and he pitied poor Felicite. How was it possible to be beloved by that sublime creature and not adore her on his knees, not believe her on the faith of a glance or a smile? He felt a desire to turn and rend that cold, pale spectre of a man. Ignorant he might be, as Felicite had told him, of the tricks of thought of the jesters of the press, but one thing he knew — Love was the human religion.

When his mother saw him entering the court-yard she uttered an exclamation of joy, and Zephirine whistled for Mariotte.

"Mariotte, the boy is coming! cook the fish!"

"I see him, mademoiselle," replied the woman.

Fanny, uneasy at the sadness she saw on her son's brow, picked up her worsted-work; the old aunt took out her knitting. The baron gave his arm-chair to his son and walked about the room, as if to stretch his legs before going out to take a turn in the garden. No Flemish or Dutch picture ever presented an interior in tones more mellow, peopled with faces and forms so harmoniously blending. The handsome young man in his black velvet coat, the mother, still so beautiful, and the aged brother and sister framed by that ancient hall, were a moving domestic harmony.

Fanny would fain have questioned Calyste, but he had already pulled a letter from his pocket, — that letter of the Marquise Beatrix, which was, perhaps, destined to destroy the happiness of this noble family. As he unfolded it, Calyste's awakened imagination showed him the marquise dressed as Camille Maupin had fancifully depicted her.

From the Marquise de Rochefide to Mademoiselle des Touches.

Genoa, July 2.

I have not written to you since our stay in Florence, my dear friend, for Venice and Rome have absorbed my time, and, as you know, happiness occupies a large part of life; so far, we have neither of us dropped from its first level. I am a little fatigued; for when one has a soul not easy to blaser, the constant succession of enjoyments naturally causes lassitude.

Our friend has had a magnificent triumph at the Scala and the Fenice, and now at the San Carlo. Three Italian operas in two years! You cannot say that love has made him idle. We have been warmly received everywhere, — though I myself would have preferred solitude and silence. Surely that is the only suitable manner of life for women who have placed themselves in direct opposition to society? I expected such a life; but love, my dear friend, is a more exacting master than marriage, — however, it is sweet to obey him; though I did not think I should have to see the world again, even by snatches, and the attentions I receive are so many stabs. I am no longer on a footing of equality with the highest rank of women; and the more attentions are paid to me, the more my inferiority is made apparent.

Gennaro could not comprehend this sensitiveness; but he has been so happy that it would ill become me not to have sacrificed my petty vanity to that great and noble thing, — the life of an artist. We women live by love, whereas men live by love and action; otherwise they would not be men. Still, there are great disadvantages for a woman in the position in which I have put myself. You have escaped them; you continue to be a person in the eyes of the world, which has no rights over you; you have your own free will, and I have lost mine. I am speaking now of the things of the heart, not those of social life, which I have utterly renounced. You can be coquettish and self-willed, and have all the graces of a woman who loves, a woman who can give or refuse her love as she pleases; you have kept the right to have caprices, in the interests even of your love. In short, to-day you still possess your right of feeling, while I, I have no longer any liberty of heart, which I think precious to exercise in love, even though the love itself may be eternal. I have no right now to that privilege of quarrelling in jest to which so many women cling, and justly; for is it not the plummet line with which to sound the hearts of men? I have no threat at my command. I must draw my power henceforth from obedience, from unlimited gentleness; I must make myself imposing by the greatness of my love. I would rather die than leave Gennaro, and my pardon lies in the sanctity of my love. Between social dignity and my petty personal dignity, I did right not to hesitate. If at times I have a few melancholy feelings, like clouds that pass through a clear blue sky, and to which all women like to yield themselves, I keep silence about them; they might seem like regrets. Ah me! I have so fully understood the obligations of my position that I have armed myself with the utmost indulgence; but so far, Gennaro has not alarmed my susceptible jealousy. I don't as yet see where that dear great genius may fail.

Dear angel, I am like those pious souls who argue with their God, for are not you my Providence? do I not owe my happiness to you? You must never doubt, therefore, that you are constantly in my thoughts.

I have seen Italy at last; seen it as you saw it, and as it ought to be seen, — lighted to our souls by love, as it is by its own bright sun and its masterpieces. I pity those who, being moved to adoration at every step, have no hand to press, no heart in which to shed the exuberance of emotions which calm themselves when shared. These two years have been to me a lifetime, in which my memory has stored rich harvests. Have you made plans, as I do, to stay forever at Chiavari, to buy a palazzo in Venice, a summer-house at Sorrento, a villa in Florence? All loving women dread society; but I, who am cast forever outside of it, ought I not to bury myself in some beautiful landscape, on flowery slopes, facing the sea, or in a valley that equals a sea, like that of Fiesole?

But alas! we are only poor artists, and want of money is bringing these two bohemians back to Paris. Gennaro does not want me to feel that I have lost my luxury, and he wishes to put his new work, a grand opera, into rehearsal at once. You will understand, of course, my dearest, that I cannot set foot in Paris. I could not, I would not, even if it costs me my love, meet one of those glances of women, or of men, which would make me think of murder or suicide. Yes, I could hack in pieces whoever insulted me with pity; like Chateauneuf, who, in the time of Henri III., I think, rode his horse at the Provost of Paris for a wrong of that kind, and trampled him under hoof.

I write, therefore, to say that I shall soon pay you a visit at Les Touches. I want to stay there, in that Chartreuse, while awaiting the success of our Gennaro's opera. You will see that I am bold with my benefactress, my sister; but I prove, at any rate, that the greatness of obligations laid upon me has not led me, as it does so many people, to ingratitude. You have told me so much of the difficulties of the land journey that I shall go to Croisic by water. This idea came to me on finding that there is a little Danish vessel now here, laden with marble, which is to touch at Croisic for a cargo of salt on its way back to the Baltic. I shall thus escape the fatigue and the cost of the land journey. Dear Felicite, you are the only person with whom I could be alone without Conti. Will it not be some pleasure to have a woman with you who understands your heart as fully as you do hers?

Adieu, a bientot. The wind is favorable, and I set sail, wafting you a kiss.

Beatrix.

"Ah! she loves, too!" thought Calyste, folding the letter sadly.

That sadness flowed to the heart of the mother as if some gleam had lighted up a gulf to her. The baron had gone out; Fanny went to the door of the tower and pushed the bolt, then she returned, and leaned upon the back of her boy's chair, like the sister of Dido in Guerin's picture, and said, —

"What is it, my Calyste? what makes you so sad? You promised to explain to me these visits to Les Touches; I am to bless its mistress, — at least, you said so."

"Yes, indeed you will, dear mother," he replied. "She has shown me the insufficiency of my education at an epoch when the nobles ought to possess a personal value in order to give life to their rank. I was as far from the age we live in as Guerande is from Paris. She has been, as it were, the mother of my intellect."

"I cannot bless her for that," said the baroness, with tears in her eyes.

"Mamma!" cried Calyste, on whose forehead those hot tears fell, two pearls of sorrowful motherhood, "mamma, don't weep! Just now, when I wanted to do her a service, and search the country round, she said, 'It will make your mother so uneasy.'"

"Did she say that? Then I can forgive her many things," replied Fanny.

"Felicite thinks only of my good," continued Calyste. "She often checks the lively, venturesome language of artists so as not to shake me in a faith which is, though she knows it not, unshakable. She has told me of the life in Paris of several young men of the highest nobility coming from their provinces, as I might do,—leaving families without fortune, but obtaining in Paris, by the power of their will and their intellect, a great career. I can do what the Baron de Rastignac, now a minister of State, has done. Felicite has taught me; I read with her; she gives me lessons on the piano; she is teaching me Italian; she has initiated me into a thousand social secrets, about which no one in Guerande knows anything at all. She could not give me the treasures of her love, but she has given me those of her vast intellect, her mind, her genius. She does not want to be a pleasure, but a light to me; she lessens not one of my faiths; she herself has faith in the nobility, she loves Brittany, she—"

"She has changed our Calyste," said his blind old aunt, interrupting him. "I do not understand one word he has been saying. You have a solid roof over your head, my good nephew; you have parents and relations who adore you, and faithful servants; you can marry some good little Breton girl, religious and accomplished, who will make you happy. Reserve your ambitions for your eldest son, who may be four times as rich as you, if you choose to live tranquilly, thriftily, in obscurity,—but in the peace of God,—in order to release the burdens on your estate. It is all as simple as a Breton heart. You will be, not so rapidly perhaps, but more solidly, a rich nobleman."

"Your aunt is right, my darling; she plans for your happiness with as much anxiety as I do myself. If I do not succeed in marrying you to my niece, Margaret, the daughter of your uncle, Lord Fitzwilliam, it is almost certain that Mademoiselle de Pen-Hoel will leave her fortune to whichever of her nieces you may choose."

"And besides, there's a little gold to be found here," added the old aunt in a low voice, with a mysterious glance about her.

"Marry! at my age!" he said, casting on his mother one of those looks which melt the arguments of mothers. "Am I to live without my beautiful fond loves? Must I never tremble or throb or fear or gasp, or lie beneath implacable looks and soften them? Am I never to know beauty in its freedom, the fantasy of the soul, the clouds that course through the azure of happiness, which the breath of pleasure dissipates? Ah! shall I never wander in those sweet by-paths moist with dew; never stand beneath the drenching of a gutter and not know it rains, like those lovers seen by Diderot; never take, like the Duc de Lorraine, a live coal in my hand? Are there no silken ladders for me, no rotten trellises to cling to and not fall? Shall I know nothing of woman but conjugal submission; nothing of love but the flame of its lamp-wick? Are my longings to be satisfied before they are roused? Must I live out my days deprived of that madness of the heart that makes a man and his power? Would you make me a married monk? No! I have eaten of the fruit of

Parisian civilization. Do you not see that you have, by the ignorant morals of this family, prepared the fire that consumes me, that *will* consume me utterly, unless I can adore the divineness I see everywhere,—in those sands gleaming in the sun, in the green foliage, in all the women, beautiful, noble, elegant, pictured in the books and in the poems I have read with Camille? Alas! there is but one such woman in Guerande, and it is you, my mother! The birds of my beautiful dream, they come from Paris, they fly from the pages of Scott, of Byron,—Parisina, Effie, Minna! yes, and that royal duchess, whom I saw on the moors among the furze and the ferns, whose very aspect sent the blood to my heart."

The baroness saw these thoughts flaming in the eyes of her son, clearer, more beautiful, more living than art can tell to those who read them. She grasped them rapidly, flung to her as they were in glances like arrows from an upset quiver. Without having read Beaumarchais, she felt, as other women would have felt, that it would be a crime to marry Calyste.

"Oh! my child!" she said, taking him in her arms, and kissing the beautiful hair that was still hers, "marry whom you will, and when you will, but be happy! My part in life is not to hamper you."

Mariotte came to lay the table. Gasselin was out exercising Calyste's horse, which the youth had not mounted for two months. The three women, mother, aunt, and Mariotte, shared in the tender feminine wiliness, which taught them to make much of Calyste when he dined at home. Breton plainness fought against Parisian luxury, now brought to the very doors of Guerande. Mariotte endeavored to wean her young master from the accomplished service of Camille Maupin's kitchen, just as his mother and aunt strove to hold him in the net of their tenderness and render all comparison impossible.

"There's a salmon-trout for dinner, Monsieur Calyste, and snipe, and pancakes such as I know you can't get anywhere but here," said Mariotte, with a sly, triumphant look as she smoothed the cloth, a cascade of snow.

After dinner, when the old aunt had taken up her knitting, and the rector and Monsieur du Halga had arrived, allured by their precious *mouche*, Calyste went back to Les Touches on the pretext of returning the letter.

Claude Vignon and Felicite were still at table. The great critic was something of a gourmand, and Felicite pampered the vice, knowing how indispensable a woman makes herself by such compliance. The dinner-table presented that rich and brilliant aspect which modern luxury, aided by the perfecting of handicrafts, now gives to its service. The poor and noble house of Guenic little knew with what an adversary it was attempting to compete, or what amount of fortune was necessary to enter the lists against the silverware, the delicate porcelain, the beautiful linen, the silver-gilt service brought from Paris by Mademoiselle des Touches, and the science of her cook. Calyste declined the liqueurs contained in one of those superb cases of precious woods, which are something like tabernacles.

"Here's the letter," he said, with innocent ostentation, looking at Claude, who was slowly sipping a glass of *liqueur-des-iles.*

"Well, what did you think of it?" asked Mademoiselle des Touches, throwing the letter across the table to Vignon, who began to read it, taking up and putting down at intervals his little glass.

"I thought—well, that Parisian women were very fortunate to have men of genius to adore who adore them."

"Ah! you are still in your village," said Felicite, laughing. "What! did you not see that she loves him less, and—"

"That is evident," said Claude Vignon, who had only read the first page. "Do people reason on their situation when they really love; are they as shrewd as the marquise, as observing, as discriminating? Your dear Beatrix is held to Conti now by pride only; she is condemned to love him *quand meme*."

"Poor woman!" said Camille.

Calyste's eyes were fixed on the table; he saw nothing about him. The beautiful woman in the fanciful dress described that morning by Felicite appeared to him crowned with light; she smiled to him, she waved her fan; the other hand, issuing from its ruffle of lace, fell white and pure on the heavy folds of her crimson velvet robe.

"She is just the thing for you," said Claude Vignon, smiling sardonically at Calyste.

The young man was deeply wounded by the words, and by the manner in which they were said.

"Don't put such ideas into Calyste's mind; you don't know how dangerous such jokes may prove to be," said Mademoiselle des Touches, hastily. "I know Beatrix, and there is something too grandiose in her nature to allow her to change. Besides, Conti will be here."

"Ha!" said Claude Vignon, satirically, "a slight touch of jealousy, eh?"

"Can you really think so?" said Camille, haughtily.

"You are more perspicacious than a mother," replied Claude Vignon, still sarcastically.

"But it would be impossible," said Camille, looking at Calyste.

"They are very well matched," remarked Vignon. "She is ten years older than he; and it is he who appears to be the girl—"

"A girl, monsieur," said Calyste, waking from his reverie, "who has been twice under fire in La Vendee! If the Cause had had twenty thousand more such girls—"

"I was giving you some well-deserved praise, and that is easier than to give you a beard," remarked Vignon.

"I have a sword for those who wear their beards too long," cried Calyste.

"And I am very good at an epigram," said the other, smiling. "We are Frenchmen; the affair can easily be arranged."

Mademoiselle des Touches cast a supplicating look on Calyste, which calmed him instantly.

"Why," said Felicite, as if to break up the discussion, "do young men like my Calyste, begin by loving women of a certain age?"

"I don't know any sentiment more artless or more generous," replied Vignon. "It is the natural consequence of the adorable qualities of youth. Besides, how would old women end if it were not for such love? You are young and beautiful, and will be for twenty years to come, so I can speak of this matter before you," he added, with a keen look at Mademoiselle des Touches. "In the first place the semi-dowagers, to whom young men pay their first court, know much better how to make love than younger women. An adolescent youth is too like a young woman himself for a young woman to please him. Such a passion trenches on the fable of Narcissus. Besides that feeling of repugnance, there is, as I think, a mutual sense of inexperience which separates them. The reason why the hearts of young women are only understood by mature men, who conceal their cleverness under a passion real or feigned, is precisely the same (allowing for the difference of minds) as that which renders a woman of a certain age more adroit in attracting youth. A young man feels that he is sure to succeed with her, and the vanities of the woman are flattered by his suit. Besides, isn't it natural for youth to fling itself on fruits? The autumn of a woman's life offers many that are very toothsome, — those looks, for instance, bold, and yet reserved, bathed with the last rays of love, so warm, so sweet; that all-wise elegance of speech, those magnificent shoulders, so nobly developed, the full and undulating outline, the dimpled hands, the hair so well arranged, so cared for, that charming nape of the neck, where all the resources of art are displayed to exhibit the contrast between the hair and the flesh-tones, and to set in full relief the exuberance of life and love. Brunettes themselves are fair at such times, with the amber colors of maturity. Besides, such women reveal in their smiles and display in their words a knowledge of the world; they know how to converse; they can call up the whole of social life to make a lover laugh; their dignity and their pride are stupendous; or, in other moods, they can utter despairing cries which touch his soul, farewells of love which they take care to render useless, and only make to intensify his passion. Their devotions are absolute; they listen to us; they love us; they catch, they cling to love as a man condemned to death clings to the veriest trifles of existence, — in short, love, absolute love, is known only through them. I think such women can never be forgotten by a man, any more than he can forget what is grand and sublime. A young woman has a thousand distractions; these women have none. No longer have they self-love, pettiness, or vanity; their love — it is the Loire at its mouth, it is vast, it is swelled by all the illusions, all the affluents of life, and this is why — but my muse is dumb," he added, observing the ecstatic attitude of Mademoiselle des Touches, who was pressing Calyste's hand with all her strength, perhaps to thank him for having been the occasion of such a moment, of such an eulogy, so lofty that she did not see the trap that it laid for her.

During the rest of the evening Claude Vignon and Felicite sparkled with wit and happy sayings; they told anecdotes, and described Parisian life to Calyste, who was charmed with Claude, for mind has immense seductions for persons who are all heart.

"I shouldn't be surprised to see the Marquise de Rochefide and Conti, who, of course, will accompany her, at the landing-place to-morrow," said Claude Vignon, as the evening ended. "When I was at Croisic this afternoon, the fishermen were saying that they had seen a little vessel, Danish, Swedish, or Norwegian, in the offing."

This speech brought a flush to the cheeks of the impassible Camille.

Again Madame du Guenic sat up till one o'clock that night, waiting for her son, unable to imagine why he should stay so late if Mademoiselle des Touches did not love him.

"He must be in their way," said this adorable mother. "What were you talking about?" she asked, when at last he came in.

"Oh, mother, I have never before spent such a delightful evening. Genius is a great, a sublime thing! Why didn't you give me genius? With genius we can make our lives, we can choose among all women the woman to love, and she must be ours."

"How handsome you are, my Calyste!"

"Claude Vignon is handsome. Men of genius have luminous foreheads and eyes, through which the lightnings flash—but I, alas! I know nothing—only to love."

"They say that suffices, my angel," she said, kissing him on the forehead.

"Do you believe it?"

"They say so, but I have never known it."

Calyste kissed his mother's hand as if it was a sacred thing.

"I will love you for all those that would have adored you," he said.

"Dear child! perhaps it is a little bit your duty to do so, for you inherit my nature. But, Calyste, do not be unwise, imprudent; try to love only noble women, if love you must."

CHAPTER IX.

A FIRST MEETING

What young man full of abounding but restrained life and emotion would not have had the glorious idea of going to Croisic to see Madame de Rochefide land, and examine her incognito? Calyste greatly surprised his father and mother by going off in the morning without waiting for the mid-day breakfast. Heaven knows with what agility the young Breton's feet sped along. Some unknown vigor seemed lent to him; he walked on air, gliding along by the walls of Les Touches that he might not be seen from the house. The adorable boy was ashamed of his ardor, and afraid of being laughed at; Felicite and Vignon were so perspicacious! besides, in such cases young fellows fancy that their foreheads are transparent.

He reached the shore, strengthened by a stone embankment, at the foot of which is a house where travellers can take shelter in storms of wind or rain. It is not always possible to cross the little arm of the sea which separates the landing-place of Guerande from Croisic; the weather may be bad, or the boats not ready; and during this time of waiting, it is necessary to put not only the passengers but their horses, donkeys, baggages, and merchandise under cover.

Calyste presently saw two boats coming over from Croisic, laden with baggage,—trunks, packages, bags, and chests,—the shape and appearance of which proved to a native of these parts that such extraordinary articles must belong to travellers of distinction. In one of the boats was a young woman in a straw bonnet with a green veil, accompanied by a man. This boat was the first to arrive. Calyste trembled until on closer view he saw they were a maid and a man-servant.

"Are you going over to Croisic, Monsieur Calyste?" said one of the boatmen; to whom he replied with a shake of the head, annoyed at being called by his name.

He was captivated by the sight of a chest covered with tarred cloth on which were painted the words, MME. LA MARQUISE DE ROCHEFIDE. The name shone before him like a talisman; he fancied there was something fateful in it. He knew in some mysterious way, which he could not doubt, that he should love that woman. Why? In the burning desert of his new and infinite desires, still vague and without an object, his fancy fastened with all its strength on the first woman that presented herself. Beatrix necessarily inherited the love which Camille had rejected.

Calyste watched the landing of the luggage, casting from time to time a glance at Croisic, from which he hoped to see another boat put out to cross to the little promontory, and show him Beatrix, already to his eyes what Beatrice was to Dante, a marble statue on which to hang his garlands and his flowers. He stood with arms folded, lost in meditation. Here is a fact worthy of remark, which, neverthe-less, has never been remarked: we often subject ourselves to sentiments by our own volition,—deliberately bind ourselves, and create our own fate; chance has not as much to do with it as we believe.

"I don't see any horses," said the maid, sitting on a trunk.

"And I don't see any road," said the footman.

"Horses have been here, though," replied the woman, pointing to the proofs of their presence. "Monsieur," she said, addressing Calyste, "is this really the way to Guerande?"

"Yes," he replied, "are you expecting some one to meet you?"

"We were told that they would fetch us from Les Touches. If they don't come," she added to the footman, "I don't know how Madame la marquise will manage to dress for dinner. You had better go and find Mademoiselle des Touches. Oh! what a land of savages!"

Calyste had a vague idea of having blundered.

"Is your mistress going to Les Touches?" he inquired.

"She is there; Mademoiselle came for her this morning at seven o'clock. Ah! here come the horses."

Calyste started toward Guerande with the lightness and agility of a chamois, doubling like a hare that he might not return upon his tracks or meet any of the servants of Les Touches. He did, however, meet two of them on the narrow cause-way of the marsh along which he went.

"Shall I go in, or shall I not?" he thought when the pines of Les Touches came in sight. He was afraid; and continued his way rather sulkily to Guerande, where he finished his excursion on the mall and continued his reflections.

"She has no idea of my agitation," he said to himself.

His capricious thoughts were so many grapnels which fastened his heart to the marquise. He had known none of these mysterious terrors and joys in his inter-course with Camille. Such vague emotions rise like poems in the untutored soul. Warmed by the first fires of imagination, souls like his have been known to pass through all phases of preparation and to reach in silence and solitude the very heights of love, without having met the object of so many efforts.

Presently Calyste saw, coming toward him, the Chevalier du Halga and Ma-demoiselle de Pen-Hoel, who were walking together on the mall. He heard them say his name, and he slipped aside out of sight, but not out of hearing. The cheva-lier and the old maid, believing themselves alone, were talking aloud.

"If Charlotte de Kergarouet comes," said the chevalier, "keep her four or five months. How can you expect her to coquette with Calyste? She is never here long enough to undertake it. Whereas, if they see each other every day, those two chil-dren will fall in love, and you can marry them next winter. If you say two words about it to Charlotte she'll say four to Calyste, and a girl of sixteen can certainly carry off the prize from a woman of forty."

Here the old people turned to retrace their steps and Calyste heard no more. But remembering what his mother had told him, he saw Mademoiselle de Pen-Hoel's intention, and, in the mood in which he then was, nothing could have been more fatal. The mere idea of a girl thus imposed upon him sent him with greater ardor into his imaginary love. He had never had a fancy for Charlotte de Kerga-rouet, and he now felt repugnance at the very thought of her. Calyste was quite unaffected by questions of fortune; from infancy he had accustomed his life to the poverty and the restricted means of his father's house. A young man brought up as he had been, and now partially emancipated, was likely to consider sentiments only, and all his sentiments, all his thought now belonged to the marquise. In presence of the portrait which Camille had drawn for him of her friend, what was that little Charlotte? the companion of his childhood, whom he thought of as a sister.

He did not go home till five in the afternoon. As he entered the hall his mother gave him, with a rather sad smile, the following letter from Mademoiselle des Touches:—

> My dear Calyste,—The beautiful marquise has come; we count on you to help us celebrate her arrival. Claude, always sarcastic, declares that you will play Bice and that she will be Dante. It is for our honor as Bretons, and yours as a du Guenic to welcome a Casteran. Come soon.
>
> > Your friend,
> > Camille Maupin.

Come as you are, without ceremony; otherwise you will put us to the blush.

Calyste gave the letter to his mother and departed.

"Who are the Casterans?" said Fanny to the baron.

"An old Norman family, allied to William the Conqueror," he replied. "They bear on a shield tierce fessed azure, gules and sable, a horse rearing argent, shod with gold. That beautiful creature for whom the Gars was killed at Fougeres in 1800 was the daughter of a Casteran who made herself a nun, and became an abbess after the Duc de Verneuil deserted her."

"And the Rochefides?"

"I don't know that name. I should have to see the blazon," he replied.

The baroness was somewhat reassured on hearing that the Marquise de Rochefide was born of a noble family, but she felt that her son was now exposed to new seductions.

Calyste as he walked along felt all sorts of violent and yet soft inward movements; his throat was tight, his heart swelled, his brain was full, a fever possessed him. He tried to walk slowly, but some superior power hurried him. This impetuosity of the several senses excited by vague expectation is known to all young men. A subtle fire flames within their breasts and darts outwardly about them, like the rays of a nimbus around the heads of divine personages in works of religious art;

through it they see all Nature glorious, and woman radiant. Are they not then like those haloed saints, full of faith, hope, ardor, purity?

The young Breton found the company assembled in the little salon of Camille's suite of rooms. It was then about six o'clock; the sun, in setting, cast through the windows its ruddy light chequered by the trees; the air was still; twilight, beloved of women, was spreading through the room.

"Here comes the future deputy of Brittany," said Camille Maupin, smiling, as Calyste raised the tapestry portiere, — "punctual as a king."

"You recognized his step just now," said Claude to Felicite in a low voice.

Calyste bowed low to the marquise, who returned the salutation with an inclination of her head; he did not look at her; but he took the hand Claude Vignon held out to him and pressed it.

"This is the celebrated man of whom we have talked so much, Gennaro Conti," said Camille, not replying to Claude Vignon's remark.

She presented to Calyste a man of medium height, thin and slender, with chestnut hair, eyes that were almost red, and a white skin, freckled here and there, whose head was so precisely the well-known head of Lord Byron (though rather better carried on his shoulders) that description is superfluous. Conti was rather proud of this resemblance.

"I am fortunate," he said, "to meet Monsieur du Guenic during the one day that I spend at Les Touches."

"It was for me to say that to you," replied Calyste, with a certain ease.

"He is handsome as an angel," said the marquise in an under tone to Felicite.

Standing between the sofa and the two ladies, Calyste heard the words confusedly. He seated himself in an arm-chair and looked furtively toward the marquise. In the soft half-light he saw, reclining on a divan, as if a sculptor had placed it there, a white and serpentine shape which thrilled him. Without being aware of it, Felicite had done her friend a service; the marquise was much superior to the unflattered portrait Camille had drawn of her the night before. Was it to do honor to the guest that Beatrix had wound into her hair those tufts of blue-bells that gave value to the pale tints of her creped curls, so arranged as to fall around her face and play upon the cheeks? The circle of her eyes, which showed fatigue, was of the purest mother-of-pearl, her skin was as dazzling as the eyes, and beneath its whiteness, delicate as the satiny lining of an egg, life abounded in the beautiful blue veins. The delicacy of the features was extreme; the forehead seemed diaphanous. The head, so sweet and fragrant, admirably joined to a long neck of exquisite moulding, lent itself to many and most diverse expressions. The waist, which could be spanned by the hands, had a charming willowy ease; the bare shoulders sparkled in the twilight like a white camellia. The throat, visible to the eye though covered with a transparent fichu, allowed the graceful outlines of the bosom to be seen with charming roguishness. A gown of white muslin, strewn with blue flowers, made with very large sleeves, a pointed body and no belt, shoes with strings crossed on the instep over Scotch thread stockings, showed a charming knowledge of the art of dress. Ear-rings of silver filagree, miracles of Genoese jewelry, destined no doubt to become the fashion, were in perfect harmony with the delightful flow of the soft curls starred with blue-bells.

Calyste's eager eye took in these beauties at a glance, and carved them on his soul. The fair Beatrix and the dark Felicite might have sat for those contrasting portraits in "keepsakes" which English designers and engravers seek so persistently. Here were the force and the feebleness of womanhood in full development, a perfect antithesis. These two women could never be rivals; each had her own empire. Here was the delicate campanula, or the lily, beside the scarlet poppy; a turquoise near a ruby. In a moment, as it were,—at first sight, as the saying is,—Calyste was seized with a love which crowned the secret work of his hopes, his fears, his uncertainties. Mademoiselle des Touches had awakened his nature; Beatrix inflamed both his heart and thoughts. The young Breton suddenly felt within him a power to conquer all things, and yield to nothing that stood in his way. He looked at Conti with an envious, gloomy, savage rivalry he had never felt for Claude Vignon. He employed all his strength to control himself; but the inward tempest went down as soon as the eyes of Beatrix turned to him, and her soft voice sounded in his ear. Dinner was announced.

"Calyste, give your arm to the marquise," said Mademoiselle des Touches, taking Conti with her right hand, and Claude Vignon with her left, and drawing back to let the marquise pass.

The descent of that ancient staircase was to Calyste like the moment of going into battle for the first time. His heart failed him, he had nothing to say; a slight sweat pearled upon his forehead and wet his back; his arm trembled so much that as they reached the lowest step the marquise said to him: "Is anything the matter?"

"Oh!" he replied, in a muffled tone, "I have never seen any woman so beautiful as you, except my mother, and I am not master of my emotions."

"But you have Camille Maupin before your eyes."

"Ah! what a difference!" said Calyste, ingenuously.

"Calyste," whispered Felicite, who was just behind him, "did I not tell you that you would forget me as if I had never existed? Sit there," she said aloud, "beside the marquise, on her right, and you, Claude, on her left. As for you, Gennaro, I retain you by me; we will keep a mutual eye on their coquetries."

The peculiar accept which Camille gave to the last word struck Claude Vignon's ear, and he cast that sly but half-abstracted look upon Camille which always denoted in him the closest observation. He never ceased to examine Mademoiselle des Touches throughout the dinner.

"Coquetries!" replied the marquis, taking off her gloves, and showing her beautiful hands; "the opportunity is good, with a poet," and she motioned to Claude, "on one side, and poesy the other."

At these words Conti turned and gave Calyste a look that was full of flattery.

By artificial light, Beatrix seemed more beautiful than before. The white gleam of the candles laid a satiny lustre on her forehead, lighted the spangles of her eyes, and ran through her swaying curls, touching them here and there into gold. She threw back the thin gauze scarf she was wearing and disclosed her neck. Calyste then saw its beautiful nape, white as milk, and hollowed near the head, until its lines were lost toward the shoulders with soft and flowing symmetry. This neck, so dissimilar to that of Camille, was the sign of a totally different character in Beatrix.

Calyste found much trouble in pretending to eat; nervous motions within him deprived him of appetite. Like other young men, his nature was in the throes and convulsions which precede love, and carve it indelibly on the soul. At his age, the ardor of the heart, restrained by moral ardor, leads to an inward conflict, which explains the long and respectful hesitations, the tender debatings, the absence of all calculation, characteristic of young men whose hearts and lives are pure. Studying, though furtively, so as not to attract the notice of Conti, the various details which made the marquise so purely beautiful, Calyste became, before long, oppressed by a sense of her majesty; he felt himself dwarfed by the hauteur of certain of her glances, by the imposing expression of a face that was wholly aristocratic, by a sort of pride which women know how to express in slight motions, turns of the head, and slow gestures, effects less plastic and less studied than we think. The false situation in which Beatrix had placed herself compelled her to watch her own behavior, and to keep herself imposing without being ridiculously so. Women of the great world know how to succeed in this, which proves a fatal reef to vulgar women.

The expression of Felicite's eyes made Beatrix aware of the inward adoration she inspired in the youth beside her, and also that it would be most unworthy on her part to encourage it. She therefore took occasion now and then to give him a few repressive glances, which fell upon his heart like an avalanche of snow. The unfortunate young fellow turned on Felicite a look in which she could read the tears he was suppressing by superhuman efforts. She asked him in a friendly tone why he was eating nothing. The question piqued him, and he began to force himself to eat and to take part in the conversation.

But whatever he did, Madame de Rochefide paid little attention to him. Mademoiselle des Touches having started the topic of her journey to Italy she related, very wittily, many of its incidents, which made Claude Vignon, Conti, and Felicite laugh.

"Ah!" thought Calyste, "how far such a woman is from me! Will she ever deign to notice me?"

Mademoiselle des Touches was struck with the expression she now saw on Calyste's face, and tried to console him with a look of sympathy. Claude Vignon intercepted that look. From that moment the great critic expanded into gaiety that overflowed in sarcasm. He maintained to Beatrix that love existed only by desire; that most women deceived themselves in loving; that they loved for reasons unknown to men and to themselves; that they wanted to deceive themselves, and that the best among them were artful.

"Keep to books, and don't criticise our lives," said Camille, glancing at him imperiously.

The dinner ceased to be gay. Claude Vignon's sarcasm had made the two women pensive. Calyste was conscious of pain in the midst of the happiness he found in looking at Beatrix. Conti looked into the eyes of the marquise to guess her thoughts. When dinner was over Mademoiselle des Touches took Calyste's arm, gave the other two men to the marquise, and let them pass before her, that she might be alone with the young Breton for a moment.

"My dear Calyste," she said, "you are acting in a manner that embarrasses the marquise; she may be delighted with your admiration, but she cannot accept it. Pray control yourself."

"She was hard to me, she will never care for me," said Calyste, "and if she does not I shall die."

"Die! you! My dear Calyste, you are a child. Would you have died for me?"

"You have made yourself my friend," he answered.

After the talk that follows coffee, Vignon asked Conti to sing something. Mademoiselle des Touches sat down to the piano. Together she and Gennaro sang the *Dunque il mio bene tu mia sarai*, the last duet of Zingarelli's "Romeo e Giulietta," one of the most pathetic pages of modern music. The passage *Di tanti palpiti* expresses love in all its grandeur. Calyste, sitting in the same arm-chair in which Felicite had told him the history of the marquise, listened in rapt devotion. Beatrix and Vignon were on either side of the piano. Conti's sublime voice knew well how to blend with that of Felicite. Both had often sung this piece; they knew its resources, and they put their whole marvellous gift into bringing them out. The music was at this moment what its creator intended, a poem of divine melancholy, the farewell of two swans to life. When it was over, all present were under the influence of feelings such as cannot express themselves by vulgar applause.

"Ah! music is the first of arts!" exclaimed the marquise.

"Camille thinks youth and beauty the first of poesies," said Claude Vignon.

Mademoiselle des Touches looked at Claude with vague uneasiness. Beatrix, not seeing Calyste, turned her head as if to know what effect the music had produced upon him, less by way of interest in him than for the gratification of Conti; she saw a white face bathed in tears. At the sight, and as if some sudden pain had seized her, she turned back quickly and looked at Gennaro. Not only had Music arisen before the eyes of Calyste, touching him with her divine wand until he stood in presence of Creation from which she rent the veil, but he was dumfounded by Conti's genius. In spite of what Camille had told him of the musician's character, he now believed in the beauty of the soul, in the heart that expressed such love. How could he, Calyste, rival such as an artist? What woman could ever cease to adore such genius? That voice entered the soul like another soul. The poor lad was overwhelmed by poesy, and his own despair. He felt himself of no account. This ingenuous admission of his nothingness could be read upon his face mingled with his admiration. He did not observe the gesture with which Beatrix, attracted to Calyste by the contagion of a true feeling, called Felicite's attention to him.

"Oh! the adorable heart!" cried Camille. "Conti, you will never obtain applause of one-half the value of that child's homage. Let us sing this trio. Beatrix, my dear, come."

When the marquise, Camille, and Conti had arranged themselves at the piano, Calyste rose softly, without attracting their attention, and flung himself on one of the sofas in the bedroom, the door of which stood open, where he sat with his head in his hands, plunged in meditation.

CHAPTER X.

DRAMA

"What is it, my child?" said Claude Vignon, who had slipped silently into the bedroom after Calyste, and now took him by the hand. "You love; you think you are disdained; but it is not so. The field will be free to you in a few days and you will reign—beloved by more than one."

"Loved!" cried Calyste, springing up, and beckoning Claude into the library, "Who loves me here?"

"Camille," replied Claude.

"Camille loves me? And you!—what of you?"

"I?" answered Claude, "I—" He stopped; sat down on a sofa and rested his head with weary sadness on a cushion. "I am tired of life, but I have not the courage to quit it," he went on, after a short silence. "I wish I were mistaken in what I have just told you; but for the last few days more than one vivid light has come into my mind. I did not wander about the marshes for my pleasure; no, upon my soul I did not! The bitterness of my words when I returned and found you with Camille were the result of wounded feeling. I intend to have an explanation with her soon. Two minds as clear-sighted as hers and mine cannot deceive each other. Between two such professional duellists the combat cannot last long. Therefore I may as well tell you now that I shall leave Les Touches; yes, to-morrow perhaps, with Conti. After we are gone strange things will happen here. I shall regret not witnessing conflicts of passion of a kind so rare in France, and so dramatic. You are very young to enter such dangerous lists; you interest me; were it not for the profound disgust I feel for women, I would stay and help you play this game. It is difficult; you may lose it; you have to do with two extraordinary women, and you feel too much for one to use the other judiciously. Beatrix is dogged by nature; Camille has grandeur. Probably you will be wrecked between those reefs, drawn upon them by the waves of passion. Beware!"

Calyste's stupefaction on hearing these words enabled Claude to say them without interruption and leave the young Breton, who remained like a traveller among the Alps to whom a guide has shown the depth of some abyss by flinging a stone into it. To hear from the lips of Claude himself that Camille loved him, at the very moment when he felt that he loved Beatrix for life, was a weight too heavy for his untried soul to bear. Goaded by an immense regret which now filled all the past, overwhelmed with a sight of his position between Beatrix whom he loved and Camille whom he had ceased to love, the poor boy sat despairing and undecided, lost in thought. He sought in vain for the reasons which had made Felicite reject his love and bring Claude Vignon from Paris to oppose it. Every now and then the voice of Beatrix came fresh and pure to his ears from the little salon; a savage desire to rush in and carry her off seized him at such moments. What would become of him? What must he do? Could he come to Les Touches? If Camille loved him how could he come there to adore Beatrix? He saw no solution to these difficulties.

Insensibly to him silence now reigned in the house; he heard, but without noticing, the opening and shutting of doors. Then suddenly midnight sounded on the clock of the adjoining bedroom, and the voices of Claude and Camille roused him fully from his torpid contemplation of the future. Before he could rise and show himself, he heard the following terrible words in the voice of Claude Vignon.

"You came to Paris last year desperately in love with Calyste," Claude was saying to Felicite, "but you were horrified at the thought of the consequences of such a passion at your age; it would lead you to a gulf, to hell, to suicide perhaps. Love cannot exist unless it thinks itself eternal, and you saw not far before you a horrible parting; old age you knew would end the glorious poem soon. You thought of 'Adolphe,' that dreadful finale of the loves of Madame de Stael and Benjamin Constant, who, however, were nearer of an age than you and Calyste. Then you took me, as soldiers use fascines to build entrenchments between the enemy and themselves. You brought me to Les Touches to mask your real feelings and leave you safe to follow your own secret adoration. The scheme was grand and ignoble both; but to carry it out you should have chosen either a common man or one so preoccupied by noble thoughts that you could easily deceive him. You thought me simple and easy to mislead as a man of genius. I am not a man of genius, I am a man of talent, and as such I have divined you. When I made that eulogy yesterday on women of your age, explaining to you why Calyste had loved you, do you suppose I took to myself your ravished, fascinated, fazzling glance? Had I not read into your soul? The eyes were turned on me, but the heart was throbbing for Calyste. You have never been loved, my poor Maupin, and you never will be after rejecting the beautiful fruit which chance has offered to you at the portals of that hell of woman, the lock of which is the numeral 50!"

"Why has love fled me?" she said in a low voice. "Tell me, you who know all."

"Because you are not lovable," he answered. "You do not bend to love; love must bend to you. You may perhaps have yielded to some follies of youth, but there was no youth in your heart; your mind has too much depth; you have never been naive and artless, and you cannot begin to be so now. Your charm comes from mystery; it is abstract, not active. Your strength repulses men of strength who fear a struggle. Your power may please young souls, like that of Calyste, which like to be protected; though, even them it wearies in the long run. You are grand, and you are sublime; bear with the consequence of those two qualities—they fatigue."

"What a sentence!" cried Camille. "Am I not a woman? Do you think me an anomaly?"

"Possibly," said Claude.

"We will see!" said the woman, stung to the quick.

"Farewell, my dear Camille; I leave to-morrow. I am not angry with you, my dear; I think you the greatest of women, but if I continued to serve you as a screen, or a shield," said Claude, with two significant inflections of his voice, "you would despise me. We can part now without pain or remorse; we have neither happiness to regret nor hopes betrayed. To you, as with some few but rare men of genius, love is not what Nature made it,—an imperious need, to the satisfaction of which she attaches great and passing joys, which die. You see love such as Christianity has created it,—an ideal kingdom, full of noble sentiments, of grand weaknesses, poesies, spiritual sensations, devotions of moral fragrance, entrancing harmonies, placed high above all vulgar coarseness, to which two creatures as one angel fly on the wings of pleasure. This is what I hoped to share; I thought I held in you a key to that door, closed to so many, by which we may advance toward the infinite. You were there already. In this you have misled me. I return to my misery,—to my vast prison of Paris. Such a deception as this, had it come to me earlier in life, would have made me flee from existence; to-day it puts into my soul a disenchantment which will plunge me forever into an awful solitude. I am without the faith which helped the Fathers to people theirs with sacred images. It is to this, my dear Camille, to this that the superiority of our mind has brought us; we may, both of us, sing that dreadful hymn which a poet has put into the mouth of Moses speaking to the Almighty: 'Lord God, Thou hast made me powerful and solitary.'"

At this moment Calyste appeared.

"I ought not to leave you ignorant that I am here," he said.

Mademoiselle des Touches showed the utmost fear; a sudden flush colored her impassible face with tints of fire. During this strange scene she was more beautiful than at any other moment of her life.

"We thought you gone, Calyste," said Claude. "But this involuntary discretion on both sides will do no harm; perhaps, indeed, you may be more at your ease at Les Touches by knowing Felicite as she is. Her silence shows me I am not mistaken as to the part she meant me to play. As I told you before, she loves you, but it is for yourself, not for herself,—a sentiment that few women are able to conceive and practise; few among them know the voluptuous pleasure of sufferings born of longing,—that is one of the magnificent passions reserved for man. But she is in some sense a man," he added, sardonically. "Your love for Beatrix will make her suffer and make her happy too."

Tears were in the eyes of Mademoiselle des Touches, who was unable to look either at the terrible Vignon or the ingenuous Calyste. She was frightened at being understood; she had supposed it impossible for a man, however keen his perception, to perceive a delicacy so self-immolating, a heroism so lofty as her own. Her evident humiliation at this unveiling of her grandeur made Calyste share the emotion of the woman he had held so high, and now beheld so stricken down. He threw himself, from an irresistible impulse, at her feet, and kissed her hands, laying his face, covered with tears, upon them.

"Claude," she said, "do not abandon me, or what will become of me?"

"What have you to fear?" replied the critic. "Calyste has fallen in love at first sight with the marquise; you cannot find a better barrier between you than that. This passion of his is worth more to you than I. Yesterday there might have been some danger for you and for him; to-day you can take a maternal interest in him," he said, with a mocking smile, "and be proud of his triumphs."

Mademoiselle des Touches looked at Calyste, who had raised his head abruptly at these words. Claude Vignon enjoyed, for his sole vengeance, the sight of their confusion.

"You yourself have driven him to Madame de Rochefide," continued Claude, "and he is now under the spell. You have dug your own grave. Had you confided in me, you would have escaped the sufferings that await you."

"Sufferings!" cried Camille Maupin, taking Calyste's head in her hands, and kissing his hair, on which her tears fell plentifully. "No, Calyste; forget what you have heard; I count for nothing in all this."

She rose and stood erect before the two men, subduing both with the lightning of her eyes, from which her soul shone out.

"While Claude was speaking," she said, "I conceived the beauty and the grandeur of love without hope; it is the sentiment that brings us nearest God. Do not love me, Calyste; but I will love you as no woman will!"

It was the cry of a wounded eagle seeking its eyrie. Claude himself knelt down, took Camille's hand, and kissed it.

"Leave us now, Calyste," she said, "it is late, and your mother will be uneasy."

Calyste returned to Guerande with lagging steps, turning again and again, to see the light from the windows of the room in which was Beatrix. He was surprised himself to find how little pity he felt for Camille. But presently he felt once more the agitations of that scene, the tears she had left upon his hair; he suffered with her suffering; he fancied he heard the moans of that noble woman, so beloved, so desired but a few short days before.

When he opened the door of his paternal home, where total silence reigned, he saw his mother through the window, as she sat sewing by the light of the curiously constructed lamp while she awaited him. Tears moistened the lad's eyes as he looked at her.

"What has happened?" cried Fanny, seeing his emotion, which filled her with horrible anxiety.

For all answer, Calyste took his mother in his arms, and kissed her on her cheeks, her forehead and hair, with one of those passionate effusions of feeling that comfort mothers, and fill them with the subtle flames of the life they have given.

"It is you I love, you!" cried Calyste,—"you, who live for me; you, whom I long to render happy!"

"But you are not yourself, my child," said the baroness, looking at him attentively. "What has happened to you?"

"Camille loves me, but I love her no longer," he answered.

The next day, Calyste told Gasselin to watch the road to Saint-Nazaire, and let him know if the carriage of Mademoiselle des Touches passed over it. Gasselin brought word that the carriage had passed.

"How many persons were in it?" asked Calyste.

"Four,—two ladies and two gentlemen."

"Then saddle my horse and my father's."

Gasselin departed.

"My, nephew, what mischief is in you now?" said his Aunt Zephirine.

"Let the boy amuse himself, sister," cried the baron. "Yesterday he was dull as an owl; to-day he is gay as a lark."

"Did you tell him that our dear Charlotte was to arrive to-day?" said Zephirine, turning to her sister-in-law.

"No," replied the baroness.

"I thought perhaps he was going to meet her," said Mademoiselle du Guenic, slyly.

"If Charlotte is to stay three months with her aunt, he will have plenty of opportunities to see her," said his mother.

"Mademoiselle de Pen-Hoel wants me to marry Charlotte, to save me from perdition," said Calyste, laughing. "I was on the mall when she and the Chevalier du Halga were talking about it. She can't see that it would be greater perdition for me to marry at my age—"

"It is written above," said the old maid, interrupting Calyste, "that I shall not die tranquil or happy. I wanted to see our family continued, and some, at least, of the estates brought back; but it is not to be. What can you, my fine nephew, put in the scale against such duties? Is it that actress at Les Touches?"

"What?" said the baron; "how can Mademoiselle des Touches hinder Calyste's marriage, when it becomes necessary for us to make it? I shall go and see her."

"I assure you, father," said Calyste, "that Felicite will never be an obstacle to my marriage."

Gasselin appeared with the horses.

"Where are you going, chevalier?" said his father.

"To Saint-Nazaire."

"Ha, ha! and when is the marriage to be?" said the baron, believing that Calyste was really in a hurry to see Charlotte de Kergarouet. "It is high time I was a grandfather. Spare the horses," he continued, as he went on the portico with Fanny to see Calyste mount; "remember that they have more than thirty miles to go."

Calyste started with a tender farewell to his mother.

"Dear treasure!" she said, as she saw him lower his head to ride through the gateway.

"God keep him!" replied the baron; "for we cannot replace him."

The words made the baroness shudder.

"My nephew does not love Charlotte enough to ride to Saint-Nazaire after her," said the old blind woman to Mariotte, who was clearing the breakfast-table.

"No; but a fine lady, a marquise, has come to Les Touches, and I'll warrant he's after her; that's the way at his age," said Mariotte.

"They'll kill him," said Mademoiselle du Guenic.

"That won't kill him, mademoiselle; quite the contrary," replied Mariotte, who seemed to be pleased with Calyste's behavior.

The young fellow started at a great pace, until Gasselin asked him if he was trying to catch the boat, which, of course, was not at all his desire. He had no wish to see either Conti or Claude again; but he did expect to be invited to drive back with the ladies, leaving Gasselin to lead his horse. He was gay as a bird, thinking to himself, —

"*She* has just passed here; *her* eyes saw those trees! — What a lovely road!" he said to Gasselin.

"Ah! monsieur, Brittany is the most beautiful country in all the world," replied the Breton. "Where could you find such flowers in the hedges, and nice cool roads that wind about like these?"

"Nowhere, Gasselin."

"*Tiens*! here comes the coach from Nazaire," cried Gasselin presently.

"Mademoiselle de Pen-Hoel and her niece will be in it. Let us hide," said Calyste.

"Hide! are you crazy, monsieur? Why, we are on the moor!"

The coach, which was coming up the sandy hill above Saint-Nazaire, was full, and, much to the astonishment of Calyste, there were no signs of Charlotte.

"We had to leave Mademoiselle de Pen-Hoel, her sister and niece; they are dreadfully worried; but all my seats were engaged by the custom-house," said the conductor to Gasselin.

"I am lost!" thought Calyste; "they will meet me down there."

When Calyste reached the little esplanade which surrounds the church of Saint-Nazaire, and from which is seen Paimboeuf and the magnificent Mouths of the Loire as they struggle with the sea, he found Camille and the marquise waving their handkerchiefs as a last adieu to two passengers on the deck of the departing steamer. Beatrix was charming as she stood there, her features softened by the shadow of a rice-straw hat, on which were tufts and knots of scarlet ribbon. She wore a muslin gown with a pattern of flowers, and was leaning with one well-gloved hand on a slender parasol. Nothing is finer to the eyes than a woman poised on a rock like a statue on its pedestal. Conti could see Calyste from the vessel as he approached Camille.

"I thought," said the young man, "that you would probably come back alone."

"You have done right, Calyste," she replied, pressing his hand.

Beatrix turned round, saw her young lover, and gave him the most imperious look in her repertory. A smile, which the marquise detected on the eloquent lips of Mademoiselle des Touches, made her aware of the vulgarity of such conduct, worthy only of a bourgeoise. She then said to Calyste, smiling,—

"Are you not guilty of a slight impertinence in supposing that I should bore Camille, if left alone with her?"

"My dear, one man to two widows is none too much," said Mademoiselle des Touches, taking Calyste's arm, and leaving Beatrix to watch the vessel till it disappeared.

At this moment Calyste heard the approaching voices of Mademoiselle de Pen-Hoel, the Vicomtesse de Kergarouet, Charlotte, and Gasselin, who were all talking at once, like so many magpies. The old maid was questioning Gasselin as to what had brought him and his master to Saint-Nazaire; the carriage of Mademoiselle des Touches had already caught her eye. Before the young Breton could get out of sight, Charlotte had seen him.

"Why, there's Calyste!" she exclaimed eagerly.

"Go and offer them seats in my carriage," said Camille to Calyste; "the maid can sit with the coachman. I saw those ladies lose their places in the mail-coach."

Calyste, who could not help himself, carried the message. As soon as Madame de Kergarouet learned that the offer came from the celebrated Camille Maupin, and that the Marquise de Rochefide was of the party, she was much surprised at the objections raised by her elder sister, who refused positively to profit by what she called the devil's carryall. At Nantes, which boasted of more civilization than Guerande, Camille was read and admired; she was thought to be the muse of Brittany and an honor to the region. The absolution granted to her in Paris by society, by fashion, was there justified by her great fortune and her early successes in Nantes, which claimed the honor of having been, if not her birthplace, at least her cradle. The viscountess, therefore, eager to see her, dragged her old sister forward, paying no attention to her jeremiads.

"Good-morning, Calyste," said Charlotte.

"Oh! good-morning, Charlotte," replied Calyste, not offering his arm.

Both were confused; she by his coldness, he by his cruelty, as they walked up the sort of ravine, which is called in Saint-Nazaire a street, following the two sisters in silence. In a moment the little girl of sixteen saw her castle in Spain, built and furnished with romantic hopes, a heap of ruins. She and Calyste had played together so much in childhood, she was so bound up with him, as it were, that she had quietly supposed her future unassailable; she arrived now, swept along by thoughtless happiness, like a circling bird darting down upon a wheat-field, and lo! she was stopped in her flight, unable to imagine the obstacle.

"What is the matter, Calyste?" she said, taking his hand.

"Nothing," replied the young man, releasing himself with cruel haste as he remembered the projects of his aunt and her friend.

Tears came into Charlotte's eyes. She looked at the handsome Calyste without ill-humor; but a first spasm of jealousy seized her, and she felt the dreadful madness of rivalry when she came in sight of the two Parisian women, and suspected the cause of his coldness.

Charlotte de Kergarouet was a girl of ordinary height, and commonplace coloring; she had a little round face, made lively by a pair of black eyes which sparkled with cleverness, abundant brown hair, a round waist, a flat back, thin arms, and the curt, decided manner of a provincial girl, who did not want to be taken for a little goose. She was the petted child of the family on account of the preference her aunt showed for her. At this moment she was wrapped in a mantle of Scotch merino in large plaids, lined with green silk, which she had worn on the boat. Her travelling-dress, of some common stuff, chastely made with a chemisette body and a pleated collar, was fated to appear, even to her own eyes, horrible in comparison with the fresh toilets of Beatrix and Camille. She was painfully aware of the stockings soiled among the rocks as she had jumped from the boat, of shabby leather shoes, chosen for the purpose of not spoiling better ones on the journey,—a fixed principle in the manners and customs of provincials.

As for the Vicomtesse de Kergarouet, she might stand as the type of a provincial woman. Tall, hard, withered, full of pretensions, which did not show themselves until they were mortified, talking much, and catching, by dint of talking (as one cannons at billiards), a few ideas, which gave her the reputation of wit, endeavoring to humiliate Parisians, whenever she met them, with an assumption of country wisdom and patronage, humbling herself to be exalted and furious at being left upon her knees; fishing, as the English say, for compliments, which she never caught; dressed in clothes that were exaggerated in style, and yet ill cared for; mistaking want of good manners for dignity, and trying to embarrass others by paying no attention to them; refusing what she desired in order to have it offered again, and to seem to yield only to entreaty; concerned about matters that others have done with, and surprised at not being in the fashion; and finally, unable to get through an hour without reference to Nantes, matters of social life in Nantes, complaints of Nantes, criticism of Nantes, and taking as personalities the remarks she forced out of absent-minded or wearied listeners.

Her manners, language, and ideas had, more or less, descended to her four daughters. To know Camille Maupin and Madame de Rochefide would be for her a future, and the topic of a hundred conversations. Consequently, she advanced toward the church as if she meant to take it by assault, waving her handkerchief, unfolded for the purpose of displaying the heavy corners of domestic embroidery, and trimmed with flimsy lace. Her gait was tolerably bold and cavalier, which, however, was of no consequence in a woman forty-seven years of age.

"Monsieur le chevalier," she said to Camille and Beatrix, pointing to Calyste, who was mournfully following with Charlotte, "has conveyed to me your friendly proposal, but we fear—my sister, my daughter, and myself—to inconvenience you."

"Sister, I shall not put these ladies to inconvenience," said Mademoiselle de Pen-Hoel, sharply; "I can very well find a horse in Saint-Nazaire to take me home."

Camille and Beatrix exchanged an oblique glance, which Calyste intercepted, and that glance sufficed to annihilate all the memories of his childhood, all his beliefs in the Kergarouets and Pen-Hoels, and to put an end forever to the projects of the three families.

"We can very well put five in the carriage," replied Mademoiselle des Touches, on whom Jacqueline turned her back, "even if we were inconvenienced, which cannot be the case, with your slender figures. Besides, I should enjoy the pleasure of doing a little service to Calyste's friends. Your maid, madame, will find a seat by the coachman, and your luggage, if you have any, can go behind the carriage; I have no footman with me."

The viscountess was overwhelming in thanks, and complained that her sister Jacqueline had been in such a hurry to see her niece that she would not give her time to come properly in her own carriage with post-horses, though, to be sure, the post-road was not only longer, but more expensive; she herself was obliged to return almost immediately to Nantes, where she had left three other little kittens, who were anxiously awaiting her. Here she put her arm round Charlotte's neck. Charlotte, in reply, raised her eyes to her mother with the air of a little victim, which gave an impression to onlookers that the viscountess bored her four daughters prodigiously by dragging them on the scene very much as Corporal Trim produces his cap in "Tristram Shandy."

"You are a fortunate mother and—" began Camille, stopping short as she remembered that Beatrix must have parted from her son when she left her husband's house.

"Oh, yes!" said the viscountess; "if I have the misfortune of spending my life in the country, and, above all, at Nantes, I have at least the consolation of being adored by my children. Have you children?" she said to Camille.

"I am Mademoiselle des Touches," replied Camille. "Madame is the Marquise de Rochefide."

"Then I must pity you for not knowing the greatest happiness that there is for us poor, simple women—is not that so, madame?" said the viscountess, turning to Beatrix. "But you, mademoiselle, have so many compensations."

The tears came into Madame de Rochefide's eyes, and she turned away toward the parapet to hide them. Calyste followed her.

"Madame," said Camille, in a low voice to the viscountess, "are you not aware that the marquise is separated from her husband? She has not seen her son for two years, and does not know when she will see him."

"You don't say so!" said Madame de Kergarouet. "Poor lady! is she legally separated?"

"No, by mutual consent," replied Camille.

"Ah, well! I understand that," said the viscountess boldly.

Old Mademoiselle de Pen-Hoel, furious at being thus dragged into the enemy's camp, had retreated to a short distance with her dear Charlotte. Calyste, after looking about him to make sure that no one could see him, seized the hand of the marquise, kissed it, and left a tear upon it. Beatrix turned round, her tears dried by anger; she was about to utter some terrible word, but it died upon her lips as she saw the grief on the angelic face of the youth, as deeply touched by her present sorrow as she was herself.

"Good heavens, Calyste!" said Camille in his ear, as he returned with Madame de Rochefide, "are you to have *that* for a mother-in-law, and the little one for a wife?"

"Because her aunt is rich," replied Calyste, sarcastically.

The whole party now moved toward the inn, and the viscountess felt herself obliged to make Camille a speech on the savages of Saint-Nazaire.

"I love Brittany, madame," replied Camille, gravely. "I was born at Guerande."

Calyste could not help admiring Mademoiselle des Touches, who, by the tone of her voice, the tranquillity of her look, and her quiet manner, put him at his ease, in spite of the terrible declarations of the preceding night. She seemed, however, a little fatigued; her eyes were enlarged by dark circles round them, showing that he had not slept; but the brow dominated the inward storm with cold placidity.

"What queens!" he said to Charlotte, calling her attention to the marquise and Camille as he gave the girl his arm, to Mademoiselle de Pen-Hoel's great satisfaction.

"What an idea your mother has had," said the old maid, taking her niece's other arm, "to put herself in the company of that reprobate woman!"

"Oh, aunt, a woman who is the glory of Brittany!"

"The shame, my dear. Mind that you don't fawn upon her in that way."

"Mademoiselle Charlotte is right," said Calyste; "you are not just."

"Oh, you!" replied Mademoiselle de Pen-Hoel, "she has bewitched you."

"I regard her," said Calyste, "with the same friendship that I feel for you."

"Since when have the du Guenics taken to telling lies?" asked the old maid.

"Since the Pen-Hoels have grown deaf," replied Calyste.

"Are you not in love with her?" demanded the old maid.

"I have been, but I am so no longer," he said.

"Bad boy! then why have you given us such anxiety? I know very well that love is only foolishness; there is nothing solid but marriage," she remarked, looking at Charlotte.

Charlotte, somewhat reassured, hoped to recover her advantages by recalling the memories of childhood. She leaned affectionately on Calyste's arm, who resolved in his own mind to have a clear explanation with the little heiress.

"Ah! what fun we shall have at *mouche*, Calyste!" she said; "what good laughs we used to have over it!"

The horses were now put in; Camille placed Madame de Kergarouet and Charlotte on the back seat. Jacqueline having disappeared, she herself, with the marquise, sat forward. Calyste was, of course, obliged to relinquish the pleasure on which he had counted, of driving back with Camille and Beatrix, but he rode beside the carriage all the way; the horses, being tired with the journey, went slowly enough to allow him to keep his eyes on Beatrix.

History must lose the curious conversations that went on between these four persons whom accident had so strangely united in this carriage, for it is impossible to report the hundred and more versions which went the round of Nantes on the remarks, replies, and witticisms which the viscountess heard from the lips of the celebrated Camille Maupin *herself*. She was, however, very careful not to repeat, not even to comprehend, the actual replies made by Mademoiselle des Touches to her absurd questions about Camille's authorship,—a penance to which all authors are subjected, and which often make them expiate the few and rare pleasures that they win.

"How do you write your books?" she began.

"Much as you do your worsted-work or knitting," replied Camille.

"But where do you find those deep reflections, those seductive pictures?"

"Where you find the witty things you say, madame; there is nothing so easy as to write books, provided you will—"

"Ah! does it depend wholly on the will? I shouldn't have thought it. Which of your compositions do you prefer?"

"I find it difficult to prefer any of my little kittens."

"I see you are *blasee* on compliments; there is really nothing new that one can say."

"I assure you, madame, that I am very sensible to the form which you give to yours."

The viscountess, anxious not to seem to neglect the marquise, remarked, looking at Beatrix with a meaning air,—

"I shall never forget this journey made between Wit and Beauty."

"You flatter me, madame," said the marquise, laughing. "I assure you that my wit is but a small matter, not to be mentioned by the side of genius; besides, I think I have not said much as yet."

Charlotte, who keenly felt her mother's absurdity, looked at her, endeavoring to stop its course; but Madame de Kergarouet went bravely on in her tilt with the satirical Parisians.

Calyste, who was trotting slowly beside the carriage, could only see the faces of the two ladies on the front seat, and his eyes expressed, from time to time, rather painful thoughts. Forced, by her position, to let herself be looked at, Beatrix constantly avoided meeting the young man's eyes, and practised a manoeuvre most exasperating to lovers; she held her shawl crossed and her hands crossed over it, apparently plunged in the deepest meditation.

At a part of the road which is shaded, dewy, and verdant as a forest glade, where the wheels of the carriage scarcely sounded, and the breeze brought down balsamic odors and waved the branches above their heads, Camille called Madame de Rochefide's attention to the harmonies of the place, and pressed her knee to make her look at Calyste.

"How well he rides!" she said.

"Oh! Calyste does everything well," said Charlotte.

"He rides like an Englishman," said the marquise, indifferently.

"His mother is Irish,—an O'Brien," continued Charlotte, who thought herself insulted by such indifference.

Camille and the marquise drove through Guerande with the viscountess and her daughter, to the great astonishment of the inhabitants of the town. They left the mother and daughter at the end of the lane leading to the Guenic mansion, where a crowd came near gathering, attracted by so unusual a sight. Calyste had ridden on to announce the arrival of the company to his mother and aunt, who expected them to dinner, that meal having been postponed till four o'clock. Then he returned to the gate to give his arm to the two ladies, and bid Camille and Beatrix adieu.

He kissed the hand of Felicite, hoping thereby to be able to do the same to that of the marquise; but she still kept her arms crossed resolutely, and he cast moist glances of entreaty at her uselessly.

"You little ninny!" whispered Camille, lightly touching his ear with a kiss that was full of friendship.

"Quite true," thought Calyste to himself as the carriage drove away. "I am forgetting her advice—but I shall always forget it, I'm afraid."

Mademoiselle de Pen-Hoel (who had intrepidly returned to Guerande on the back of a hired horse), the Vicomtesse de Kergarouet, and Charlotte found dinner ready, and were treated with the utmost cordiality, if luxury were lacking, by the du Guenics. Mademoiselle Zephirine had ordered the best wine to be brought from the cellar, and Mariotte had surpassed herself in her Breton dishes.

The viscountess, proud of her trip with the illustrious Camille Maupin, endeavored to explain to the assembled company the present condition of modern literature, and Camille's place in it. But the literary topic met the fate of whist; neither the du Guenics, nor the abbe, nor the Chevalier du Halga understood one word of it. The rector and the chevalier had arrived in time for the liqueurs at dessert.

As soon as Mariotte, assisted by Gasselin and Madame de Kergarouet's maid, had cleared the table, there was a general and enthusiastic cry for *mouche*. Joy appeared to reign in the household. All supposed Calyste to be free of his late entanglement, and almost as good as married to the little Charlotte. The young man alone kept silence. For the first time in his life he had instituted comparisons between his life-long friends and the two elegant women, witty, accomplished, and tasteful, who, at the present moment, must be laughing heartily at the provincial mother and daughter, judging by the look he intercepted between them.

He was seeking in vain for some excuse to leave his family on this occasion, and go up as usual to Les Touches, when Madame de Kergarouet mentioned that she regretted not having accepted Mademoiselle des Touches' offer of her carriage for the return journey to Saint-Nazaire, which for the sake of her three other "dear kittens," she felt compelled to make on the following day.

Fanny, who alone saw her son's uneasiness, and the little hold which Charlotte's coquetries and her mother's attentions were gaining on him, came to his aid.

"Madame," she said to the viscountess, "you will, I think, be very uncomfortable in the carrier's vehicle, and especially at having to start so early in the morning. You would certainly have done better to take the offer made to you by Mademoiselle des Touches. But it is not too late to do so now. Calyste, go up to Les Touches and arrange the matter; but don't be long; return to us soon."

"It won't take me ten minutes," cried Calyste, kissing his mother violently as she followed him to the door.

CHAPTER XI.

FEMALE DIPLOMACY

Calyste ran with the lightness of a young fawn to Les Touches and reached the portico just as Camille and Beatrix were leaving the grand salon after their dinner. He had the sense to offer his arm to Felicite.

"So you have abandoned your viscountess and her daughter for us," she said, pressing his arm; "we are able now to understand the full merit of that sacrifice."

"Are these Kergarouets related to the Portendueres, and to old Admiral de Kergarouet, whose widow married Charles de Vandenesse?" asked Madame de Rochefide.

"The viscountess is the admiral's great-niece," replied Camille.

"Well, she's a charming girl," said Beatrix, placing herself gracefully in a Gothic chair. "She will just do for you, Monsieur du Guenic."

"The marriage will never take place," said Camille hastily.

Mortified by the cold, calm air with which the marquise seemed to consider the Breton girl as the only creature fit to mate him, Calyste remained speechless and even mindless.

"Why so, Camille?" asked Madame de Rochefide.

"Really, my dear," said Camille, seeing Calyste's despair, "you are not generous; did I advise Conti to marry?"

Beatrix looked at her friend with a surprise that was mingled with indefinable suspicions.

Calyste, unable to understand Camille's motive, but feeling that she came to his assistance and seeing in her cheeks that faint spot of color which he knew to mean the presence of some violent emotion, went up to her rather awkwardly and took her hand. But she left him and seated herself carelessly at the piano, like a woman so sure of her friend and lover that she can afford to leave him with another woman. She played variations, improvising them as she played, on certain themes chosen, unconsciously to herself, by the impulse of her mind; they were melancholy in the extreme.

Beatrix seemed to listen to the music, but she was really observing Calyste, who, much too young and artless for the part which Camille was intending him to play, remained in rapt adoration before his real idol.

After about an hour, during which time Camille continued to play, Beatrix rose and retired to her apartments. Camille at once took Calyste into her chamber and closed the door, fearing to be overheard; for women have an amazing instinct of distrust.

"My child," she said, "if you want to succeed with Beatrix, you must seem to love me still, or you will fail. You are a child; you know nothing of women; all you know is how to love. Now loving and making one's self beloved are two very different things. If you go your own way you will fall into horrible suffering, and I wish to see you happy. If you rouse, not the pride, but the self-will, the obstinacy which is a strong feature in her character, she is capable of going off at any moment to Paris and rejoining Conti; and what will you do then?"

"I shall love her."

"You won't see her again."

"Oh! yes, I shall," he said.

"How?"

"I shall follow her."

"Why, you are as poor as Job, my dear boy."

"My father, Gasselin, and I lived for three months in Vendee on one hundred and fifty francs, marching night and day."

"Calyste," said Mademoiselle des Touches, "now listen to me. I know that you have too much candor to play a part, too much honesty to deceive; and I don't want to corrupt such a nature as yours. Yet deception is the only way by which you can win Beatrix; I take it therefore upon myself. In a week from now she shall love you."

"Is it possible?" he said clasping his hands.

"Yes," replied Camille, "but it will be necessary to overcome certain pledges which she has made to herself. I will do that for you. You must not interfere in the rather arduous task I shall undertake. The marquise has a true aristocratic delicacy of perception; she is keenly distrustful; no hunter could meet with game more wary or more difficult to capture. You are wholly unable to cope with her; will you promise me a blind obedience?"

"What must I do?" replied the youth.

"Very little," said Camille. "Come here every day and devote yourself to me. Come to my rooms; avoid Beatrix if you meet her. We will stay together till four o'clock; you shall employ the time in study, and I in smoking. It will be hard for you not to see her, but I will find you a number of interesting books. You have read nothing as yet of George Sand. I will send one of my people this very evening to Nantes to buy her works and those of other authors whom you ought to know. The evenings we will spend together, and I permit you to make love to me if you can—it will be for the best."

"I know, Camille, that your affection for me is great and so rare that it makes me wish I had never met Beatrix," he replied with simple good faith; "but I don't see what you hope from all this."

"I hope to make her love you."

"Good heavens! it cannot be possible!" he cried, again clasping his hands toward Camille, who was greatly moved on seeing the joy that she gave him at her own expense.

"Now listen to me carefully," she said. "If you break the agreement between us, if you have—not a long conversation—but a mere exchange of words with the marquise in private, if you let her question you, if you fail in the silent part I ask you to play, which is certainly not a very difficult one, I do assure you," she said in a serious tone, "you will lose her forever."

"I don't understand the meaning of what you are saying to me," cried Calyste, looking at Camille with adorable naivete.

"If you did understand it, you wouldn't be the noble and beautiful Calyste that you are," she replied, taking his hand and kissing it.

Calyste then did what he had never before done; he took Camille round the waist and kissed her gently, not with love but with tenderness, as he kissed his mother. Mademoiselle des Touches did not restrain her tears.

"Go now," she said, "my child; and tell your viscountess that my carriage is at her command."

Calyste wanted to stay longer, but he was forced to obey her imperious and imperative gesture.

He went home gaily; he believed that in a week the beautiful Beatrix would love him. The players at *mouche* found him once more the Calyste they had missed for the last two months. Charlotte attributed this change to herself. Mademoiselle de Pen-Hoel was charming to him. The Abbe Grimont endeavored to make out what was passing in the mother's mind. The Chevalier du Halga rubbed his hands. The two old maids were as lively as lizards. The viscountess lost one hundred sous by accumulated *mouches*, which so excited the cupidity of Zephirine that she regretted not being able to see the cards, and even spoke sharply to her sister-in-law, who acted as the proxy of her eyes.

The party lasted till eleven o'clock. There were two defections, the baron and the chevalier, who went to sleep in their respective chairs. Mariotte had made galettes of buckwheat, the baroness produced a tea-caddy. The illustrious house of du Guenic served a little supper before the departure of its guests, consisting of fresh butter, fruits, and cream, in addition to Mariotte's cakes; for which festal event issued from their wrappings a silver teapot and some beautiful old English china sent to the baroness by her aunts. This appearance of modern splendor in the ancient hall, together with the exquisite grace of its mistress, brought up like a true Irish lady to make and pour out tea (that mighty affair to Englishwomen), had something charming about them. The most exquisite luxury could never have attained to the simple, modest, noble effect produced by this sentiment of joyful hospitality.

A few moments after Calyste's departure from Les Touches, Beatrix, who had heard him go, returned to Camille, whom she found with humid eyes lying back on her sofa.

"What is it, Felicite?" asked the marquise.

"I am forty years old, and I love him!" said Mademoiselle des Touches, with dreadful tones of agony in her voice, her eyes becoming hard and brilliant. "If you knew, Beatrix, the tears I have shed over the lost years of my youth! To be loved out of pity! to know that one owes one's happiness only to perpetual care, to the slyness of cats, to traps laid for innocence and all the youthful virtues—oh, it is infamous! If it were not that one finds absolution in the magnitude of love, in the power of happiness, in the certainty of being forever above all other women in his memory, the first to carve on that young heart the ineffaceable happiness of an absolute devotion, I would—yes, if he asked it,—I would fling myself into the sea. Sometimes I find myself wishing that he would ask it; it would then be an oblation, not a suicide. Ah, Beatrix, by coming here you have, unconsciously, set me a hard task. I know it will be difficult to keep him against you; but you love Conti, you are noble and generous, you will not deceive me; on the contrary, you will help me to retain my Calyste's love. I expected the impression you would make upon him, but I have not committed the mistake of seeming jealous; that would only have added fuel to the flame. On the contrary, before you came, I described you in such glowing colors that you hardly realize the portrait, although you are, it seems to me, more beautiful than ever."

This vehement elegy, in which truth was mingled with deception, completely duped the marquise. Claude Vignon had told Conti the reasons for his departure, and Beatrix was, of course, informed of them. She determined therefore to behave with generosity and give the cold shoulder to Calyste; but at the same instant there came into her soul that quiver of joy which vibrates in the heart of every woman when she finds herself beloved. The love a woman inspires in any man's heart is flattery without hypocrisy, and it is impossible for some women to forego it; but when that man belongs to a friend, his homage gives more than pleasure,—it gives delight. Beatrix sat down beside her friend and began to coax her prettily.

"You have not a white hair," she said; "you haven't even a wrinkle; your temples are just as fresh as ever; whereas I know more than one woman of thirty who is obliged to cover hers. Look, dear," she added, lifting her curls, "see what that journey to Italy has cost me."

Her temples showed an almost imperceptible withering of the texture of the delicate skin. She raised her sleeves and showed Camille the same slight withering of the wrists, where the transparent tissue suffered the blue network of swollen veins to be visible, and three deep lines made a bracelet of wrinkles.

"There, my dear, are two spots which—as a certain writer ferreting for the miseries of women, has said—never lie," she continued. "One must needs have suffered to know the truth of his observation. Happily for us, most men know nothing about it; they don't read us like that dreadful author."

"Your letter told me all," replied Camille; "happiness ignores everything but itself. You boasted too much of yours to be really happy. Truth is deaf, dumb, and blind where love really is. Consequently, seeing very plainly that you have your reasons for abandoning Conti, I have feared to have you here. My dear, Calyste is an angel; he is as good as he is beautiful; his innocent heart will not resist your eyes; already he admires you too much not to love you at the first encouragement; your coldness can alone preserve him to me. I confess to you, with the cowardice of true passion, that if he were taken from me I should die. That dreadful book of Benjamin Constant, 'Adolphe,' tells us only of Adolphe's sorrows; but what about those of the woman, hey? The man did not observe them enough to describe them; and what woman would have dared to reveal them? They would dishonor her sex, humiliate its virtues, and pass into vice. Ah! I measure the abyss before me by my fears, by these sufferings that are those of hell. But, Beatrix, I will tell you this: in case I am abandoned, my choice is made."

"What is it?" cried Beatrix, with an eagerness that made Camille shudder.

The two friends looked at each other with the keen attention of Venetian inquisitors; their souls clashed in that rapid glance, and struck fire like flints. The marquise lowered her eyes.

"After man, there is nought but God," said the celebrated woman. "God is the Unknown. I shall fling myself into that as into some vast abyss. Calyste has sworn to me that he admires you only as he would a picture; but alas! you are but twenty-eight, in the full magnificence of your beauty. The struggle thus begins between him and me by falsehood. But I have one support; happily I know a means to keep him true to me, and I shall triumph."

"What means?"

"That is my secret, dear. Let me have the benefits of my age. If Claude Vignon, as Conti has doubtless told you, flings me back into the gulf, I, who had climbed to a rock which I thought inaccessible, — I will at least gather the pale and fragile, but delightful flowers that grow in its depths."

Madame de Rochefide was moulded like wax in those able hands. Camille felt an almost savage pleasure in thus entrapping her rival in her toils. She sent her to bed that night piqued by curiosity, floating between jealousy and generosity, but most assuredly with her mind full of the beautiful Calyste.

"She will be enchanted to deceive me," thought Camille, as she kissed her good-night.

Then, when she was alone, the author, the constructor of dramas, gave place to the woman, and she burst into tears. Filling her hookah with tobacco soaked in opium, she spent the greater part of the night in smoking, dulling thus the sufferings of her soul, and seeing through the clouds about her the beautiful young head of her late lover.

"What a glorious book to write, if I were only to express my pain!" she said to herself. "But it is written already; Sappho lived before me. And Sappho was young. A fine and touching heroine truly, a woman of forty! Ah! my poor Camille, smoke your hookah; you haven't even the resource of making a poem of your misery—that's the last drop of anguish in your cup!"

The next morning Calyste came before mid-day and slipped upstairs, as he was told, into Camille's own room, where he found the books. Felicite sat before the window, smoking, contemplating in turn the marshes, the sea, and Calyste, to whom she now and then said a few words about Beatrix. At one time, seeing the marquise strolling about the garden, she raised a curtain in a way to attract her attention, and also to throw a band of light across Calyste's book.

"To-day, my child, I shall ask you to stay to dinner; but you must refuse, with a glance at the marquise, which will show her how much you regret not staying."

When the three actors met in the salon, and this comedy was played, Calyste felt for a moment his equivocal position, and the glance that he cast on Beatrix was far more expressive than Felicite expected. Beatrix had dressed herself charmingly.

"What a bewitching toilet, my dearest!" said Camille, when Calyste had departed.

These manoeuvres lasted six days, during which time many conversations, into which Camille Maupin put all her ability, took place, unknown to Calyste, between herself and the marquise. They were like the preliminaries of a duel between two women,—a duel without truce, in which the assault was made on both sides with snares, feints, false generosities, deceitful confessions, crafty confidences, by which one hid and the other bared her love; and in which the sharp steel of Camille's treacherous words entered the heart of her friend, and left its poison there. Beatrix at last took offence at what she thought Camille's distrust; she considered it out of place between them. At the same time she was enchanted to find the great writer a victim to the pettiness of her sex, and she resolved to enjoy the pleasure of showing her where her greatness ended, and how even she could be humiliated.

"My dear, what is to be the excuse to-day for Monsieur du Guenic's not dining with us?" she asked, looking maliciously at her friend. "Monday you said we had engagements; Tuesday the dinner was poor; Wednesday you were afraid his mother would be angry; Thursday you wanted to take a walk with me; and yesterday you simply dismissed him without a reason. To-day I shall have my way, and I mean that he shall stay."

"Already, my dear!" said Camille, with cutting irony. The marquise blushed. "Stay, Monsieur du Guenic," said Camille, in the tone of a queen.

Beatrix became cold and hard, contradictory in tone, epigrammatic, and almost rude to Calyste, whom Felicite sent home to play *mouche* with Charlotte de Kergarouet.

"*She* is not dangerous at any rate," said Beatrix, sarcastically.

Young lovers are like hungry men; kitchen odors will not appease their hunger; they think too much of what is coming to care for the means that bring it. As Calyste walked back to Guerande, his soul was full of Beatrix; he paid no heed to the profound feminine cleverness which Felicite was displaying on his behalf. During this week the marquise had only written once to Conti, a symptom of indifference which had not escaped the watchful eyes of Camille, who imparted it to Calyste. All Calyste's life was concentrated in the short moment of the day during which he was allowed to see the marquise. This drop of water, far from allaying his thirst, only redoubled it. The magic promise, "Beatrix shall love you," made by Camille, was the talisman with which he strove to restrain the fiery ardor of his passion. But he knew not how to consume the time; he could not sleep, and spent the hours of the night in reading; every evening he brought back with him, as Mariotte remarked, cartloads of books.

His aunt called down maledictions on the head of Mademoiselle des Touches; but his mother, who had gone on several occasions to his room on seeing his light burning far into the night, knew by this time the secret of his conduct. Though for her love was a sealed book, and she was even unaware of her own ignorance, Fanny rose through maternal tenderness into certain ideas of it; but the depths of such sentiment being dark and obscured by clouds to her mind, she was shocked at the state in which she saw him; the solitary uncomprehended desire of his soul, which was evidently consuming him, simply terrified her. Calyste had but one thought; Beatrix was always before him. In the evenings, while cards were being played, his abstraction resembled his father's somnolence. Finding him so different from what he was when he loved Camille, the baroness became aware, with a sort of horror, of the symptoms of real love,—a species of possession which had seized upon her son,—a love unknown within the walls of that old mansion.

Feverish irritability, a constant absorption in thought, made Calyste almost doltish. Often he would sit for hours with his eyes fixed on some figure in the tapestry. One morning his mother implored him to give up Les Touches, and leave the two women forever.

"Not go to Les Touches!" he cried.

"Oh! yes, yes, go! do not look so, my darling!" she cried, kissing him on the eyes that had flashed such flames.

Under these circumstances Calyste often came near losing the fruit of Camille's plot through the Breton fury of his love, of which he was ceasing to be the master. Finally, he swore to himself, in spite of his promise to Felicite, to see Beatrix, and speak to her. He wanted to read her eyes, to bathe in their light, to examine every detail of her dress, breathe its perfume, listen to the music of her voice, watch the graceful composition of her movements, embrace at a glance the whole figure, and study her as a general studies the field where he means to win a decisive battle. He willed as lovers will; he was grasped by desires which closed his ears and darkened his intellect, and threw him into an unnatural state in which he was conscious of neither obstacles, nor distances, nor the existence even of his own body.

One morning he resolved to go to Les Touches at an earlier hour than that agreed upon, and endeavor to meet Beatrix in the garden. He knew she walked there daily before breakfast.

Mademoiselle des Touches and the marquise had gone, as it happened, to see the marshes and the little bay with its margin of fine sand, where the sea penetrates and lies like a lake in the midst of the dunes. They had just returned, and were walking up a garden path beside the lawn, conversing as they walked.

"If the scenery pleases you," said Camille, "we must take Calyste and make a trip to Croisic. There are splendid rocks there, cascades of granite, little bays with natural basins, charmingly unexpected and capricious things, besides the sea itself, with its store of marble fragments,—a world of amusement. Also you will see women making fuel with cow-dung, which they nail against the walls of their houses to dry in the sun, after which they pile it up as we do peat in Paris."

"What! will you really risk Calyste?" cried the marquise, laughing, in a tone which proved that Camille's ruse had answered its purpose.

"Ah, my dear," she replied, "if you did but know the angelic soul of that dear child, you would understand me. In him, mere beauty is nothing; one must enter that pure heart, which is amazed at every step it takes into the kingdom of love. What faith! what grace! what innocence! The ancients were right enough in the worship they paid to sacred beauty. Some traveller, I forget who, relates that when wild horses lose their leader they choose the handsomest horse in the herd for his successor. Beauty, my dear, is the genius of things; it is the ensign which Nature hoists over her most precious creations; it is the truest of symbols as it is the greatest of accidents. Did any one ever suppose that angels could be deformed? are they not necessarily a combination of grace and strength? What is it that makes us stand for hours before some picture in Italy, where genius has striven through years of toil to realize but one of those accidents of Nature? Come, call up your sense of the truth of things and answer me; is it not the Idea of Beauty which our souls associate with moral grandeur? Well, Calyste is one of those dreams, those visions, realized. He has the regal power of a lion, tranquilly unsuspicious of its royalty. When he feels at his ease, he is witty; and I love his girlish timidity. My soul rests in his heart away from all corruptions, all ideas of knowledge, literature, the world, society, politics,—those useless accessories under which we stifle happiness. I am what I have never been,—a child! I am sure of him, but I like to play at jealousy; he likes it too. Besides, that is part of my secret."

Beatrix walked on pensively, in silence. Camille endured unspeakable martyrdom, and she cast a sidelong look at her companion which looked like flame.

"Ah, my dear; but *you* are happy," said Beatrix presently, laying her hand on Camille's arm like a woman wearied out with some inward struggle.

"Yes, happy indeed!" replied Felicite, with savage bitterness.

The two women dropped upon a bench from a sense of exhaustion. No creature of her sex was ever played upon like an instrument with more Machiavellian penetration than the marquise throughout this week.

"Yes, you are happy, but I!" she said,—"to know of Conti's infidelities, and have to bear them!"

"Why not leave him?" said Camille, seeing the hour had come to strike a decisive blow.

"Can I?"

"Oh! poor boy!"

Both were gazing into a clump of trees with a stupefied air.

Camille rose.

"I will go and hasten breakfast; my walk has given me an appetite," she said.

"Our conversation has taken away mine," remarked Beatrix.

The marquise in her morning dress was outlined in white against the dark greens of the foliage. Calyste, who had slipped through the salon into the garden, took a path, along which he sauntered as though he were meeting her by accident. Beatrix could not restrain a quiver as he approached her.

"Madame, in what way did I displease you yesterday?" he said, after the first commonplace sentences had been exchanged.

"But you have neither pleased me nor displeased me," she said, in a gentle voice.

The tone, air, and manner in which the marquise said these words encouraged Calyste.

"Am I so indifferent to you?" he said in a troubled voice, as the tears came into his eyes.

"Ought we not to be indifferent to each other?" replied the marquise. "Have we not, each of us, another, and a binding attachment?"

"Oh!" cried Calyste, "if you mean Camille, I did love her, but I love her no longer."

"Then why are you shut up together every morning?" she said, with a treacherous smile. "I don't suppose that Camille, in spite of her passion for tobacco, prefers her cigar to you, or that you, in your admiration for female authors, spend four hours a day in reading their romances."

"So then you know —" began the guileless young Breton, his face glowing with the happiness of being face to face with his idol.

"Calyste!" cried Camille, angrily, suddenly appearing and interrupting him. She took his arm and drew him away to some distance. "Calyste, is this what you promised me?"

Beatrix heard these words of reproach as Mademoiselle des Touches disappeared toward the house, taking Calyste with her. She was stupefied by the young man's assertion, and could not comprehend it; she was not as strong as Claude Vignon. In truth, the part being played by Camille Maupin, as shocking as it was grand, is one of those wicked grandeurs which women only practise when driven to extremity. By it their hearts are broken; in it the feelings of their sex are lost to them; it begins an abnegation which ends by either plunging them to hell, or lifting them to heaven.

During breakfast, which Calyste was invited to share, the marquise, whose sentiments could be noble and generous, made a sudden return upon herself, resolving to stifle the germs of love which were rising in her heart. She was neither cold nor hard to Calyste, but gently indifferent,—a course which tortured him. Felicite brought forward a proposition that they should make, on the next day but one, an excursion into the curious and interesting country lying between Les Touches, Croisic, and the village of Batz. She begged Calyste to employ himself on the morrow in hiring a boat and sailors to take them across the little bay, undertaking herself to provide horses and provisions, and all else that was necessary for a party of pleasure, in which there was to be no fatigue. Beatrix stopped the matter short, however, by saying that she did not wish to make excursions round the country. Calyste's face, which had beamed with delight at the prospect, was suddenly overclouded.

"What are you afraid of, my dear?" asked Camille.

"My position is so delicate I do not wish to compromise—I will not say my reputation, but my happiness," she said, meaningly, with a glance at the young Breton. "You know very well how suspicious Conti can be; if he knew—"

"Who will tell him?"

"He is coming back here to fetch me," said Beatrix.

Calyste turned pale. In spite of all that Camille could urge, in spite of Calyste's entreaties, Madame de Rochefide remained inflexible, and showed what Camille had called her obstinacy. Calyste left Les Touches the victim of one of those depressions of love which threaten, in certain men, to turn into madness. He began to revolve in his mind some decided means of coming to an explanation with Beatrix.

CHAPTER XII.

CORRESPONDENCE

When Calyste reached home, he did not leave his room until dinner time; and after dinner he went back to it. At ten o'clock his mother, uneasy at his absence, went to look for him, and found him writing in the midst of a pile of blotted and half-torn paper. He was writing to Beatrix, for distrust of Camille had come into his mind. The air and manner of the marquise during their brief interview in the garden had singularly encouraged him.

No first love-letter ever was or ever will be, as may readily be supposed, a brilliant effort of the mind. In all young men not tainted by corruption such a letter is written with gushings from the heart, too overflowing, too multifarious not to be the essence, the elixir of many other letters begun, rejected, and rewritten.

Here is the one that Calyste finally composed and which he read aloud to his poor, astonished mother. To her the old mansion seemed to have taken fire; this love of her son flamed up in it like the glare of a conflagration.

Calyste to Madame la Marquise de Rochefide.

Madame,—I loved you when you were to me but a dream; judge, therefore, of the force my love acquired when I saw you. The dream was far surpassed by the reality. It is my grief and my misfortune to have nothing to say to you that you do not know already of your beauty and your charms; and yet, perhaps, they have awakened in no other heart so deep a sentiment as they have in me.

In so many ways you are beautiful; I have studied you so much while thinking of you day and night that I have penetrated the mysteries of your being, the secrets of your heart, and your delicacy, so little appreciated. Have you ever been loved, understood, adored as you deserve to be?

Let me tell you now that there is not a trait in your nature which my heart does not interpret; your pride is understood by mine; the grandeur of your glance, the grace of your bearing, the distinction of your movements,—all things about your person are in harmony with the thoughts, the hopes, the desires hidden in the depths of your soul; it is because I have divined them all that I think myself worthy of your notice. If I had not become, within the last few days, another yourself, I could not speak to you of myself; this letter, indeed, relates far more to you than it does to me.

Beatrix, in order to write to you, I have silenced my youth, I have laid aside myself, I have aged my thoughts,—or, rather, it is you who have aged them, by this week of dreadful sufferings caused, innocently indeed, by you.

Do not think me one of those common lovers at whom I have heard you laugh so justly. What merit is there in loving a young and beautiful and wise and noble woman. Alas! I have no merit! What can I be to you? A child, attracted by effulgence of beauty and by moral grandeur, as the insects are attracted to the light. You cannot do otherwise than tread upon the flowers of my soul; they are there at your feet, and all my happiness consists in your stepping on them.

Absolute devotion, unbounded faith, love unquenchable,—all these treasures of a true and tender heart are nothing, nothing! they serve only to love with, they cannot win the love we crave. Sometimes I do not understand why a worship so ardent does not warm its idol; and when I meet your eye, so cold, so stern, I turn to ice within me. Your disdain, that is the acting force between us, not my worship. Why? You cannot hate me as much as I love you; why, then, does the weaker feeling rule the stronger? I loved Felicite with all the powers of my heart; yet I forgot her in a day, in a moment, when I saw you. She was my error; you are my truth.

You have, unknowingly, destroyed my happiness, and yet you owe me nothing in return. I loved Camille without hope, and I have no hope from you; nothing is changed but my divinity. I was a pagan; I am now a Christian, that is all—

Except this: you have taught me that to love is the greatest of all joys; the joy of being loved comes later. According to Camille, it is not loving to love for a short time only; the love that does not grow from day to day, from hour to hour, is a mere wretched passion. In order to grow, love must not see its end; and she saw the end of ours, the setting of our sun of love. When I beheld you, I understood her words, which, until then, I had disputed with all my youth, with all the ardor of my desires, with the despotic sternness of twenty years. That grand and noble Camille mingled her tears with mine, and yet she firmly rejected the love she saw must end. Therefore I am free to love you here on earth and in the heaven above us, as we love God. If you loved me, you would have no such arguments as Camille used to overthrow my love. We are both young; we could fly on equal wing across our sunny heaven, not fearing storms as that grand eagle feared them.

But ha! what am I saying? my thoughts have carried me beyond the humility of my real hopes. Believe me, believe in the submission, the patience, the mute adoration which I only ask you not to wound uselessly. I know, Beatrix, that you cannot love me without the loss of your self-esteem; therefore I ask for no return. Camille once said there was some hidden fatality in names, a propos of hers. That fatality I felt for myself on the jetty of Guerande, when I read on the shores of the ocean your name. Yes, you will pass through my life as Beatrice passed through that of Dante. My heart will be a pedestal for that white statue, cold, distant, jealous, and oppressive.

It is forbidden to you to love me; I know that. You will suffer a thousand deaths, you will be betrayed, humiliated, unhappy; but you have in you a devil's pride, which binds you to that column you have once embraced,—you are like Samson, you will perish by holding to it. But this I have not divined; my love is too blind for that; Camille has told it to me. It is not my mind that speaks to you of this, it is hers. I have no mind with which to reason when I think of you; blood gushes from my heart, and its hot wave darkens my intellect, weakens my strength, paralyzes my tongue, and bends my knees. I can only adore you, whatever you may do to me.

Camille calls your resolution obstinacy; I defend you, and I call it virtue. You are only the more beautiful because of it. I know my destiny, and the pride of a Breton can rise to the height of the woman who makes her pride a virtue.

Therefore, dear Beatrix, be kind, be consoling to me. When victims were selected, they crowned them with flowers; so do you to me; you owe me the flowers of pity, the music of my sacrifice. Am I not a proof of your grandeur? Will you not rise to the level of my disdained love,—disdained in spite of its sincerity, in spite of its immortal passion?

Ask Camille how I behaved to her after the day she told me, on her return to Les Touches, that she loved Claude Vignon. I was mute; I suffered in silence. Well, for you I will show even greater strength,—I will bury my feelings in my heart, if you will not drive me to despair, if you will only understand my heroism. A single word of praise from you is enough to make me bear the pains of martyrdom.

But if you persist in this cold silence, this deadly disdain, you will make me think you fear me. Ah, Beatrix, be with me what you are,—charming, witty, gay, and tender. Talk to me of Conti, as Camille has talked to me of Claude. I have no other spirit in my soul, no other genius but that of love; nothing is there that can make you fear me; I will be in your presence as if I loved you not.

Can you reject so humble a prayer?—the prayer of a child who only asks that his Light shall lighten him, that his Sun may warm him.

He whom you love can be with you at all times, but I, poor Calyste! have so few days in which to see you; you will soon be freed from me. Therefore I may return to Les Touches to-morrow, may I not? You will not refuse my arm for that excursion? We shall go together to Croisic and to Batz? If you do not go I shall take it for an answer,—Calyste will understand it!

There were four more pages of the same sort in close, fine writing, wherein Calyste explained the sort of threat conveyed in the last words, and related his youth and life; but the tale was chiefly told in exclamatory phrases, with many of those points and dashes of which modern literature is so prodigal when it comes to crucial passages,—as though they were planks offered to the reader's imagination, to help him across crevasses. The rest of this artless letter was merely repetition. But if it was not likely to touch Madame de Rochefide, and would very slightly interest the admirers of strong emotions, it made the mother weep, as she said to her son, in her tender voice,—

"My child, you are not happy."

This tumultuous poem of sentiments which had arisen like a storm in Calyste's heart, terrified the baroness; for the first time in her life she read a love-letter.

Calyste was standing in deep perplexity; how could he send that letter? He followed his mother back into the salon with the letter in his pocket and burning in his heart like fire. The Chevalier du Halga was still there, and the last deal of a lively *mouche* was going on. Charlotte de Kergarouet, in despair at Calyste's indifference, was paying attention to his father as a means of promoting her marriage. Calyste wandered hither and thither like a butterfly which had flown into the room by mistake. At last, when *mouche* was over, he drew the Chevalier du Halga into the great salon, from which he sent away Mademoiselle de Pen-Hoel's page and Mariotte.

"What does he want of the chevalier?" said old Zephirine, addressing her friend Jacqueline.

"Calyste strikes me as half-crazy," replied Mademoiselle de Pen-Hoel. "He pays Charlotte no more attention than if she were a *paludiere.*"

Remembering that the Chevalier du Halga had the reputation of having navigated in his youth the waters of gallantry, it came into Calyste's head to consult him.

"What is the best way to send a letter secretly to one's mistress," he said to the old gentleman in a whisper.

"Well, you can slip it into the hand of her maid with a louis or two underneath it; for sooner or later the maid will find out the secret, and it is just as well to let her into it at once," replied the chevalier, on whose face was the gleam of a smile. "But, on the whole, it is best to give the letter yourself."

"A louis or two!" exclaimed Calyste.

He snatched up his hat and ran to Les Touches, where he appeared like an apparition in the little salon, guided thither by the voices of Camille and Beatrix. They were sitting on the sofa together, apparently on the best of terms. Calyste, with the headlong impulse of love, flung himself heedlessly on the sofa beside the marquise, took her hand, and slipped the letter within it. He did this so rapidly that Felicite, watchful as she was, did not perceive it. Calyste's heart was tingling with an emotion half sweet, half painful, as he felt the hand of Beatrix press his own, and saw her, without interrupting her words, or seeming in the least disconcerted, slip the letter into her glove.

"You fling yourself on a woman's dress without mercy," she said, laughing.

"Calyste is a boy who is wanting in common-sense," said Felicite, not sparing him an open rebuke.

Calyste rose, took Camille's hand, and kissed it. Then he went to the piano and ran his finger-nail over the notes, making them all sound at once, like a rapid scale. This exuberance of joy surprised Camille, and made her thoughtful; she signed to Calyste to come to her.

"What is the matter with you?" she whispered in his ear.

"Nothing," he replied.

"There is something between them," thought Mademoiselle des Touches.

The marquise was impenetrable. Camille tried to make Calyste talk, hoping that his artless mind would betray itself; but the youth excused himself on the ground that his mother expected him, and he left Les Touches at eleven o'clock, — not, however, without having faced the fire of a piercing glance from Camille, to whom that excuse was made for the first time.

After the agitations of a wakeful night filled with visions of Beatrix, and after going a score of times through the chief street of Guerande for the purpose of meeting the answer to his letter, which did not come, Calyste finally received the following reply, which the marquise's waiting-woman, entering the hotel du Guenic, presented to him. He carried it to the garden, and there, in the grotto, he read as follows: —

Madame de Rochefide to Calyste.

You are a noble child, but you are only a child. You are bound to Camille, who adores you. You would not find in me either the perfections that distinguish her or the happiness that she can give you. Whatever you may think, she is young and I am old; her heart is full of treasures, mine is empty; she has for you a devotion you ill appreciate; she is unselfish; she lives only for you and in you. I, on the other hand, am full of doubts; I should drag you down to a wearisome life, without grandeur of any kind, —a life ruined by my own conduct. Camille is free; she can go and come as she will; I am a slave.

You forget that I love and am beloved. The situation in which I have placed myself forbids my accepting homage. That a man should love me, or say he loves me, is an insult. To turn to another would be to place myself at the level of the lowest of my sex.

You, who are young and full of delicacy, how can you oblige me to say these things, which rend my heart as they issue from it?

I preferred the scandal of an irreparable deed to the shame of constant deception; my own loss of station to a loss of honesty. In the eyes of many persons whose esteem I value, I am still worthy; but if I permitted another man to love me, I should fall indeed. The world is indulgent to those whose constancy covers, as with a mantle, the irregularity of their happiness; but it is pitiless to vice.

You see I feel neither disdain nor anger; I am answering your letter frankly and with simplicity. You are young; you are ignorant of the world; you are carried away by fancy; you are incapable, like all whose lives are pure, of making the reflections which evil suggests. But I will go still further.

Were I destined to be the most humiliated of women, were I forced to hide fearful sorrows, were I betrayed, abandoned, —which, thank God, is wholly impossible, —no one in this world would see me more. Yes, I believe I should find courage to kill a man who, seeing me in that situation, should talk to me of love.

You now know my mind to its depths. Perhaps I ought to thank you for having written to me. After receiving your letter, and, above all, after making you this reply, I could be at my ease with you in Camille's house, I could act out my natural self, and be what you ask of me; but I hardly need speak to you of the bitter ridicule that would overwhelm me if my eyes or my manner ceased to express the sentiments of which you complain. A second robbery from Camille would be a proof of her want of power which no woman could twice forgive. Even if I loved you, if I were blind to all else, if I forgot all else, I should still see Camille! Her love for you is a barrier too high to be o'erleaped by any power, even by the wings of an angel; none but a devil would fail to recoil before such treachery. In this, my dear Calyste, are many motives which delicate and noble women keep to themselves, of which you men know nothing; nor could you understand them, even though you were all as like our sex as you yourself appear to be at this moment.

My child, you have a mother who has shown you what you ought to be in life. She is pure and spotless; she fulfils her destiny nobly; what I have heard of her has filled my eyes with tears, and in the depths of my heart I envy her. I, too, might have been what she is! Calyste, that is the woman your wife should be, and such should be her life. I will never send you back, in jest, as I have done, to that little Charlotte, who would weary you to death; but I do commend you to some divine young girl who is worthy of your love.

If I were yours, your life would be blighted. You would have given me your whole existence, and I—you see, I am frank—I should have taken it; I should have gone with you, Heaven knows where, far from the world! But I should have made you most unhappy; for I am jealous. I see lions lurking in the path, and monsters in drops of water. I am made wretched by trifles that most women put up with; inexorable thoughts—from my heart, not yours—would poison our existence and destroy my life. If a man, after ten years' happiness, were not as respectful and as delicate as he was to me at first, I should resent the change; it would abase me in my own eyes! Such a lover could not believe in the Amadis and the Cyrus of my dreams. To-day true love is but a dream, not a reality. I see in yours only the joy of a desire the end of which is, as yet, unperceived by you.

For myself, I am not forty years old; I have not bent my pride beneath the yoke of experience,—in short, I am a woman too young to be anything but odious. I will not answer for my temper; my grace and charm are all external. Perhaps I have not yet suffered enough to have the indulgent manners and the absolute tenderness which come to us from cruel disappointments. Happiness has its insolence, and I, I fear, am insolent. Camille will be always your devoted slave; I should be an unreasonable tyrant. Besides, Camille was brought to you by your guardian angel, at the turning point of your life, to show you the career you ought to follow,—a career in which you cannot fail.

I know Felicite! her tenderness is inexhaustible; she may ignore the graces of our sex, but she possesses that fruitful strength, that genius for constancy, that noble intrepidity which makes us willing to accept the rest. She will marry you to some young girl, no matter what she suffers. She will find you a free Beatrix—if it is a Beatrix indeed who answers to your desires in a wife, and to your dreams; she will smooth all the difficulties in your way. The sale of a single acre of her ground in Paris would free your property in Brittany; she will make you her heir; are you not already her son by adoption?

Alas! what could I do for your happiness? Nothing. Do not betray that infinite love which contents itself with the duties of motherhood. Ah! I think her very fortunate, my Camille! She can well afford to forgive your feeling for poor Beatrix; women of her age are indulgent to such fancies. When they are sure of being loved, they will pardon a passing infidelity; in fact, it is often one of their keenest pleasures to triumph over a younger rival. Camille is above such women, and that remark does not refer to her; but I make it to ease your mind.

I have studied Camille closely; she is, to my eyes, one of the greatest women of our age. She has mind and she has goodness,—two qualities almost irreconcilable in woman; she is generous and simple,—two other grandeurs seldom found together in our sex. I have seen in the depths of her soul such treasures that the beautiful line of Dante on eternal happiness, which I heard her interpreting to you the other day, "Senza brama sicura ricchezza," seems as if made for her. She has talked to me of her career; she has related her life, showing me how love, that object of our prayers, our dreams, has ever eluded her. I replied that she seemed to me an instance of the difficulty, if not the impossibility, of uniting in one person two great glories.

You, Calyste, are one of the angelic souls whose mate it seems impossible to find; but Camille will obtain for you, even if she dies in doing so, the hand of some young girl with whom you can make a happy home.

For myself, I hold out to you a friendly hand, and I count, not on your heart, but on your mind, to make you in future a brother to me, as I shall be a sister to you; and I desire that this letter may terminate a correspondence which, between Les Touches and Guerande, is rather absurd.

Beatrix de Casteran.

The baroness, stirred to the depths of her soul by the strange exhibitions and the rapid changes of her boy's emotions, could no longer sit quietly at her work in the ancient hall. After looking at Calyste from time to time, she finally rose and came to him in a manner that was humble, and yet bold; she wanted him to grant a favor which she felt she had a right to demand.

"Well," she said, trembling, and looking at the letter, but not directly asking for it.

Calyste read it aloud to her. And these two noble souls, so simple, so guileless, saw nothing in that wily and treacherous epistle of the malice or the snares which the marquise had written into it.

"She is a noble woman, a grand woman!" said the baroness, with moistened eyes. "I will pray to God for her. I did not know that a woman could abandon her husband and child, and yet preserve a soul so virtuous. She is indeed worthy of pardon."

"Have I not every reason to adore her?" cried Calyste.

"But where will this love lead you?" said the baroness. "Ah, my child, how dangerous are women with noble sentiments! There is less to fear in those who are bad! Marry Charlotte de Kergarouet and release two-thirds of the estate. By selling a few farms, Mademoiselle de Pen-Hoel can bestow that grand result upon you in the marriage contract, and she will also help you, with her experience, to make the most of your property. You will be able to leave your children a great name, and a fine estate."

"Forget Beatrix!" said Calyste, in a muffled voice, with his eyes on the ground.

He left the baroness, and went up to his own room to write an answer to the marquise.

Madame du Guenic, whose heart retained every word of Madame de Roche-fide's letter, felt the need of some help in comprehending it more clearly, and also the grounds of Calyste's hope. At this hour the Chevalier du Halga was always to be seen taking his dog for a walk on the mall. The baroness, certain of finding him there, put on her bonnet and shawl and went out.

The sight of the Baronne du Guenic walking in Guerande elsewhere than to church, or on the two pretty roads selected as promenades on *fete* days, accompanied by the baron and Mademoiselle de Pen-Hoel, was an event so remarkable that two hours later, throughout the whole town, people accosted each other with the remark,—

"Madame du Guenic went out to-day; did you meet her?"

As soon as this amazing news reached the ears of Mademoiselle de Pen-Hoel, she said to her niece,—

"Something very extraordinary is happening at the du Guenics."

"Calyste is madly in love with that beautiful Marquise de Rochefide," said Charlotte. "I ought to leave Guerande and return to Nantes."

The Chevalier du Halga, much surprised at being sought by the baroness, released the chain of his little dog, aware that he could not divide himself between the two interests.

"Chevalier," began the baroness, "you used to practise gallantry?"

Here the Chevalier du Halga straightened himself up with an air that was not a little vain. Madame du Guenic, without naming her son or the marquise, repeated, as nearly as possible, the love-letter, and asked the chevalier to explain to her the meaning of such an answer. Du Halga snuffed the air and stroked his chin; he listened attentively; he made grimaces; and finally, he looked fixedly at the baroness with a knowing air, as he said,—

"When thoroughbred horses want to leap a barrier, they go up to reconnoitre it, and smell it over. Calyste is a lucky dog!"

"Oh, hush!" she cried.

"I'm mute. Ah! in the olden time I knew all about it," said the old chevalier, striking an attitude. "The weather was fine, the breeze nor'east. *Tudieu!* how the 'Belle-Poule' kept close to the wind that day when—Oh!" he cried, interrupting himself, "we shall have a change of weather; my ears are buzzing, and I feel the pain in my ribs! You know, don't you, that the battle of the 'Belle-Poule' was so famous that women wore head-dresses '*a la* Belle-Poule.' Madame de Kergarouet was the first to come to the opera in that head-dress, and I said to her: 'Madame, you are dressed for conquest.' The speech was repeated from box to box all through the house."

The baroness listened pleasantly to the old hero, who, faithful to the laws of gallantry, escorted her to the alley of her house, neglecting Thisbe. The secret of Thisbe's existence had once escaped him. Thisbe was the granddaughter of a delightful Thisbe, the pet of Madame l'Amirale de Kergarouet, first wife of the Comte de Kergarouet, the chevalier's commanding officer. The present Thisbe was eighteen years old.

The baroness ran up to Calyste's room. He was absent; she saw a letter, not sealed, but addressed to Madame de Rochefide, lying on the table. An invincible curiosity compelled the anxious mother to read it. This act of indiscretion was cruelly punished. The letter revealed to her the depths of the gulf into which his passion was hurling Calyste.

Calyste to Madame la Marquise de Rochefide.

What care I for the race of the du Guenics in these days, Beatrix? what is their name to me? My name is Beatrix; the happiness of Beatrix is my happiness; her life is my life, and all my fortune is in her heart. Our estates have been mortgaged these two hundred years, and so they may remain for two hundred more; our farmers have charge of them; no one can take them from us. To see you, to love you,—that is my property, my object, my religion!

You talk to me of marrying! the very thought convulses my heart. Is there another Beatrix? I will marry no one but you; I will wait for you twenty years, if need be. I am young, and you will be ever beautiful. My mother is a saint. I do not blame her, but she has never loved. I know now what she has lost, and what sacrifices she has made. You have taught me, Beatrix, to love her better; she is in my heart with you, and no other can ever be there; she is your only rival,—is not this to say that you reign in that heart supreme? Therefore your arguments have no force upon my mind.

As for Camille, you need only say the word, or give me a mere sign, and I will ask her to tell you herself that I do not love her. She is the mother of my intellect; nothing more, nothing less. From the moment that I first saw you she became to me a sister, a friend, a comrade, what you will of that kind; but we have no rights other than those of friendship upon each other. I took her for a woman until I saw you. You have proved to me that Camille is a man; she swims, hunts, smokes, drinks, rides on horseback, writes and analyzes hearts and books; she has no weaknesses; she marches on in all her strength; her motions even have no resemblance to your graceful movements, to your step, airy as the flight of a bird. Neither has she your voice of love, your tender eyes, your gracious manner; she is Camille Maupin; there is nothing of the woman about her, whereas in you are all the things of womanhood that I love. It has seemed to me, from the first moment when I saw you, that you were mine.

You will laugh at that fancy, but it has grown and is growing. It seems to me unnatural, anomalous that we should be apart. You are my soul, my life; I cannot live where you are not!

Let me love you! Let us fly! let us go into some country where you know no one, where only God and I can reach your heart! My mother, who loves you, might some day follow us. Ireland is full of castles; my mother's family will lend us one. Ah, Beatrix, let us go! A boat, a few sailors, and we are there, before any one can know we have fled this world you fear so much.

You have never been loved. I feel it as I re-read your letter, in which I fancy I can see that if the reasons you bring forward did not exist, you would let yourself be loved by me. Beatrix, a sacred love wipes out the past. Yes, I love you so truly that I could wish you doubly shamed if so my love might prove itself by holding you a saint!

You call my love an insult. Oh, Beatrix, you do not think it so! The love of noble youth—and you have called me that—would honor a queen. Therefore, to-morrow let us walk as lovers, hand in hand, among the rocks and beside the sea; your step upon the sands of my old Brittany will bless them anew to me! Give me this day of happiness; and that passing alms, unremembered, alas! by you, will be eternal riches to your

Calyste.

The baroness let fall the letter, without reading all of it. She knelt upon a chair, and made a mental prayer to God to save her Calyste's reason, to put his madness, his error far away from him; to lead him from the path in which she now beheld him.

"What are you doing, mother?" said Calyste, entering the room.

"I am praying to God for you," she answered, simply, turning her tearful eyes upon him. "I have committed the sin of reading that letter. My Calyste is mad!"

"A sweet madness!" said the young man, kissing her.

"I wish I could see that woman," she sighed.

"Mamma," said Calyste, "we shall take a boat to-morrow and cross to Croisic. If you are on the jetty you can see her."

So saying, he sealed his letter and departed for Les Touches.

That which, above all, terrified the baroness was to see a sentiment attaining, by the force of its own instinct, to the clear-sightedness of practised experience. Calyste's letter to Beatrix was such as the Chevalier du Halga, with his knowledge of the world, might have dictated.

CHAPTER XIII.

DUEL BETWEEN WOMEN

Perhaps one of the greatest enjoyments that small minds or inferior minds can obtain is that of deceiving a great soul, and laying snares for it. Beatrix knew herself far beneath Camille Maupin. This inferiority lay not only in the collection of mental and moral qualities which we call *talent*, but in the things of the heart called *passion*.

At the moment when Calyste was hurrying to Les Touches with the impetuosity of a first love borne on the wings of hope, the marquise was feeling a keen delight in knowing herself the object of the first love of so charming a young man. She did not go so far as to wish herself a sharer in the sentiment, but she thought it heroism on her part to repress the *capriccio*, as the Italians say. She thought she was equalling Camille's devotion, and told herself, moreover, that she was sacrificing herself to her friend. The vanities peculiar to Frenchwomen, which constitute the celebrated coquetry of which she was so signal an instance, were flattered and deeply satisfied by Calyste's love. Assailed by such powerful seduction, she was resisting it, and her virtues sang in her soul a concert of praise and self-approval.

The two women were half-sitting, half lying, in apparent indolence on the divan of the little salon, so filled with harmony and the fragrance of flowers. The windows were open, for the north wind had ceased to blow. A soothing southerly breeze was ruffling the surface of the salt lake before them, and the sun was glittering on the sands of the shore. Their souls were as deeply agitated as the nature before them was tranquil, and the heat within was not less ardent.

Bruised by the working of the machinery which she herself had set in motion, Camille was compelled to keep watch for her safety, fearing the amazing cleverness of the friendly enemy, or, rather, the inimical friend she had allowed within her borders. To guard her own secrets and maintain herself aloof, she had taken of late to contemplations of nature; she cheated the aching of her own heart by seeking a meaning in the world around her, finding God in that desert of heaven and earth. When an unbeliever once perceives the presence of God, he flings himself unreservedly into Catholicism, which, viewed as a system, is complete.

That morning Camille's brow had worn the halo of thoughts born of these researches during a night-time of painful struggle. Calyste was ever before her like a celestial image. The beautiful youth, to whom she had secretly devoted herself, had become to her a guardian angel. Was it not he who led her into those loftier regions, where suffering ceased beneath the weight of incommensurable infinity?

and now a certain air of triumph about Beatrix disturbed her. No woman gains an advantage over another without allowing it to be felt, however much she may deny having taken it. Nothing was ever more strange in its course than the dumb, moral struggle which was going on between these two women, each hiding from the other a secret,—each believing herself generous through hidden sacrifices.

Calyste arrived, holding the letter between his hand and his glove, ready to slip it at some convenient moment into the hand of Beatrix. Camille, whom the subtle change in the manner of her friend had not escaped, seemed not to watch her, but did watch her in a mirror at the moment when Calyste was just entering the room. That is always a crucial moment for women. The cleverest as well as the silliest of them, the frankest as the shrewdest, are seldom able to keep their secret; it bursts from them, at any rate, to the eyes of another woman. Too much reserve or too little; a free and luminous look; the mysterious lowering of eyelids,—all betray, at that sudden moment, the sentiment which is the most difficult of all to hide; for real indifference has something so radically cold about it that it can never be simulated. Women have a genius for shades,—shades of detail, shades of character; they know them all. There are times when their eyes take in a rival from head to foot; they can guess the slightest movement of a foot beneath a gown, the almost imperceptible motion of the waist; they know the significance of things which, to a man, seem insignificant. Two women observing each other play one of the choicest scenes of comedy that the world can show.

"Calyste has committed some folly," thought Camille, perceiving in each of her guests an indefinable air of persons who have a mutual understanding.

There was no longer either stiffness or pretended indifference on the part of Beatrix; she now regarded Calyste as her own property. Calyste was even more transparent; he colored, as guilty people, or happy people color. He announced that he had come to make arrangements for the excursion on the following day.

"Then you really intend to go, my dear?" said Camille, interrogatively.

"Yes," said Beatrix.

"How did you know it, Calyste?" asked Mademoiselle des Touches.

"I came here to find out," replied Calyste, on a look flashed at him by Madame de Rochefide, who did not wish Camille to gain the slightest inkling of their correspondence.

"They have an agreement together," thought Camille, who caught the look in the powerful sweep of her eye.

Under the pressure of that thought a horrible discomposure overspread her face and frightened Beatrix.

"What is the matter, my dear?" she cried.

"Nothing. Well, then, Calyste, send my horses and yours across to Croisic, so that we may drive home by way of Batz. We will breakfast at Croisic, and get home in time for dinner. You must take charge of the boat arrangements. Let us start by half-past eight. You will see some fine sights, Beatrix, and one very strange one;

you will see Cambremer, a man who does penance on a rock for having wilfully killed his son. Oh! you are in a primitive land, among a primitive race of people, where men are moved by other sentiments than those of ordinary mortals. Calyste shall tell you the tale; it is a drama of the seashore."

She went into her bedroom, for she was stifling. Calyste gave his letter to Beatrix and followed Camille.

"Calyste, you are loved, I think; but you are hiding something from me; you have done some foolish thing."

"Loved!" he exclaimed, dropping into a chair.

Camille looked into the next room; Beatrix had disappeared. The fact was odd. Women do not usually leave a room which contains the man they admire, unless they have either the certainty of seeing him again, or something better still. Mademoiselle des Touches said to herself:—

"Can he have given her a letter?"

But she thought the innocent Breton incapable of such boldness.

"If you have disobeyed me, all will be lost, through your own fault," she said to him very gravely. "Go, now, and make your preparations for to-morrow."

She made a gesture which Calyste did not venture to resist.

As he walked toward Croisic, to engage the boatmen, fears came into Calyste's mind. Camille's speech foreshadowed something fatal, and he believed in the second sight of her maternal affection. When he returned, four hours later, very tired, and expecting to dine at Les Touches, he found Camille's maid keeping watch over the door, to tell him that neither her mistress nor the marquise could receive him that evening. Calyste, much surprised, wished to question her, but she bade him hastily good-night and closed the door.

Six o'clock was striking on the steeple of Guerande as Calyste entered his own house, where Mariotte gave him his belated dinner; after which, he played *mouche* in gloomy meditation. These alternations of joy and gloom, happiness and unhappiness, the extinction of hopes succeeding the apparent certainty of being loved, bruised and wounded the young soul which had flown so high on outstretched wings that the fall was dreadful.

"Does anything trouble you, my Calyste?" said his mother.

"Nothing," he replied, looking at her with eyes from which the light of the soul and the fire of love were withdrawn.

It is not hope, but despair, which gives the measure of our ambitions. The finest poems of hope are sung in secret, but grief appears without a veil.

"Calyste, you are not nice," said Charlotte, after vainly attempting on him those little provincial witcheries which degenerate usually into teasing.

"I am tired," he said, rising, and bidding the company good-night.

"Calyste is much changed," remarked Mademoiselle de Pen-Hoel.

"We haven't beautiful dresses trimmed with lace; we don't shake our sleeves like this, or twist our bodies like that; we don't know how to give sidelong glances, and turn our eyes," said Charlotte, mimicking the air, and attitude, and glances of the marquise. "*We* haven't that head voice, nor the interesting little cough, *heu! heu!* which sounds like the sigh of a spook; *we* have the misfortune of being healthy and robust, and of loving our friends without coquetry; and when we look at them, we don't pretend to stick a dart into them, or to watch them slyly; *we* can't bend our heads like a weeping willow, just to look the more interesting when we raise them—this way."

Mademoiselle de Pen-Hoel could not help laughing at her niece's gesture; but neither the chevalier nor the baron paid any heed to this truly provincial satire against Paris.

"But the Marquise de Rochefide is a very handsome woman," said the old maid.

"My dear," said the baroness to her husband, "I happen to know that she is going over to Croisic to-morrow. Let us walk on the jetty; I should like to see her."

While Calyste was racking his brains to imagine what could have closed the doors of Les Touches to him, a scene was passing between Camille and Beatrix which was to have its influence on the events of the morrow.

Calyste's last letter had stirred in Madame de Rochefide's heart emotions hitherto unknown to it. Women are not often the subject of a love so young, guileless, sincere, and unconditional as that of this youth, this child. Beatrix had loved more than she had been loved. After being all her life a slave, she suddenly felt an inexplicable desire to be a tyrant. But, in the midst of her pleasure, as she read and re-read the letter, she was pierced through and through with a cruel idea.

What were Calyste and Camille doing together ever since Claude Vignon's departure? If, as Calyste said, he did not love Camille, and if Camille knew it, how did they employ their mornings, and why were they alone together? Memory suddenly flashed into her mind, in answer to these questions, certain speeches of Camille; a grinning devil seemed to show her, as in a magic mirror, the portrait of that heroic woman, with certain gestures, certain aspects, which suddenly enlightened her. What! instead of being her equal, was she crushed by Felicite? instead of over-reaching her, was she being over-reached herself? was she only a toy, a pleasure, which Camille was giving to her child, whom she loved with an extraordinary passion that was free from all vulgarity?

To a woman like Beatrix this thought came like a thunder-clap. She went over in her mind minutely the history of the past week. In a moment the part which Camille was playing, and her own, unrolled themselves to their fullest extent before her eyes; she felt horribly belittled. In her fury of jealous anger, she fancied she could see in Camille's conduct an intention of vengeance against Conti. Was the hidden wrath of the past two years really acting upon the present moment?

Once on the path of these doubts and superstitions, Beatrix did not pause. She walked up and down her room, driven to rapid motion by the impetuous movements of her soul, sitting down now and then, and trying to decide upon a course, but unable to do so. And thus she remained, a prey to indecision until the dinner hour, when she rose hastily, and went downstairs without dressing. No sooner did Camille see her, than she felt that a crisis had come. Beatrix, in her morning gown, with a chilling air and a taciturn manner, indicated to an observer as keen as Maupin the coming hostilities of an embittered heart.

Camille instantly left the room and gave the order which so astonished Calyste; she feared that he might arrive in the midst of the quarrel, and she determined to be alone, without witnesses, in fighting this duel of deception on both sides. Beatrix, without an auxiliary, would infallibly succumb. Camille well knew the barrenness of that soul, the pettiness of that pride, to which she had justly applied the epithet of obstinate.

The dinner was gloomy. Camille was gentle and kind; she felt herself the superior being. Beatrix was hard and cutting; she felt she was being managed like a child. During dinner the battle began with glances, gestures, half-spoken sentences,—not enough to enlighten the servants, but enough to prepare an observer for the coming storm. When the time to go upstairs came, Camille offered her arm maliciously to Beatrix, who pretended not to see it, and sprang up the stairway alone. When coffee had been served Mademoiselle des Touches said to the footman, "You may go,"—a brief sentence, which served as a signal for the combat.

"The novels you make, my dear, are more dangerous than those you write," said the marquise.

"They have one advantage, however," replied Camille, lighting a cigarette.

"What is that?" asked Beatrix.

"They are unpublished, my angel."

"Is the one in which you are putting me to be turned into a book?"

"I've no fancy for the role of OEdipus; I know you have the wit and beauty of a sphinx, but don't propound conundrums. Speak out, plainly, my dear Beatrix."

"When, in order to make a man happy, amuse him, please him, and save him from ennui, we allow the devil to help us—"

"That man would reproach us later for our efforts on his behalf, and would think them prompted by the genius of depravity," said Camille, taking the cigarette from her lips to interrupt her friend.

"He forgets the love which carried us away, and is our sole justification— but that's the way of men, they are all unjust and ungrateful," continued Beatrix. "Women among themselves know each other; they know how proud and noble their own minds are, and, let us frankly say so, how virtuous! But, Camille, I have just recognized the truth of certain criticisms upon your nature, of which you have sometimes complained. My dear, you have something of the man about you; you behave like a man; nothing restrains you; if you haven't all a man's advantages, you have a man's spirit in all your ways; and you share his contempt for women. I have no reason, my dear, to be satisfied with you, and I am too frank to hide my dissatisfaction. No one has ever given or ever will give, perhaps, so cruel a wound to my heart as that from which I am now suffering. If you are not a woman in love, you are one in vengeance. It takes a *woman* of genius to discover the most sensitive spot of all in another woman's delicacy. I am talking now of Calyste, and the trickery, my dear,—that is the word,—*trickery*,—you have employed against me. To what depths have you descended, Camille Maupin! and why?"

"More and more sphinx-like!" said Camille, smiling.

"You want me to fling myself at Calyste's head; but I am still too young for that sort of thing. To me, love is sacred; love is love with all its emotions, jealousies, and despotisms. I am not an author; it is impossible for me to see ideas where the heart feels sentiments."

"You think yourself capable of loving foolishly!" said Camille. "Make yourself easy on that score; you still have plenty of sense. My dear, you calumniate yourself; I assure you that your nature is cold enough to enable your head to judge of every action of your heart."

The marquise colored high; she darted a look of hatred, a venomous look, at Camille, and found, without searching, the sharpest arrows in her quiver. Camille smoked composedly as she listened to a furious tirade, which rang with such cutting insults that we do not reproduce it here. Beatrix, irritated by the calmness of her adversary, condescended even to personalities on Camille's age.

"Is that all?" said Felicite, when Beatrix paused, letting a cloud of smoke exhale from her lips. "Do you love Calyste?"

"No; of course not."

"So much the better," replied Camille. "I do love him—far too much for my own peace of mind. He may, perhaps, have had a passing fancy for you; for you are, you know, enchantingly fair, while I am as black as a crow; you are slim and willowy, while I have a portly dignity; in short, you are *young*!—that's the final word, and you have not spared it to me. You have abused your advantages as a woman against me. I have done my best to prevent what has now happened. However little of a woman you may think me, I am woman enough, my dear, not to allow a rival to triumph over me unless I choose to help her." (This remark, made in apparently the most innocent manner, cut the marquise to the heart). "You take me for a very silly person if you believe all that Calyste tries to make you think of me. I am neither so great nor so small; I am a woman, and very much of a woman. Come, put off your grand airs, and give me your hand!" continued Camille, taking Madame de Rochefide's hand. "You do not love Calyste, you say; that is true, is it not? Don't be angry, therefore; be hard, and cold, and stern to him to-morrow; he will end by submitting to his fate, especially after certain little reproaches which I mean to make to him. Still, Calyste is a Breton, and very persistent; if he should continue to pay court to you, tell me frankly, and I will lend you my little country house near Paris, where you will find all the comforts of life, and where Conti can come out and see you. You said just now that Calyste calumniated me. Good heavens! what of that? The purest love lies twenty times a day; its deceptions only prove its strength."

Camille's face wore an air of such superb disdain that the marquise grew fearful and anxious. She knew not how to answer. Camille dealt her a last blow.

"I am more confiding and less bitter than you," she said. "I don't suspect you of attempting to cover by a quarrel a secret injury, which would compromise my very life. You know me; I shall never survive the loss of Calyste, but I must lose him sooner or later. Still, Calyste loves me now; of that I am sure."

"Here is what he answered to a letter of mine, urging him to be true to you," said Beatrix, holding out Calyste's last letter.

Camille took it and read it; but as she read it, her eyes filled with tears; and presently she wept as women weep in their bitterest sorrows.

"My God!" she said, "how he loves her! I shall die without being understood — or loved," she added.

She sat for a few moments with her head leaning against the shoulder of her companion; her grief was genuine; she felt to the very core of her being the same terrible blow which the Baronne du Guenic had received in reading that letter.

"Do you love him?" she said, straightening herself up, and looking fixedly at Beatrix. "Have you that infinite worship for him which triumphs over all pains, survives contempt, betrayal, the certainty that he will never love you? Do you love him for himself, and for the very joy of loving him?"

"Dear friend," said the marquise, tenderly, "be happy, be at peace; I will leave this place to-morrow."

"No, do not go; he loves you, I see that. Well, I love him so much that I could not endure to see him wretched and unhappy. Still, I had formed plans for him, projects; but if he loves you, all is over."

"And I love him, Camille," said the marquise, with a sort of *naivete*, and coloring.

"You love him, and yet you cast him off!" cried Camille. "Ah! that is not loving; you do not love him."

"I don't know what fresh virtue he has roused in me, but certainly he has made me ashamed of my own self," said Beatrix. "I would I were virtuous and free, that I might give him something better than the dregs of a heart and the weight of my chains. I do not want a hampered destiny either for him or for myself."

"Cold brain!" exclaimed Camille, with a sort of horror. "To love and calculate!"

"Call it what you like," said Beatrix, "but I will not spoil his life, or hang like a millstone round his neck, to become an eternal regret to him. If I cannot be his wife, I shall not be his mistress. He has — you will laugh at me? No? Well, then, he has purified me."

Camille cast on Beatrix the most sullen, savage look that female jealousy ever cast upon a rival.

"On that ground, I believed I stood alone," she said. "Beatrix, those words of yours must separate us forever; we are no longer friends. Here begins a terrible conflict between us. I tell you now; you will either succumb or fly."

So saying, Camille bounded into her room, after showing her face, which was that of a maddened lioness, to the astonished Beatrix. Then she raised the portiere and looked in again.

"Do you intend to go to Croisic to-morrow," she asked.

"Certainly," replied the marquise, proudly. "I shall not fly, and I shall not succumb."

"I play above board," replied Camille; "I shall write to Conti."

Beatrix became as white as the gauze of her scarf.

"We are staking our lives on this game," she replied, not knowing what to say or do.

The violent passions roused by this scene between the two women calmed down during the night. Both argued with their own minds and returned to those treacherously temporizing courses which are so attractive to the majority of women,—an excellent system between men and women, but fatally unsafe among women alone. In the midst of this tumult of their souls Mademoiselle des Touches had listened to that great Voice whose counsels subdue the strongest will; Beatrix heard only the promptings of worldly wisdom; she feared the contempt of society.

Thus Felicite's last deception succeeded; Calyste's blunder was repaired, but a fresh indiscretion might be fatal to him.

CHAPTER XIV.

AN EXCURSION TO CROISIC

It was now the end of August, and the sky was magnificently clear. Near the horizon the sea had taken, as it is wont to do in southern climes, a tint of molten silver; on the shore it rippled in tiny waves. A sort of glowing vapor, an effect of the rays of the sun falling plumb upon the sands, produced an atmosphere like that of the tropics. The salt shone up like bunches of white violets on the surface of the marsh. The patient *paludiers*, dressed in white to resist the action of the sun, had been from early morning at their posts, armed with long rakes. Some were leaning on the low mud-walls that divided the different holdings, whence they watched the process of this natural chemistry, known to them from childhood. Others were playing with their wives and children. Those green dragons, otherwise called custom-house officers, were tranquilly smoking their pipes.

There was something foreign, perhaps oriental, about the scene; at any rate a Parisian suddenly transported thither would never have supposed himself in France. The baron and baroness, who had made a pretext of coming to see how the salt harvest throve, were on the jetty, admiring the silent landscape, where the sea alone sounded the moan of her waves at regular intervals, where boats and vessels tracked a vast expanse, and the girdle of green earth richly cultivated, produced an effect that was all the more charming because so rare on the desolate shores of ocean.

"Well, my friends, I wanted to see the marshes of Guerande once more before I die," said the baron to the *paludiers*, who had gathered about the entrance of the marshes to salute him.

"Can a Guenic die?" said one of them.

Just then the party from Les Touches arrived through the narrow pathway. The marquise walked first alone; Calyste and Camille followed arm-in-arm. Gasselin brought up the rear.

"There are my father and mother," said the young man to Camille.

The marquise stopped short. Madame du Guenic felt the most violent repulsion at the appearance of Beatrix, although the latter was dressed to much advantage. A Leghorn hat with wide brims and a wreath of blue-bells, her crimped hair fluffy beneath it, a gown of some gray woollen stuff, and a blue sash with floating ends gave her the air of a princess disguised as a milkmaid.

"She has no heart," thought the baroness.

"Mademoiselle," said Calyste to Camille, "this is Madame du Guenic, and this is my father." Then he said turning to the baron and baroness, "Mademoiselle des Touches, and Madame la Marquise de Rochefide, *nee* de Casteran, father."

The baron bowed to Mademoiselle des Touches, who made a respectful bow, full of gratitude, to the baroness.

"That one," thought Fanny, "really loves my boy; she seems to thank me for bringing him into the world."

"I suppose you have come to see, as I have, whether the harvest is a good one. But I believe you have better reasons for doing so than I," said the baron to Camille. "You have property here, I think, mademoiselle."

"Mademoiselle is the largest of all the owners," said one of the *paludiers* who were grouped about them, "and may God preserve her to us, for she's a *good* lady."

The two parties bowed and separated.

"No one would suppose Mademoiselle des Touches to be more than thirty," said the baron to his wife. "She is very handsome. And Calyste prefers that haggard Parisian marquise to a sound Breton girl!"

"I fear he does," replied the baroness.

A boat was waiting at the steps of the jetty, where the party embarked without a smile. The marquise was cold and dignified. Camille had lectured Calyste on his disobedience, explaining to him clearly how matters stood. Calyste, a prey to black despair, was casting glances at Beatrix in which anger and love struggled for the mastery. Not a word was said by any of them during the short passage from the jetty of Guerande to the extreme end of the port of Croisic, the point where the boats discharge the salt, which the peasant-women then bear away on their heads in huge earthen jars after the fashion of caryatides. These women go barefooted with very short petticoats. Many of them let the kerchiefs which cover their bosoms fly carelessly open. Some wear only shifts, and are the more dignified; for the less clothing a woman wears, the more nobly modest is her bearing.

The little Danish vessel had just finished lading, therefore the landing of the two handsome ladies excited much curiosity among the female salt-carriers; and as much to avoid their remarks as to serve Calyste, Camille sprang forward toward the rocks, leaving him to follow with Beatrix, while Gasselin put a distance of some two hundred steps between himself and his master.

The peninsula of Croisic is flanked on the sea side by granite rocks the shapes of which are so strangely fantastic that they can only be appreciated by travellers who are in a position to compare them with other great spectacles of primeval Nature. Perhaps the rocks of Croisic have the same advantage over sights of that kind as that accorded to the road to the Grande Chartreuse over all other narrow valleys. Neither the coasts of Croisic, where the granite bulwark is split into strange reefs, nor those of Sardinia, where Nature is dedicated to grandiose and terrible effects, nor even the basaltic rocks of the northern seas can show a character so unique and so complete. Fancy has here amused itself by composing interminable arabesques where the most fantastic figures wind and twine. All forms are here.

The imagination is at last fatigued by this vast gallery of abnormal shapes, where in stormy weather the sea makes rough assaults which have ended in polishing all ruggedness.

You will find under a naturally vaulted roof, of a boldness imitated from afar by Brunelleschi (for the greatest efforts of art are always the timid copying of effects of nature), a rocky hollow polished like a marble bath-tub and floored with fine white sand, in which is four feet of tepid water where you can bathe without danger. You walk on, admiring the cool little covers sheltered by great portals; roughly carved, it is true, but majestic, like the Pitti palace, that other imitation of the whims of Nature. Curious features are innumerable; nothing is lacking that the wildest imagination could invent or desire.

There even exists a thing so rare on the rocky shores of ocean that this may be the solitary instance of it,—a large bush of box. This bush, the greatest curiosity of Croisic, where trees have never grown, is three miles distant from the harbor, on the point of rocks that runs farthest into the sea. On this granite promontory, which rises to a height that neither the waves nor the spray can touch, even in the wildest weather, and faces southerly, diluvian caprice has constructed a hollow basin, which projects about four feet. Into this basin, or cleft, chance, possibly man, has conveyed enough vegetable earth for the growth of a box-plant, compact, well-nourished, and sown, no doubt, by birds. The shape of the roots would indicate to a botanist an existence of at least three hundred years. Above it the rock has been broken off abruptly. The natural convulsion which did this, the traces of which are ineffaceably written here, must have carried away the broken fragments of the granite I know not where.

The sea rushes in, meeting no reefs, to the foot of this cliff, which rises to a height of some four or five hundred feet; at its base lie several scattered rocks, just reaching the surface at high water, and describing a semi-circle. It requires some nerve and resolution to climb to the summit of this little Gibraltar, the shape of which is nearly round, and from which a sudden gust of wind might precipitate the rash gazer into the sea, or, still more to be feared, upon the rocks.

This gigantic sentinel resembles the look-out towers of old castles, from which the inhabitants could look the country over and foresee attacks. Thence we see the clock towers and the arid fields of Croisic, with the sandy dunes, which injure cultivation, and stretch as far as Batz. A few old men declare that in days long past a fortress occupied the spot. The sardine-fishers have given the rock, which can be seen far out at sea, a name; but it is useless to write it here, its Breton consonants being as difficult to pronounce as to remember.

Calyste led Beatrix to this point, whence the view is magnificent, and where the natural sculpture of the granite is even more imposing to the spectator than the mass of the huge breastwork when seen from the sandy road which skirts the shore.

Is it necessary to explain why Camille had rushed away alone? Like some wounded wild animal, she longed for solitude, and went on and on, threading her way among the fissures and caves and little peaks of nature's fortress. Not to be hampered in climbing by women's clothing, she wore trousers with frilled edges, a short blouse, a peaked cap, and, by way of staff, she carried a riding-whip, for Camille has always had a certain vanity in her strength and her agility. Thus arrayed, she looked far handsomer than Beatrix. She wore also a little shawl of crimson China crape, crossed on her bosom and tied behind, as they dress a child. For some time Beatrix and Calyste saw her flitting before them over the peaks and chasms like a ghost or vision; she was trying to still her inward sufferings by confronting some imaginary peril.

She was the first to reach the rock in which the box-bush grew. There she sat down in the shade of a granite projection, and was lost in thought. What could a woman like herself do with old age, having already drunk the cup of fame which all great talents, too eager to sip slowly the stupid pleasures of vanity, quaff at a single draught? She has since admitted that it was here—at this moment, and on this spot—that one of those singular reflections suggested by a mere nothing, by one of those chance accidents that seem nonsense to common minds, but which, to noble souls, do sometimes open vast depths of thought, decided her to take the extraordinary step by which she was to part forever from social life.

She drew from her pocket a little box, in which she had put, in case of thirst, some strawberry lozenges; she now ate several; and as she did so, the thought crossed her mind that the strawberries, which existed no longer, lived nevertheless in their qualities. Was it not so with ourselves? The ocean before her was an image of the infinite. No great spirit can face the infinite, admitting the immortality of the soul, without the conviction of a future of holiness. The thought filled her mind. How petty then seemed the part that she was playing! there was no real greatness in giving Beatrix to Calyste! So thinking, she felt the earthly woman die within her, and the true woman, the noble and angelic being, veiled until now by flesh, arose in her place. Her great mind, her knowledge, her attainments, her false loves had brought her face to face with what? Ah! who would have thought it?—with the bounteous mother, the comforter of troubled spirits, with the Roman Church, ever kind to repentance, poetic to poets, childlike with children, and yet so profound, so full of mystery to anxious, restless minds that they can burrow there and satisfy all longings, all questionings, all hopes. She cast her eyes, as it were, upon the strangely devious way—like the tortuous rocky path before her—over which her love for Calyste had led her. Ah! Calyste was indeed a messenger from heaven, her divine conductor! She had stifled earthly love, and a divine love had come from it.

After walking for some distance in silence, Calyste could not refrain, on a remark of Beatrix about the grandeur of the ocean, so unlike the smiling beauty of the Mediterranean, from comparing in depth, purity, extent, unchanging and eternal duration, that ocean with his love.

"It is met by a rock!" said Beatrix, laughing.

"When you speak thus," he answered, with a sublime look, "I hear you, I see you, and I can summon to my aid the patience of the angels; but when I am alone, you would pity me if you could see me then. My mother weeps for my suffering."

"Listen to me, Calyste; we must put an end to all this," said the marquise, gazing down upon the sandy road. "Perhaps we have now reached the only propitious place to say these things, for never in my life did I see nature more in keeping with my thoughts. I have seen Italy, where all things tell of love; I have seen Switzerland, where all is cool and fresh, and tells of happiness,—the happiness of labor; where the verdure, the tranquil waters, the smiling slopes, are oppressed by the snow-topped Alps; but I have never seen anything that so depicts the burning barrenness of my life as that little arid plain down there, dried by the salt sea winds, corroded by the spray, where a fruitless agriculture tries to struggle against the will of that great ocean. There, Calyste, you have an image of this Beatrix. Don't cling to it. I love you, but I will never be yours in any way whatever, for I have the sense of my inward desolation. Ah! you do not know how cruel I am to myself in speaking thus to you. No, you shall never see your idol diminished; she shall never fall from the height at which you have placed her. I now have a horror of any love which disregards the world and religion. I shall remain in my present bonds; I shall be that sandy plain we see before us, without fruit or flowers or verdure."

"But if you are abandoned?" said Calyste.

"Then I should beg my pardon of the man I have offended. I will never run the risk of taking a happiness I know would quickly end."

"End!" cried Calyste.

The marquise stopped the passionate speech into which her lover was about to launch, by repeating the word "End!" in a tone that silenced him.

This opposition roused in the young man one of those mute inward furies known only to those who love without hope. They walked on several hundred steps in total silence, looking neither at the sea, nor the rocks, nor the plain of Croisic.

"I would make you happy," said Calyste.

"All men begin by promising that," she answered, "and they end by abandonment and disgust. I have no reproach to cast on him to whom I shall be faithful. He made me no promises; I went to him; but my only means of lessening my fault is to make it eternal."

"Say rather, madame, that you feel no love for me. I, who love you, I know that love cannot argue; it is itself; it sees nothing else. There is no sacrifice I will not make to you; command it, and I will do the impossible. He who despised his mistress for flinging her glove among the lions, and ordering him to bring it back to her, did not *love!* He denied your right to test our hearts, and to yield yourselves only to our utmost devotion. I will sacrifice to you my family, my name, my future."

"But what an insult in that word 'sacrifice'!" she said, in reproachful tones, which made poor Calyste feel the folly of his speech.

None but women who truly love, or inborn coquettes, know how to use a word as a point from which to make a spring.

"You are right," said Calyste, letting fall a tear; "that word can only be said of the cruel struggles which you ask of me."

"Hush!" said Beatrix, struck by an answer in which, for the first time, Calyste had really made her feel his love. "I have done wrong enough; tempt me no more."

At this moment they had reached the base of the rock on which grew the plant of box. Calyste felt a thrill of delight as he helped the marquise to climb the steep ascent to the summit, which she wished to reach. To the poor lad it was a precious privilege to hold her up, to make her lean upon him, to feel her tremble; she had need of him. This unlooked-for pleasure turned his head; he saw nought else but Beatrix, and he clasped her round the waist.

"What!" she said, with an imposing air.

"Will you never be mine?" he demanded, in a voice that was choked by the tumult of his blood.

"Never, my friend," she replied. "I can only be to you a Beatrix,—a dream. But is not that a sweet and tender thing? We shall have no bitterness, no grief, no repentance."

"Will you return to Conti?"

"I must."

"You shall never belong to any man!" cried Calyste, pushing her from him with frenzied violence.

He listened for her fall, intending to spring after her, but he heard only a muffled sound, the tearing of some stuff, and then the thud of a body falling on the ground. Instead of being flung head foremost down the precipice, Beatrix had only slipped some eight or ten feet into the cavity where the box-bush grew; but she might from there have rolled down into the sea if her gown had not caught upon a point of rock, and by tearing slowly lowered the weight of her body upon the bush.

Mademoiselle des Touches, who saw the scene, was unable in her horror to cry out, but she signed to Gasselin to come. Calyste was leaning forward with an expression of savage curiosity; he saw the position in which Beatrix lay, and he shuddered. Her lips moved,—she seemed to be praying; in fact, she thought she was about to die, for she felt the bush beginning to give way. With the agility which danger gives to youth, Calyste slid down to the ledge below the bush, where he was able to grasp the marquise and hold her, although at the risk of their both sliding down into the sea. As he held her, he saw that she had fainted; but in that aerial spot he could fancy her all his, and his first emotion was that of pleasure.

"Open your eyes," he said, "and forgive me; we will die together."

"Die?" she said, opening her eyes and unclosing her pallid lips.

Calyste welcomed that word with a kiss, and felt the marquise tremble under it convulsively, with passionate joy. At that instant Gasselin's hob-nailed shoes sounded on the rock above them. The old Breton was followed by Camille, and together they sought for some means of saving the lovers.

"There's but one way, mademoiselle," said Gasselin. "I must slide down there, and they can climb on my shoulders, and you must pull them up."

"And you?" said Camille.

The man seemed surprised that he should be considered in presence of the danger to his young master.

"You must go to Croisic and fetch a ladder," said Camille.

Beatrix asked in a feeble voice to be laid down, and Calyste placed her on the narrow space between the bush and its background of rock.

"I saw you, Calyste," said Camille from above. "Whether Beatrix lives or dies, remember that this must be an accident."

"She will hate me," he said, with moistened eyes.

"She will adore you," replied Camille. "But this puts an end to our excursion. We must get her back to Les Touches. Had she been killed, Calyste, what would have become of you?"

"I should have followed her."

"And your mother?" Then, after a pause, she added, feebly, "and me?"

Calyste was deadly pale; he stood with his back against the granite motionless and silent. Gasselin soon returned from one of the little farms scattered through the neighborhood, bearing a ladder which he had borrowed. By this time Beatrix had recovered a little strength. The ladder being placed, she was able, by the help of Gasselin, who lowered Camille's red shawl till she could grasp it, to reach the round top of the rock, where the Breton took her in his arms and carried her to the shore as though she were an infant.

"I should not have said no to death—but suffering!" she murmured to Felicite, in a feeble voice.

The weakness, in fact the complete prostration, of the marquise obliged Camille to have her taken to the farmhouse from which the ladder had been borrowed. Calyste, Gasselin, and Camille took off what clothes they could spare and laid them on the ladder, making a sort of litter on which they carried Beatrix. The farmers gave her a bed. Gasselin then went to the place where the carriage was awaiting them, and, taking one of the horses, rode to Croisic to obtain a doctor, telling the boatman to row to the landing-place that was nearest to the farmhouse.

Calyste, sitting on a stool, answered only by motions of the head, and rare monosyllables when spoken to; Camille's uneasiness, roused for Beatrix, was still further excited by Calyste's unnatural condition. When the physician arrived, and Beatrix was bled, she felt better, began to talk, and consented to embark; so that by five o'clock they reached the jetty at Guerande, whence she was carried to Les Touches. The news of the accident had already spread through that lonely and almost uninhabited region with incredible rapidity.

Calyste passed the night at Les Touches, sitting at the foot of Beatrix's bed, in company with Camille. The doctor from Guerande had assured them that on the following day a little stiffness would be all that remained of the accident. Across the despair of Calyste's heart there came a gleam of joy. He was there, at her feet; he could watch her sleeping or waking; he might study her pallid face and all its expressions. Camille smiled bitterly as her keen mind recognized in Calyste the symptoms of a passion such as man can feel but once,—a passion which dyes his soul and his faculties by mingling with the fountain of his life at a period when neither thoughts nor cares distract or oppose the inward working of this emotion. She saw that Calyste would never, could never see the real woman that was in Beatrix.

And with what guileless innocence the young Breton allowed his thoughts to be read! When he saw the beautiful green eyes of the sick woman turned to him, expressing a mixture of love, confusion, and even mischief, he colored, and turned away his head.

"Did I not say truly, Calyste, that you men promised happiness, and ended by flinging us down a precipice?"

When he heard this little jest, said in sweet, caressing tones which betrayed a change of heart in Beatrix, Calyste knelt down, took her moist hand which she yielded to him, and kissed it humbly.

"You have the right to reject my love forever," he said, "and I, I have no right to say one word to you."

"Ah!" cried Camille, seeing the expression on Beatrix's face and comparing it with that obtained by her diplomacy, "love has a wit of its own, wiser than that of all the world! Take your composing-draught, my dear friend, and go to sleep."

That night, spent by Calyste beside Mademoiselle des Touches, who read a book of theological mysticism while Calyste read "Indiana,"—the first work of Camille's celebrated rival, in which is the captivating image of a young man loving with idolatry and devotion, with mysterious tranquillity and for all his life, a woman placed in the same false position as Beatrix (a book which had a fatal influence upon him),—that night left ineffaceable marks upon the heart of the poor young fellow, whom Felicite soothed with the assurance that unless a woman were a monster she must be flattered in all her vanities by being the object of such a crime.

"You would never have flung *me* into the water," said Camille, brushing away a tear.

Toward morning, Calyste, worn-out with emotion, fell asleep in his arm-chair; and the marquise in her turn, watched his charming face, paled by his feelings and his vigil of love. She heard him murmur her name as he slept.

"He loves while sleeping," she said to Camille.

"We must send him home," said Felicite, waking him.

No one was anxious at the hotel du Guenic, for Mademoiselle des Touches had written a line to the baroness telling her of the accident.

Calyste returned to dinner at Les Touches and found Beatrix up and dressed, but pale, feeble, and languid. No longer was there any harshness in her words or any coldness in her looks. After this evening, filled with music by Camille, who went to her piano to leave Calyste free to take and press the hands of Beatrix (though both were unable to speak), no storms occurred at Les Touches. Felicite completely effaced herself.

Cold, fragile, thin, hard women like Madame de Rochefide, women whose necks turn in a manner to give them a vague resemblance to the feline race, have souls of the same pale tint as their light eyes, green or gray; and to melt them, to fuse those blocks of stone it needs a thunderbolt. To Beatrix, Calyste's fury of love and his mad action came as the thunderbolt that nought resists, which changes all natures, even the most stubborn. She felt herself inwardly humbled; a true, pure love bathed her heart with its soft and limpid warmth. She breathed a sweet and genial atmosphere of feelings hitherto unknown to her, by which she felt herself magnified, elevated; in fact, she rose into that heaven where Bretons throughout all time have placed the Woman. She relished with delight the respectful adoration of the youth, whose happiness cost her little, for a gesture, a look, a word was enough to satisfy him. The value which Calyste's heart gave to these trifles touched her exceedingly; to hold her gloved hand was more to that young angel than the possession of her whole person to the man who ought to have been faithful to her. What a contrast between them!

Few women could resist such constant deification. Beatrix felt herself sure of being obeyed and understood. She might have asked Calyste to risk his life for the slightest of her caprices, and he would never have reflected for a moment. This consciousness gave her a certain noble and imposing air. She saw love on the side of its grandeur; and her heart sought for some foothold on which she might remain forever the loftiest of women in the eyes of her young lover, over whom she now wished her power to be eternal.

Her coquetries became the more persistent because she felt within herself a certain weakness. She played the invalid for a whole week with charming hypocrisy. Again and again she walked about the velvet turf which lay between the house and garden leaning on Calyste's arm in languid dependence.

"Ah! my dear, you are taking him a long journey in a small space," said Mademoiselle des Touches one day.

Before the excursion to Croisic, the two women were discoursing one evening about love, and laughing at the different ways that men adopted to declare it; admitting to themselves that the cleverest men, and naturally the least loving, did not like to wander in the labyrinths of sentimentality and went straight to the point,—in which perhaps they were right; for the result was that those who loved most deeply and reservedly were, for a time at least, ill-treated.

"They go to work like La Fontaine, when he wanted to enter the Academy," said Camille.

Madame de Rochefide had unbounded power to restrain Calyste within the limits where she meant to keep him; it sufficed her to remind him by a look or gesture of his horrible violence on the rocks. The eyes of her poor victim would fill with tears, he was silent, swallowing down his prayers, his arguments, his sufferings with a heroism that would certainly have touched any other woman. She finally brought him by her infernal coquetry to such a pass that he went one day to Camille imploring her advice.

Beatrix, armed with Calyste's own letter, quoted the passage in which he said that to love was the first happiness, that of being loved came later; and she used that axiom to restrain his passion to the limits of respectful idolatry, which pleased her well. She liked to feel her soul caressed by those sweet hymns of praise and adoration which nature suggests to youth; in them is so much artless art; such innocent seduction is in their cries, their prayers, their exclamations, their pledges of themselves in the promissory notes which they offer on the future; to all of which Beatrix was very careful to give no definite answer. Yes, she heard him; but she doubted! Love was not yet the question; what he asked of her was permission to love. In fact, that was all the poor lad really asked for; his mind still clung to the strongest side of love, the spiritual side. But the woman who is firmest in words is often the feeblest in action. It is strange that Calyste, having seen the progress his suit had made by pushing Beatrix into the sea, did not continue to urge it violently. But love in young men is so ecstatic and religious that their inmost desire is to win its fruition through moral conviction. In that is the sublimity of their love.

Nevertheless the day came when the Breton, driven to desperation, complained to Camille of Beatrix's conduct.

"I meant to cure you by making you quickly understand her," replied Mademoiselle des Touches; "but you have spoiled all. Ten days ago you were her master; to-day, my poor boy, you are her slave. You will never have the strength now to do as I advise."

"What ought I to do?"

"Quarrel with her on the ground of her hardness. A woman is always over-excited when she discusses; let her be angry and ill-treat you, and then stay away; do not return to Les Touches till she herself recalls you."

In all extreme illness there is a moment when the patient is willing to accept the cruellest remedy and submits to the most horrible operation. Calyste had reached that point. He listened to Camille's advice and stayed at home two whole days; but on the third he was scratching at Beatrix's door to let her know that he and Camille were waiting breakfast for her.

"Another chance lost!" Camille said to him when she saw him re-appear so weakly.

During his two days' absence, Beatrix had frequently looked through the window which opens on the road to Guerande. When Camille found her doing so, she talked of the effect produced by the gorse along the roadway, the golden blooms of which were dazzling in the September sunshine.

The marquise kept Camille and Calyste waiting long for breakfast; and the delay would have been significant to any eyes but those of Calyste, for when she did appear, her dress showed an evident intention to fascinate him and prevent another absence. After breakfast she went to walk with him in the garden and filled his simple heart with joy by expressing a wish to go again to that rock where she had so nearly perished.

"Will you go with me alone?" asked Calyste, in a troubled voice.

"If I refused to do so," she replied, "I should give you reason to suppose I thought you dangerous. Alas! as I have told you again and again I belong to another, and I must be his only; I chose him knowing nothing of love. The fault was great, and bitter is my punishment."

When she talked thus, her eyes moist with the scanty tears shed by that class of woman, Calyste was filled with a compassion that reduced his fiery ardor; he adored her then as he did a Madonna. We have no more right to require different characters to be alike in the expression of feelings than we have to expect the same fruits from different trees. Beatrix was at this moment undergoing an inward struggle; she hesitated between herself and Calyste,—between the world she still hoped to re-enter, and the young happiness offered to her; between a second and an unpardonable love, and social rehabilitation. She began, therefore, to listen, without even acted displeasure, to the talk of the youth's blind passion; she allowed his soft pity to soothe her. Several times she had been moved to tears as she listened to Calyste's promises; and she suffered him to commiserate her for being bound to an evil genius, a man as false as Conti. More than once she related to him the misery and anguish she had gone through in Italy, when she first became aware that she was not alone in Conti's heart. On this subject Camille had fully informed Calyste and given him several lectures on it, by which he profited.

"I," he said, "will love you only, you absolutely. I have no triumphs of art, no applause of crowds stirred by my genius to offer you; my only talent is to love you; my honor, my pride are in your perfections. No other woman can have merit in my eyes; you have no odious rivalry to fear. You are misconceived and wronged, but I know you, and for every misconception, for every wrong, I will make you feel my comprehension day by day."

She listened to such speeches with bowed head, allowing him to kiss her hands, and admitting silently but gracefully that she was indeed an angel misunderstood.

"I am too humiliated," she would say; "my past has robbed the future of all security."

It was a glorious day for Calyste when, arriving at Les Touches at seven in the morning, he saw from afar Beatrix at a window watching for him, and wearing the same straw hat she had worn on the memorable day of their first excursion. For a moment he was dazzled and giddy. These little things of passion magnify the world itself. It may be that only Frenchwomen possess the art of such scenic effects; they owe it to the grace of their minds; they know how to put into sentiment as much of the picturesque as the particular sentiment can bear without a loss of vigor or of force.

Ah! how lightly she rested on Calyste's arm! Together they left Les Touches by the garden-gate which opens on the dunes. Beatrix thought the sands delightful; she spied the hardy little plants with rose-colored flowers that grew there, and she gathered a quantity to mix with the Chartreux pansies which also grow in that arid desert, dividing them significantly with Calyste, to whom those flowers and their foliage were to be henceforth an eternal and dreadful relic.

"We'll add a bit of box," she said smiling.

They sat some time together on the jetty, and Calyste, while waiting for the boat to come over, told her of his juvenile act on the day of her arrival.

"I knew of your little escapade," she said, "and it was the cause of my sternness to you that first night."

During their walk Madame de Rochefide had the lightly jesting tone of a woman who loves, together with a certain tenderness and abandonment of manner. Calyste had reason to think himself beloved. But when, wandering along the shore beneath the rocks, they came upon one of those charming creeks where the waves deposit the most extraordinary mosaic of brilliant pebbles, and they played there like children gathering the prettiest, when Calyste at the summit of happiness asked her plainly to fly with him to Ireland, she resumed her dignified and distant air, asked for his arm, and continued their walk in silence to what she called her Tarpeian rock.

"My friend," she said, mounting with slow steps the magnificent block of granite of which she was making for herself a pedestal, "I have not the courage to conceal what you are to me. For ten years I have had no happiness comparable to that which we have just enjoyed together, searching for shells among those rocks, exchanging pebbles of which I shall make a necklace more precious far to me than if it were made of the finest diamonds. I have been once more a little girl, a child, such as I was at fourteen or sixteen—when I was worthy of you. The love I have had the happiness to inspire in your heart has raised me in my own eyes. Understand these words to their magical extent. You have made me the proudest and happiest of my sex, and you will live longer in my remembrance, perhaps, than I in yours."

At this moment they reached the summit of the rock, whence they saw the vast ocean on one side and Brittany on the other, with its golden isles, its feudal towers, and its gorse. Never did any woman stand on a finer scene to make a great avowal.

"But," she continued, "I do not belong to myself; I am more bound by my own will than I was by the law. You must be punished for my misdeed, but be satisfied to know that we suffer together. Dante never saw his Beatrice again; Petrarch never possessed his Laura. Such disasters fall on none but noble souls. But, if I should be abandoned, if I fall lower yet into shame and ignominy, if your Beatrix is cruelly misjudged by the world she loathes, if indeed she is the lowest of women,—then, my child, my adored child," she said, taking his hand, "to you she will still be first of all; you will know that she rises to heaven as she leans on you; but then, my friend," she added, giving him an intoxicating look, "then if you wish to cast her down do not fail of your blow; after your love, death!"

Calyste clasped her round the waist and pressed her to his heart. As if to confirm her words Madame de Rochefide laid a tender, timid kiss upon his brow. When they turned and walked slowly back; talking together like those who have a perfect comprehension of each other,—she, thinking she had gained a truce, he not doubting of his happiness; and both deceived. Calyste, from what Camille had told him, was confident that Conti would be enchanted to find an opportunity to part from Beatrix; Beatrix, yielding herself up to the vagueness of her position, looked to chance to arrange the future.

They reached Les Touches in the most delightful of all states of mind, entering by the garden gate, the key of which Calyste had taken with him. It was nearly six o'clock. The luscious odors, the warm atmosphere, the burnished rays of the evening sun were all in harmony with their feelings and their tender talk. Their steps were taken in unison,—the gait of all lovers,—their movements told of the union of their thoughts. The silence that reigned about Les Touches was so profound that the noise which Calyste made in opening and shutting the gate must have echoed through the garden. As the two had said all to each other that could be said, and as their day's excursion, so filled with emotion, had physically tired them, they walked slowly, saying nothing.

Suddenly, at the turn of a path, Beatrix was seized with a horrible trembling, with that contagious horror which is caused by the sight of a snake, and which Calyste felt before he saw the cause of it. On a bench, beneath the branches of a weeping ash, sat Conti, talking with Camille Maupin.

CHAPTER XV.

CONTI

The inward and convulsive trembling of the marquise was more apparent than she wished it to be; a tragic drama developed at that moment in the souls of all present.

"You did not expect me so soon, I fancy," said Conti, offering his arm to Beatrix.

The marquise could not avoid dropping Calyste's arm and taking that of Conti. This ignoble transit, imperiously demanded, so dishonoring to the new love, overwhelmed Calyste who threw himself on the bench beside Camille, after exchanging the coldest of salutations with his rival. He was torn by conflicting emotions. Strong in the thought that Beatrix loved him, he wanted at first to fling himself upon Conti and tell him that Beatrix was his; but the violent trembling of the woman betraying how she suffered—for she had really paid the penalty of her faults in that one moment—affected him so deeply that he was dumb, struck like her with a sense of some implacable necessity.

Madame de Rochefide and Conti passed in front of the seat where Calyste had dropped beside Camille, and as she passed, the marquise looked at Camille, giving her one of those terrible glances in which women have the art of saying all things. She avoided the eyes of Calyste and turned her attention to Conti, who appeared to be jesting with her.

"What will they say to each other?" Calyste asked of Camille.

"Dear child, you don't know as yet the terrible rights which an extinguished love still gives to a man over a woman. Beatrix could not refuse to take his arm. He is, no doubt, joking her about her new love; he must have guessed it from your attitudes and the manner in which you approached us."

"Joking her!" cried the impetuous youth, starting up.

"Be calm," said Camille, "or you will lose the last chances that remain to you. If he wounds her self-love, she will crush him like a worm under her foot. But he is too astute for that; he will manage her with greater cleverness. He will seem not even to suppose that the proud Madame de Rochefide could betray him; *she* could never be guilty of such depravity as loving a man for the sake of his beauty. He will represent you to her as a child ambitious to have a marquise in love with him, and to make himself the arbiter of the fate of two women. In short, he will fire a broadside of malicious insinuations. Beatrix will then be forced to parry with false assertions and denials, which he will simply make use of to become once more her master."

"Ah!" cried Calyste, "he does not love her. I would leave her free. True love means a choice made anew at every moment, confirmed from day to day. The morrow justifies the past, and swells the treasury of our pleasures. Ah! why did he not stay away a little longer? A few days more and he would not have found her. What brought him back?"

"The jest of a journalist," replied Camille. "His opera, on the success of which he counted, has fallen flat. Some journalist, probably Claude Vignon, remarked in the foyer: 'It is hard to lose fame and mistress at the same moment,' and the speech cut him in all his vanities. Love based on petty sentiments is always pitiless. I have questioned him; but who can fathom a nature so false and deceiving? He appeared to be weary of his troubles and his love,—in short, disgusted with life. He regrets having allied himself so publicly with the marquise, and made me, in speaking of his past happiness, a melancholy poem, which was somewhat too clever to be true. I think he hoped to worm out of me the secret of your love, in the midst of the joy he expected his flatteries to cause me."

"What else?" said Calyste, watching Beatrix and Conti, who were now coming towards them; but he listened no longer to Camille's words.

In talking with Conti, Camille had held herself prudently on the defensive; she had betrayed neither Calyste's secret nor that of Beatrix. The great artist was capable of treachery to every one, and Mademoiselle des Touches warned Calyste to distrust him.

"My dear friend," she said, "this is by far the most critical moment for you. You need caution and a sort of cleverness you do not possess; I am afraid you will let yourself be tricked by the most wily man I have ever known, and I can do nothing to help you."

The bell announced dinner. Conti offered his arm to Camille; Calyste gave his to Beatrix. Camille drew back to let the marquise pass, but the latter had found a moment in which to look at Calyste, and impress upon him, by putting her finger on her lips, the absolute necessity of discretion.

Conti was extremely gay during the dinner; perhaps this was only one way of probing Madame de Rochefide, who played her part extremely ill. If her conduct had been mere coquetry, she might have deceived even Conti; but her new love was real, and it betrayed her. The wily musician, far from adding to her embarrassment, pretended not to have perceived it. At dessert, he brought the conversation round to women, and lauded the nobility of their sentiments. Many a woman, he said, who might have been willing to abandon a man in prosperity, would sacrifice all to him in misfortune. Women had the advantage over men in constancy; nothing ever detached them from their first lover, to whom they clung as a matter of honor, unless he wounded them; they felt that a second love was unworthy of them, and so forth. His ethics were of the highest order; shedding incense on the altar where he knew that one heart at least, pierced by many a blow, was bleeding. Camille and Beatrix alone understood the bitterness of the sarcasms shot forth in the guise of eulogy. At times they both flushed scarlet, but they were forced to control themselves. When dinner was over, they took each other by the arm to return to Camille's salon, and, as if by mutual consent, they turned aside into the great salon, where they could be alone for an instant in the darkness.

"It is dreadful to let Conti ride over me roughshod; and yet I can't defend myself," said Beatrix, in a low voice. "The galley-slave is always a slave to his chain-companion. I am lost; I must needs return to my galleys! And it is you, Camille, who have cast me there! Ah! you brought him back a day too soon, or a day too late. I recognize your infernal talent as author. Well, your revenge is complete, the finale perfect!"

"I may have told you that I would write to Conti, but to do it was another matter," cried Camille. "I am incapable of such baseness. But you are unhappy, and I will forgive the suspicion."

"What will become of Calyste?" said the marquise, with naive self-conceit.

"Then Conti carries you off, does he?" asked Camille.

"Ah! you think you triumph!" cried Beatrix.

Anger distorted her handsome face as she said those bitter words to Camille, who was trying to hide her satisfaction under a false expression of sympathy. Unfortunately, the sparkle in her eyes belied the sadness of her face, and Beatrix was learned in such deceptions. When, a few moments later, the two women were seated under a strong light on that divan where the first three weeks so many comedies had been played, and where the secret tragedy of many thwarted passions had begun, they examined each other for the last time, and felt they were forever parted by an undying hatred.

"Calyste remains to you," said Beatrix, looking into Camille's eyes; "but I am fixed in his heart, and no woman can ever drive me out of it."

Camille replied, with an inimitable tone of irony that struck the marquise to the heart, in the famous words of Mazarin's niece to Louis XIV.,—

"You reign, you love, and you depart!"

Neither Camille nor Beatrix was conscious during this sharp and bitter scene of the absence of Conti and Calyste. The composer had remained at table with his rival, begging him to keep him company in finishing a bottle of champagne.

"We have something to say to each other," added Conti, to prevent all refusal on the part of Calyste.

Placed as they both were, it was impossible for the young Breton to refuse this challenge.

"My dear friend," said the composer, in his most caressing voice, as soon as the poor lad had drunk a couple of glasses of champagne, "we are both good fellows, and we can speak to each other frankly. I have not come here suspiciously. Beatrix loves me,"—this with a gesture of the utmost self-conceit—"but the truth is, I have ceased to love her. I am not here to carry her away with me, but to break off our relations, and to leave her the honors of the rupture. You are young; you don't yet know how useful it is to appear to be the victim when you are really the executioner. Young men spit fire and flame; they leave a woman with noise and fury; they often despise her, and they make her hate them. But wise men do as I am doing; they get themselves dismissed, assuming a mortified air, which leaves regret in the woman's heart and also a sense of her superiority. You don't yet know, luckily for you, how hampered men often are in their careers by the rash promises which women are silly enough to accept when gallantry obliges us to make nooses to catch our happiness. We swear eternal faithfulness, and declare that we desire to pass our lives with them, and seem to await a husband's death impatiently. Let him die, and there are some provincial women obtuse or silly or malicious enough to say: 'Here am I, free at last.' The spent ball suddenly comes to life again, and falls plumb in the midst of our finest triumphs or our most carefully planned happiness. I have seen that you love Beatrix. I leave her therefore in a position where she loses nothing of her precious majesty; she will certainly coquet with you, if only to tease and annoy that angel of a Camille Maupin. Well, my dear fellow, take her, love her, you'll do me a great service; I want her to turn against me. I have been afraid of her pride and her virtue. Perhaps, in spite of my approval of the matter, it may take some time to effect this *chassez-croissez*. On such occasions the wisest plan is to take no step at all. I did, just now, as we walked about the lawn, attempt to let her see that I knew all, and was ready to congratulate her on her new happiness. Well, she was furious! At this moment I am desperately in love with the youngest and handsomest of our prima-donnas, Mademoiselle Falcon of the Grand Opera. I think of marrying her; yes, I have got as far as that. When you come to Paris you will see that I have changed a marquise for a queen."

Calyste, whose candid face revealed his satisfaction, admitted his love for Beatrix, which was all that Conti wanted to discover. There is no man in the world, however *blasé* or depraved he may be, whose love will not flame up again the moment he sees it threatened by a rival. He may wish to leave a woman, but he will never willingly let her leave him. When a pair of lovers get to this extremity, both the man and the woman strive for priority of action, so deep is the wound to their vanity. Questioned by the composer, Calyste related all that had happened during the last three weeks at Les Touches, delighted to find that Conti, who concealed his fury under an appearance of charming good-humor, took it all in good part.

"Come, let us go upstairs," said the latter. "Women are so distrustful; those two will wonder how we can sit here together without tearing each other's hair out; they are even capable of coming down to listen. I'll serve you faithfully, my dear boy. You'll see me rough and jealous with the marquise; I shall seem to suspect her; there's no better way to drive a woman to betray you. You will be happy, and I shall be free. Seem to pity that angel for belonging to a man without delicacy; show her a tear—for you can weep, you are still young. I, alas! can weep no more; and that's a great advantage lost."

Calyste and Conti went up to Camille's salon. The composer, begged by his young rival to sing, gave them that greatest of musical masterpieces viewed as execution, the famous *"Pria che spunti l'aurora,"* which Rubini himself never attempted without trembling, and which had often been Conti's triumph. Never was his singing more extraordinary than on this occasion, when so many feelings were contending in his breast. Calyste was in ecstasy. As Conti sang the first words of the cavatina, he looked intently at the marquise, giving to those words a cruel signification which was fully understood. Camille, who accompanied him, guessed the order thus conveyed, which bowed the head of the luckless Beatrix. She looked at Calyste, and felt sure that the youth had fallen into some trap in spite of her advice. This conviction became certainty when the evidently happy Breton came up to bid Beatrix good-night, kissing her hand, and pressing it with a little air of happy confidence.

By the time Calyste had reached Guerande, the servants were packing Conti's travelling-carriage, and "by dawn," as the song had said, the composer was carrying Beatrix away with Camille's horses to the first relay. The morning twilight enabled Madame de Rochefide to see Guerande, its towers, whitened by the dawn, shining out upon the still dark sky. Melancholy thoughts possessed her; she was leaving there one of the sweetest flowers of all her life,—a pure love, such as a young girl dreams of; the only true love she had ever known or was ever to conceive of. The woman of the world obeyed the laws of the world; she sacrificed love to their demands just as many women sacrifice it to religion or to duty. Sometimes mere pride can rise in acts as high as virtue. Read thus, this history is that of many women.

The next morning Calyste went to Les Touches about mid-day. When he reached the spot from which, the day before, he had seen Beatrix watching for him at the window, he saw Camille, who instantly ran down to him. She met him at the foot of the staircase and told the cruel truth in one word,—

"Gone!"

"Beatrix?" asked Calyste, thunderstruck.

"You have been duped by Conti; you told me nothing, and I could do nothing for you."

She led the poor fellow to her little salon, where he flung himself on the divan where he had so often seen the marquise, and burst into tears. Felicite smoked her hookah and said nothing, knowing well that no words or thoughts are capable of arresting the first anguish of such pain, which is always deaf and dumb. Calyste, unable even to think, much less to choose a course, sat there all day in a state of complete torpidity. Just before dinner was served, Camille tried to say a few words, after begging him, very earnestly, to listen to her.

"Friend," she said, "you caused me the bitterest suffering, and I had not, like you, a beautiful young life before me in which to heal myself. For me, life has no longer any spring, nor my soul a love. So, to find consolation, I have had to look above. Here, in this room, the day before Beatrix came here, I drew you her portrait; I did not do her injustice, or you might have thought me jealous. I wanted you to know her as she is, for that would have kept you safe. Listen now to the full truth. Madame de Rochefide is wholly unworthy of you. The scandal of her fall was not necessary; she did the thing deliberately in order to play a part in the eyes of society. She is one of those women who prefer the celebrity of a scandal to tranquil happiness; they fly in the face of society to obtain the fatal alms of a rebuke; they desire to be talked about at any cost. Beatrix was eaten up with vanity. Her fortune and her wit had not given her the feminine royalty that she craved; they had not enabled her to reign supreme over a salon. She then bethought herself of seeking the celebrity of the Duchesse de Langeais and the Vicomtesse de Beauseant. But the world, after all, is just; it gives the homage of its interest to real feelings only. Beatrix playing comedy was judged to be a second-rate actress. There was no reason whatever for her flight; the sword of Damocles was not suspended over her head; she is neither sincere, nor loving, nor tender; if she were, would she have gone away with Conti this morning?"

Camille talked long and eloquently; but this last effort to open Calyste's eyes was useless, and she said no more when he expressed to her by a gesture his absolute belief in Beatrix.

She forced him to come down into the dining-room and sit there while she dined; though he himself was unable to swallow food. It is only during extreme youth that these contractions of the bodily functions occur. Later, the organs have acquired, as it were, fixed habits, and are hardened. The reaction of the mental and moral system upon the physical is not enough to produce a mortal illness unless the physical system retains its primitive purity. A man resists the violent grief that kills a youth, less by the greater weakness of his affection than by the greater strength of his organs.

Therefore Mademoiselle des Touches was greatly alarmed by the calm, resigned attitude which Calyste took after his burst of tears had subsided. Before he left her, he asked permission to go into Beatrix's bedroom, where he had seen her on the night of her illness, and there he laid his head on the pillow where hers had lain.

"I am committing follies," he said, grasping Camille's hand, and bidding her good-night in deep dejection.

He returned home, found the usual company at *mouche*, and passed the remainder of the evening sitting beside his mother. The rector, the Chevalier du Halga, and Mademoiselle de Pen-Hoel all knew of Madame de Rochefide's departure, and were rejoicing in it. Calyste would now return to them; and all three watched him cautiously. No one in that old manor-house was capable of imagining the result of a first love, the love of youth in a heart so simple and so true as that of Calyste.

CHAPTER XVI.

SICKNESS UNTO DEATH

For several days Calyste went regularly to Les Touches. He paced round and round the lawn, where he had sometimes walked with Beatrix on his arm. He often went to Croisic to stand upon that fateful rock, or lie for hours in the bush of box; for, by studying the footholds on the sides of the fissure, he had found a means of getting up and down.

These solitary trips, his silence, his gravity, made his mother very anxious. After about two weeks, during which time this conduct, like that of a caged animal, lasted, this poor lover, caged in his despair, ceased to cross the bay; he had scarcely strength to drag himself along the road from Guerande to the spot where he had seen Beatrix watching from her window. The family, delighted at the departure of "those Parisians," to use a term of the provinces, saw nothing fatal or diseased about the lad. The two old maids and the rector, pursuing their scheme, had kept Charlotte de Kergarouet, who nightly played off her little coquetries on Calyste, obtaining in return nothing better than advice in playing *mouche*. During these long evenings, Calyste sat between his mother and the little Breton girl, observed by the rector and Charlotte's aunt, who discussed his greater or less depression as they walked home together. Their simple minds mistook the lethargic indifference of the hapless youth for submission to their plans. One evening when Calyste, wearied out, went off suddenly to bed, the players dropped their cards upon the table and looked at each other as the young man closed the door of his chamber. One and all had listened to the sound of his receding steps with anxiety.

"Something is the matter with Calyste," said the baroness, wiping her eyes.

"Nothing is the matter," replied Mademoiselle de Pen-Hoel; "but you should marry him at once."

"Do you believe that marriage would divert his mind?" asked the chevalier.

Charlotte looked reprovingly at Monsieur du Halga, whom she now began to think ill-mannered, depraved, immoral, without religion, and very ridiculous about his dog,—opinions which her aunt, defending the old sailor, combated.

"I shall lecture Calyste to-morrow morning," said the baron, whom the others had thought asleep. "I do not wish to go out of this world without seeing my grandson, a little pink and white Guenic with a Breton cap on his head."

"Calyste doesn't say a word," said old Zephirine, "and there's no making out what's the matter with him. He doesn't eat; I don't see what he lives on. If he gets his meals at Les Touches, the devil's kitchen doesn't nourish him."

"He is in love," said the chevalier, risking that opinion very timidly.

"Come, come, old gray-beard, you've forgotten to put in your stake!" cried Mademoiselle de Pen-Hoel. "When you begin to think of your young days you forget everything."

"Come to breakfast to-morrow," said old Zephirine to her friend Jacqueline; "my brother will have had a talk with his son, and we can settle the matter finally. One nail, you know, drives out another."

"Not among Bretons," said the chevalier.

The next day Calyste saw Charlotte, as she arrived dressed with unusual care, just after the baron had given him, in the dining-room, a discourse on matrimony, to which he could make no answer. He now knew the ignorance of his father and mother and all their friends; he had gathered the fruits of the tree of knowledge, and knew himself to be as much isolated as if he did not speak the family language. He merely requested his father to give him a few days' grace. The old baron rubbed his hands with joy, and gave fresh life to the baroness by whispering in her ear what he called the good news.

Breakfast was gay; Charlotte, to whom the baron had given a hint, was sparkling. After the meal was over, Calyste went out upon the portico leading to the garden, followed by Charlotte; he gave her his arm and led her to the grotto. Their parents and friends were at the window, looking at them with a species of tenderness. Presently Charlotte, uneasy at her suitor's silence, looked back and saw them, which gave her an opportunity of beginning the conversation by saying to Calyste, —

"They are watching us."

"They cannot hear us," he replied.

"True; but they see us."

"Let us sit down, Charlotte," replied Calyste, gently taking her hand.

"Is it true that your banner used formerly to float from that twisted column?" asked Charlotte, with a sense that the house was already hers; how comfortable she should be there! what a happy sort of life! "You will make some changes inside the house, won't you, Calyste?" she said.

"I shall not have time, my dear Charlotte," said the young man, taking her hands and kissing them. "I am going now to tell you my secret. I love too well a person whom you have seen, and who loves me, to be able to make the happiness of any other woman; though I know that from our childhood you and I have been destined for each other by our friends."

"But she is married, Calyste."

"I shall wait," replied the young man.

"And I, too," said Charlotte, her eyes filling with tears. "You cannot long love a woman like that, who, they say, has gone off with a singer—"

"Marry, my dear Charlotte," said Calyste, interrupting her. "With the fortune your aunt intends to give you, which is enormous for Brittany, you can choose some better man than I. You could marry a titled man. I have brought you here, not to tell you what you already knew, but to entreat you, in the name of our childish friendship, to take this rupture upon yourself, and say that you have rejected me. Say that you do not wish to marry a man whose heart is not free; and thus I shall be spared at least the sense that I have done you public wrong. You do not know, Charlotte, how heavy a burden life now is to me. I cannot bear the slightest struggle; I am weakened like a man whose vital spark is gone, whose soul has left him. If it were not for the grief I should cause my mother, I would have flung myself before now into the sea; I have not returned to the rocks at Croisic since the day that temptation became almost irresistible. Do not speak of this to any one. Good-bye, Charlotte."

He took the young girl's head and kissed her hair; then he left the garden by the postern-gate and fled to Les Touches, where he stayed near Camille till past midnight. On returning home, at one in the morning, he found his mother awaiting him with her worsted-work. He entered softly, clasped her hand in his, and said,—

"Is Charlotte gone?"

"She goes to-morrow, with her aunt, in despair, both of them," answered the baroness. "Come to Ireland with me, my Calyste."

"Many a time I have thought of flying there—"

"Ah!" cried the baroness.

"With Beatrix," he added.

Some days after Charlotte's departure, Calyste joined the Chevalier du Halga in his daily promenade on the mall with his little dog. They sat down in the sunshine on a bench, where the young man's eyes could wander from the vanes of Les Touches to the rocks of Croisic, against which the waves were playing and dashing their white foam. Calyste was thin and pale; his strength was diminishing, and he was conscious at times of little shudders at regular intervals, denoting fever. His eyes, surrounded by dark circles, had that singular brilliancy which a fixed idea gives to the eyes of hermits and solitary souls, or the ardor of contest to those of the strong fighters of our present civilization. The chevalier was the only person with whom he could exchange a few ideas. He had divined in that old man an apostle of his own religion; he recognized in his soul the vestiges of an eternal love.

"Have you loved many women in your life?" he asked him on the second occasion, when, as seamen say, they sailed in company along the mall.

"Only one," replied Du Halga.

"Was she free?"

"No," exclaimed the chevalier. "Ah! how I suffered! She was the wife of my best friend, my protector, my chief—but we loved each other so!"

"Did she love you?" said Calyste.

"Passionately," replied the chevalier, with a fervency not usual with him.

"You were happy?"

"Until her death; she died at the age of forty-nine, during the emigration, at St. Petersburg, the climate of which killed her. She must be very cold in her coffin. I have often thought of going there to fetch her, and lay her in our dear Brittany, near to me! But she lies in my heart."

The chevalier brushed away his tears. Calyste took his hand and pressed it.

"I care for this little dog more than for life itself," said the old man, pointing to Thisbe. "The little darling is precisely like the one she held on her knees and stroked with her beautiful hands. I never look at Thisbe but what I see the hands of Madame l'Amirale."

"Did you see Madame de Rochefide?" asked Calyste.

"No," replied the chevalier. "It is sixty-eight years since I have looked at any woman with attention—except your mother, who has something of Madame l'Amirale's complexion."

Three days later, the chevalier said to Calyste, on the mall,—

"My child, I have a hundred and forty *louis* laid by. When you know where Madame de Rochefide is, come and get them and follow her."

Calyste thanked the old man, whose existence he envied. But now, from day to day, he grew morose; he seemed to love no one; all things hurt him; he was gentle and kind to his mother only. The baroness watched with ever increasing anxiety the progress of his madness; she alone was able, by force of prayer and entreaty, to make him swallow food. Toward the end of October the sick lad ceased to go even to the mall in search of the chevalier, who now came vainly to the house to tempt him out with the coaxing wisdom of an old man.

"We can talk of Madame de Rochefide," he would say. "I'll tell you my first adventure."

"Your son is ill," he said privately to the baroness, on the day he became convinced that all such efforts were useless.

Calyste replied to questions about his health that he was perfectly well; but like all young victims of melancholy, he took pleasure in the thought of death. He no longer left the house, but sat in the garden on a bench, warming himself in the pale and tepid sunshine, alone with his one thought, and avoiding all companionship.

Soon after the day when Calyste ceased to go even to Les Touches, Felicite requested the rector of Guerande to come and see her. The assiduity with which the Abbe Grimont called every morning at Les Touches, and sometimes dined there, became the great topic of the town; it was talked of all over the region, and even reached Nantes. Nevertheless, the rector never missed a single evening at the hotel du Guenic, where desolation reigned. Masters and servants were all afflicted at Calyste's increasing weakness, though none of them thought him in danger; how could it ever enter the minds of these good people that youth might die of love? Even the chevalier had no example of such a death among his memories of life and travel. They attributed Calyste's thinness to want of food. His mother implored him to eat. Calyste endeavored to conquer his repugnance in order to comfort her; but nourishment taken against his will served only to increase the slow fever which was now consuming the beautiful young life.

During the last days of October the cherished child of the house could no longer mount the stairs to his chamber, and his bed was placed in the lower hall, where he was surrounded at all hours by his family. They sent at last for the Guerande physician, who broke the fever with quinine and reduced it in a few days, ordering Calyste to take exercise, and find something to amuse him. The baron, on this, came out of his apathy and recovered a little of his old strength; he grew younger as his son seemed to age. With Calyste, Gasselin, and his two fine dogs, he started for the forest, and for some days all three hunted. Calyste obeyed his father and went where he was told, from forest to forest, visiting friends and acquaintances in the neighboring chateaus. But the youth had no spirit or gaiety; nothing brought a smile to his face; his livid and contracted features betrayed an utterly passive being. The baron, worn out at last by fatigue consequent on this spasm of exertion, was forced to return home, bringing Calyste in a state of exhaustion almost equal to his own. For several days after their return both father and son were so dangerously ill that the family were forced to send, at the request of the Guerande physician himself, for two of the best doctors in Nantes.

The baron had received a fatal shock on realizing the change now so visible in Calyste. With that lucidity of mind which nature gives to the dying, he trembled at the thought that his race was about to perish. He said no word, but he clasped his hands and prayed to God as he sat in his chair, from which his weakness now prevented him from rising. The father's face was turned toward the bed where the son lay, and he looked at him almost incessantly. At the least motion Calyste made, a singular commotion stirred within him, as if the flame of his own life were flickering. The baroness no longer left the room where Zephirine sat knitting in the chimney-corner in horrible uneasiness. Demands were made upon the old woman for wood, father and son both suffering from the cold, and for supplies and provisions, so that, finally, not being agile enough to supply these wants, she had given her precious keys to Mariotte. But she insisted on knowing everything; she questioned Mariotte and her sister-in-law incessantly, asking in a low voice to be told, over and over again, the state of her brother and nephew. One night, when father and son were dozing, Mademoiselle de Pen-Hoel told her that she must resign herself to the death of her brother, whose pallid face was now the color of wax. The old woman dropped her knitting, fumbled in her pocket for a while, and at length drew out an old chaplet of black wood, on which she began to pray with a fervor which gave to her old and withered face a splendor so vigorous that the other old woman imitated her friend, and then all present, on a sign from the rector, joining in the spiritual uplifting of Mademoiselle de Guenic.

"Alas! I prayed to God," said the baroness, remembering her prayer after reading the fatal letter written by Calyste, "and he did not hear me."

"Perhaps it would be well," said the rector, "if we begged Mademoiselle des Touches to come and see Calyste."

"She!" cried old Zephirine, "the author of all our misery! she who has turned him from his family, who has taken him from us, led him to read impious books, taught him an heretical language! Let her be accursed, and may God never pardon her! She has destroyed the du Guenics!"

"She may perhaps restore them," said the rector, in a gentle voice. "Mademoiselle des Touches is a saintly woman; I am her surety for that. She has none but good intentions to Calyste. May she only be enabled to carry them out."

"Let me know the day when she sets foot in this house, that I may get out of it," cried the old woman passionately. "She has killed both father and son. Do you think I don't hear death in Calyste's voice? he is so feeble now that he has barely strength to whisper."

It was at this moment that the three doctors arrived. They plied Calyste with questions; but as for his father, the examination was short; they were surprised that he still lived on. The Guerande doctor calmly told the baroness that as to Calyste, it would probably be best to take him to Paris and consult the most experienced physicians, for it would cost over a hundred *louis* to bring one down.

"People die of something, but not of love," said Mademoiselle de Pen-Hoel.

"Alas! whatever be the cause, Calyste is dying," said the baroness. "I see all the symptoms of consumption, that most horrible disease of my country, about him."

"Calyste dying!" said the baron, opening his eyes, from which rolled two large tears which slowly made their way, delayed by wrinkles, along his cheeks,—the only tears he had probably ever shed in his life. Suddenly he rose to his feet, walked the few steps to his son's bedside, took his hand, and looked earnestly at him.

"What is it you want, father?" said Calyste.

"That you should live!" cried the baron.

"I cannot live without Beatrix," replied Calyste.

The old man dropped into a chair.

"Oh! where could we get a hundred *louis* to bring doctors from Paris? There is still time," cried the baroness.

"A hundred *louis!*" cried Zephirine; "will that save him?"

Without waiting for her sister-in-law's reply, the old maid ran her hands through the placket-holes of her gown, unfastened the petticoat beneath it, which gave forth a heavy sound as it dropped to the floor. She knew so well the places where she had sewn in her *louis* that she now ripped them out with the rapidity of magic. The gold pieces rang as they fell, one by one, into her lap. The old Pen-Hoel gazed at this performance in stupefied amazement.

"But they'll see you!" she whispered in her friend's ear.

"Thirty-seven," answered Zephirine, continuing to count.

"Every one will know how much you have."

"Forty-two."

"Double *louis!* all new! How did you get them, you who can't see clearly?"

"I felt them. Here's one hundred and four *louis*," cried Zephirine. "Is that enough?"

"What is all this?" asked the Chevalier du Halga, who now came in, unable to understand the attitude of his old blind friend, holding out her petticoat which was full of gold coins.

Mademoiselle de Pen-Hoel explained.

"I knew it," said the chevalier, "and I have come to bring a hundred and forty *louis* which I have been holding at Calyste's disposition, as he knows very well."

The chevalier drew the *rouleaux* from his pocket and showed them. Mariotte, seeing such wealth, sent Gasselin to lock the doors.

"Gold will not give him health," said the baroness, weeping.

"But it can take him to Paris, where he can find her. Come, Calyste."

"Yes," cried Calyste, springing up, "I will go."

"He will live," said the baron, in a shaking voice; "and I can die—send for the rector!"

The words cast terror on all present. Calyste, seeing the mortal paleness on his father's face, for the old man was exhausted by the cruel emotions of the scene, came to his father's side. The rector, after hearing the report of the doctors, had gone to Mademoiselle des Touches, intending to bring her back with him to Calyste, for in proportion as the worthy man had formerly detested her, he now admired her, and protected her as a shepherd protects the most precious of his flock.

When the news of the baron's approaching end became known in Guerande, a crowd gathered in the street and lane; the peasants, the *paludiers*, and the servants knelt in the court-yard while the rector administered the last sacraments to the old Breton warrior. The whole town was agitated by the news that the father was dying beside his half-dying son. The probable extinction of this old Breton race was felt to be a public calamity.

The solemn ceremony affected Calyste deeply. His filial sorrow silenced for a moment the anguish of his love. During the last hour of the glorious old defender of the monarchy, he knelt beside him, watching the coming on of death. The old man died in his chair in presence of the assembled family.

"I die faithful to God and his religion," he said. "My God! as the reward of my efforts grant that Calyste may live!"

"I shall live, father; and I will obey you," said the young man.

"If you wish to make my death as happy as Fanny has made my life, swear to me to marry."

"I promise it, father."

It was a touching sight to see Calyste, or rather his shadow, leaning on the arm of the old Chevalier du Halga—a spectre leading a shade—and following the baron's coffin as chief mourner. The church and the little square were crowded with the country people coming in to the funeral from a circuit of thirty miles.

But the baroness and Zephirine soon saw that, in spite of his intention to obey his father's wishes, Calyste was falling back into a condition of fatal stupor. On the day when the family put on their mourning, the baroness took her son to a bench in the garden and questioned him closely. Calyste answered gently and submissively, but his answers only proved to her the despair of his soul.

"Mother," he said, "there is no life in me. What I eat does not feed me; the air that enters my lungs does not refresh me; the sun feels cold; it seems to you to light that front of the house, and show you the old carvings bathed in its beams, but to me it is all a blur, a mist. If Beatrix were here, it would be dazzling. There is but one only thing left in this world that keeps its shape and color to my eyes,—this flower, this foliage," he added, drawing from his breast the withered bunch the marquise had given him at Croisic.

The baroness dared not say more. Her son's answer seemed to her more indicative of madness than his silence of grief. She saw no hope, no light in the darkness that surrounded them.

The baron's last hours and death had prevented the rector from bringing Mademoiselle des Touches to Calyste, as he seemed bent on doing, for reasons which he did not reveal. But on this day, while mother and son still sat on the garden bench, Calyste quivered all over on perceiving Felicite through the opposite windows of the court-yard and garden. She reminded him of Beatrix, and his life revived. It was therefore to Camille that the poor stricken mother owed the first motion of joy that lightened her mourning.

"Well, Calyste," said Mademoiselle des Touches, when they met, "I want you to go to Paris with me. We will find Beatrix," she added in a low voice.

The pale, thin face of the youth flushed red, and a smile brightened his features.

"Let us go," he said.

"We shall save him," said Mademoiselle des Touches to the mother, who pressed her hands and wept for joy.

A week after the baron's funeral, Mademoiselle des Touches, the Baronne du Guenic and Calyste started for Paris, leaving the household in charge of old Zephirine.

CHAPTER XVII.

A DEATH: A MARRIAGE

Felicite's tender love was preparing for Calyste a prosperous future. Being allied to the family of Grandlieu, the ducal branch of which was ending in five daughters for lack of a male heir, she had written to the Duchesse de Grandlieu, describing Calyste and giving his history, and also stating certain intentions of her own, which were as follows: She had lately sold her house in the rue du Mont-Blanc, for which a party of speculators had given her two millions five hundred thousand francs. Her man of business had since purchased for her a charming new house in the rue de Bourbon for seven hundred thousand francs; one million she intended to devote to the recovery of the du Guenic estates, and the rest of her fortune she desired to settle upon Sabine de Grandlieu. Felicite had long known the plans of the duke and duchess as to the settlement of their five daughters: the youngest was to marry the Vicomte de Grandlieu, the heir to their ducal title; Clotilde-Frederique, the second daughter, desired to remain unmarried, in memory of a man she had deeply loved, Lucien de Rubempre, while, at the same time, she did not wish to become a nun like her eldest sister; two of the remaining sisters were already married, and the youngest but one, the pretty Sabine, just twenty years old, was the only disposable daughter left. It was Sabine on whom Felicite resolved to lay the burden of curing Calyste's passion for Beatrix.

During the journey to Paris Mademoiselle des Touches revealed to the baroness these arrangements. The new house in the rue de Bourbon was being decorated, and she intended it for the home of Sabine and Calyste if her plans succeeded.

The party had been invited to stay at the hotel de Grandlieu, where the baroness was received with all the distinction due to her rank as the wife of a du Guenic and the daughter of a British peer. Mademoiselle des Touches urged Calyste to see Paris, while she herself made the necessary inquiries about Beatrix (who had disappeared from the world, and was travelling abroad), and she took care to throw him into the midst of diversions and amusements of all kinds. The season for balls and fetes was just beginning, and the duchess and her daughters did the honors of Paris to the young Breton, who was insensibly diverted from his own thoughts by the movement and life of the great city. He found some resemblance of mind between Madame de Rochefide and Sabine de Grandlieu, who was certainly one of the handsomest and most charming girls in Parisian society, and this fancied likeness made him give to her coquetries a willing attention which no other woman could possibly have obtained from him. Sabine herself was greatly pleased with Calyste, and matters went so well that during the winter of 1837 the young Baron du Guenic, whose youth and health had returned to him, listened without repugnance to his mother when she reminded him of the promise made to his dying father and proposed to him a marriage with Sabine de Grandlieu. Still, while agreeing to fulfil his promise, he concealed within his soul an indifference to all things, of which the baroness alone was aware, but which she trusted would be conquered by the pleasures of a happy home.

On the day when the Grandlieu family and the baroness, accompanied by her relations who came from England for this occasion, assembled in the grand salon of the hotel de Grandlieu to sign the marriage contract, and Leopold Hannequin, the family notary, explained the preliminaries of that contract before reading it, Calyste, on whose forehead every one present might have noticed clouds, suddenly and curtly refused to accept the benefactions offered him by Mademoiselle des Touches. Did he still count on Felicite's devotion to recover Beatrix? In the midst of the embarrassment and stupefaction of the assembled families, Sabine de Grandlieu entered the room and gave him a letter, explaining that Mademoiselle des Touches had requested her to give it to him on this occasion.

Calyste turned away from the company to the embrasure of a window and read as follows:—

Camille Maupin to Calyste.

Calyste, before I enter my convent cell I am permitted to cast a look upon the world I am now to leave for a life of prayer and solitude. That look is to you, who have been the whole world to me in these last months. My voice will reach you, if my calculations do not miscarry, at the moment of a ceremony I am unable to take part in.

On the day when you stand before the altar giving your hand and name to a young and charming girl who can love you openly before earth and heaven, I shall be before another altar in a convent at Nantes betrothed forever to Him who will neither fail nor betray me. But I do not write to sadden you,—only to entreat you not to hinder by false delicacy the service I have wished to do you since we first met. Do not contest my rights so dearly bought.

If love is suffering, ah! I have loved you indeed, my Calyste. But feel no remorse; the only happiness I have known in life I owe to you; the pangs were caused by my own self. Make me compensation, then, for all those pangs, those sorrows, by causing me an everlasting joy. Let the poor Camille, who is no longer, still be something in the material comfort you enjoy. Dear, let me be like the fragrance of flowers in your life, mingling myself with it unseen and not importunate.

To you, Calyste, I shall owe my eternal happiness; will you not accept a few paltry and fleeting benefits from me? Surely you will not be wanting in generosity? Do you not see in this the last message of a renounced love? Calyste, the world without you had nothing more for me; you made it the most awful of solitudes; and you have thus brought Camille Maupin, the unbeliever, the writer of books, which I am soon to repudiate solemnly—you have cast her, daring and perverted, bound hand and foot, before God.

I am to-day what I might have been, what I was born to be, —innocent, and a child. I have washed my robes in the tears of repentance; I can come before the altar whither my guardian angel, my beloved Calyste, has led me. With what tender comfort I give you that name, which the step I now take sanctifies. I love you without self-seeking, as a mother loves her son, as the Church loves her children. I can pray for you and for yours without one thought or wish except for your happiness. Ah! if you only knew the sublime tranquillity in which I live, now that I have risen in thought above all petty earthly interests, and how precious is the thought of DOING (as your noble motto says) our duty, you would enter your beautiful new life with unfaltering step and never a glance behind you or about you. Above all, my earnest prayer to you is that you be faithful to yourself and to those belonging to you. Dear, society, in which you are to live, cannot exist without the religion of duty, and you will terribly mistake it, as I mistook it, if you allow yourself to yield to passion and to fancy, as I did. Woman is the equal of man only in making her life a continual offering, as that of man is a perpetual action; my life has been, on the contrary, one long egotism. If may be that God placed you, toward evening, by the door of my house, as a messenger from Himself, bearing my punishment and my pardon.

Heed this confession of a woman to whom fame has been like a pharos, warning her of the only true path. Be wise, be noble; sacrifice your fancy to your duties, as head of your race, as husband, as father. Raise the fallen standard of the old du Guenics; show to this century of irreligion and want of principle what a gentleman is in all his grandeur and his honor. Dear child of my soul, let me play the part of a mother to you; your own mother will not be jealous of this voice from a tomb, these hands uplifted to heaven, imploring blessings on you. To-day, more than ever, does rank and nobility need fortune. Calyste, accept a part of mine, and make a worthy use of it. It is not a gift; it is a trust I place in your hands. I have thought more of your children and of your old Breton house than of you in offering you the profits which time has brought to my property in Paris.

"Let us now sign the contract," said the young baron, returning to the assembled company.

The Abbe Grimont, to whom the honor of the conversion of this celebrated woman was attributed, became, soon after, vicar-general of the diocese.

The following week, after the marriage ceremony, which, according to the custom of many families of the faubourg Saint-Germain, was celebrated at seven in the morning at the church of Saint Thomas d'Aquin, Calyste and Sabine got into their pretty travelling-carriage, amid the tears, embraces, and congratulations of a score of friends, collected under the awning of the hotel de Grandlieu. The congratulations came from the four witnesses, and the men present; the tears were in the eyes of the Duchesse de Grandlieu and her daughter Clotilde, who both trembled under the weight of the same thought, —

"She is launched upon the sea of life! Poor Sabine! at the mercy of a man who does not marry entirely of his own free will."

Marriage is not wholly made up of pleasures, —as fugitive in that relation as in all others; it involves compatibility of temper, physical sympathies, harmonies of character, which make of that social necessity an eternal problem. Marriageable daughters, as well as mothers, know the terms as well as the dangers of this lottery; and that is why women weep at a wedding while men smile; men believe that they risk nothing, while women know, or very nearly know, what they risk.

In another carriage, which preceded the married pair, was the Baronne du Guenic, to whom the duchess had said at parting, —

"You are a mother, though you have only had one son; try to take my place to my dear Sabine."

On the box of the bridal carriage sat a *chasseur*, who acted as courier, and in the rumble were two waiting-maids. The four postilions dressed in their finest uniforms, for each carriage was drawn by four horses, appeared with bouquets on their breasts and ribbons on their hats, which the Duc de Grandlieu had the utmost difficulty in making them relinquish, even by bribing them with money. The French postilion is eminently intelligent, but he likes his fun. These fellows took their bribes and replaced their ribbons at the barrier.

"Well, good-bye, Sabine," said the duchess; "remember your promise; write to me often. Calyste, I say nothing more to you, but you understand me."

Clotilde, leaning on the youngest sister Athenais, who was smiling to the Vicomte de Grandlieu, cast a reflecting look through her tears at the bride, and followed the carriage with her eyes as it disappeared to the clacking of four whips, more noisy than the shots of a pistol gallery. In a few minutes the gay convoy had reached the esplanade of the Invalides, the barrier of Passy by the quay of the Pont d'Iena, and were fairly on the high-road to Brittany.

Is it not a singular thing that the artisans of Switzerland and Germany, and the great families of France and England should, one and all, follow the custom of setting out on a journey after the marriage ceremony? The great people shut themselves in a box which rolls along; the little people gaily tramp the roads, sitting down in the woods, banqueting at the inns, as long as their joy, or rather their money lasts. A moralist is puzzled to decide on which side is the finer sense of modesty, — that which hides from the public eye and inaugurates the domestic hearth and bed in private, as to the worthy burghers of all lands, or that which withdraws from the family and exhibits itself publicly on the high-roads and in face of strangers. One would think that delicate souls might desire solitude and seek to escape both the world and their family. The love which begins a marriage is a pearl, a diamond, a jewel cut by the choicest of arts, a treasure to bury in the depths of the soul.

Who can relate a honeymoon, unless it be the bride? How many women reading this history will admit to themselves that this period of uncertain duration is the forecast of conjugal life? The first three letters of Sabine to her mother will depict a situation not surprising to some young brides and to many old women. All those who find themselves the sick-nurses, so to speak, of a husband's heart, do not, as Sabine did, discover this at once. But young girls of the faubourg Saint-Germain, if intelligent, are women in mind. Before marriage, they have received from their mothers and the world they live in the baptism of good manners; though women of rank, anxious to hand down their traditions, do not always see the bearing of their own lessons when they say to their daughters: "That is a motion that must not be made;" "Never laugh at such things;" "No lady ever flings herself on a sofa; she sits down quietly;" "Pray give up such detestable ways;" "My dear, that is a thing which is never done," etc.

Many bourgeois critics unjustly deny the innocence and virtue of young girls who, like Sabine, are truly virgin at heart, improved by the training of their minds, by the habit of noble bearing, by natural good taste, while, from the age of sixteen, they have learned how to use their opera-glasses. Sabine was a girl of this school, which was also that of Mademoiselle de Chaulieu. This inborn sense of the fitness of things, these gifts of race made Sabine de Grandlieu as interesting a young woman as the heroine of the "Memoirs of two young Married Women." Her letters to her mother during the honeymoon, of which we here give three or four, will show the qualities of her mind and temperament.

Guerande, April, 1838.

To Madame la Duchesse de Grandlieu:

Dear Mamma,—You will understand why I did not write to you during the journey,—our wits are then like wheels. Here I am, for the last two days, in the depths of Brittany, at the hotel du Guenic, —a house as covered with carving as a sandal-wood box. In spite of the affectionate devotion of Calyste's family, I feel a keen desire to fly to you, to tell you many things which can only be trusted to a mother.

Calyste married, dear mamma, with a great sorrow in his heart. We all knew that, and you did not hide from me the difficulties of my position; but alas! they are greater than you thought. Ah! my dear mother, what experience we acquire in the short space of a few days—I might even say a few hours! All your counsels have proved fruitless; you will see why from one sentence: I love Calyste as if he were not my husband,—that is to say, if I were married to another, and were travelling with Calyste, I should love Calyste and hate my husband.

Now think of a man beloved so completely, involuntarily, absolutely, and all the other adverbs you may choose to employ, and you will see that my servitude is established in spite of your good advice. You told me to be grand, noble, dignified, and self-respecting in order to obtain from Calyste the feelings that are never subject to the chances and changes of life,—esteem, honor, and the consideration which sanctifies a woman in the bosom of her family. I remember how you blamed, I dare say justly, the young women of the present day, who, under pretext of living happily with their husbands, begin by compliance, flattery, familiarity, an abandonment, you called it, a little too wanton (a word I did not fully understand), all of which, if I must believe you, are relays that lead rapidly to indifference and possibly to contempt. "Remember that you are a Grandlieu!" yes, I remember that you told me all that—

But oh! that advice, filled with the maternal eloquence of a female Daedelus has had the fate of all things mythological. Dear, beloved mother, could you ever have supposed it possible that I should begin by the catastrophe which, according to you, ends the honeymoon of the young women of the present day?

When Calyste and I were fairly alone in the travelling carriage, we felt rather foolish in each other's company, understanding the importance of the first word, the first look; and we both, bewildered by the solemnity, looked out of our respective windows. It became so ridiculous that when we reached the barrier monsieur began, in a rather troubled tone of voice, a set discourse, prepared, no doubt, like other improvisations, to which I listened with a beating heart, and which I take the liberty of here abridging.

"My dear Sabine," he said, "I want you to be happy, and, above all, do I wish you to be happy in your own way. Therefore, in the situation in which we are, instead of deceiving ourselves mutually about our characters and our feelings by noble compliances, let us endeavor to be to each other at once what we should be years hence. Think always that you have a friend and a brother in me, as I shall feel I have a sister and a friend in you."

Though it was all said with the utmost delicacy, I found nothing in this first conjugal love-speech which responded to the feelings in my soul, and I remained pensive after replying that I was animated by the same sentiments. After this declaration of our rights to mutual coldness, we talked of weather, relays, and scenery in the most charming manner,—I with rather a forced little laugh, he absent-mindedly.

At last, as we were leaving Versailles, I turned to Calyste—whom I called my dear Calyste, and he called me my dear Sabine—and asked him plainly to tell me the events which had led him to the point of death, and to which I was aware that I owed the happiness of being his wife. He hesitated long. In fact, my request gave rise to a little argument between us, which lasted through three relays,—I endeavoring to maintain the part of an obstinate girl, and trying to sulk; he debating within himself the question which the newspapers used to put to Charles X.: "Must the king yield or not?" At last, after passing Verneuil, and exchanging oaths enough to satisfy three dynasties never to reproach him for his folly, and never to treat him coldly, etc., etc., he related to me his love for Madame de Rochefide.

"I do not wish," he said, in conclusion, "to have any secrets between us."

Poor, dear Calyste, it seems, was ignorant that his friend, Mademoiselle des Touches, and you had thought it right to tell me the truth. Well, mother,—for I can tell all to a mother as tender as you,—I was deeply hurt by perceiving that he had yielded less to my request than to his own desire to talk of that strange passion. Do you blame me, darling mother, for having wished to reconnoitre the extent of the grief, the open wound of the heart of which you warned me?

So, eight hours after receiving the rector's blessing at Saint-Thomas d'Aquin, your Sabine was in the rather false position of a young wife listening to a confidence, from the very lips of her husband, of his misplaced love for an unworthy rival. Yes, there I was, in the drama of a young woman learning, officially, as it were, that she owed her marriage to the disdainful rejection of an old and faded beauty!

Still, I gained what I sought. "What was that?" you will ask. Ah! mother dear, I have seen too much of love going on around me not to know how to put a little of it into practice. Well, Calyste ended the poem of his miseries with the warmest protestations of an absolute forgetting of what he called his madness. All kinds of affirmations have to be signed, you know. The happy unhappy one took my hand, carried it to his lips, and, after that, he kept it for a long time clasped in his own. A declaration followed. That one seemed to me more conformable than the first to the demands of our new condition, though our lips never said a word. Perhaps I owed it to the vigorous indignation I felt and showed at the bad taste of a woman foolish enough not to love my beautiful, my glorious Calyste.

They are calling me to play a game of cards, which I do not yet understand. I will finish my letter to-morrow. To leave you at this moment to make a fifth at mouche (that is the name of the game) can only be done in the depths of Brittany—Adieu.

Your Sabine.
Guerande, May, 1838.

I take up my Odyssey. On the third day your children no longer used the ceremonious "you;" they thee'd and thou'd each other like lovers. My mother-in-law, enchanted to see us so happy, is trying to take your place to me, dear mother, and, as often happens when people play a part to efface other memories, she has been so charming that she is, almost, you to me.

I think she has guessed the heroism of my conduct, for at the beginning of our journey she tried to hide her anxiety with such care that it was visible from excessive precaution.

When I saw the towers of Guerande rising in the distance, I whispered in the ear of your son-in-law, "Have you really forgotten her?" My husband, now become my angel, can't know anything, I think, about sincere and simple love, for the words made him wild with happiness. Still, I think the desire to put Madame de Rochefide forever out of his mind led me too far. But how could I help it? I love, and I am half a Portuguese,—for I am much more like you, mamma, than like my father.

Calyste accepts all from me as spoilt children accept things, they think it their right; he is an only child, I remember that. But, between ourselves, I will not give my daughter (if I have any daughters) to an only son. I see a variety of tyrants in an only son. So, mamma, we have rather inverted our parts, and I am the devoted half of the pair. There are dangers, I know, in devotion, though we profit by it; we lose our dignity, for one thing. I feel bound to tell you of the wreck of that semi-virtue. Dignity, after all, is only a screen set up before pride, behind which we rage as we please; but how could I help it? you were not here, and I saw a gulf opening before me. Had I remained upon my dignity, I should have won only the cold joys (or pains) of a sort of brotherhood which would soon have drifted into indifference. What sort of future might that have led to? My devotion has, I know, made me Calyste's slave; but shall I regret it? We shall see.

As for the present, I am delighted with it. I love Calyste; I love him absolutely, with the folly of a mother, who thinks that all her son may do is right, even if he tyrannizes a trifle over her.

Guerande, May 15th.

Up to the present moment, dear mamma, I find marriage a delightful affair, I can spend all my tenderness on the noblest of men whom a foolish woman disdained for a fiddler,—for that woman evidently was a fool, and a cold fool, the worst kind! I, in my legitimate love, am charitable; I am curing his wounds while I lay my heart open to incurable ones. Yes, the more I love Calyste, the more I feel that I should die of grief if our present happiness ever ceased.

I must tell you how the whole family and the circle which meets at the hotel de Guenic adore me. They are all personages born under tapestries of the highest warp; in fact, they seem to have stepped from those old tapestries as if to prove that the impossible may exist. Some day, when we are alone together, I will describe to you my Aunt Zephirine, Mademoiselle de Pen-Hoel, the Chevalier du Halga, the Demoiselles de Kergarouet, and others. They all, even to the two servants, Gasselin and Mariotte (whom I wish they would let me take to Paris), regard me as an angel sent from heaven; they tremble when I speak. Dear people! they ought to be preserved under glass.

My mother-in-law has solemnly installed us in the apartments formerly occupied by herself and her late husband. The scene was touching. She said to us,—

"I spent my whole married life, a happy woman, in these rooms; may the omen be a happy one for you, my children."

She has taken Calyste's former room for hers. Saintly soul! she seems intent on laying off her memories and all her conjugal dignities to invest us with them. The province of Brittany, this town, this family of ancient morals and ancient customs has, in spite of certain absurdities which strike the eye of a frivolous Parisian girl, something inexplicable, something grandiose even in its trifles, which can only be defined by the word sacred.

All the tenants of the vast domains of the house of Guenic, bought back, as you know, by Mademoiselle des Touches (whom we are going to visit in her convent), have been in a body to pay their respects to us. These worthy people, in their holiday costumes, expressing their genuine joy in the fact that Calyste has now become really and truly their master, made me understand Brittany, the feudal system and old France. The whole scene was a festival I can't describe to you in writing, but I will tell you about it when we meet. The terms of the leases have been proposed by the gars themselves. We shall sign them, after making a tour of inspection round the estates, which have been mortgaged away from us for one hundred and fifty years! Mademoiselle de Pen-Hoel told me that the gars have reckoned up the revenues and estimated the rentals with a veracity and justice Parisians would never believe.

We start in three days on horseback for this trip. I will write you on my return, dear mother. I shall have nothing more to tell you about myself, for my happiness is at its height—and how can that be told? I shall write you only what you know already, and that is, how I love you.

Nantes, June, 1838.

Having now played the role of a chatelaine, adored by her vassals as if the revolutions of 1789 and 1830 had lowered no banners; and after rides through forests, and halts at farmhouses, dinners on oaken tables, covered with centenary linen, bending under Homeric viands served on antediluvian dishes; after drinking the choicest wines in goblets to volleys of musketry, accompanied by cries of "Long live the Guenics!" till I was deafened; after balls, where the only orchestra was a bagpipe, blown by a man for ten hours; and after bouquets, and young brides who wanted us to bless them, and downright weariness, which made me find in my bed a sleep I never knew before, with delightful awakenings when love shone radiant as the sun pouring in upon me, and scintillating with a million of flies, all buzzing in the Breton dialect!—in short, after a most grotesque residence in the Chateau du Guenic, where the windows are gates and the cows graze peacefully on the grass in the halls (which castle we have sworn to repair and to inhabit for a while very year to the wild acclamations of the clan du Guenic, a gars of which bore high our banner)—ouf! I am at Nantes.

But oh! what a day was that when we arrived at the old castle! The rector came out, mother, with all his clergy, crowned with flowers, to receive us and bless us, expressing such joy,—the tears are in my eyes as I think of it. And my noble Calyste! who played his part of seigneur like a personage in Walter Scott! My lord received his tenants' homage as if he were back in the thirteenth century. I heard the girls and the women saying to each other, "Oh, what a beautiful seigneur we have!" for all the world like an opera chorus. The old men talked of Calyste's resemblance to the former Guenics whom they had known in their youth. Ah! noble, sublime Brittany! land of belief and faith! But progress has got its eye upon it; bridges are being built, roads made, ideas are coming, and then farewell to the sublime! The peasants will certainly not be as free and proud as I have now seen them, when progress has proved to them that they are Calyste's equals —if, indeed, they could ever be got to believe it.

After this poem of our pacific Restoration had been sung, and the contracts and leases signed, we left that ravishing land, all flowery, gay, solemn, lonely by turns, and came here to kneel with our happiness at the feet of her who gave it to us.

Calyste and I both felt the need of thanking the sister of the Visitation. In memory of her he has quartered his own arms with those of Des Touches, which are: party couped, tranche and taille or and sinople, on the latter two eagles argent. He means to take one of the eagles argent for his own supporter and put this motto in its beak: Souviegne-vous.

Yesterday we went to the convent of the ladies of the Visitation, to which we were taken by the Abbe Grimont, a friend of the du Guenic family, who told us that your dear Felicite, mamma, was indeed a saint. She could not very well be anything else to him, for her conversion, which was thought to be his doing, has led to his appointment as vicar-general of the diocese. Mademoiselle des Touches declined to receive Calyste, and would only see me. I found her slightly changed, thinner and paler; but she seemed much pleased at my visit.

"Tell Calyste," she said, in a low voice, "that it is a matter of conscience with me not to see him, for I am permitted to do so. I prefer not to buy that happiness by months of suffering. Ah, you do not know what it costs me to reply to the question, 'Of what are you thinking?' Certainly the mother of the novices has no conception of the number and extent of the ideas which are rushing through my mind when she asks that question. Sometimes I am seeing Italy or Paris, with all its sights; always thinking, however, of Calyste, who is"—she said this in that poetic way you know and admire so much—"who is the sun of memory to me. I found," she continued, "that I was too old to be received among the Carmelites, and I have entered the order of Saint-Francois de Sales solely because he said, 'I will bare your heads instead of your feet,'—objecting, as he did, to austerities which mortified the body only. It is, in truth, the head that sins. The saintly bishop was right to make his rule austere toward the intellect, and terrible against the will. That is what I sought; for my head was the guilty part of me. It deceived me as to my heart until I reached that fatal age of forty, when, for a few brief moments, we are forty times happier than young women, and then, speedily, fifty times more unhappy. But, my child, tell me," she asked, ceasing with visible satisfaction to speak of herself, "are you happy?"

"You see me under all the enchantments of love and happiness," I answered.

"Calyste is as good and simple as he is noble and beautiful," she said, gravely. "I have made you my heiress in more things than property; you now possess the double ideal of which I dreamed. I rejoice in what I have done," she continued, after a pause. "But, my child, make no mistake; do yourself no wrong. You have easily won happiness; you have only to stretch out your hand to take it, and it is yours; but be careful to preserve it. If you had come here solely to carry away with you the counsels that my knowledge of your husband alone can give you, the journey would be well repaid. Calyste is moved at this moment by a communicated passion, but you have not inspired it. To make your happiness lasting, try, my dear child, to give him something of his former emotions. In the interests of both of you, be capricious, be coquettish; to tell you the truth, you must be. I am not advising any odious scheming, or petty tyranny; this that I tell you is the science of a woman's life. Between usury and prodigality, my child, is economy. Study, therefore, to acquire honorably a certain empire over Calyste. These are the last words on earthly interests that I shall ever utter, and I have kept them to say as we part; for there are times when I tremble in my conscience lest to save Calyste I may have sacrificed you. Bind him to you, firmly, give him children, let him respect their mother in you—and," she added, in a low and trembling voice, "manage, if you can, that he shall never again see Beatrix."

That name plunged us both into a sort of stupor; we looked into each other's eyes, exchanging a vague uneasiness.

"Do you return to Guerande?" she asked me.

"Yes," I said.

"Never go to Les Touches. I did wrong to give him that property."

"Why?" I asked.

"Child!" she answered, "Les Touches for you is Bluebeard's chamber. There is nothing so dangerous as to wake a sleeping passion."

I have given you, dear mamma, the substance, or at any rate, the meaning of our conversation. If Mademoiselle des Touches made me talk to her freely, she also gave me much to think of; and all the more because, in the delight of this trip, and the charm of these relations with my Calyste, I had well-nigh forgotten the serious situation of which I spoke to you in my first letter, and about which you warned me.

But oh! mother, it is impossible for me to follow these counsels. I cannot put an appearance of opposition or caprice into my love; it would falsify it. Calyste will do with me what he pleases. According to your theory, the more I am a woman the more I make myself his toy; for I am, and I know it, horribly weak in my happiness; I cannot resist a single glance of my lord. But no! I do not abandon myself to love; I only cling to it, as a mother presses her infant to her breast, fearing some evil.

Note.—When "Beatrix" was first published, in 1839, the volume ended with the following paragraph: "Calyste, rich and married to the most beautiful woman in Paris, retains a sadness in his soul which nothing dissipates,—not even the birth of a son at Guerande, in 1839, to the great joy of Zephirine du Guenic. Beatrix lives still in the depths of his heart, and it is impossible to foresee what disasters might result should he again meet with Madame de Rochefide." In 1842 this concluding paragraph was suppressed and the story continued as here follows.—TR.

CHAPTER XVIII.

THE END OF A HONEY-MOON

Guerande, July, 1838.

To Madame la Duchesse de Grandlieu:

Ah, my dear mamma! at the end of three months to know what it is to be jealous! My heart completes its experience; I now feel the deepest hatred and the deepest love! I am more than betrayed,—I am not loved. How fortunate for me to have a mother, a heart on which to cry out as I will!

It is enough to say to wives who are still half girls: "Here's a key rusty with memories among those of your palace; go everywhere, enjoy everything, but keep away from Les Touches!" to make us eager to go there hot-foot, our eyes shining with the curiosity of Eve. What a root of bitterness Mademoiselle des Touches planted in my love! Why did she forbid me to go to Les Touches? What sort of happiness is mine if it depends on an excursion, on a visit to a paltry house in Brittany? Why should I fear? Is there anything to fear? Add to this reasoning of Mrs. Blue-Beard the desire that nips all women to know if their power is solid or precarious, and you'll understand how it was that I said one day, with an unconcerned little air:—

"What sort of place is Les Touches?"

"Les Touches belongs to you," said my divine, dear mother-in-law.

"If Calyste had never set foot in Les Touches!"—cried my aunt Zephirine, shaking her head.

"He would not be my husband," I added.

"Then you know what happened there?" said my mother-in-law, slyly.

"It is a place of perdition!" exclaimed Mademoiselle de Pen-Hoel. "Mademoiselle des Touches committed many sins there, for which she is now asking the pardon of God."

"But they saved the soul of that noble woman, and made the fortune of a convent," cried the Chevalier du Halga. "The Abbe Grimont told me she had given a hundred thousand francs to the nuns of the Visitation."

"Should you like to go to Les Touches?" asked my mother-in-law. "It is worth seeing."

"No, no!" I said hastily.

Doesn't this little scene read to you like a page out of some diabolical drama?

It was repeated again and again under various pretexts. At last my mother-in-law said to me: "I understand why you do not go to Les Touches, and I think you are right."

Oh! you must admit, mamma, that an involuntary, unconscious stab like that would have decided you to find out if your happiness rested on such a frail foundation that it would perish at a mere touch. To do Calyste justice, he never proposed to me to visit that hermitage, now his property. But as soon as we love we are creatures devoid of common-sense, and this silence, this reserve piqued me; so I said to him one day: "What are you afraid of at Les Touches, that you alone never speak of the place?"

"Let us go there," he replied.

So there I was caught,—like other women who want to be caught, and who trust to chance to cut the Gordian knot of their indecision. So to Les Touches we went.

It is enchanting, in a style profoundly artistic. I took delight in that place of horror where Mademoiselle des Touches had so earnestly forbidden me to go. Poisonous flowers are all charming; Satan sowed them—for the devil has flowers as well as God; we have only to look within our souls to see the two shared in the making of us. What delicious acrity in a situation where I played, not with fire, but—with ashes! I studied Calyste; the point was to know if that passion was thoroughly extinct. I watched, as you may well believe, every wind that blew; I kept an eye upon his face as he went from room to room and from one piece of furniture to another, exactly like a child who is looking for some hidden thing. Calyste seemed thoughtful, but at first I thought that I had vanquished the past. I felt strong enough to mention Madame de Rochefide-whom in my heart I called la Rocheperfide. At last we went to see the famous bush were Beatrix was caught when he flung her into the sea that she might never belong to another man.

"She must be light indeed to have stayed there," I said laughing. Calyste kept silence, so I added, "We'll respect the dead."

Still Calyste was silent.

"Have I displeased you?" I asked.

"No; but cease to galvanize that passion," he answered.

What a speech! Calyste, when he saw me all cast down by it, redoubled his care and tenderness.

August.

I was, alas! at the edge of a precipice, amusing myself, like the innocent heroines of all melodramas, by gathering flowers. Suddenly a horrible thought rode full tilt through my happiness, like the horse in the German ballad. I thought I saw that Calyste's love was increasing through his reminiscences; that he was expending on me the stormy emotions I revived by reminding him of the coquetries of that hateful Beatrix,—just think of it! that cold, unhealthy nature, so persistent yet so flabby, something between a mollusk and a bit of coral, dares to call itself Beatrix, Beatrice!

Already, dearest mother, I am forced to keep one eye open to suspicion, when my heart is all Calyste's; and isn't it a great catastrophe when the eye gets the better of the heart, and suspicion at last finds itself justified? It came to pass in this way: —

"This place is dear to me," I said to Calyste one morning, "because I owe my happiness to it; and so I forgive you for taking me sometimes for another woman."

The loyal Breton blushed, and I threw my arms around his neck. But all the same I have left Les Touches, and never will I go back there again.

The very strength of hatred which makes me long for Madame de Rochefide's death—ah, heavens! a natural death, pleurisy, or some accident—makes me also understand to its fullest extent the power of my love for Calyste. That woman has appeared to me to trouble my sleep,—I see her in a dream; shall I ever encounter her bodily? Ah! the postulant of the Visitation was right,—Les Touches is a fatal spot; Calyste has there recovered his past emotions, and they are, I see it plainly, more powerful than the joys of our love. Ascertain, my dear mamma, if Madame de Rochefide is in Paris, for if she is, I shall stay in Brittany. Poor Mademoiselle des Touches might well repent of her share in our marriage if she knew to what extent I am taken for our odious rival! But this is prostitution! I am not myself; I am ashamed of it all. A frantic desire seizes me sometimes to fly from Guerande and those sands of Croisic.

August 25th.

I am determined to go and live in the ruins of the old chateau. Calyste, worried by my restlessness, agrees to take me. Either he knows life so little that he guesses nothing, or he does know the cause of my flight, in which case he cannot love me. I tremble so with fear lest I find the awful certainty I seek that, like a child, I put my hands before my eyes not to hear the explosion—

Oh, mother! I am not loved with the love that I feel in my heart. Calyste is charming to me, that's true! but what man, unless he were a monster, would not be, as Calyste is, amiable and gracious when receiving all the flowers of the soul of a young girl of twenty, brought up by you, pure, loving, and beautiful, as many women have said to you that I am.

Guenic, September 18.

Has he forgotten her? That's the solitary thought which echoes through my soul like a remorse. Ah! dear mamma, have all women to struggle against memories as I do? None but innocent young men should be married to pure young girls. But that's a deceptive Utopia; better have one's rival in the past than in the future.

Ah! mother, pity me, though at this moment I am happy as a woman who fears to lose her happiness and so clings fast to it,—one way of killing it, says that profoundly wise Clotilde.

I notice that for the last five months I think only of myself, that is, of Calyste.

Tell sister Clotilde that her melancholy bits of wisdom often recur to me. She is happy in being faithful to the dead; she fears no rival. A kiss to my dear Athenais, about whom I see Juste is beside himself. From what you told me in your last letter it is evident he fears you will not give her to him. Cultivate that fear as a precious product. Athenais will be sovereign lady; but I who fear lest I can never win Calyste back from himself shall always be a servant.

A thousand tendernesses, dear mamma. Ah! if my terrors are not delusions, Camille Maupin has sold me her fortune dearly. My affectionate respects to papa.

These letters give a perfect explanation of the secret relation between husband and wife. Sabine thought of a love marriage where Calyste saw only a marriage of expediency. The joys of the honey-moon had not altogether conformed to the legal requirements of the social system.

During the stay of the married pair in Brittany the work of restoring and furnishing the hotel du Guenic had been carried on by the celebrated architect Grindot, under the superintendence of Clotilde and the Duc and Duchesse de Grandlieu, all arrangements having been made for the return of the young household to Paris in December, 1838. Sabine installed herself in the rue de Bourbon with pleasure,—less for the satisfaction of playing mistress of a great household than for that of knowing what her family would think of her marriage.

Calyste, with easy indifference, was quite willing to let his sister-in-law Clotilde and his mother-in-law the duchess guide him in all matters of social life, and they were both very grateful for his obedience. He obtained the place in society which was due to his name, his fortune, and his alliance. The success of his wife, who was regarded as one of the most charming women in Paris, the diversions of high society, the duties to be fulfilled, the winter amusements of the great city, gave a certain fresh life to the happiness of the young household by producing a series of excitements and interludes. Sabine, considered happy by her mother and sister, who saw in Calyste's coolness an effect of his English education, cast aside her gloomy notions; she heard her lot so envied by many unhappily married women that she drove her terrors from her into the region of chimeras, until the time when her pregnancy gave additional guarantees to this neutral sort of union, guarantees which are usually augured well of by experienced women. In October, 1839, the young Baronne du Guenic had a son, and committed the mistake of nursing it herself, on the theory of most women in such cases. How is it possible, they think, not to be wholly the mother of the child of an idolized husband?

Toward the end of the following summer, in August, 1840, Sabine had nearly reached the period when the duty of nursing her first child would come to an end. Calyste, during his two years' residence in Paris, had completely thrown off that innocence of mind the charm of which had so adorned his earliest appearance in the world of passion. He was now the comrade of the young Duc Georges de Maufrigneuse, lately married, like himself, to an heiress, Berthe de Cinq-Cygne; of the Vicomte Savinien de Portenduere, the Duc and Duchesse de Rhetore, the Duc and Duchesse de Lenoncourt-Chaulieu, and all the *habitues* of his mother-in-law's salon; and he fully understood by this time the differences that separated Parisian life from the life of the provinces. Wealth has fatal hours, hours of leisure and idleness, which Paris knows better than all other capitals how to amuse, charm, and divert. Contact with those young husbands who deserted the noblest and sweetest of creatures for the delights of a cigar and whist, for the glorious conversations of a club, or the excitements of "the turf," undermined before long many of the domestic virtues of the young Breton noble. The motherly solicitude of a wife who is anxious not to weary her husband always comes to the support of the dissipations of young men. A wife is proud to see her husband return to her when she has allowed him full liberty of action.

One evening, on October of that year, to escape the crying of the newly weaned child, Calyste, on whose forehead Sabine could not endure to see a frown, went, urged by her, to the Varietes, where a new play was to be given for the first time. The footman whose business it was to engage a stall had taken it quite near to that part of the theatre which is called the *avant-scene*. As Calyste looked about him during the first interlude, he saw in one of the two proscenium boxes on his side, and not ten steps from him, Madame de Rochefide. Beatrix in Paris! Beatrix in public! The two thoughts flew through Calyste's heart like arrows. To see her again after nearly three years! How shall we depict the convulsion in the soul of this lover, who, far from forgetting the past, had sometimes substituted Beatrix for his wife so plainly that his wife had perceived it? Beatrix was light, life, motion, and the Unknown. Sabine was duty, dulness, and the expected. One became, in a moment, pleasure; the other, weariness. It was the falling of a thunderbolt.

From a sense of loyalty, the first thought of Sabine's husband was to leave the theatre. As he left the door of the orchestra stalls, he saw the door of the proscenium box half-open, and his feet took him there in spite of his will. The young Breton found Beatrix between two very distinguished men, Canalis and Raoul Nathan, a statesman and a man of letters. In the three years since Calyste had seen her, Madame de Rochefide was amazingly changed; and yet, although the transformation had seriously affected her as a woman, she was only the more poetic and the more attractive to Calyste. Until the age of thirty the pretty women of Paris ask nothing more of their toilet than clothing; but after they pass through the fatal portal of the thirties, they look for weapons, seductions, embellishments among their *chiffons;* out of these they compose charms, they find means, they take a style, they seize youth, they study the slightest accessory,—in a word, they pass from nature to art.

Madame de Rochefide had just come through the vicissitudes of a drama which, in this history of the manners and morals of France in the nineteenth century may be called that of the Deserted Woman. Deserted by Conti, she became, naturally, a great artist in dress, in coquetry, in artificial flowers of all kinds.

"Why is Conti not here?" inquired Calyste in a low voice of Canalis, after going through the commonplace civilities with which even the most solemn interviews begin when they take place publicly.

The former great poet of the faubourg Saint-Germain, twice a cabinet minister, and now for the fourth time an orator in the Chamber, and aspiring to another ministry, laid a warning finger significantly on his lip. That gesture explained everything.

"I am happy to see you," said Beatrix, demurely. "I said to myself when I recognized you just now, before you saw me, that *you* at least would not disown me. Ah! my Calyste," she added in a whisper, "why did you marry?—and with such a little fool!"

As soon as a woman whispers in the ear of a new-comer and makes him sit beside her, men of the world find an immediate excuse for leaving the pair alone together.

"Come, Nathan," said Canalis, "Madame la marquise will, I am sure, allow me to go and say a word to d'Arthez, whom I see over there with the Princesse de Cadignan; it relates to some business in the Chamber to-morrow."

This well-bred departure gave Calyste time to recover from the shock he had just received; but he nearly lost both his strength and his senses once more, as he inhaled the perfume, to him entrancing though venomous, of the poem composed by Beatrix. Madame de Rochefide, now become bony and gaunt, her complexion faded and almost discolored, her eyes hollow with deep circles, had that evening brightened those premature ruins by the cleverest contrivances of the *article Paris*. She had taken it into her head, like other deserted women, to assume a virgin air, and recall by clouds of white material the maidens of Ossian, so poetically painted by Girodet. Her fair hair draped her elongated face with a mass of curls, among which rippled the rays of the foot-lights attracted by the shining of a perfumed oil. Her white brow sparkled. She had applied an imperceptible tinge of rouge to her cheeks, upon the faded whiteness of a skin revived by bran and water. A scarf so delicate in texture that it made one doubt if human fingers could have fabricated such gossamer, was wound about her throat to diminish its length, and partly conceal it; leaving imperfectly visible the treasures of the bust which were cleverly enclosed in a corset. Her figure was indeed a masterpiece of composition.

As for her pose, one word will suffice—it was worthy of the pains she had taken to arrange it. Her arms, now thin and hard, were scarcely visible within the puffings of her very large sleeves. She presented that mixture of false glitter and brilliant fabrics, of silken gauze and craped hair, of vivacity, calmness, and motion which goes by the term of the *Je ne sais quoi*. Everybody knows in what that consists, namely: great cleverness, some taste, and a certain composure of manner. Beatrix might now be called a decorative scenic effect, changed at will, and wonderfully manipulated. The presentation of this fairy effect, to which is added clever dialogue, turns the heads of men who are endowed by nature with frankness, until they become possessed, through the law of contrasts, by a frantic desire to play with artifice. It is false, though enticing; a pretence, but agreeable; and certain men adore women who play at seduction as others do at cards. And this is why: The desire of the man is a syllogism which draws conclusions from this external science as to the secret promises of pleasure. The inner consciousness says, without words: "A woman who can, as it were, create herself beautiful must have many other resources for love." And that is true. Deserted women are usually those who merely love; those who retain love know the *art* of loving. Now, though her Italian lesson had very cruelly maltreated the self-love and vanity of Madame de Rochefide, her nature was too instinctively artificial not to profit by it.

"It is not a question of loving a man," she was saying a few moments before Calyste had entered her box; "we must tease and harass him if we want to keep him. That's the secret of all those women who seek to retain you men. The dragons who guard treasures are always armed with claws and wings."

"I shall make a sonnet on that thought," replied Canalis at the very moment when Calyste entered the box.

With a single glance Beatrix divined the state of Calyste's heart; she saw the marks of the collar she had put upon him at Les Touches, still fresh and red. Calyste, however, wounded by the speech made to him about his wife, hesitated between his dignity as a husband, Sabine's defence, and a harsh word cast upon a heart which held such memories for him, a heart which he believed to be bleeding. The marquise observed his hesitation; she had made that speech expressly that she might know how far her empire over Calyste still extended. Seeing his weakness, she came at once to his succor to relieve his embarrassment.

"Well, dear friend, you find me alone," she said, as soon as the two gentlemen had left the box,—"yes, alone in the world!"

"You forget me!" said Calyste.

"You!" she replied, "but you are married. That was one of my griefs, among the many I have endured since I saw you last. Not only—I said to myself—do I lose love, but I have lost a friendship which I thought was Breton. Alas! we can make ourselves bear everything. Now I suffer less, but I am broken, exhausted! This is the first outpouring of my heart for a long, long time. Obliged to seem proud before indifferent persons, and arrogant as if I had never fallen in presence of those who pay court to me, and having lost my dear Felicite, there was no ear into which I could cast the words, *I suffer!* But to you I can tell the anguish I endured on seeing you just now so near to me. Yes," she said, replying to a gesture of Calyste's, "it is almost fidelity. That is how it is with misery; a look, a visit, a mere nothing is everything to us. Ah! you once loved me—you—as I deserved to be loved by him who has taken pleasure in trampling under foot the treasures I poured out upon him. And yet, to my sorrow, I cannot forget; I love, and I desire to be faithful to a past that can never return."

Having uttered this tirade, improvised for the hundredth time, she played the pupils of her eyes in a way to double the effect of her words, which seemed to be dragged from the depths of her soul by the violence of a torrent long restrained. Calyste, incapable of speech, let fall the tears that gathered in his eyes. Beatrix caught his hand and pressed it, making him turn pale.

"Thank you, Calyste, thank you, my poor child; that is how a true friend responds to the grief of his friend. We understand each other. No, don't add another word; leave me now; people are looking at us; it might cause trouble to your wife if some one chanced to tell her that we were seen together,—innocently enough, before a thousand people! There, you see I am strong; adieu—"

She wiped her eyes, making what might be called, in woman's rhetoric, an antithesis of action.

"Let me laugh the laugh of a lost soul with the careless creatures who amuse me," she went on. "I live among artists, writers, in short the world I knew in the salon of our poor Camille—who may indeed have acted wisely. To enrich the man we love and then to disappear saying, 'I am too old for him!' that is ending like the martyrs,—and the best end too, if one cannot die a virgin."

She began to laugh, as it to remove the melancholy impression she had made upon her former adorer.

"But," said Calyste, "where can I go to see you?"

"I am hidden in the rue de Chartres opposite the Parc de Monceaux, in a little house suitable to my means; and there I cram my head with literature—but only for myself, to distract my thoughts; God keep me from the mania of literary women! Now go, leave me; I must not allow the world to talk of me; what will it not say on seeing us together! Adieu—oh! Calyste, my friend, if you stay another minute I shall burst into tears!"

Calyste withdrew, after holding out his hand to Beatrix and feeling for the second time that strange and deep sensation of a double pressure—full of seductive tingling.

"Sabine never knew how to stir my soul in that way," was the thought that assailed him in the corridor.

During the rest of the evening the Marquise de Rochefide did not cast three straight glances at Calyste, but there were many sidelong looks which tore of the soul of the man now wholly thrown back into his first, repulsed love.

When the baron du Guenic reached home the splendor of his apartments made him think of the sort of mediocrity of which Beatrix had spoken, and he hated his wealth because it could not belong to that fallen angel. When he was told that Sabine had long been in bed he rejoiced to find himself rich in the possession of a night in which to live over his emotions. He cursed the power of divination which love had bestowed upon Sabine. When by chance a man is adored by his wife, she reads on his face as in a book; she learns every quiver of its muscles, she knows whence comes its calmness, she asks herself the reason of the slightest sadness, seeking to know if haply the cause is in herself; she studies the eyes; for her the eyes are tinted with the dominant thought,—they love or they do not love. Calyste knew himself to be the object of so deep, so naive, so jealous a worship that he doubted his power to compose a cautious face that should not betray the change in his moral being.

"How shall I manage to-morrow morning?" he said to himself as he went to sleep, dreading the sort of inspection to which Sabine would have recourse. When they came together at night, and sometimes during the day, Sabine would ask him, "Do you still love me?" or, "I don't weary you, do I?" Charming interrogations, varied according to the nature or the cleverness of women, which hide their anxieties either feigned or real.

To the surface of the noblest and purest hearts the mud and slime cast up by hurricanes must come. So on that morrow morning, Calyste, who certainly loved his child, quivered with joy on learning that Sabine feared the croup, and was watching for the cause of slight convulsions, not daring to leave her little boy. The baron made a pretext of business and went out, thus avoiding the home breakfast. He escaped as prisoners escape, happy in being afoot, and free to go by the Pont Louis XVI. and the Champs Elysees to a cafe on the boulevard where he had liked to breakfast when he was a bachelor.

What is there in love? Does Nature rebel against the social yoke? Does she need that impulse of her given life to be spontaneous, free, the dash of an impetuous torrent foaming against rocks of opposition and of coquetry, rather than a tranquil stream flowing between the two banks of the church and the legal ceremony? Has she her own designs as she secretly prepares those volcanic eruptions to which, perhaps, we owe great men?

It would be difficult to find a young man more sacredly brought up than Calyste, of purer morals, less stained by irreligion; and yet he bounded toward a woman unworthy of him, when a benign and radiant chance had given him for his wife a young creature whose beauty was truly aristocratic, whose mind was keen and delicate, a pious, loving girl, attached singly to him, of angelic sweetness, and made more tender still by love, a love that was passionate in spite of marriage, like his for Beatrix. Perhaps the noblest men retain some clay in their constitutions; the slough still pleases them. If this be so, the least imperfect human being is the woman, in spite of her faults and her want of reason. Madame de Rochefide, it must be said, amid the circle of poetic pretensions which surrounded her, and in spite of her fall, belonged to the highest nobility; she presented a nature more ethereal than slimy, and hid the courtesan she was meant to be beneath an aristocratic exterior. Therefore the above explanation does not fully account for Calyste's strange passion.

Perhaps we ought to look for its cause in a vanity so deeply buried in the soul that moralists have not yet uncovered that side of vice. There are men, truly noble, like Calyste, handsome as Calyste, rich, distinguished, and well-bred, who tire—without their knowledge, possibly—of marriage with a nature like their own; beings whose own nobleness is not surprised or moved by nobleness in others; whom grandeur and delicacy consonant with their own does not affect; but who seek from inferior or fallen natures the seal of their own superiority—if indeed they do not openly beg for praise. Calyste found nothing to protect in Sabine, she was irreproachable; the powers thus stagnant in his heart were now to vibrate for Beatrix. If great men have played before our eyes the Saviour's part toward the woman taken in adultery, why should ordinary men be wiser in their generation than they?

Calyste reached the hour of two o'clock living on one sentence only, "I shall see her again!"—a poem which has often paid the costs of a journey of two thousand miles. He now went with a light step to the rue de Chartres, and recognized the house at once although he had never before seen it. Once there, he stood—he, the son-in-law of the Duc de Grandlieu, he, rich, noble as the Bourbons—at the foot of the staircase, stopped short by the interrogation of the old footman: "Monsieur's name?" Calyste felt that he ought to leave to Beatrix her freedom of action in receiving or not receiving him; and he waited, looking into the garden, with its walls furrowed by those black and yellow lines produced by rain upon the stucco of Paris.

Madame de Rochefide, like nearly all great ladies who break their chain, had left her fortune to her husband when she fled from him; she could not beg from her tyrant. Conti and Mademoiselle des Touches had spared Beatrix all the petty worries of material life, and her mother had frequently send her considerable sums of money. Finding herself now on her own resources, she was forced to an economy that was rather severe for a woman accustomed to every luxury. She had therefore gone to the summit of the hill on which lies the Parc de Monceaux, and there she had taken refuge in a "little house" formerly belonging to a great seigneur, standing on the street, but possessed of a charming garden, the rent of which did not exceed eighteen hundred francs. Still served by an old footman, a maid, and a cook from Alencon, who were faithful to her throughout her vicissitudes, her penury, as she thought it, would have been opulence to many an ambitious bourgeoise.

Calyste went up a staircase the steps of which were well pumiced and the landings filled with flowering plants. On the first floor the old servant opened, in order to admit the baron into the apartment, a double door of red velvet with lozenges of red silk studded with gilt nails. Silk and velvet furnished the rooms through which Calyste passed. Carpets in grave colors, curtains crossing each other before the windows, portieres, in short all things within contrasted with the mean external appearance of the house, which was ill-kept by the proprietor. Calyste awaited Beatrix in a salon of sober character, where all the luxury was simple in style. This room, hung with garnet velvet heightened here and there with dead-gold silken trimmings, the floor covered with a dark red carpet, the windows resembling conservatories, with abundant flowers in the jardinieres, was lighted so faintly that Calyste could scarcely see on a mantel-shelf two cases of old celadon, between which gleamed a silver cup attributed to Benvenuto Cellini, and brought from Italy by Beatrix. The furniture of gilded wood with velvet coverings, the magnificent consoles, on one of which was a curious clock, the table with its Persian cloth, all bore testimony to former opulence, the remains of which had been well applied. On a little table Calyste saw jewelled knick-knacks, a book in course of reading, in which glittered the handle of a dagger used as a paper-cutter — symbol of criticism! Finally, on the walls, ten water-colors richly framed, each representing one of the diverse bedrooms in which Madame de Rochefide's wandering life had led her to sojourn, gave the measure of what was surely superior impertinence.

The rustle of a silk dress announced the poor unfortunate, who appeared in a studied toilet which would certainly have told a *roue* that his coming was awaited. The gown, made like a wrapper to show the line of a white bosom, was of pearl-gray moire with large open sleeves, from which issued the arms covered with a second sleeve of puffed tulle, divided by straps and trimmed with lace at the wrists. The beautiful hair, which the comb held insecurely, escaped from a cap of lace and flowers.

"Already!" she said, smiling. "A lover could not have shown more eagerness. You must have secrets to tell me, have you not?"

And she posed herself gracefully on a sofa, inviting Calyste by a gesture to sit beside her. By chance (a selected chance, possibly, for women have two memories, that of angels and that of devils) Beatrix was redolent of the perfume which she used at Les Touches during her first acquaintance with Calyste. The inhaling of this scent, contact with that dress, the glance of those eyes, which in the semi-darkness gathered the light and returned it, turned Calyste's brain. The luckless man was again impelled to that violence which had once before almost cost Beatrix her life; but this time the marquise was on the edge of a sofa, not on that of a rock; she rose to ring the bell, laying a finger on his lips. Calyste, recalled to order, controlled himself, all the more because he saw that Beatrix had no inimical intention.

"Antoine, I am not at home—for every one," she said. "Put some wood on the fire. You see, Calyste, that I treat you as a friend," she continued with dignity, when the old man had left the room; "therefore do not treat me as you would a mistress. I have two remarks to make to you. In the first place, I should not deny myself foolishly to any man I really loved; and secondly, I am determined to belong to no other man on earth, for I believed, Calyste, that I was loved by a species of Rizzio, whom no engagement trammelled, a man absolutely free, and you see to what that fatal confidence has led me. As for you, you are now under the yoke of the most sacred of duties; you have a young, amiable, delightful wife; moreover, you are a father. I should be, as you are, without excuse—we should be two fools—"

"My dear Beatrix, all these reasons vanish before a single word—I have never loved but you on earth, and I was married against my will."

"Ah! a trick played upon us by Mademoiselle des Touches," she said, smiling.

Three hours passed, during which Madame de Rochefide held Calyste to the consideration of conjugal faith, pointing out to him the horrible alternative of an utter renunciation of Sabine. Nothing else could reassure her, she said, in the dreadful situation to which Calyste's love would reduce her. Then she affected to regard the sacrifice of Sabine as a small matter, she knew her so well!

"My dear child," she said, "that's a woman who fulfils all the promises of her girlhood. She is a Grandlieu, to be sure, but she's as brown as her mother the Portuguese, not to say yellow, and as dry and stiff as her father. To tell the truth, your wife will never go wrong; she's a big boy who can take care of herself. Poor Calyste! is that the sort of woman you needed? She has fine eyes, but such eyes are very common in Italy and in Spain and Portugal. Can any woman be tender with bones like hers. Eve was fair; brown women descend from Adam, blondes come from the hand of God, which left upon Eve his last thought after he had created her."

About six o'clock Calyste, driven to desperation, took his hat to depart.

"Yes, go, my poor friend," she said; "don't give her the annoyance of dining without you."

Calyste stayed. At his age it was so easy to snare him on his worst side.

"What! you dare to dine with me?" said Beatrix, playing a provocative amazement. "My poor food does not alarm you? Have you enough independence of soul to crown me with joy by this little proof of your affection?"

"Let me write a note to Sabine; otherwise she will wait dinner for me till nine o'clock."

"Here," said Beatrix, "this is the table at which I write."

She lighted the candles herself, and took one to the table to look over what he was writing.

"My dear Sabine—"

"'My dear'?—can you really say that your wife is still dear to you?" she asked, looking at him with a cold eye that froze the very marrow of his bones. "Go,—you had better go and dine with her."

"I dine at a restaurant with some friends."

"A lie. Oh, fy! you are not worthy to be loved either by her or by me. Men are all cowards in their treatment of women. Go, monsieur, go and dine with your dear Sabine."

Calyste flung himself back in his arm-chair and became as pale as death. Bretons possess a courage of nature which makes them obstinate under difficulties. Presently the young baron sat up, put his elbow on the table, his chin in his hand, and looked at the implacable Beatrix with a flashing eye. He was so superb that a Northern or a Southern woman would have fallen at his feet saying, "Take me!" But Beatrix, born on the borders of Normandy and Brittany, belonged to the race of Casterans; desertion had developed in her the ferocity of the Frank, the spitefulness of the Norman; she wanted some terrible notoriety as a vengeance, and she yielded to no weakness.

"Dictate what I ought to write," said the luckless man. "But, in that case—"

"Well, yes!" she said, "you shall love me then as you loved me at Guerande. Write: *I dine out; do not expect me.*"

"What next?" said Calyste, thinking something more would follow.

"Nothing; sign it. Good," she said, darting on the note with restrained joy. "I will send it by a messenger."

"And now," cried Calyste, rising like a happy man.

"Ah! I have kept, I believe, my freedom of action," she said, turning away from him and going to the fireplace, where she rang the bell. "Here, Antoine," she said, when the old footman entered, "send this note to its address. Monsieur dines here."

CHAPTER XIX.

THE FIRST LIE OF A PIOUS DUCHESS

Calyste returned to his own house about two in the morning. After waiting for him till half-past twelve, Sabine had gone to bed overwhelmed with fatigue. She slept, although she was keenly distressed by the laconic wording of her husband's note. Still, she explained it. The true love of a woman invariably begins by explaining all things to the advantage of the man beloved. Calyste was pressed for time, she said.

The next morning the child was better; the mother's uneasiness subsided, and Sabine came with a smiling face, and little Calyste on her arm, to present him to his father before breakfast with the pretty fooleries and senseless words which gay young mothers do and say. This little scene gave Calyste the chance to maintain a countenance. He was charming to his wife, thinking in his heart that he was a monster, and he played like a child with Monsieur le chevalier; in fact he played too well,—he overdid the part; but Sabine had not reached the stage at which a woman recognizes so delicate a distinction.

At breakfast, however, she asked him suddenly:—

"What did you do yesterday?"

"Portenduere kept me to dinner," he replied, "and after that we went to the club to play whist."

"That's a foolish life, my Calyste," said Sabine. "Young noblemen in these days ought to busy themselves about recovering in the eyes of the country the ground lost by their fathers. It isn't by smoking cigars, playing whist, idling away their leisure, and saying insolent things of parvenus who have driven them from their positions, nor yet by separating themselves from the masses whose soul and intellect and providence they ought to be, that the nobility will exist. Instead of being a party, you will soon be a mere opinion, as de Marsay said. Ah! if you only knew how my ideas on this subject have enlarged since I have nursed and cradled your child! I'd like to see that grand old name of Guenic become once more historical!" Then suddenly plunging her eyes into those of Calyste, who was listening to her with a pensive air, she added: "Admit that the first note you ever wrote me was rather stiff."

"I did not think of sending you word till I got to the club."

"But you wrote on a woman's note-paper; it had a perfume of feminine elegance."

"Those club directors are such dandies!"

The Vicomte de Portenduere and his wife, formerly Mademoiselle Mirouet, had become of late very intimate with the du Guenics, so intimate that they shared their box at the Opera by equal payments. The two young women, Ursula and Sabine, had been won to this friendship by the delightful interchange of counsels, cares, and confidences apropos of their first infants.

While Calyste, a novice in falsehood, was saying to himself, "I must warn Savinien," Sabine was thinking, "I am sure that paper bore a coronet." This reflection passed through her mind like a flash, and Sabine scolded herself for having made it. Nevertheless, she resolved to find the paper, which in the midst of her terrors of the night before she had flung into her letter-box.

After breakfast Calyste went out, saying to his wife that he should soon return. Then he jumped into one of those little low carriages with one horse which were just beginning to supersede the inconvenient cabriolet of our ancestors. He drove in a few minutes to the vicomte's house and begged him to do him the service, with rights of return, of fibbing in case Sabine should question the vicomtesse. Thence Calyste, urging his coachman to speed, rushed to the rue de Chartres in order to know how Beatrix had passed the rest of the night. He found that unfortunate just from her bath, fresh, embellished, and breakfasting with a very good appetite. He admired the grace with which his angel ate her boiled eggs, and he marvelled at the beauty of the gold service, a present from a monomaniac lord, for whom Conti had composed a few ballads on *ideas* of the lord, who afterwards published them as his own!

Calyste listened entranced to the witty speeches of his idol, whose great object was to amuse him, until she grew angry and wept when he rose to leave her. He thought he had been there only half an hour, but it was past three before he reached home. His handsome English horse, a present from the Vicomtesse de Grandlieu, was so bathed in sweat that it looked as though it had been driven through the sea. By one of those chances which all jealous women prepare for themselves, Sabine was at a window which looked on the court-yard, impatient at Calyste's non-return, uneasy without knowing why. The condition of the horse with its foaming mouth surprised her.

"Where can he have come from?"

The question was whispered in her ear by that power which is not exactly consciousness, nor devil, nor angel; which sees, forebodes, shows us the unseen, and creates belief in mental beings, creatures born of our brains, going and coming and living in the world invisible of ideas.

"Where do you come from, dear angel?" Sabine said to Calyste, meeting him on the first landing of the staircase. "Abd-el-Kader is nearly foundered. You told me you would be gone but a moment, and I have been waiting for you these three hours."

"Well, well," thought Calyste, who was making progress in dissimulation, "I must get out of it by a present—Dear little mother," he said aloud, taking her round the waist with more cajolery than he would have used if he had not been conscious of guilt, "I see that it is quite impossible to keep a secret, however innocent, from the woman who loves us—"

"Well, don't tell secrets on the staircase," she said, laughing. "Come in."

In the middle of a salon which adjoined their bedroom, she caught sight in a mirror of Calyste's face, on which, not aware that it could be seen, he allowed his real feelings and his weariness to appear.

"Now for your secret?" she said, turning round.

"You have shown such heroism as a nurse," he said, "that the heir presumptive of the Guenics is dearer to me than ever, and I wanted to give you a surprise, precisely like any bourgeois of the rue Saint Denis. They are finishing for you at this moment a dressing-table at which true artists have worked, and my mother and aunt Zephirine have contributed."

Sabine clasped him in her arms, and held him tightly to her breast with her head on his neck, faint with the weight of happiness, not for the piece of furniture, but for the dispersion of her first dark doubt. It was one of those magnificent transports which can be counted, and which no love, however excessive, can prodigally spend, or life would be too soon burned out. Then, indeed, men should fall at the feet of women to adore them, for such moments are sublime, moments when the forces of the heart and intellect gush forth like the waters of sculptured nymphs from their inclining urns. Sabine burst into tears.

Suddenly as if bitten by a viper, she left Calyste, threw herself on a sofa and fainted away, for the reaction of a chill to her glowing heart came near to killing her. As she held Calyste in her arms, her nose at his cravat, abandoned to her joy, she smelt the perfume of that letter paper! Another woman's head had lain there, whose hair and face had left that adulterous odor! She had just kissed the spot where the kisses of her rival were still warm.

"What is the matter?" asked Calyste, after he had brought Sabine back to consciousness by passing a damp cloth over her face and making her smell salts.

"Fetch the doctor and my nurse, both! Yes, my milk has turned, I feel it. They won't come at once unless you fetch them yourself—go!"

Calyste, alarmed, rushed out. The moment Sabine heard the closing of the porte-cochere she started up like a frightened doe, and walked about the salon as if beside herself, crying out, "My God! my God! my God!"

Those two words took the place of all ideas. The crisis she had seized upon as a pretext in reality took place. The hairs of her head were like so many red-hot needles heated in the fire of a nervous fever. Her boiling blood seemed to her to mingle with her nerves and yet try to issue from all her pores. She was blind for a few moments, and cried aloud, "I am dying!"

At that terrible cry of the injured wife and mother her maid ran in. After she was laid upon her bed and recovered both sight and mind, the first act of her intelligence was to send the maid to her friend, Madame de Portenduere. Sabine felt that her ideas were whirling in her brain like straws at the will of a waterspout. "I saw," she said later, "myriads all at once."

She rang for the footman and in the transport of her fever she found strength to write the following letter, for she was mastered by one mad desire—to have certainty:—

To Madame la Baronne du Guenic:

Dear Mamma,—When you come to Paris, as you allow us to hope you will, I shall thank you in person for the beautiful present by which you and my aunt Zephirine and Calyste wish to reward me for doing my duty. I was already well repaid by my own happiness in doing it. I can never express the pleasure you have given me in that beautiful dressing-table, but when you are with me I shall try to do so. Believe me, when I array myself before that treasure, I shall think, like the Roman matron, that my noblest jewel is our little angel, etc.

She directed the letter to Guerande and gave it to the footman to post.

When the Vicomtesse de Portenduere came, the shuddering chill of reaction had succeeded in poor Sabine this first paroxysm of madness.

"Ursula, I think I am going to die," she said.

"What is the matter, dear?"

"Where did Savinien and Calyste go after they dined with you yesterday?"

"Dined with me?" said Ursula, to whom her husband had said nothing, not expecting such immediate inquiry. "Savinien and I dined alone together and went to the Opera without Calyste."

"Ursula, dearest, in the name of your love for Savinien, keep silence about what you have just said to me and what I shall now tell you. You alone shall know why I die—I am betrayed! at the end of three years, at twenty-two years of age!"

Her teeth chattered, her eyes were dull and frozen, her face had taken on the greenish tinge of an old Venetian mirror.

"You! so beautiful! For whom?"

"I don't know yet. But Calyste has told me two lies. Do not pity me, do not seem incensed, pretend ignorance and perhaps you can find out who *she* is through Savinien. Oh! that letter of yesterday!"

Trembling, shaking, she sprang from her bed to a piece of furniture from which she took the letter.

"See," she said, lying down again, "the coronet of a marquise! Find out if Madame de Rochefide has returned to Paris. Am I to have a heart in which to weep and moan? Oh, dearest!—to see one's beliefs, one's poesy, idol, virtue, happiness, all, all in pieces, withered, lost! No God in the sky! no love upon earth! no life in my heart! no anything! I don't know if there's daylight; I doubt the sun. I've such anguish in my soul I scarcely feel the horrible sufferings in my body. Happily, the baby is weaned; my milk would have poisoned him."

At that idea the tears began to flow from Sabine's eyes which had hitherto been dry.

Pretty Madame de Portenduere, holding in her hand the fatal letter, the perfume of which Sabine again inhaled, was at first stupefied by this true sorrow, shocked by this agony of love, without as yet understanding it, in spite of Sabine's incoherent attempts to relate the facts. Suddenly Ursula was illuminated by one of those ideas which come to none but sincere friends.

"I must save her!" she thought to herself. "Trust me, Sabine," she cried. "Wait for my return; I will find out the truth."

"Ah! in my grave I'll love you," exclaimed Sabine.

The viscountess went straight to the Duchesse de Grandlieu, pledged her to secrecy, and then explained to her fully her daughter's situation.

"Madame," she said as she ended, "do you not think with me, that in order to avoid some fatal illness—perhaps, I don't know, even madness—we had better confide the whole truth to the doctor, and invent some tale to clear that hateful Calyste and make him seem for the time being innocent?"

"My dear child," said the duchess, who was chilled to the heart by this confidence, "friendship has given you for the moment the experience of a woman of my age. I know how Sabine loves her husband; you are right, she might become insane."

"Or lose her beauty, which would be worse," said the viscountess.

"Let us go to her!" cried the duchess.

Fortunately they arrived a few moments before the famous *accoucheur*, Dommanget, the only one of the two men of science whom Calyste had been able to find.

"Ursula has told me everything," said the duchess to her daughter, "and you are mistaken. In the first place, Madame de Rochefide is not in Paris. As for what your husband did yesterday, my dear, I can tell you that he lost a great deal of money at cards, so that he does not even know how to pay for your dressing-table."

"But *that?*" said Sabine, holding out to her mother the fatal letter.

"That!" said the duchess, laughing; "why, that is written on the Jockey Club paper; everybody writes nowadays on coroneted paper; even our stewards will soon be titled."

The prudent mother threw the unlucky paper into the fire as she spoke.

When Calyste and Dommanget arrived, the duchess, who had given instructions to the servants, was at once informed. She left Sabine to the care of Madame de Portenduere and stopped the *accoucheur* and Calyste in the salon.

"Sabine's life is at stake, monsieur," she said to Calyste; "you have betrayed her for Madame de Rochefide."

Calyste blushed, like a girl still respectable, detected in a fault.

"And," continued the duchess, "as you do not know how to deceive, you have behaved in such a clumsy manner that Sabine has guessed the truth. But I have for the present repaired your blunder. You do not wish the death of my daughter, I am sure—All this, Monsieur Dommanget, will put you on the track of her real illness and its cause. As for you, Calyste, an old woman like me understands your error, though she does not pardon it. Such pardons can only be brought by a lifetime of after happiness. If you wish me to esteem you, you must, in the first place, save my daughter; next, you must forget Madame de Rochefide; she is only worth having once. Learn to lie; have the courage of a criminal, and his impudence. I have just told a lie myself, and I shall have to do hard penance for that mortal sin."

She then told the two men the lies she had invented. The clever physician sitting at the bedside of his patient studied in her symptoms the means of repairing the ill, while he ordered measures the success of which depended on great rapidity of execution. Calyste sitting at the foot of the bed strove to put into his glance an expression of tenderness.

"So it was play which put those black circles round your eyes?" Sabine said to him in a feeble voice.

The words made the doctor, the mother, and the viscountess tremble, and they all three looked at one another covertly. Calyste turned as red as a cherry.

"That's what comes of nursing a child," said Dommanget brutally, but cleverly. "Husbands are lonely when separated from their wives, and they go to the club and play. But you needn't worry over the thirty thousand francs which Monsieur le baron lost last night—"

"Thirty thousand francs!" cried Ursula, in a silly tone.

"Yes, I know it," replied Dommanget. "They told me this morning at the house of the young Duchesse Berthe de Maufrigneuse that it was Monsieur de Trailles who won that money from you," he added, turning to Calyste. "Why do you play with such men? Frankly, monsieur le baron, I can well believe you are ashamed of it."

Seeing his mother-in-law, a pious duchess, the young viscountess, a happy woman, and the old *accoucheur*, a confirmed egotist, all three lying like a dealer in bric-a-brac, the kind and feeling Calyste understood the greatness of the danger, and two heavy tears rolled from his eyes and completely deceived Sabine.

"Monsieur," she said, sitting up in bed and looking angrily at Dommanget, "Monsieur du Guenic can lose thirty, fifty, a hundred thousand francs if it pleases him, without any one having a right to think it wrong or read him a lesson. It is far better that Monsieur de Trailles should win his money than that we should win Monsieur de Trailles'."

Calyste rose, took his wife round the neck, kissed her on both cheeks and whispered:—

"Sabine, you are an angel!"

Two days later the young wife was thought to be out of danger, and the next day Calyste was at Madame de Rochefide's making a merit of his infamy.

"Beatrix," he said, "you owe me happiness. I have sacrificed my poor little wife to you; she has discovered all. That fatal paper on which you made me write, bore your name and your coronet, which I never noticed—I saw but you! Fortunately the 'B' was by chance effaced. But the perfume you left upon me and the lies in which I involved myself like a fool have betrayed my happiness. Sabine nearly died of it; her milk went to the head; erysipelas set in, and possibly she may bear the marks for the rest of her days."

As Beatrix listened to this tirade her face was due North, icy enough to freeze the Seine had she looked at it.

"So much the better," she said; "perhaps it will whiten her for you."

And Beatrix, now become as hard as her bones, sharp as her voice, harsh as her complexion, continued a series of atrocious sarcasms in the same tone. There is no greater blunder than for a man to talk of his wife, if she is virtuous, to his mistress, unless it be to talk of his mistress, if she is beautiful, to his wife. But Calyste had not received that species of Parisian education which we must call the politeness of the passions. He knew neither how to lie to his wife, nor how to tell his mistress the truth,—two apprenticeships a man in his position must make in order to manage women. He was therefore compelled to employ all the power of passion to obtain from Beatrix a pardon which she forced him to solicit for two hours; a pardon refused by an injured angel who raised her eyes to the ceiling that she might not see the guilty man, and who put forth reasons sacred to marquises in a voice quivering with tears which were furtively wiped with the lace of her handkerchief.

"To speak to me of your wife on the very day after my fall!" she cried. "Why did you not tell me she is a pearl of virtue? I know she thinks you handsome; pure depravity! I, I love your soul! for let me tell you, my friend, you are ugly compared to many shepherds on the Campagna of Rome," etc., etc.

Such speeches may surprise the reader, but they were part of a system profoundly meditated by Beatrix in this her third incarnation,—for at each passion a woman becomes another being and advances one step more into profligacy, the only word which properly renders the effect of the experience given by such adventures. Now, the Marquise de Rochefide had sat in judgment on herself before the mirror. Clever women are never deceived about themselves; they count their wrinkles, they assist at the birth of their crow's-feet, they know themselves by heart, and even own it by the greatness of their efforts at preservation. Therefore to struggle successfully against a splendid young woman, to carry away from her six triumphs a week, Beatrix had recourse to the knowledge and the science of courtesans. Without acknowledging to herself the baseness of this plan, led away to the employment of such means by a Turkish passion for Calyste's beauty, she had resolved to make him think himself unpleasant, ugly, ill-made, and to behave as if she hated him. No system is more fruitful with men of a conquering nature. To such natures the presence of repugnance to be vanquished is the renewal of the triumph of the first day on all succeeding days. And it is something even better. It is flattery in the guise of dislike. A man then says to himself, "I am irresistible," or "My love is all-powerful because it conquers her repugnance." If you deny this principle, divined by all coquettes and courtesans throughout all social zones, you may as well reject all seekers after knowledge, all delvers into secrets, repulsed through years in their duel with hidden causes. Beatrix added to the use of contempt as a moral piston, a constant comparison of her own poetic, comfortable home with the hotel du Guenic. All deserted wives who abandon themselves in despair, neglect also their surroundings, so discouraged are they. On this, Madame de Rochefide counted, and presently began an underhand attack on the luxury of the faubourg Saint-Germain, which she characterized as stupid.

The scene of reconciliation, in which Beatrix made Calyste swear and reswear hatred to the wife, who, she said, was playing comedy, took place in a perfect bower where she played off her graces amid ravishing flowers, and rare plants of the costliest luxury. The science of nothings, the trifles of the day, she carried to excess. Fallen into a mortifying position through Conti's desertion, Beatrix was determined to have, at any rate, the fame which unprincipled conduct gives. The misfortune of the poor young wife, a rich and beautiful Grandlieu, should be her pedestal.

CHAPTER XX.

A SHORT TREATISE ON CERTAINTY: BUT NOT FROM PASCAL'S POINT OF VIEW

When a woman returns to ordinary life after the nursing of her first child she reappears in the world embellished and charming. This phase of maternity, while it rejuvenates the women of a certain age, gives to young women a splendor of freshness, a gay activity, a *brio* of mere existence,—if it is permissible to apply to the body a word which Italy has discovered for the mind. In trying to return to the charming habits of the honeymoon, Sabine discovered that her husband was not the former Calyste. Again she observed him, unhappy girl, instead of resting securely in her happiness. She sought for the fatal perfume, and smelt it. This time she no longer confided in her friend, nor in the mother who had so charitably deceived her. She wanted certainty, and Certainty made no long tarrying. Certainty is never wanting, it is like the sun; and presently shades are asked for to keep it out. It is, in matters of the heart, a repetition of the fable of the woodman calling upon Death,—we soon ask Certainty to leave us blind.

One morning, about two weeks after the first crisis, Sabine received this terrible letter:—

Guerande.

To Madame la Baronne du Guenic:

My dear Daughter,—Your aunt Zephirine and I are lost in conjectures about the dressing-table of which you tell us in your letter. I have written to Calyste about it, and I beg you to excuse our ignorance. You can never doubt our hearts, I am sure. We are piling up riches for you here. Thanks to the advice of Mademoiselle de Pen-Hoel on the management of your property, you will find yourself within a few years in possession of a considerable capital without losing any of your income.

Your letter, dear child as dearly loved as if I had borne you in my bosom and fed you with my milk, surprised me by its brevity, and above all by your silence about my dearest little Calyste. You told me nothing of the great Calyste either; but then, I know that he is happy, etc.

Sabine wrote across this letter these words, "Noble Brittany does not always lie." She then laid the paper on Calyste's desk.

Calyste found the letter and read it. Seeing Sabine's sentence and recognizing her handwriting he flung the letter into the fire, determined to pretend that he had never received it. Sabine spent a whole week in an agony the secrets of which are known only to angelic or solitary souls whom the wing of the bad angel has never overshadowed. Calyste's silence terrified her.

"I, who ought to be all gentleness, all pleasure to him, I have displeased him, wounded him! My virtue has made itself hateful. I have no doubt humiliated my idol," she said to herself. These thoughts plowed furrows in her heart. She wanted to ask pardon for her fault, but Certainty let loose upon her other proofs. Grown bold and insolent, Beatrix wrote to Calyste at his own home; Madame du Guenic received the letter, and gave it to her husband without opening it, but she said to him, in a changed voice and with death in her soul: "My friend, that letter is from the Jockey Club; I recognize both the paper and the perfume."

Calyste colored, and put the letter into his pocket.

"Why don't you read it?"

"I know what it is about."

The young wife sat down. No longer did fever burn her, she wept no more; but madness such as, in feeble beings, gives birth to miracles of crime, madness which lays hands on arsenic for themselves or for their rivals, possessed her. At this moment little Calyste was brought in, and she took him in her arms to dance him. The child, just awakened, sought the breast beneath the gown.

"He remembers,—he, at any rate," she said in a low voice.

Calyste went to his own room to read his letter. When he was no longer present the poor young woman burst into tears, and wept as women weep when they are all alone.

Pain, as well as pleasure, has its initiation. The first crisis, like that in which poor Sabine nearly succumbed, returns no more than the first fruits of other things return. It is the first wedge struck in the torture of the heart; all others are expected, the shock to the nerves is known, the capital of our forces has been already drawn upon for vigorous resistance. So Sabine, sure of her betrayal, spent three hours with her son in her arms beside the fire in a way that surprised herself, when Gasselin, turned into a footman, came to say:—

"Madame is served."

"Let monsieur know."

"Monsieur does not dine at home, Madame la baronne."

Who knows what torture there is for a young woman of twenty-three in finding herself alone in the great dining-room of an old mansion, served by silent servants, under circumstances like these?

"Order the carriage," she said suddenly; "I shall go to the Opera."

She dressed superbly; she wanted to exhibit herself alone and smiling like a happy woman. In the midst of her remorse for the addition she had made to Madame de Rochefide's letter she had resolved to conquer, to win back Calyste by loving kindness, by the virtues of a wife, by the gentleness of the paschal lamb. She wished, also, to deceive all Paris. She loved, — loved as courtesans and as angels love, with pride, with humility. But the opera chanced to be "Otello." When Rubini sang *Il mio cor si divide*, she rushed away. Music is sometimes mightier than actor or poet, the two most powerful of all natures, combined. Savinien de Portenduere accompanied Sabine to the peristyle and put her in the carriage without being able to understand this sudden flight.

Madame du Guenic now entered a phase of suffering which is peculiar to the aristocracy. Envious, poor, and miserable beings, — when you see on the arms of such women golden serpents with diamond heads, necklaces clasped around their necks, say to yourselves that those vipers sting, those slender bonds burn to the quick through the delicate flesh. All such luxury is dearly bought. In situations like that of Sabine, women curse the pleasures of wealth; they look no longer at the gilding of their salons; the silk of the divans is jute in their eyes, exotic flowers are nettles, perfumes poison, the choicest cookery scrapes their throat like barley-bread, and life becomes as bitter as the Dead Sea.

Two or three examples may serve to show this reaction of luxury upon happiness; so that all those women who have endured it may behold their own experience.

Fully aware now of this terrible rivalry, Sabine studied her husband when he left the house, that she might divine, if possible, the future of his day. With what restrained fury does a woman fling herself upon the red-hot spikes of that savage martyrdom! What delirious joy if she could think he did not go to the rue de Chartres! Calyste returned, and then the study of his forehead, his hair, his eyes, his countenance, his demeanor, gave a horrible interest to mere nothings, to observations pursued even to matters of toilet, in which a woman loses her self-respect and dignity. These fatal investigations, concealed in the depths of her heart, turn sour and rot the delicate roots from which should spring to bloom the azure flowers of sacred confidence, the golden petals of the One only love, with all the perfumes of memory.

One day Calyste looked about him discontentedly; he had stayed at home! Sabine made herself caressing and humble, gay and sparkling.

"You are vexed with me, Calyste; am I not a good wife? What is there here that displeases you?" she asked.

"These rooms are so cold and bare," he replied; "you don't understand arranging things."

"Tell me what is wanting."

"Flowers."

"Ah!" she thought to herself, "Madame de Rochefide likes flowers."

Two days later, the rooms of the hotel du Guenic had assumed another aspect. No one in Paris could flatter himself to have more exquisite flowers than those that now adorned them.

Some time later Calyste, one evening after dinner, complained of the cold. He twisted about in his chair, declaring there was a draught, and seemed to be looking for something. Sabine could not at first imagine what this new fancy signified, she, whose house possessed a calorifere which heated the staircases, antechambers, and passages. At last, after three days' meditation, she came to the conclusion that her rival probably sat surrounded by a screen to obtain the half-lights favorable to faded faces; so Sabine had a screen, but hers was of glass and of Israelitish splendor.

"From what quarter will the next storm come?" she said to herself.

These indirect comparisons with his mistress were not yet at an end. When Calyste dined at home he ate his dinner in a way to drive Sabine frantic; he would motion to the servants to take away his plates after pecking at two or three mouthfuls.

"Wasn't it good?" Sabine would ask, in despair at seeing all the pains she had taken in conference with her cook thrown away.

"I don't say that, my angel," replied Calyste, without anger; "I am not hungry, that is all."

A woman consumed by a legitimate passion, who struggles thus, falls at last into a fury of desire to get the better of her rival, and often goes too far, even in the most secret regions of married life. So cruel, burning, and incessant a combat in the obvious and, as we may call them, exterior matters of a household must needs become more intense and desperate in the things of the heart. Sabine studied her attitudes, her toilets; she took heed about herself in all the infinitely little trifles of love.

The cooking trouble lasted nearly a month. Sabine, assisted by Mariotte and Gasselin, invented various little vaudeville schemes to ascertain the dishes which Madame de Rochefide served to Calyste. Gasselin was substituted for Calyste's groom, who had fallen conveniently ill. This enabled Gasselin to consort with Madame de Rochefide's cook, and before long, Sabine gave Calyste the same fare, only better; but still he made difficulties.

"What is wanting now?" she said.

"Oh, nothing," he answered, looking round the table for something he did not find.

"Ah!" exclaimed Sabine, as she woke the next morning, "Calyste wanted some of those Indian sauces they serve in England in cruets. Madame de Rochefide accustoms him to all sorts of condiments."

She bought the English cruets and the spiced sauces; but it soon became impossible for her to make such discoveries in all the preparations invented by her rival.

This period lasted some months; which is not surprising when we remember the sort of attraction presented by such a struggle. It is life. And that is preferable, with its wounds and its anguish, to the gloomy darkness of disgust, to the poison of contempt, to the void of abdication, to that death of the heart which is called indifference. But all Sabine's courage abandoned her one evening when she appeared in a toilet such as women are inspired to wear in the hope of eclipsing a rival, and about which Calyste said, laughing:—

"In spite of all you can do, Sabine, you'll never be anything but a handsome Andalusian."

"Alas!" she said, dropping on a sofa, "I may never make myself a blonde, but I know if this continues I shall soon be thirty-five years old."

She refused to go to the Opera as she intended, and chose to stay at home the whole evening. But once alone she pulled the flowers from her hair and stamped upon them; she tore off the gown and scarf and trampled them underfoot, like a goat caught in the tangle of its tether, which struggles till death comes. Then she went to bed.

CHAPTER XXI.

THE WICKEDNESS OF A GOOD WOMAN

Playing for these terrible stakes Sabine grew thin; grief consumed her; but she never for a moment forsook the role she had imposed upon herself. Sustained by a sort of fever, her lips drove back into her throat the bitter words that pain suggested; she repressed the flashing of her glorious dark eyes, and made them soft even to humility. But her failing health soon became noticeable. The duchess, an excellent mother, though her piety was becoming more and more Portuguese, recognized a moral cause in the physically weak condition in which Sabine now took satisfaction. She knew the exact state of the relation between Beatrix and Calyste; and she took great pains to draw her daughter to her own house, partly to soothe the wounds of her heart, but more especially to drag her away from the scene of her martyrdom. Sabine, however, maintained the deepest silence for a long time about her sorrows, fearing lest some one might meddle between herself and Calyste. She declared herself happy! At the height of her misery she recovered her pride, and all her virtues.

But at last, after some months during which her sister Clotilde and her mother had caressed and petted her, she acknowledged her grief, confided her sorrows, cursed life, and declared that she saw death coming with delirious joy. She begged Clotilde, who was resolved to remain unmarried, to be a mother to her little Calyste, the finest child that any royal race could desire for heir presumptive.

One evening, as she sat with her young sister Athenais (whose marriage to the Vicomte de Grandlieu was to take place at the end of Lent), and with Clotilde and the duchess, Sabine gave utterance to the supreme cries of her heart's anguish, excited by the pangs of a last humiliation.

"Athenais," she said, when the Vicomte Juste de Grandlieu departed at eleven o'clock, "you are going to marry; let my example be a warning to you. Consider it a crime to display your best qualities; resist the pleasure of adorning yourself to please Juste. Be calm, dignified, cold; measure the happiness you give by that which you receive. This is shameful, but it is necessary. Look at me. I perish through my best qualities. All that I *know* was fine and sacred and grand within me, all my virtues, were rocks on which my happiness is wrecked. I have ceased to please because I am not thirty-six years old. In the eyes of some men youth is thought an inferiority. There is nothing to imagine on an innocent face. I laugh frankly, and that is wrong; to captivate I ought to play off the melancholy half-smile of the fallen angel, who wants to hide her yellowing teeth. A fresh complexion is monotonous; some men prefer their doll's wax made of rouge and spermaceti and cold cream. I am straightforward; but duplicity is more pleasing. I am loyally passionate, as an honest woman may be, but I ought to be manoeuvring, tricky, hypocritical, and simulate a coldness I have not,—like any provincial actress. I am intoxicated with the happiness of having married one of the most charming men in France; I tell him, naively, how distinguished he is, how graceful his movements are, how handsome I think him; but to please him I ought to turn away my head with pretended horror, to love nothing with real love, and tell him his distinction is mere sickliness. I have the misfortune to admire all beautiful things without setting myself up for a wit by caustic and envious criticism of whatever shines from poesy and beauty. I don't seek to make Canalis and Nathan say of *me* in verse and prose that my intellect is superior. I'm only a poor little artless child; I care only for Calyste. Ah! if I had scoured the world like *her*, if I had said as *she* has said, 'I love,' in every language of Europe, I should be consoled, I should be pitied, I should be adored for serving the regal Macedonian with cosmopolitan love! We are thanked for our tenderness if we set it in relief against our vice. And I, a noble woman, must teach myself impurity and all the tricks of prostitutes! And Calyste is the dupe of such grimaces! Oh, mother! oh, my dear Clotilde! I feel that I have got my death-blow. My pride is only a sham buckler; I am without defence against my misery; I love my husband madly, and yet to bring him back to me I must borrow the wisdom of indifference."

"Silly girl," whispered Clotilde, "let him think you will avenge yourself—"

"I wish to die irreproachable and without the mere semblance of doing wrong," replied Sabine. "A woman's vengeance should be worthy of her love."

"My child," said the duchess to her daughter, "a mother must of course see life more coolly than you can see it. Love is not the end, but the means, of the Family. Do not imitate that poor Baronne de Macumer. Excessive passion is unfruitful and deadly. And remember, God sends us afflictions with knowledge of our needs. Now that Athenais' marriage is arranged, I can give all my thoughts to you. In fact, I have already talked of this delicate crisis in your life with your father and the Duc de Chaulieu, and also with d'Ajuda; we shall certainly find means to bring Calyste back to you."

"There is always one resource with the Marquise de Rochefide," remarked Clotilde, smiling, to her sister; "she never keeps her adorers long."

"D'Ajuda, my darling," continued the duchess, "was Monsieur de Rochefide's brother-in-law. If our dear confessor approves of certain little manoeuvres to which we must have recourse to carry out a plan which I have proposed to your father, I can guarantee to you the recovery of Calyste. My conscience is repugnant to the use of such means, and I must first submit them to the judgment of the Abbe Brossette. We shall not wait, my child, till you are *in extremis* before coming to your relief. Keep a good heart! Your grief to-night is so bitter that my secret escapes me; but it is impossible for me not to give you a little hope."

"Will it make Calyste unhappy?" asked Sabine, looking anxiously at the duchess.

"Oh, heavens! shall I ever be as silly as that!" cried Athenais, naively.

"Ah, little girl, you know nothing of the precipices down which our virtue flings us when led by love," replied Sabine, making a sort of moral revelation, so distraught was she by her woe.

The speech was uttered with such incisive bitterness that the duchess, enlightened by the tone and accent and look of her daughter, felt certain there was some hidden trouble.

"My dears, it is midnight; come, go to bed," she said to Clotilde and Athenais, whose eyes were shining.

"In spite of my thirty-five years I appear to be *de trop*," said Clotilde, laughing. While Athenais kissed her mother, Clotilde leaned over Sabine and said in her ear: "You will tell what it is? I'll dine with you to-morrow. If my mother's conscience won't let her act, I—I myself will get Calyste out of the hands of the infidels."

"Well, Sabine," said the duchess, taking her daughter into her bedroom, "tell me, what new trouble is there, my child?"

"Mamma, I am lost!"

"But how?"

"I wanted to get the better of that horrible woman—I conquered for a time—I am pregnant again—and Calyste loves her so that I foresee a total abandonment. When she hears of it she will be furious. Ah! I suffer such tortures that I cannot endure them long. I know when he is going to her, I know it by his joy; and his peevishness tells me as plainly when he leaves her. He no longer troubles himself to conceal his feelings; I have become intolerable to him. She has an influence over him as unhealthy as she is herself in soul and body. You'll see! she will exact from him, as the price of forgiveness, my public desertion, a rupture like her own; she will take him away from me to Switzerland or Italy. He is beginning now to say it is ridiculous that he knows nothing of Europe. I can guess what those words mean, flung out in advance. If Calyste is not cured of her in three months I don't know what he may become; but as for me, I will kill myself."

"But your soul, my unhappy child? Suicide is a mortal sin."

"Don't you understand? She may give him a child. And if Calyste loved the child of that woman more than mine—Oh! that's the end of my patience and all my resignation."

She fell into a chair. She had given vent to the deepest thought in her heart; she had no longer a hidden grief; and secret sorrow is like that iron rod that sculptors put within the structure of their clay,—it supports, it is a force.

"Come, go home, dear sufferer. In view of such misery the abbe will surely give me absolution for the venial sins which the deceits of the world compel us to commit. Leave me now, my daughter," she said, going to her *prie-Dieu*. "I must pray to our Lord and the Blessed Virgin for you, with special supplication. Good-bye, my dear Sabine; above all things, do not neglect your religious duties if you wish us to succeed."

"And if we do triumph, mother, we shall only save the family. Calyste has killed within me the holy fervor of love, — killed it by sickening me with all things. What a honey-moon was mine, in which I was made to feel on that first day the bitterness of a retrospective adultery!"

The next day, about two in the afternoon, one of the vicars of the faubourg Saint-Germain appointed to a vacant bishopric in 1840 (an office refused by him for the third time), the Abbe Brossette, one of the most distinguished priests in Paris, crossed the court-yard of the hotel de Grandlieu, with a step which we must needs call the ecclesiastical step, so significant is it of caution, mystery, calmness, gravity, and dignity. He was a thin little man about fifty years of age, with a face as white as that of an old woman, chilled by priestly austerities, and hollowed by all the sufferings which he espoused. Two black eyes, ardent with faith yet softened by an expression more mysterious than mystical, animated that truly apostolical face. He was smiling as he mounted the steps of the portico, so little did he believe in the enormity of the cases about which his penitent sent for him; but as the hand of the duchess was an open palm for charity, she was worth the time which her innocent confessions stole from the more serious miseries of the parish.

When the vicar was announced the duchess rose, and made a few steps toward him in the salon, — a distinction she granted only to cardinals, bishops, simple priests, duchesses older then herself, and persons of royal blood.

"My dear abbe," she said, pointing to a chair and speaking in a low voice, "I need the authority of your experience before I throw myself into a rather wicked intrigue, although it is one which must result in great good; and I desire to know from you whether I shall make hindrances to my own salvation in the course I propose to follow."

"Madame la duchesse," replied the abbe, "do not mix up spiritual things with worldly things; they are usually irreconcilable. In the first place, what is this matter?"

"You know that my daughter Sabine is dying of grief; Monsieur du Guenic has left her for Madame de Rochefide."

"It is very dreadful, very serious; but you know what our dear Saint Francois de Sales says on that subject. Remember too how Madame Guyon complained of the lack of mysticism in the proofs of conjugal love; she would have been very willing to see her husband with a Madame de Rochefide."

"Sabine is only too gentle; she is almost too completely a Christian wife; but she has not the slightest taste for mysticism."

"Poor young woman!" said the abbe, maliciously. "What method will you take to remedy the evil?"

"I have committed the sin, my dear director, of thinking how to launch upon Madame de Rochefide a little man, very self-willed and full of the worst qualities, who will certainly induce her to dismiss my son-in-law."

"My daughter," replied the abbe, stroking his chin, "we are not now in the confessional; I am not obliged to make myself your judge. From the world's point of view, I admit that the result would be decisive—"

"The means seem to me odious," she said.

"Why? No doubt the duty of a Christian woman is to withdraw a sinning woman from an evil path, rather than push her along it; but when a woman has advanced upon that path as far as Madame de Rochefide, it is not the hand of man, but that of God, which recalls such a sinner; she needs a thunderbolt."

"Father," replied the duchess, "I thank you for your indulgence; but the thought has occurred to me that my son-in-law is brave and a Breton. He was heroic at the time of the rash affair of that poor MADAME. Now, if the young fellow who undertook to make Madame de Rochefide love him were to quarrel with Calyste, and a duel should ensue—"

"You have thought wisely, Madame la duchesse; and it only proves that in crooked paths you will always find rocks of stumbling."

"I have discovered a means, my dear abbe, to do a great good; to withdraw Madame de Rochefide from the fatal path in which she now is; to restore Calyste to his wife, and possibly to save from hell a poor distracted creature."

"In that case, why consult me?" asked the vicar, smiling.

"Ah!" replied the duchess, "Because I must permit myself some rather nasty actions—"

"You don't mean to rob anybody?"

"On the contrary, I shall apparently have to spend a great deal of money."

"You will not calumniate, or—"

"Oh! oh!"

"—injure your neighbor?"

"I don't know about that."

"Come, tell me your plan," said the abbe, now becoming curious.

"Suppose, instead of driving out one nail by another,—this is what I thought at my *prie-Dieu* after imploring the Blessed Virgin to enlighten me,—I were to free Calyste by persuading Monsieur de Rochefide to take back his wife? Instead of lending a hand to evil for the sake of doing good to my daughter, I should do one great good by another almost as great—"

The vicar looked at the Portuguese lady, and was pensive.

"That is evidently an idea that came to you from afar," he said, "so far that—"

"I have thanked the Virgin for it," replied the good and humble duchess; "and I have made a vow—not counting a novena—to give twelve hundred francs to some poor family if I succeed. But when I communicated my plan to Monsieur de Grandlieu he began to laugh, and said: 'Upon my honor, at your time of life I think you women have a devil of your own.'"

"Monsieur le duc made as a husband the same reply I was about to make when you interrupted me," said the abbe, who could not restrain a smile.

"Ah! Father, if you approve of the idea, will you also approve of the means of execution? It is necessary to do to a certain Madame Schontz (a Beatrix of the quartier Saint-Georges) what I proposed to do to Madame de Rochefide."

"I am certain that you will not do any real wrong," said the vicar, cleverly, not wishing to hear any more, having found the result so desirable. "You can consult me later if you find your conscience muttering," he added. "But why, instead of giving that person in the rue Saint-Georges a fresh occasion for scandal, don't you give her a husband?"

"Ah! my dear director, now you have rectified the only bad thing I had in my plan. You are worthy of being an archbishop, and I hope I shall not die till I have had the opportunity of calling you Your Eminence."

"I see only one difficulty in all this," said the abbe.

"What is that?"

"Suppose Madame de Rochefide chooses to keep your son-in-law after she goes back to her husband?"

"That's my affair," replied the duchess; "when one doesn't often intrigue, one does so—"

"Badly, very badly," said the abbe. "Habit is necessary for everything. Try to employ some of those scamps who live by intrigue, and don't show your own hand."

"Ah! monsieur l'abbe, if I make use of the means of hell, will Heaven help me?"

"You are not at confession," repeated the abbe. "Save your child."

The worthy duchess, delighted with her vicar, accompanied him to the door of the salon.

CHAPTER XXII.

THE NORMAL HISTORY OF AN UPPER-CLASS GRI-SETTE

A storm was gathering, as we see, over Monsieur de Rochefide, who enjoyed at that moment the greatest amount of happiness that a Parisian can desire in being to Madame Schontz as much a husband as he had been to Beatrix. It seemed therefore, as the duke had very sensibly said to his wife, almost an impossibility to upset so agreeable and satisfactory an existence. This opinion will oblige us to give certain details on the life led by Monsieur de Rochefide after his wife had placed him in the position of a *deserted husband*. The reader will then be enabled to understand the enormous difference which our laws and our morals put between the two sexes in the same situation. That which turns to misery for the woman turns to happiness for the man. This contrast may inspire more than one young woman with the determination to remain in her own home, and to struggle there, like Sabine du Guenic, by practising (as she may select) the most aggressive or the most inoffensive virtues.

Some days after Beatrix had abandoned him, Arthur de Rochefide, now an only child in consequence of the death of his sister, the first wife of the Marquis d'Ajuda-Pinto, who left no children, found himself sole master of the hotel de Rochefide, rue d'Anjou Saint-Honore, and of two hundred thousand francs a year left to him by his father. This rich inheritance, added to the fortune which Arthur possessed when he married, brought his income, including that from the fortune of his wife, to a thousand francs a day. To a gentleman endowed with a nature such as Mademoiselle des Touches had described it in a few words to Calyste, such wealth was happiness enough. While his wife continued in her home and fulfilled the duties of maternity, Rochefide enjoyed this immense fortune; but he did not spend it any more than he expended the faculties of his mind. His good, stout vanity, gratified by the figure he presented as a handsome man (to which he owed a few successes that authorized him to despise women), allowed itself free scope in the matter of brains. Gifted with the sort of mind which we must call a reflector, he appropriated the sallies of others, the wit of the stage and the *petits journaux*, by his method of repeating them, and applied them as formulas of criticism. His military joviality (he had served in the Royal Guard) seasoned conversation with so much point that women without any intellects proclaimed him witty, and the rest did not dare to contradict them.

This system Arthur pursued in all things; he owed to nature the convenient genius of imitation without mimicry; he imitated seriously. Thus without any taste of his own, he knew how to be the first to adopt and the first to abandon a new fashion. Accused of nothing worse than spending too much time at his toilet and wearing a corset, he presented the type of those persons who displease no one by adopting incessantly the ideas and the follies of everbody, and who, astride of circumstance, never grow old.

As a husband, he was pitied; people thought Beatrix inexcusable for deserting the best fellow on earth, and social jeers only touched the woman. A member of all clubs, subscriber to all the absurdities generated by patriotism or party spirit ill-understood (a compliance which put him in the front rank *a propos* of all such matters), this loyal, brave, and very silly nobleman, whom unfortunately so many rich men resemble, would naturally desire to distinguish himself by adopting some fashionable mania. Consequently, he glorified his name principally in being the sultan of a four-footed harem, governed by an old English groom, which cost him monthly from four to five thousand francs. His specialty was *running horses;* he protected the equine race and supported a magazine devoted to hippic questions; but, for all that, he knew very little of the animals, and from shoes to bridles he depended wholly on his groom, — all of which will sufficiently explain to you that this semi-bachelor had nothing actually of his own, neither mind, taste, position, or absurdity; even his fortune came from his fathers. After having tasted the displeasures of marriage he was so content to find himself once more a bachelor that he said among his friends, "I was born with a caul" (that is, to good luck).

Pleased above all things to be able to live without the costs of making an appearance, to which husbands are constrained, his house, in which since the death of his father nothing had been changed, resembled those of masters who are travelling; he lived there little, never dined, and seldom slept there. Here follows the reason for such indifference.

After various amorous adventures, bored by women of fashion of the kind who are truly bores, and who plant too many thorny hedges around happiness, he had married after a fashion, as we shall see, a certain Madame Schontz, celebrated in the world of Fanny Beaupre, Susanne du Val-Noble, Florine, Mariette, Jenny Cadine, etc. This world, — of which one of our artists wittily remarked at the frantic moment of an opera *galop,* "When one thinks that all *that* is lodged and clothed and lives well, what a fine idea it gives us of mankind!" — this world has already irrupted elsewhere into this history of French manners and customs of the nineteenth century; but to paint it with fidelity, the historian should proportion the number of such personages to the diverse endings of their strange careers, which terminate either in poverty under its most hideous aspect, or by premature death often self-inflicted, or by lucky marriages, occasionally by opulence.

Madame Schontz, known at first under the name of La Petite-Aurelie, to distinguish her from one of her rivals far less clever than herself, belongs to the highest class of those women whose social utility cannot be questioned by the prefect of the Seine, nor by those who are interested in the welfare of the city of Paris. Certainly the Rat, accused of demolishing fortunes which frequently never existed, might better be compared to a beaver. Without the Aspasias of the Notre-Dame de

Lorette quarter, far fewer houses would be built in Paris. Pioneers in fresh stucco, they have gone, towed by speculation, along the heights of Montmartre, pitching their tents in those solitudes of carved free-stone, the like of which adorns the European streets of Amsterdam, Milan, Stockholm, London, and Moscow, architectural steppes where the wind rustles innumerable papers on which a void is divulged by the words, *Apartments to let*.

The situation of these dames is determined by that which they take in the apocryphal regions. If the house is near the line traced by the rue de Provence, the woman has an income, her budget prospers; but if she approaches the farther line of the Boulevard Exterieur or rises towards the horrid town of Batignolles, she is without resources. When Monsieur de Rochefide first encountered Madame Schontz, she lived on the third floor of the only house that remained in the rue de Berlin; thus she was camping on the border-land between misery and its reverse. This person was not really named, as you may suppose, either Schontz or Aurelie. She concealed the name of her father, an old soldier of the Empire, that perennial colonel who always appears at the dawn of all these feminine existences either as father or seducer. Madame Schontz had received the gratuitous education of Saint-Denis, where young girls are admirably brought up, but where, unfortunately, neither husbands nor openings in life are offered to them when they leave the school,—an admirable creation of the Emperor, which now lacks but one thing, the Emperor himself!

"I shall be there, to provide for the daughters of my faithful legions," he replied to a remark of one of his ministers, who foresaw the future.

Napoleon had also said, "I shall be there!" for the members of the Institute; to whom they had better give no salary than send them eighty francs each month, a wage that is less than that of certain clerks!

Aurelie was really the daughter of the intrepid Colonel Schiltz, a leader of those bold Alsacian guerillas who came near saving the Emperor in the campaign of France. He died at Metz,—robbed, pillaged, ruined. In 1814 Napoleon put the little Josephine Schiltz, then about nine years old, at Saint-Denis. Having lost both father and mother and being without a home and without resources, the poor child was not dismissed from the institution on the second return of the Bourbons. She was under-mistress of the school till 1827, but then her patience gave way; her beauty seduced her. When she reached her majority Josephine Schiltz, the Empress's goddaughter, was on the verge of the adventurous life of a courtesan, persuaded to that doubtful future by the fatal example of some of her comrades like herself without resources, who congratulated themselves on their decision. She substituted *on* for *il* in her father's name and placed herself under the patronage of Saint-Aurelie.

Lively, witty, and well-educated, she committed more faults than her duller companions, whose misdemeanors had invariably self-interest for their base. After knowing various writers, poor but dishonest, clever but deeply in debt; after trying certain rich men as calculating as they were foolish; and after sacrificing solid interests to one true love,—thus going through all the schools in which experience is taught, — on a certain day of extreme misery, when, at Valentino's (the first stage to Musard) she danced in a gown, hat, and mantle that were all borrowed, she attracted the attention of Arthur de Rochefide, who had come there to see the famous *galop*. Her cleverness instantly captivated the man who at that time knew not what passion to devote himself to. So that two years after his desertion by Beatrix, the memory of whom often humiliated him, the marquis was not blamed by any one for marrying, so to speak, in the thirteenth arrondissement, a substitute for his wife.

Let us sketch the four periods of this happiness. It is necessary to show that the theory of marriage in the thirteenth arrondissement affects in like manner all who come within its rule.[2] Marquis in the forties, sexagenary retired shopkeeper, quadruple millionnaire or moderate-income man, great seigneur or bourgeois, the strategy of passion (except for the differences inherent in social zones) never varies. The heart and the money-box are always in the same exact and clearly defined relation. Thus informed, you will be able to estimate the difficulties the duchess was certain to encounter in her charitable enterprise.

Who knows the power in France of witty sayings upon ordinary minds, or what harm the clever men who invent them have done? For instance, no book-keeper could add up the figures of the sums remaining unproductive and lost in the depths of generous hearts and strong-boxes by that ignoble phrase, *"tirer une carotte!"*

The saying has become so popular that it must be allowed to soil this page. Besides, if we penetrate within the 13th arrondissement, we are forced to accept its picturesque patois. *Tirer une carotte* has a dozen allied meanings, but it suffices to give it here as: *To dupe.* Monsieur de Rochefide, like all little minds, was terribly afraid of being *carotte*. The noun has become a verb. From the very start of his passion for Madame Schontz, Arthur was on his guard, and he was, therefore, very *rat*, to use another word of the same vocabulary. The word *rat*, when applied to a young girl, means the guest or the one entertained, but applied to a man it signifies the giver of the feast who is niggardly.

Madame Schontz had too much sense and she knew men too well not to conceive great hopes from such a beginning. Monsieur de Rochefide allowed her five hundred francs a month, furnished for her, rather shabbily, an apartment costing twelve hundred francs a year on a second floor in the rue Coquenard, and set himself to study Aurelie's character, while she, perceiving his object, gave him a character to study. Consequently, Rochefide became happy in meeting with a woman of noble nature. But he saw nothing surprising in that; her mother was a Barnheim of Baden, a well-bred woman. Besides, Aurelie was so well brought up herself! Speaking English, German, and Italian, she possessed a thorough knowledge of foreign literatures. She could hold her own against all second-class pianists. And, remark this! she behaved about her talents like a well-bred woman; she never mentioned them. She picked up a brush in a painter's studio, used it half jestingly, and produced a head which caused general astonishment. For mere amusement during the time she pined as under-mistress at Saint-Denis, she had

[2] Before 1859 there was no 13th arrondissement in Paris, hence the saying. — TR.

made some advance in the domain of the sciences, but her subsequent life had covered these good seeds with a coating of salt, and she now gave Arthur the credit of the sprouting of the precious germs, re-cultivated for him.

Thus Aurelie began by showing a disinterestedness equal to her other charms, which allowed this weak corvette to attach its grapnels securely to the larger vessel. Nevertheless, about the end of the first year, she made ignoble noises in the antechamber with her clogs, coming in about the time when the marquis was awaiting her, and hiding, as best she could, the draggled tail of an outrageously muddy gown. In short, she had by this time so perfectly persuaded her *gros papa* that all her ambition, after so many ups and downs, was to obtain honorably a comfortable little bourgeois existence, that, about ten months after their first meeting, the second phase of happiness declared itself.

Madame Schontz then obtained a fine apartment in the rue Neuve-Saint-Georges. Arthur, who could no longer conceal the amount of his fortune, gave her splendid furniture, a complete service of plate, twelve hundred francs a month, a low carriage with one horse,—this, however, was hired; but he granted a tiger very graciously. Madame Schontz was not the least grateful for this munificence; she knew the motive of her Arthur's conduct, and recognized the calculations of the male *rat*. Sick of living at a restaurant, where the fare is usually execrable, and where the least little *gourmet* dinner costs sixty francs for one, and two hundred francs if you invite three friends, Rochefide offered Madame Schontz forty francs a day for his dinner and that of a friend, everything included. Aurelie accepted.

Thus having made him take up all her moral letters of credit, drawn one by one on Monsieur de Rochefide's comfort, she was listened to with favor when she asked for five hundred francs more a month for her dress, in order not to shame her *gros papa*, whose friends all belonged to the Jockey Club.

"It would be a pretty thing," she said, "if Rastignac, Maxime de Trailles, d'Esgrignon, La Roche-Hugon, Ronqueroles, Laginski, Lenoncourt, found you with a sort of Madame Everard. Besides, have confidence in me, papa, and you'll be the gainer."

In fact, Aurelie contrived to display new virtues in this second phase. She laid out for herself a house-keeping role for which she claimed much credit. She made, so she said, both ends meet at the close of the month on two thousand five hundred francs without a debt,—a thing unheard of in the faubourg Saint-Germain of the 13th arrondissement,—and she served dinners infinitely superior to those of Nucingen, at which exquisite wines were drunk at twelve francs a bottle. Rochefide, amazed, and delighted to be able to invite his friends to the house with economy, declared, as he caught her round the waist,—

"She's a treasure!"

Soon after he hired one-third of a box at the Opera for her; next he took her to first representations. Then he began to consult his Aurelie, and recognized the excellence of her advice. She let him take the clever sayings she said about most things for his own, and, these being unknown to others, raised his reputation as an amusing man. He now acquired the certainty of being loved truly, and for himself alone. Aurelie refused to make the happiness of a Russian prince who offered her five thousand francs a month.

"You are a lucky man, my dear marquis," cried old Prince Galathionne as he finished his game of whist at the club. "Yesterday, after you left us alone, I tried to get Madame Schontz away from you, but she said: 'Prince, you are not handsomer, but you are a great deal older than Rochefide; you would beat me, but he is like a father to me; can you give me one-tenth of a reason why I should change? I've never had the grand passion for Arthur that I once had for little fools in varnished boots and whose debts I paid; but I love him as a wife loves her husband when she is an honest woman.' And thereupon she showed me the door."

This speech, which did not seem exaggerated, had the effect of greatly increasing the state of neglect and degradation which reigned in the hotel de Rochefide. Arthur now transported his whole existence and his pleasures to Madame Schontz, and found himself well off; for at the end of three years he had four hundred thousand francs to invest.

The third phase now began. Madame Schontz became the tenderest of mothers to Arthur's son; she fetched him from school and took him back herself; she overwhelmed with presents and dainties and pocket-money the child who called her his "little mamma," and who adored her. She took part in the management of Arthur's property; she made him buy into the Funds when low, just before the famous treaty of London which overturned the ministry of March 1st. Arthur gained two hundred thousand francs by that transaction and Aurelie did not ask for a penny of it. Like the gentleman that he was, Rochefide invested his six hundred thousand francs in stock of the Bank of France and put half of that sum in the name of Josephine Schiltz. A little house was now hired in the rue de La Bruyere and given to Grindot, that great decorative architect, with orders to make it a perfect bonbon-box.

Henceforth, Rochefide no longer managed his affairs. Madame Schontz received the revenues and paid the bills. Become, as it were, practically his wife, his woman of business, she justified the position by making her *gros papa* more comfortable than ever; she had learned all his fancies, and gratified them as Madame de Pompadour gratified those of Louis XV. In short, Madame Schontz reigned an absolute mistress. She then began to patronize a few young men, artists, men of letters, new-fledged to fame, who rejected both ancients and moderns, and strove to make themselves a great reputation by accomplishing little or nothing.

The conduct of Madame Schontz, a triumph of tactics, ought to reveal to you her superiority. In the first place, these ten or a dozen young fellows amused Arthur; they supplied him with witty sayings and clever opinions on all sorts of topics, and did not put in doubt the fidelity of the mistress; moreover, they proclaimed her a woman who was eminently intelligent. These living advertisements, these perambulating articles, soon set up Madame Schontz as the most agreeable woman to be found in the borderland which separates the thirteenth arrondissement from the twelve others. Her rivals — Suzanne Gaillard, who, in 1838, had won the advantage over her of becoming a wife married in legitimate marriage, Fanny

Beaupre, Mariette, Antonia—spread calumnies that were more than droll about the beauty of those young men and the complacent good-nature with which Monsieur de Rochefide welcomed them. Madame Schontz, who could distance, as she said, by three *blagues* the wit of those ladies, said to them one night at a supper given by Nathan to Florine, after recounting her fortune and her success, "Do as much yourselves!"—a speech which remained in their memory.

It was during this period that Madame Schontz made Arthur sell his race-horses, through a series of considerations which she no doubt derived from the critical mind of Claude Vignon, one of her *habitues*.

"I can conceive," she said one night, after lashing the horses for some time with her lively wit, "that princes and rich men should set their hearts on horse-flesh, but only for the good of the country, not for the paltry satisfactions of a betting man. If you had a stud farm on your property and could raise a thousand or twelve hundred horses, and if all the horses of France and of Navarre could enter into one great solemn competition, it would be fine; but you buy animals as the managers of theatres trade in artists; you degrade an institution to a gambling game; you make a Bourse of legs, as you make a Bourse of stocks. It is unworthy. Don't you spend sixty thousand francs sometimes merely to read in the newspapers: 'Lelia, belonging to Monsieur de Rochefide beat by a length Fleur-de-Genet the property of Monsieur le Duc de Rhetore'? You had much better give that money to poets, who would carry you in prose and verse to immortality, like the late Montyon."

By dint of being prodded, the marquis was brought to see the hollowness of the turf; he realized that economy of sixty thousand francs; and the next year Madame Schontz remarked to him,—

"I don't cost you anything now, Arthur."

Many rich men envied the marquis and endeavored to entice Madame Schontz away from him, but like the Russian prince they wasted their old age.

"Listen to me," she said to Finot, now become immensely rich. "I am certain that Rochefide would forgive me a little passion if I fell in love with any one, but one doesn't leave a marquis with a kind heart like that for a *parvenu* like you. You couldn't keep me in the position in which Arthur has placed me; he has made me half a wife and a lady, and that's more than you could do even if you married me."

This was the last nail which clinched the fetters of that happy galley-slave, for the speech of course reached the ears for which it was intended.

The fourth phase had begun, that of *habit*, the final victory in these plans of campaign, which make the women of this class say of a man, "I hold him!" Rochefide, who had just bought the little hotel in the name of Mademoiselle Josephine Schiltz (a trifle of eighty thousand francs), had reached, at the moment the Duchesse de Grandlieu was forming plans about him, the stage of deriving vanity from his mistress (whom he now called Ninon II.), by vaunting her scrupulous honesty, her excellent manners, her education, and her wit. He had merged his own defects, merits, tastes, and pleasures in Madame Schontz, and he found himself at this period of his life, either from lassitude, indifference, or philosophy, a man unable to change, who clings to wife or mistress.

We may understand the position won in five years by Madame Schontz from the fact that presentation at her house had to be proposed some time before it was granted. She refused to receive dull rich people and smirched people; and only departed from this rule in favor of certain great names of the aristocracy.

"They," she said, "have a right to be stupid because they are well-bred."

She possessed ostensibly the three hundred thousand francs which Rochefide had given her, and which a certain good fellow, a broker named Gobenheim (the only man of that class admitted to her house) invested and reinvested for her. But she manipulated for herself secretly a little fortune of two hundred thousand francs, the result of her savings for the last three years and of the constant movement of the three hundred thousand francs, — for she never admitted the possession of more than that known sum.

"The more you make, the less you get rich," said Gobenheim to her one day.

"Water is so dear," she answered.

This secret hoard was increased by jewels and diamonds, which Aurelie wore a month and then sold. When any one called her rich, Madame Schontz replied that at the rate of interest in the Funds three hundred thousand francs produced only twelve thousand, and she had spent as much as that in the hardest days of her life.

CHAPTER XXIII.

ONE OF THE DISEASES OF THE AGE

Such conduct implied a plan, and Madame Schontz had, as you may well believe, a plan. Jealous for the last two years of Madame du Bruel, she was consumed with the ambition to be married by church and mayor. All social positions have their forbidden fruit, some little thing magnified by desire until it has become the weightiest thing in life. This ambition of course involved a second Arthur; but no espial on the part of those about her had as yet discovered Rochefide's secret rival. Bixiou fancied he saw the favored one in Leon de Lora; the painter saw him in Bixiou, who had passed his fortieth year and ought to be making himself a fate of some kind. Suspicions were also turned on Victor de Vernisset, a poet of the school of Canalis, whose passion for Madame Schontz was desperate; but the poet accused Stidmann, a young sculptor, of being his fortune rival. This artist, a charming lad, worked for jewellers, for manufacturers in bronze and silver-smiths; he longed to be another Benvenuto Cellini. Claude Vignon, the young Comte de la Palferine, Gobenheim, Vermanton a cynical philosopher, all frequenters of this amusing salon, were severally suspected, and proved innocent. No one had fathomed Madame Schontz, certainly not Rochefide, who thought she had a penchant for the young and witty La Palferine; she was virtuous from self-interest and was wholly bent on making a good marriage.

Only one man of equivocal reputation was ever seen in Madame Schontz's salon, namely Couture, who had more than once made his brother speculators howl; but Couture had been one of Madame Schontz's earliest friends, and she alone remained faithful to him. The false alarm of 1840 swept away the last vestige of this stock-gambler's credit; Aurelie, seeing his run of ill-luck, made Rochefide play, as we have seen, in the other direction. Thankful to find a place for himself at Aurelie's table, Couture, to whom Finot, the cleverest or, if you choose, the luckiest of all parvenus, occasionally gave a note of a thousand francs, was alone wise and calculating enough to offer his hand and name to madame Schontz, who studied him to see if the bold speculator had sufficient power to make his way in politics and enough gratitude not to desert his wife. Couture, a man about forty-three years of age, half worn-out, did not redeem the unpleasant sonority of his name by birth; he said little of the authors of his days.

Madame Schontz was bemoaning to herself the rarity of eligible men, when Couture presented to her a provincial, supplied with the two handles by which women take hold of such pitchers when they wish to keep them. To sketch this person will be to paint a portion of the youth of the day. The digression is history.

In 1838, Fabien du Ronceret, son of a chief-justice of the Royal court at Caen (who had lately died), left his native town of Alencon, resigning his judgeship (a position in which his father had compelled him, he said, to waste his time), and came to Paris, with the intention of making a noise there,—a Norman idea, difficult to realize, for he could scarcely scrape together eight thousand francs a year; his mother still being alive and possessing a life-interest in a valuable estate in Alencon. This young man had already, during previous visits to Paris, tried his rope, like an acrobat, and had recognized the great vice of the social replastering of 1830. He meant to turn it to his own profit, following the example of the longest heads of the bourgeoisie. This requires a rapid glance on one of the effects of the new order of things.

Modern equality, unduly developed in our day, has necessarily developed in private life, on a line parallel with political life, the three great divisions of the social *I;* namely, pride, conceit, and vanity. Fools wish to pass for wits; wits want to be thought men of talent; men of talent wish to be treated as men of genius; as for men of genius, they are more reasonable; they consent to be only demigods. This tendency of the public mind of these days, which, in the Chamber, makes the manufacturer jealous of the statesman, and the administrator jealous of the writer, leads fools to disparage wits, wits to disparage men of talent, men of talent to disparage those who outstrip them by an inch or two, and the demigods to threaten institutions, the throne, or whatever does not adore them unconditionally. So soon as a nation has, in a very unstatesmanlike spirit, pulled down all recognized social superiorities, she opens the sluice through which rushes a torrent of secondary ambitions, the meanest of which resolves to lead. She had, so democrats declare, an evil in her aristocracy; but a defined and circumscribed evil; she exchanges it for a dozen armed and contending aristocracies—the worst of all situations. By proclaiming the equality of all, she has promulgated a declaration of the rights of Envy. We inherit to-day the saturnalias of the Revolution transferred to the domain, apparently peaceful, of the mind, of industry, of politics; it now seems that reputations won by toil, by services rendered, by talent, are privileges granted at the expense of the masses. Agrarian law will spread to the field of glory. Never, in any age, have men demanded the affixing of their names on the nation's posters for reasons more puerile. Distinction is sought at any price, by ridicule, by an affectation of interest in the cause of Poland, in penitentiaries, in the future of liberated galley-slaves, in all the little scoundrels above and below twelve years, and in every other social misery. These diverse manias create fictitious dignities, presidents, vice-presidents, and secretaries of societies, the number of which is greater than that of the social questions they seek to solve. Society on its grand scale has been demolished to make a million of little ones in the image of the defunct. These parasitic organizations reveal decomposition; are they not the swarming of maggots in the dead body? All these societies are the daughters of one mother, Vanity. It is not thus that Catholic charity or true beneficence proceeds; *they* study evils in wounds and cure them; they don't perorate in public meetings upon deadly ills for the pleasure of perorating.

Fabien du Ronceret, without being a superior man, had divined, by the exercise of that greedy common-sense peculiar to a Norman, the gain he could derive from this public vice. Every epoch has its character which clever men make use of. Fabien's mind, though not clever, was wholly bent on making himself talked about.

"My dear fellow, a man must make himself talked about, if he wants to be anything," he said, on parting from the king of Alencon, a certain du Bousquier, a friend of his father. "In six months I shall be better known than you are!"

It was thus that Fabien interpreted the spirit of his age; he did not rule it, he obeyed it. He made his debut in Bohemia, a region in the moral topography of Paris where he was known as "The Heir" by reason of certain premeditated prodigalities. Du Ronceret had profited by Couture's follies for the pretty Madame Cadine, for whom, during his ephemeral opulence, he had arranged a delightful ground-floor apartment with a garden in the rue Blanche. The Norman, who wanted his luxury ready-made, bought Couture's furniture and all the improvements he was forced to leave behind him, — a kiosk in the garden, where he smoked, a gallery in rustic wood, with India mattings and adorned with potteries, through which to reach the kiosk if it rained. When the Heir was complimented on his apartment, he called it his *den*. The provincial took care not to say that Grindot, the architect, had bestowed his best capacity upon it, as did Stidmann on the carvings, and Leon de Lora on the paintings, for Fabien's crowning defect was the vanity which condescends to lie for the sake of magnifying the individual self.

The Heir complimented these magnificences by a greenhouse which he built along a wall with a southern exposure, — not that he loved flowers, but he meant to attack through horticulture the public notice he wanted to excite. At the present moment he had all but attained his end. Elected vice-president of some sort of floral society presided over by the Duc de Vissembourg, brother of the Prince de Chiavari, youngest son of the late Marechal Vernon, he adorned his coat with the ribbon of the Legion of honor on the occasion of an exhibition of products, the opening speech at which, delivered by him, and bought of Lousteau for five hundred francs, was boldly pronounced to be his own brew. He also made himself talked about by a flower, given to him by old Blondet of Alencon, father of Emile Blondet, which he presented to the horticultural world as the product of his own greenhouse.

But this success was nothing. The Heir, who wished to be accepted as a wit, had formed a plan of consorting with clever celebrities and so reflecting their fame, — a plan somewhat hard to execute on a basis of an exchequer limited to eight thousand francs a year. With this end in view, Fabien du Ronceret had addressed himself again and again, without success, to Bixiou, Stidmann, and Leon de Lora, asking them to present him to Madame Schontz, and allow him to take part in that menagerie of lions of all kinds. Failing in those directions he applied to Couture, for whose dinners he had so often paid that the late speculator felt obliged to prove categorically to Madame Schontz that she ought to acquire such an original, if it was only to make him one of those elegant footmen without wages whom the mistresses of households employ to do errands, when servants are lacking.

In the course of three evenings Madame Schontz read Fabien like a book and said to herself,—

"If Couture does not suit me, I am certain of saddling that one. My future can go on two legs now."

This queer fellow whom everybody laughed at was really the chosen one,—chosen, however, with an intention which made such preference insulting. The choice escaped all public suspicion by its very improbability. Madame Schontz intoxicated Fabien with smiles given secretly, with little scenes played on the threshold when she bade him good-night, if Monsieur de Rochefide stayed behind. She often made Fabien a third with Arthur in her opera-box and at first representations; this she excused by saying he had done her such or such a service and she did not know how else to repay him. Men have a natural conceit as common to them as to women,—that of being loved exclusively. Now of all flattering passions there is none more prized than that of a Madame Schontz, for the man she makes the object of a love she calls "from the heart," in distinction from another sort of love. A woman like Madame Schontz, who plays the great lady, and whose intrinsic value is real, was sure to be an object of pride to Fabien, who fell in love with her to the point of never presenting himself before her eyes except in full dress, varnished boots, lemon-kid gloves, embroidered shirt and frill, waistcoat more or less variegated,—in short, with all the external symptoms of profound worship.

A month before the conference of the duchess and her confessor, Madame Schontz had confided the secret of her birth and her real name to Fabien, who did not in the least understand the motive of the confidence. A fortnight later, Madame Schontz, surprised at this want of intelligence, suddenly exclaimed to herself:—

"Heavens! how stupid I am! he expects me to love him for himself."

Accordingly the next day she took the Heir in her *caleche* to the Bois, for she now had two little carriages, drawn by two horses. In the course of this public *tete-a-tete* she opened the question of her future, and declared that she wished to marry.

"I have seven hundred thousand francs," she said, "and I admit to you that if I could find a man full of ambition, who knew how to understand my character, I would change my position; for do you know what is the dream of my life? To become a true bourgeoise, enter an honorable family, and make my husband and children truly happy."

The Norman would fain be "distinguished" by Madame Schontz, but as for marrying her, that folly seemed debatable to a bachelor of thirty-eight whom the revolution of July had made a judge. Seeing his hesitation, Madame Schontz made the Heir the butt of her wit, her jests, and her disdain, and turned to Couture. Within a week, the latter, whom she put upon the scent of her fortune, had offered his hand, and heart, and future,—three things of about the same value.

The manoeuvres of Madame Schontz had reached this stage of proceeding, when Madame de Grandlieu began her inquiries into the life and habits of the Beatrix of the Place Saint-Georges.

CHAPTER XXIV.

THE INFLUENCE OF SOCIAL RELATIONS AND PO-SITION

In accordance with the advice of the Abbe Brossette the Duchesse de Grandlieu asked the Marquis d'Ajuda to bring her that king of political cut-throats, the celebrated Comte Maxime de Trailles, archduke of Bohemia, the youngest of young men, though he was now fully fifty years of age. Monsieur d'Ajuda arranged to dine with Maxime at the club in the rue de Beuane, and proposed to him after dinner to go and play dummy whist with the Duc de Grandlieu, who had an attack of gout and was all alone.

Though the son-in-law of the duke and the cousin of the duchess had every right to present him in a salon where he had never yet set foot, Maxime de Trailles did not deceive himself as to the meaning of an invitation thus given. He felt certain that the duke or the duchess had some need of him. Club life where men play cards with other men whom they do not receive in their own houses is by no means one of the most trifling signs of the present age.

The Duc de Grandlieu did Maxime the honor of appearing to suffer from his gout. After several games of whist he went to bed, leaving his wife *tete-a-tete* with Maxime and d'Ajuda. The duchess, seconded by the marquis, communicated her project to Monsieur de Trailles, and asked his assistance, while ostensibly asking only for his advice. Maxime listened to the end without committing himself, and waited till the duchess should ask point-blank for his co-operation before replying.

"Madame, I fully understand you," he then said, casting on her and the marquis one of those shrewd, penetrating, astute, comprehensive glances by which such great scamps compromise their interlocutors. "D'Ajuda will tell you that if any one in Paris can conduct that difficult negotiation, it is I,—of course without mixing you up in it; without its being even known that I have come here this evening. Only, before anything is done, we must settle preliminaries. How much are you willing to sacrifice?"

"All that is necessary."

"Very well, then, Madame la duchesse. As the price of my efforts you must do me the honor to receive in your house and seriously protect Madame la Comtesse de Trailles."

"What! are you married?" cried d'Ajuda.

"I shall be married within a fortnight to the heiress of a rich but extremely bourgeois family,—a sacrifice to opinion! I imbibe the very spirit of my government, and start upon a new career. Consequently, Madame la duchesse will understand how important it is to me to have my wife adopted by her and by her family. I am certain of being made deputy by the resignation of my father-in-law, and I am promised a diplomatic post in keeping with my new fortune. I do not see why my wife should not be as well received as Madame de Portenduere in that society of young women which includes Mesdames de la Bastie, Georges de Maufrigneuse, de L'Estorade, du Guenic, d'Ajuda, de Restaud, de Rastignac, de Vandenesse. My wife is pretty, and I will undertake to *un-cotton-night-cap* her. Will this suit you, Madame la duchesse? You are religious, and if you say yes, your promise, which I know to be sacred, will greatly aid in my change of life. It will be one more good action to your account. Alas! I have long been the king of *mauvais sujets*, and I want to make an end of it. After all, we bear, azure, a wivern or, darting fire, ongle gules, and scaled vert, a chief ermine, from the time of Francois I., who thought proper to ennoble the valet of Louis XI., and we have been counts since Catherine de' Medici."

"I will receive and protect your wife," said the duchess, solemnly, "and my family will not turn its back upon her; I give you my word."

"Ah! Madame la duchesse," cried Maxime, visibly touched, "if Monsieur le duc would also deign to treat me with some kindness, I promise you to make your plan succeed without its costing you very much. But," he continued after a pause, "you must take upon yourself to follow my instructions. This is the last intrigue of my bachelor life; it must be all the better managed because it concerns a good action," he added, smiling.

"Follow your instructions!" said the duchess. "Then I must appear in all this."

"Ah! madame, I will not compromise you," cried Maxime. "I esteem you too much to demand guarantees. I merely mean that you must follow my advice. For example, it will be necessary that du Guenic be taken away by his wife for at least two years; she must show him Switzerland, Italy, Germany,—in short, all possible countries."

"Ah! you confirm a fear of my director," said the duchess, naively, remembering the judicious objection of the Abbe Brossette.

Maxime and d'Ajuda could not refrain from smiling at the idea of this agreement between heaven and hell.

"To prevent Madame de Rochefide from ever seeing Calyste again," she continued, "we will all travel, Juste and his wife, Calyste, Sabine, and I. I will leave Clotilde with her father—"

"It is too soon to sing victory, madame," said Maxime. "I foresee enormous difficulties; though I shall no doubt vanquish them. Your esteem and your protection are rewards which would make me commit the vilest actions, but these will be—"

"The vilest actions!" cried the duchess, interrupting this modern condottiere, and showing on her countenance as much disgust as amazement.

"And you would share them, madame, inasmuch as I am only your agent. But are you ignorant of the degree of blindness to which Madame de Rochefide has brought your son-in-law? I know it from Canalis and Nathan, between whom she was hesitating when Calyste threw himself into the lioness's jaws. Beatrix has contrived to persuade that serious Breton that she has never loved any one but him; that she is virtuous; that Conti was merely a sentimental head-love in which neither the heart nor the rest of it had any part,—a musical love, in short! As for Rochefide, that was duty. So, you understand, she is virgin!—a fact she proves by forgetting her son, whom for more than a year she has not made the slightest attempt to see. The truth is, the little count will soon be twelve years old, and he finds in Madame Schontz a mother who is all the more a mother because maternity is, as you know, a passion with women of that sort. Du Guenic would let himself be cut in pieces, and would chop up his wife for Beatrix; and you think it is an easy matter to drag a man from the depths of such credulity! Ah! madame, Shakespeare's Iago would lose all his handkerchiefs. People think that Othello, or his younger brother, Orosmanes, or Saint-Preux, Rene, Werther, and other lovers now in possession of fame, represented love! Never did their frosty-hearted fathers know what absolute love is; Moliere alone conceived it. Love, Madame la duchesse, is not loving a noble woman, a Clarissa—a great effort, faith! Love is to say to one's self: 'She whom I love is infamous; she deceives me, she will deceive me; she is an abandoned creature, she smells of the frying of hell-fire;' but we rush to her, we find there the blue of heaven, the flowers of Paradise. That is how Moliere loved, and how we, scamps that we are! how we love. As for me, I weep at the great scene of Arnolphe. Now, that is how your son-in-law loves Beatrix. I shall have trouble separating Rochefide from Madame Schontz; but Madame Schontz will no doubt lend herself to the plot; I shall study her interior. But as for Calyste and Beatrix, they will need the blows of an axe, far deeper treachery, and so base an infamy that your virtuous imagination could never descend to it—unless indeed your director gave you a hand. You have asked the impossible, you shall be obeyed. But in spite of my settled intention to war with fire and sword, I cannot absolutely promise you success. I have known lovers who did not recoil before the most awful disillusions. You are too virtuous to know the full power of women who are not virtuous."

"Do not enter upon those infamous actions until I have consulted the Abbe Brossette to know how far I may be your accomplice," cried the duchess, with a naivete which disclosed what selfishness there is in piety.

"You shall be ignorant of everything, my dear mother," interposed d'Ajuda.

On the portico, while the carriage of the marquis was drawing up, d'Ajuda said to Maxime:—

"You frightened that good duchess."

"But she has no idea of the difficulty of what she asks. Let us go to the Jockey Club; Rochefide must invite me to dine with Madame Schontz to-morrow, for to-night my plan will be made, and I shall have chosen the pawns on my chess-board to carry it out. In the days of her splendor Beatrix refused to receive me; I intend to pay off that score, and I will avenge your sister-in-law so cruelly that perhaps she will find herself too well revenged."

The next day Rochefide told Madame Schontz that Maxime de Trailles was coming to dinner. That meant notifying her to display all her luxury, and prepare the choicest food for this connoisseur emeritus, whom all the women of the Madame Schontz type were in awe of. Madame Schontz herself thought as much of her toilet as of putting her house in a state to receive this personage.

In Paris there are as many royalties as there are varieties of art, mental and moral specialties, sciences, professions; the strongest and most capable of the men who practise them has a majesty which is all his own; he is appreciated, respected by his peers, who know the difficulties of his art or profession, and whose admiration is given to the man who surmounts them. Maxime was, in the eyes of *rats* and courtesans, an extremely powerful and capable man, who had known how to make himself excessively loved. He was also admired by men who knew how difficult it is to live in Paris on good terms with creditors; in short, he had never had any other rival in elegance, deportment, and wit than the illustrious de Marsay, who frequently employed him on political missions. All this will suffice to explain his interview with the duchess, his prestige with Madame Schontz, and the authority of his words in a conference which he intended to have on the boulevard des Italiens with a young man already well-known, though lately arrived, in the Bohemia of Paris.

CHAPTER XXV.
A PRINCE OF BOHEMIA

The next day, when Maxime de Trailles rose, Finot (whom he had summoned the night before) was announced. Maxime requested his visitor to arrange, as if by accident, a breakfast at the cafe Anglais, where Finot, Couture, and Lousteau should gossip beside him. Finot, whose position toward the Comte de Trailles was that of a sub-lieutenant before a marshall of France, could refuse him nothing; it was altogether too dangerous to annoy that lion. Consequently, when Maxime came to the breakfast, he found Finot and his two friends at table and the conversation already started on Madame Schontz, about whom Couture, well manoeuvred by Finot and Lousteau (Lousteau being, though not aware of it, Finot's tool), revealed to the Comte de Trailles all that he wanted to know about her.

About one o'clock, Maxime was chewing a toothpick and talking with du Tillet on Tortoni's portico, where speculation held a little Bourse, a sort of prelude to the great one. He seemed to be engaged in business, but he was really awaiting the Comte de la Palferine, who, within a given time, was certain to pass that way. The boulevard des Italiens is to-day what the Pont Neuf was in 1650; all persons known to fame pass along it once, at least, in the course of the day. Accordingly, at the end of about ten minutes, Maxime dropped du Tillet's arm, and nodding to the young Prince of Bohemia said, smiling: —

"One word with you, count."

The two rivals in their own principality, the one orb on its decline, the other like the rising sun, sat down upon four chairs before the Cafe de Paris. Maxime took care to place a certain distance between himself and some old fellows who habitually sunned themselves like wall-fruit at that hour in the afternoon, to dry out their rheumatic affections. He had excellent reasons for distrusting old men.

"Have you debts?" said Maxime, to the young count.

"If I had none, should I be worthy of being your successor?" replied La Palferine.

"In putting that question to you I don't place the matter in doubt; I only want to know if the total is reasonable; if it goes to the five or the six?"

"Six what?"

"Figures; whether you owe fifty or one hundred thousand? I have owed, myself, as much as six hundred thousand."

La Palferine raised his hat with an air as respectful as it was humorous.

"If I had sufficient credit to borrow a hundred thousand francs," he replied, "I should forget my creditors and go and pass my life in Venice, amid masterpieces of painting and pretty women and—"

"And at my age what would you be?" asked Maxime.

"I should never reach it," replied the young count.

Maxime returned the civility of his rival, and touched his hat lightly with an air of laughable gravity.

"That's one way of looking at life," he replied in the tone of one connoisseur to another. "You owe—?"

"Oh! a mere trifle, unworthy of being confessed to an uncle; he would disinherit me for such a paltry sum,—six thousand."

"One is often more hampered by six thousand than by a hundred thousand," said Maxime, sententiously. "La Palferine, you've a bold spirit, and you have even more spirit than boldness; you can go far, and make yourself a position. Let me tell you that of all those who have rushed into the career at the close of which I now am, and who have tried to oppose me, you are the only one who has ever pleased me."

La Palferine colored, so flattered was he by this avowal made with gracious good-humor by the leader of Parisian adventurers. This action of his own vanity was however a recognition of inferiority which wounded him; but Maxime divined that unpleasant reaction, easy to foresee in so clever a mind, and he applied a balm instantly by putting himself at the discretion of the young man.

"Will you do something for me that will facilitate my retreat from the Olympic circus by a fine marriage? I will do as much for you."

"You make me very proud; it realizes the fable of the Rat and the Lion," said La Palferine.

"I shall begin by lending you twenty thousand francs," continued Maxime.

"Twenty thousand francs! I knew very well that by dint of walking up and down this boulevard—" said La Palferine, in the style of a parenthesis.

"My dear fellow, you must put yourself on a certain footing," said Maxime, laughing. "Don't go on your own two feet, have six; do as I do, I never get out of my tilbury."

"But you must be going to ask me for something beyond my powers."

"No, it is only to make a woman love you within a fortnight."

"Is it a lorette?"

"Why?"

"Because that's impossible; but if it concerns a woman, and a well-bred one who is also clever—"

"She is a very illustrious marquise."

"You want her letters?" said the young count.

"Ah! you are after my own heart!" cried Maxime. "No, that's not it."

"Then you want me to love her?"

"Yes, in the real sense—"

"If I am to abandon the aesthetic, it is utterly impossible," said La Palferine. "I have, don't you see, as to women a certain honor; we may play the fool with them, but not—"

"Ah! I was not mistaken!" cried Maxime. "Do you think I'm a man to propose mere twopenny infamies to you? No, you must go, and dazzle, and conquer. My good mate, I give you twenty thousand francs, and ten days in which to triumph. Meet me to-night at Madame Schontz'."

"I dine there."

"Very good," returned Maxime. "Later, when you have need of me, Monsieur le comte, you will find me," he added in the tone of a king who binds himself, but promises nothing.

"This poor woman must have done you some deadly harm," said La Palferine.

"Don't try to throw a plummet-line into my waters, my boy; and let me tell you that in case of success you will obtain such powerful influence that you will be able, like me, to retire upon a fine marriage when you are bored with your bohemian life."

"Comes there a time when it is a bore to amuse one's self," said La Palferine, "to be nothing, to live like the birds, to hunt the fields of Paris like a savage, and laugh at everything?"

"All things weary, even hell," said de Trailles, laughing. "Well, this evening."

The two *roues*, the old and the young, rose. As Maxime got into his one-horse equipage, he thought to himself: "Madame d'Espard can't endure Beatrix; she will help me. Hotel de Grandlieu," he called out to the coachman, observing that Rastignac was just passing him.

Find a great man without some weakness!

The duchess, Madame du Guenic, and Clotilde were evidently weeping.

"What is the matter?" he asked the duchess.

"Calyste did not come home; this is the first time; my poor daughter is in despair."

"Madame la duchesse," said Maxime, drawing the pious lady into the embrasure of a window, "for Heaven's sake keep the utmost secrecy as to my efforts, and ask d'Ajuda to do the same; for if Calyste ever hears of our plot there will be a duel between him and me to the death. When I told you that the affair would not cost much, I meant that you would not be obliged to spend enormous sums; but I do want twenty thousand francs; the rest is my affair; there may be important places to be given, a receiver-generalship possibly."

The duchess and Maxime left the room. When Madame de Grandlieu returned to her daughter, she again listened to Sabine's dithyrambics inlaid with family facts even more cruel than those which had already crushed the young wife's happiness.

"Don't be so troubled, my darling," said the duchess. "Beatrix will pay dear for your tears and sufferings; the hand of Satan is upon her; she will meet with ten humiliations for every one she has inflicted upon you."

Madame Schontz had invited Claude Vignon, who, on several occasions, had expressed a wish to know Maxime de Trailles personally. She also invited Couture, Fabien, Bixiou, Leon de Lora, La Palferine, and Nathan. The latter was asked by Rochefide on account of Maxime. Aurelie thus expected nine guests, all men of the first ability, with the exception of du Ronceret; but the Norman vanity and the brutal ambition of the Heir were fully on a par with Claude Vignon's literary power, Nathan's poetic gift, La Palferine's *finesse*, Couture's financial eye, Bixiou's wit, Finot's shrewdness, Maxime's profound diplomacy, and Leon de Lora's genius.

Madame Schontz, anxious to appear both young and beautiful, armed herself with a toilet which that sort of woman has the art of making. She wore a guipure pelerine of spidery texture, a gown of blue velvet, the graceful corsage of which was buttoned with opals, and her hair in bands as smooth and shining as ebony. Madame Schontz owed her celebrity as a pretty woman to the brilliancy and freshness of a complexion as white and warm as that of Creoles, to a face full of spirited details, the features of which were clearly and firmly drawn, —a type long presented in perennial youth by the Comtesse Merlin, and which is perhaps peculiar to Southern races. Unhappily, little Madame Schontz had tended towards ebonpoint ever since her life had become so happy and calm. Her neck, of exquisite roundness, was beginning to take on flesh about the shoulders; but in France the heads of women are principally treasured; so that fine heads will often keep an ill-formed body unobserved.

"My dear child," said Maxime, coming in and kissing Madame Schontz on the forehead, "Rochefide wanted me to see your establishment; why, it is almost in keeping with his four hundred thousand francs a year. Well, well, he would never have had them if he hadn't known you. In less than five years you have made him save what others—Antonia, Malaga, Cadine, or Florentine—would have made him lose."

"I am not a lorette, I am an artist," said Madame Schontz, with a sort of dignity, "I hope to end, as they say on the stage, as the progenitrix of honest men."

"It is dreadful, but we are all marrying," returned Maxime, throwing himself into an arm-chair beside the fire. "Here am I, on the point of making a Comtesse Maxime."

"Oh, how I should like to see her!" exclaimed Madame Schontz. "But permit me to present to you Monsieur Claude Vignon—Monsieur Claude Vignon, Monsieur de Trailles."

"Ah, so you are the man who allowed Camille Maupin, the innkeeper of literature, to go into a convent?" cried Maxime. "After you, God. I never received such an honor. Mademoiselle des Touches treated you, monsieur, as though you were Louis XIV."

"That is how history is written!" replied Claude Vignon. "Don't you know that her fortune was used to free the Baron du Guenic's estates? Ah! if she only knew that Calyste now belongs to her ex-friend," (Maxime pushed the critic's foot, motioning to Rochefide), "she would issue from her convent, I do believe, to tear him from her."

"Upon my word, Rochefide, if I were you," said Maxime, finding that his warning did not stop Vignon, "I should give back my wife's fortune, so that the world couldn't say she attached herself to Calyste from necessity."

"Maxime is right," remarked Madame Schontz, looking at Arthur, who colored high. "If I have helped you to gain several thousand francs a year, you couldn't better employ them. I shall have made the happiness of husband *and* wife; what a feather in my cap!"

"I never thought of it," replied the marquis; "but a man should be a gentleman before he's a husband."

"Let me tell you when is the time to be generous," said Maxime.

"Arthur," said Aurelie, "Maxime is right. Don't you see, old fellow, that generous actions are like Couture's investments?—you should make them in the nick of time."

At that moment Couture, followed by Finot, came in; and, soon after, all the guests were assembled in the beautiful blue and gold salon of the hotel Schontz, a title which the various artists had given to their inn after Rochefide purchased it for his Ninon II. When Maxime saw La Palferine, the last to arrive, enter, he walked up to his lieutenant, and taking him aside into the recess of a window, gave him notes for twenty thousand francs.

"Remember, my boy, you needn't economize them," he said, with the particular grace of a true scamp.

"There's none but you who can double the value of what you seem to give," replied La Palferine.

"Have you decided?"

"Surely, inasmuch as I take the money," said the count, with a mixture of haughtiness and jest.

"Well, then, Nathan, who is here to-night, will present you two days hence at the house of Madame la Marquise de Rochefide."

La Palferine started when he heard the name.

"You are to be madly in love with her, and, not to rouse suspicion, drink heavily, wines, liqueurs! I'll tell Aurelie to place you beside Nathan at dinner. One thing more, my boy: you and I must meet every night, on the boulevard de la Madeleine at one in the morning,—you to give me an account of progress, I to give you in-structions."

"I shall be there, my master," said the young count, bowing.

"Why do you make us dine with that queer fellow dressed like the head-wait-er of a restaurant?" whispered Maxime to Madame Schontz, with a sign toward Fabien du Ronceret.

"Have you never met the Heir? Du Ronceret of Alencon."

"Monsieur," said Maxime to Fabien, "I think you must know my friend d'Es-grignon?"

"Victurnien has ceased to know me for some time," replied Fabien, "but we used to be very intimate in our youth."

The dinner was one of those which are given nowhere but in Paris by these great female spendthrifts, for the choiceness of their preparations often surprise the most fastidious of guests. It was at just such a supper, at the house of a cour-tesan as handsome and rich as Madame Schontz, that Paganini declared he had never eaten such fare at the table of any sovereign, nor drunk such wines with any prince, nor heard such witty conversation, nor seen the glitter of such coquettish luxury.

Maxime and Madame Schontz were the first to re-enter the salon, about ten o'clock, leaving the other guests, who had ceased to tell anecdotes and were now boasting of their various good qualities, with their viscous lips glued to the glasses which they could not drain.

"Well, my dear," said Maxime, "you are not mistaken; yes, I have come for your *beaux yeux* and for help in a great affair. You must leave Arthur; but I pledge myself to make him give you two hundred thousand francs."

"Why should I leave the poor fellow?"

"To marry that idiot, who seems to have been sent from Alencon expressly for the purpose. He has been a judge, and I'll have him made chief-justice in place of Emile Blondet's father, who is getting to be eighty years old. Now, if you know how to sail your boat, your husband can be elected deputy. You will both be per-sonages, and you can then look down on Madame la Comtesse du Bruel."

"Never!" said Madame Schontz; "she's a countess."

"Hasn't he condition enough to be made a count?"

"By the bye, he bears arms," cried Aurelie, hunting for a letter in an elegant bag hanging at the corner of the fireplace, and giving it to Maxime. "What do they mean? Here are combs."

"He bears: per fesse argent and azure; on the first, three combs gules, two and one, crossed by three bunches grapes purpure, leaved vert, one and two; on the second, four feathers or, placed fretwise, with *Servir* for motto, and a squire's hel-met. It is not much; it seems they were ennobled under Louis XIV.; some mercer was doubtless their grandfather, and the maternal line must have made its money in wines; the du Ronceret whom the king ennobled was probably an usher. But if you get rid of Arthur and marry du Ronceret, I promise you he shall be a baron at the very least. But you see, my dear, you'll have to soak yourself for five or six years in the provinces if you want to bury La Schontz in a baroness. That queer creature has been casting looks at you, the meaning of which is perfectly clear. You've got him."

"No," replied Aurelie, "when my hand was offered to him he remained, like the brandies I read of to-day in the market reports, *dull*."

"I will undertake to decide him—if he is drunk. Go and see where they all are."

"It is not worth while to go; I hear no one but Bixiou, who is making jokes to which nobody listens. But I know my Arthur; he feels bound to be polite, and he is probably looking at Bixiou with his eyes shut."

"Let us go back, then."

"*Ah ca!*" said Madame Schontz, suddenly stopping short, "in whose interest shall I be working?"

"In that of Madame de Rochefide," replied Maxime, promptly. "It is impossible to reconcile her with Rochefide as long as you hold him. Her object is to recover her place as head of his household and the enjoyment of four hundred thousand francs a year."

"And she offers me only two hundred thousand! I want three hundred thousand, since the affair concerns her. What! haven't I taken care of her brat and her husband? I have filled her place in every way—and does she think to bargain with me? With that, my dear Maxime, I shall have a million; and if you'll promise me the chief-justiceship at Alencon, I can hold my own as Madame du Ronceret."

"That's settled," said Maxime.

"Oh! won't it be dull to live in that little town!" cried Aurelie, philosophically. "I have heard so much of that province from d'Esgrignon and the Val-Noble that I seem to have lived there already."

"Suppose I promise you the support of the nobility?"

"Ah! Maxime, you don't mean that?—but the pigeon won't fly."

"And he is very ugly with his purple skin and bristles for whiskers; he looks like a wild boar with the eyes of a bird of prey. But he'll make the finest chief-justice of a provincial court. Now don't be uneasy! in ten minutes he shall be singing to you Isabelle's air in the fourth act of Robert le Diable: 'At thy feet I kneel'—you promise, don't you? to send Arthur back to Beatrix?"

"It will be difficult; but perseverance wins."

About half-past ten o'clock the guests returned to the salon for coffee. Under the circumstances in which Madame Schontz, Couture, and du Ronceret were placed, it is easy to imagine the effect produced upon the Heir by the following conversation which Maxime held with Couture in a corner and in a low voice, but so placed that Fabien could listen to them.

"My dear Couture, if you want to lead a steady life you had better accept a receiver-generalship which Madame de Rochefide will obtain for you. Aurelie's million will furnish the security, and you'll share the property in marrying her. You can be made deputy, if you know how to trim your sails; and the premium I want for thus saving you is your vote in the chamber."

"I shall always be proud to be a follower of yours."

"Ah! my dear fellow, you have had quite an escape. Just imagine! Aurelie took a fancy for that Norman from Alencon; she asked to have him made a baron, and chief-justice in his native town, and officer of the Legion of honor! The fool never guessed her value, and you will owe your fortune to her disappointment. You had better not leave that clever creature time for reflection. As for me, I am already putting the irons in the fire."

And Maxime left Couture at the summit of happiness, saying to La Palferine, "Shall I drive you home, my boy?"

By eleven o'clock Aurelie was alone with Couture, Fabien, and Rochefide. Arthur was asleep on a sofa. Couture and Fabien each tried to outstay the other, without success; and Madame Schontz finally terminated the struggle by saying to Couture,—

"Good-night, I shall see you to-morrow."

A dismissal which he took in good part.

"Mademoiselle," said Fabien, in a low voice, "because you saw me thoughtful at the offer which you indirectly made to me, do not think there was the slightest hesitation on my part. But you do not know my mother; she would never consent to my happiness."

"You have reached an age for respectful summons," retorted Aurelie, insolently. "But if you are afraid of mamma you won't do for me."

"Josephine!" said the Heir, tenderly, passing his arm audaciously round Madame Schontz' waist, "I thought you loved me!"

"Well?"

"Perhaps I could appease my mother, and obtain her consent."

"How?"

"If you would employ your influence—"

"To have you made baron, officer of the Legion of honor, and chief-justice at Alencon,—is that it, my friend? Listen to me: I have done so many things in my life that I am capable of virtue. I can be an honest woman and a loyal wife; and I can push my husband very high. But I wish to be loved by him without one look or one thought being turned away from me. Does that suit you? Don't bind yourself imprudently; it concerns your whole life, my little man."

"With a woman like you I can do it blind," cried Fabien, intoxicated by the glance she gave him as much as by the liqueurs des Iles.

"You shall never repent that word, my dear; you shall be peer of France. As for that poor old fellow," she continued, looking at Rochefide, who was sound asleep, "after to-day I have d-o-n-e with him."

Fabien caught Madame Schontz around the waist and kissed her with an impulse of fury and joy, in which the double intoxication of wine and love was secondary to ambition.

"Remember, my dear child," she said, "the respect you ought to show to your wife; don't play the lover; leave me free to retire from my mud-hole in a proper manner. Poor Couture, who thought himself sure of wealth and a receiver-generalship!"

"I have a horror of that man," said Fabien; "I wish I might never see him again."

"I will not receive him any more," replied Madame Schontz, with a prudish little air. "Now that we have come to an understanding, my Fabien, you must go; it is one o'clock."

This little scene gave birth in the household of Arthur and Aurelie (so completely happy until now) to a phase of domestic warfare produced in the bosom of all homes by some secret and alien interest in one of the partners. The next day when Arthur awoke he found Madame Schontz as frigid as that class of woman knows how to make herself.

"What happened last night?" he said, as he breakfasted, looking at Aurelie.

"What often happens in Paris," she replied, "one goes to bed in damp weather and the next morning the pavements are dry and frozen so hard that they are dusty. Do you want a brush?"

"What's the matter with you, dearest?"

"Go and find your great scarecrow of a wife!"

"My wife!" exclaimed the poor marquis.

"Don't I know why you brought Maxime here? You mean to make up with Madame de Rochefide, who wants you perhaps for some indiscreet brat. And I, whom you call so clever, I advised you to give back her fortune! Oh! I see your scheme. At the end of five years Monsieur is tired of me. I'm getting fat, Beatrix is all bones—it will be a change for you! You are not the first I've known to like skeletons. Your Beatrix knows how to dress herself, that's true; and you are man who likes figure-heads. Besides, you want to send Monsieur du Guenic to the right-about. It will be a triumph! You'll cut quite an appearance in the world! How people will talk of it! Why! you'll be a hero!"

Madame Schontz did not make an end of her sarcasms for two hours after mid-day, in spite of Arthur's protestations. She then said she was invited out to dinner, and advised her "faithless one" to go without her to the Opera, for she herself was going to the Ambigu-Comique to meet Madame de la Baudraye, a charming woman, a friend of Lousteau. Arthur proposed, as proof of his eternal attachment to his little Aurelie and his detestation of his wife, to start the next day for Italy, and live as a married couple in Rome, Naples, Florence,—in short, wherever she liked, offering her a gift of sixty thousand francs.

"All that is nonsense," she said. "It won't prevent you from making up with your wife, and you'll do a wise thing."

Arthur and Aurelie parted on this formidable dialogue, he to play cards and dine at the club, she to dress and spend the evening *tete-a-tete* with Fabien.

Monsieur de Rochefide found Maxime at the club, and complained to him like a man who feels that his happiness is being torn from his heart by the roots, every fibre of which clung to it. Maxime listened to his moans, as persons of social politeness are accustomed to listen, while thinking of other things.

"I'm a man of good counsel in such matters, my dear fellow," he answered. "Well, let me tell you, you are on the wrong road in letting Aurelie see how dear she is to you. Allow me to present you to Madame Antonia. There's a heart to let. You'll soon see La Schontz with other eyes. She is thirty-seven years old, that Schontz of yours, and Madame Antonia is only twenty-six! And what a woman! I may say she is my pupil. If Madame Schontz persists in keeping on the hind heels of her pride, don't you know what that means?"

"Faith, no!"

"That she wants to marry, and if that's the case, nothing can hinder her from leaving you. After a lease of six years a woman has a right to do so. Now, if you will only listen to me, you can do a better thing for yourself. Your wife is to-day worth more than all the Schontzes and Antonias of the quartier Saint-Georges. I admit the conquest is difficult, but it is not impossible; and after all that has happened she will make you as happy as an Orgon. In any case, you mustn't look like a fool; come and sup to-night with Antonia."

"No, I love Aurelie too well; I won't give her any reason to complain of me."

"Ah! my dear fellow, what a future you are preparing for yourself!" cried Maxime.

"It is eleven o'clock; she must have returned from the Ambigu," said Rochefide, leaving the club.

And he called out his coachman to drive at top speed to the rue de la Bruyere.

Madame Schontz had given precise directions; monsieur could enter as master with the fullest understanding of madame; but, warned by the noise of monsieur's arrival, madame had so arranged that the sound of her dressing-door closing as women's doors do close when they are surprised, was to reach monsieur's ears. Then, at a corner of the piano, Fabien's hat, forgotten intentionally, was removed very awkwardly by a maid the moment after monsieur had entered the room.

"Did you go to the Ambigu, my little girl?"

"No, I changed my mind, and stayed at home to play music."

"Who came to see you?" asked the marquis, good-humoredly, seeing the hat carried off by the maid.

"No one."

At that audacious falsehood Arthur bowed his head; he passed beneath the Caudine forks of submission. A real love descends at times to these sublime meannesses. Arthur behaved with Madame Schontz as Sabine with Calyste, and Calyste with Beatrix.

Within a week the transition from larva to butterfly took place in the young, handsome, and clever Charles-Edouard, Comte Rusticoli de la Palferine. Until this moment of his life he had lived miserably, covering his deficits with an audacity equal to that of Danton. But he now paid his debts; he now, by advice of Maxime, had a little carriage; he was admitted to the Jockey Club and to the club of the rue de Gramont; he became supremely elegant, and he published in the "Journal des Debats" a novelette which won him in a few days a reputation which authors by profession obtain after years of toil and successes only; for there is nothing so usurping in Paris as that which ought to be ephemeral. Nathan, very certain that the count would never publish anything else, lauded the graceful and presuming young man so highly to Beatrix that she, spurred by the praise of the poet, expressed a strong desire to see this king of the vagabonds of good society.

"He will be all the more delighted to come here," replied Nathan, "because, as I happen to know, he has fallen in love with you to the point of committing all sorts of follies."

"But I am told he has already committed them."

"No, not all; he has not yet committed that of falling in love with a virtuous woman."

Some ten days after the scheme plotted on the boulevard between Maxime and his henchman, the seductive Charles-Edouard, the latter, to whom Nature had given, no doubt sarcastically, a face of charming melancholy, made his first irruption into the nest of the dove of the rue de Chartres, who took for his reception an evening when Calyste was obliged to go to a party with his wife.

If you should ever meet La Palferine you will understand perfectly the success obtained in a single evening by that sparkling mind, that animated fancy, especially if you take into consideration the admirable adroitness of the showman who consented to superintend this debut. Nathan was a good comrade, and he made the young count shine, as a jeweller showing off an ornament in hopes to sell it, makes the diamonds glitter. La Palferine was, discreetly, the first to withdraw; he left Nathan and the marquise together, relying on the collaboration of the celebrated author, which was admirable. Seeing that Beatrix was quite astounded, Raoul put fire into her heart by pretended reticences which stirred the fibres of a curiosity she did not know she possessed. Nathan hinted that La Palferine's wit was not so much the cause of his success with women as his superiority in the art of love; a statement which magnified the count immensely.

This is the place to record a new effect of that great law of contraries, which produces so many crises in the human heart and accounts for such varied eccentricities that we are forced to remember it sometimes as well as its counterpart, the law of similitudes. All courtesans preserve in the depths of their heart a perennial desire to recover their liberty; to this they would sacrifice everything. They feel this antithetical need with such intensity that it is rare to meet with one of these women who has not aspired several times to a return to virtue through love. They are not discouraged by the most cruel deceptions. On the other hand, women restrained by their education, by the station they occupy, chained by the rank of their families, living in the midst of opulence, and wearing a halo of virtue, are drawn at times, secretly be it understood, toward the tropical regions of love. These two natures of woman, so opposed to each other, have at the bottom of their hearts, the one that faint desire for virtue, the other that faint desire for libertinism which Jean-Jacques Rousseau was the first to have the courage to diagnose. In one, it is a last reflexion of the ray divine that is not extinct; in the other, it is the last remains of our primitive clay.

This claw of the beast was rapped, this hair of the devil was pulled by Nathan with extreme cleverness. The marquise began to ask herself seriously if, up to the present time, she had not been the dupe of her head, and whether her education was complete. Vice—what is it? Possibly only the desire to know everything.

CHAPTER XXVI.

DISILLUSIONS—IN ALL BUT LA FONTAINE'S FABLES

The next day Calyste seemed to Beatrix just what he was: a perfect and loyal gentleman without imagination or cleverness. In Paris, a man called clever must have spontaneous brilliancy, as the fountains have water; men of the world and Parisians in general are in that way very clever. But Calyste loved too deeply, he was too much absorbed in his own sentiments to perceive the change in Beatrix, and to satisfy her need by displaying new resources. To her, he seemed pale indeed, after the brilliancy of the night before, and he caused not the faintest emotion to the hungry Beatrix. A great love is a credit opened to a power so voracious that bankruptcy is sure to come sooner or later.

In spite of the fatigue of this day (the day when a woman is bored by a lover) Beatrix trembled with fear at the thought of a possible meeting between La Palferine and Calyste, a man of courage without assertion. She hesitated to see the count again; but the knot of her hesitation was cut by a decisive event.

Beatrix had taken the third of a box at the Opera, obscurely situated on the lower tier for the purpose of not being much in sight. For the last few days Calyste, grown bolder, had escorted the marquise to her box, placing himself behind her, and timing their arrival at a late hour so as to meet no one in the corridors. Beatrix, on these occasions, left the box alone before the end of the last act, and Calyste followed at a distance to watch over her, although old Antoine was always there to attend his mistress. Maxime and La Palferine had studied this strategy, which was prompted by respect for the proprieties, also by that desire for concealment which characterizes the idolators of the little god, and also, again, by the fear which oppresses all women who have been constellations in the world and whom love has caused to fall from their zodiacal eminence. Public humiliation is dreaded as an agony more cruel than death itself. But, by a manoeuvre of Maxime's, that blow to her pride, that outrage which women secure of their rank in Olympus cast upon others who have fallen from their midst, was now to descend on Beatrix.

At a performance of "Lucia," which ends, as every one knows, with one of the finest triumphs of Rubini, Madame de Rochefide, whom Antoine had not yet come to fetch, reached the peristyle of the opera-house by the lower corridor just as the staircase was crowded by fashionable women ranged on the stairs or standing in groups below it, awaiting the announcement of their carriages. Beatrix was instantly recognized; whispers which soon became a murmur arose in every group.

In a moment the crowd dispersed; the marquise was left alone like a leper. Calyste dared not, seeing his wife on the staircase, advance to accompany her, though twice she vainly cast him a tearful glance, a prayer, that he would come to her. At that moment, La Palferine, elegant, superb, charming, left two ladies with whom he had been talking, and came down to the marquise.

"Take my arm," he said, bowing, "and walk proudly out. I will find your carriage."

"Will you come home with me and finish the evening?" she answered, getting into her carriage and making room for him.

La Palferine said to his groom, "Follow the carriage of madame," and then he jumped into it beside her to the utter stupefaction of Calyste, who stood for a moment planted on his two legs as if they were lead. It was the sight of him standing thus, pale and livid, that caused Beatrix to make the sign to La Palferine to enter her carriage. Doves can be Robespierres in spite of their white wings. Three carriages reached the rue de Chartres with thundering rapidity,—that of Calyste, that of the marquise, and that of La Palferine.

"Oh! you here?" said Beatrix, entering her salon on the arm of the young count, and finding Calyste, whose horse had outstripped those of the other carriages.

"Then you know monsieur?" said Calyste, furiously.

"Monsieur le Comte de la Palferine was presented to me ten days ago by Nathan," she replied; "but you, monsieur, *you* have known me four years!—"

"And I am ready, madame," said Charles-Edouard, "to make the Marquise d'Espard repent to her third generation for being the first to turn away from you."

"Ah! it was *she*, was it?" cried Beatrix; "I will make her rue it."

"To revenge yourself thoroughly," said the young man in her ear, "you ought to recover your husband; and I am capable of bringing him back to you."

The conversation, thus begun, went on till two in the morning, without allowing Calyste, whose anger was again and again repressed by a look from Beatrix, to say one word to her in private. La Palferine, though he did not like Beatrix, showed a superiority of grace, good taste, and cleverness equal to the evident inferiority of Calyste, who wriggled in his chair like a worm cut in two, and actually rose three times as if to box the ears of La Palferine. The third time that he made a dart forward, the young count said to him, "Are you in pain, monsieur?" in a manner which sent Calyste back to his chair, where he sat as rigid as a mile-stone.

The marquise conversed with the ease of a Celimene, pretending to ignore that Calyste was there. La Palferine had the cleverness to depart after a brilliant witticism, leaving the two lovers to a quarrel.

Thus, by Maxime's machinations, the fire of discord flamed in the separate households of Monsieur and of Madame de Rochefide. The next day, learning the success of this last scene from La Palferine at the Jockey Club, where the young count was playing whist, Maxime went to the hotel Schontz to ascertain with what success Aurelie was rowing her boat.

"My dear," said Madame Schontz, laughing at Maxime's expression, "I am at an end of my expedients. Rochefide is incurable. I end my career of gallantry by perceiving that cleverness is a misfortune."

"Explain to me that remark."

"In the first place, my dear friend, I have kept Arthur for the last week to a regimen of kicks on the shin and perpetual wrangling and jarring; in short, all we have that is most disagreeable in our business. 'You are ill,' he says to me with paternal sweetness, 'for I have been good to you always and I love you to adoration.' 'You are to blame for one thing, my dear,' I answered; 'you bore me.' 'Well, if I do, haven't you the wittiest and handsomest young man in Paris to amuse you?' said the poor man. I was caught. I actually felt I loved him."

"Ah!" said Maxime.

"How could I help it? Feeling is stronger than we; one can't resist such things. So I changed pedals. I began to entice my judicial wild-boar, now turned like Arthur to a sheep; I gave him Arthur's sofa. Heavens! how he bored me. But, you understand, I had to have Fabien there to let Arthur surprise us."

"Well," cried Maxime, "go on; what happened? Was Arthur furious?"

"You know nothing about it, my old fellow. When Arthur came in and 'surprised' us, Fabien and me, he retreated on the tips of his toes to the dining-room, where he began to clear his throat, 'broum, broum!' and cough, and knock the chairs about. That great fool of a Fabien, to whom, of course, I can't explain the whole matter, was frightened. There, my dear Maxime, is the point we have reached."

Maxime nodded his head, and played for a few moments with his cane.

"I have known such natures," he said. "And the only way for you to do is to pitch Arthur out of the window and lock the door upon him. This is how you must manage it. Play that scene over again with Fabien; when Arthur surprises you, give Fabien a glance Arthur can't mistake; if he gets angry, that will end the matter; if he still says, 'broum, broum!' it is just as good; you can end it a better way."

"How?"

"Why, get angry, and say: 'I believed you loved me, respected me; but I see you've no feeling at all, not even jealousy,'—you know the tirade. 'In a case like this, Maxime' (bring me in) 'would kill his man on the spot' (then weep). 'And Fabien, he' (mortify him by comparing him with that fellow), 'Fabien whom I love, Fabien would have drawn a dagger and stabbed you to the heart. Ah, that's what it is to love! Farewell, monsieur; take back your house and all your property; I shall marry Fabien; *he* gives me his name; *he* marries me in spite of his old mother—but *you*—'"

"I see! I see!" cried Madame Schontz. "I'll be superb! Ah! Maxime, there will never be but one Maxime, just as there's only one de Marsay."

"La Palferine is better than I," replied the Comte de Trailles, modestly. "He'll make his mark."

"La Palferine has tongue, but you have fist and loins. What weights you've carried! what cuffs you've given!"

"La Palferine has all that, too; he is deep and he is educated, whereas I am ignorant," replied Maxime. "I have seen Rastignac, who has made an arrangement with the Keeper of the Seals. Fabien is to be appointed chief-justice at once, and officer of the Legion of honor after one year's service."

"I shall make myself *devote*," said Madame Schontz, accenting that speech in a manner which obtained a nod of approbation from Maxime.

"Priests can do more than even we," he replied sententiously.

"Ah! can they?" said Madame Schontz. "Then I may still find some one in the provinces fit to talk to. I've already begun my role. Fabien has written to his mother that grace has enlightened me; and he has fascinated the good woman with my million and the chief-justiceship. She consents that we shall live with her, and sends me her portrait, and wants mine. If Cupid looked at hers he would die on the spot. Come, go away, Maxime. I must put an end to my poor Arthur to-night, and it breaks my heart."

Two days later, as they met on the threshold of the Jockey Club, Charles-Edouard said to Maxime, "It is done."

The words, which contained a drama accomplished in part by vengeance, made Maxime smile.

"Now come in and listen to Rochefide bemoaning himself; for you and Aurelie have both touched goal together. Aurelie has just turned Arthur out of doors, and now it is our business to get him a home. He must give Madame du Ronceret three hundred thousand francs and take back his wife; you and I must prove to him that Beatrix is superior to Aurelie."

"We have ten days before us to do it in," said Charles-Edouard, "and in all conscience that's not too much."

"What will you do when the shell bursts?"

"A man has always mind enough, give him time to collect it; I'm superb at that sort of preparation."

The two conspirators entered the salon together, and found Rochefide aged by two years; he had not even put on his corset, his beard had sprouted, and all his elegance was gone.

"Well, my dear marquis?" said Maxime.

"Ah, my dear fellow, my life is wrecked."

Arthur talked for ten minutes, and Maxime listened gravely, thinking all the while of his own marriage, which was now to take place within a week.

"My dear Arthur," he replied at last; "I told you the only means I knew to keep Aurelie, but you wouldn't—"

"What was it?"

"Didn't I advise you to go and sup with Antonia?"

"Yes, you did. But how could I? I love, and you, you only make love—"

"Listen to me, Arthur; give Aurelie three hundred thousand francs for that little house, and I'll promise to find some one to suit you better. I'll talk to you about it later, for there's d'Ajuda making signs that he wants to speak to me."

And Maxime left the inconsolable man for the representative of a family in need of consolation.

"My dear fellow," said d'Ajuda in his ear, "the duchess is in despair. Calyste is having his trunks packed secretly, and he has taken out a passport. Sabine wants to follow them, surprise Beatrix, and maul her. She is pregnant, and it takes the turn of murderous ideas; she has actually and openly bought pistols."

"Tell the duchess that Madame de Rochefide will not leave Paris, but within a fortnight she will have left Calyste. Now, d'Ajuda, shake hands. Neither you nor I have ever said, or known, or done anything about this; we admire the chances of life, that's all."

"The duchess has already made me swear on the holy Gospels to hold my tongue."

"Will you receive my wife a month hence?"

"With pleasure."

"Then every one, all round, will be satisfied," said Maxime. "Only remind the duchess that she must make that journey to Italy with the du Guenics, and the sooner the better."

For ten days Calyste was made to bear the weight of an anger all the more invincible because it was in part the effect of a real passion. Beatrix now experienced the love so brutally but faithfully described to the Duchesse de Grandlieu by Maxime de Trailles. Perhaps no well-organized beings exist who do not experience that terrible passion once in the course of their lives. The marquise felt herself mastered by a superior force,—by a young man on whom her rank and quality did not impose, who, as noble as herself, regarded her with an eye both powerful and calm, and from whom her greatest feminine arts and efforts could with difficulty obtain even a smile of approval. In short, she was oppressed by a tyrant who never left her that she did not fall to weeping, bruised and wounded, yet believing herself to blame. Charles-Edouard played upon Madame de Rochefide the same comedy Madame de Rochefide had played on Calyste for the last six months.

Since her public humiliation at the Opera, Beatrix had never ceased to treat Monsieur du Guenic on the basis of the following proposition:—

"You have preferred your wife and the opinion of the world to me. If you wish to prove that you love me, sacrifice your wife and the world to me. Abandon Sabine, and let us live in Switzerland, Italy, or Germany."

Entrenched in that hard *ultimatum*, she established the blockade which women declare by frigid glances, disdainful gestures, and a certain fortress-like demeanor, if we may so call it. She thought herself delivered from Calyste, supposing that he would never dare to break openly with the Grandlieus. To desert Sabine, to whom Mademoiselle des Touches had left her fortune, would doom him to penury.

But Calyste, half-mad with despair, had secretly obtained a passport, and had written to his mother begging her to send him at once a considerable sum of money. While awaiting the arrival of these funds he set himself to watch Beatrix, consumed by the fury of Breton jealousy. At last, nine days after the communication made by La Palferine to Maxime at the club, Calyste, to whom his mother had forwarded thirty thousand francs, went to Madame de Rochefide's house with the firm intention of forcing the blockade, driving away La Palferine, and leaving Paris with his pacified angel. It was one of those horrible alternatives in which women who have hitherto retained some little respect for themselves plunge at once and forever into the degradations of vice, — though it is possible to return thence to virtue. Until this moment Madame de Rochefide had regarded herself as a virtuous woman in heart, upon whom two passions had fallen; but to adore Charles-Edouard and still let Calyste adore her, would be to lose her self-esteem, — for where deception begins, infamy begins. She had given rights to Calyste, and no human power could prevent the Breton from falling at her feet and watering them with the tears of an absolute repentance. Many persons are surprised at the glacial insensibility under which women extinguish their loves. But if they did not thus efface their past, their lives could have no dignity, they could never maintain themselves against the fatal familiarity to which they had once submitted. In the entirely new situation in which Beatrix found herself, she might have evaded the alternatives presented to her by Calyste had La Palferine entered the room; but the vigilance of her old footman, Antoine, defeated her.

Hearing a carriage stop before the door, she said to Calyste, "Here come visitors!" and she rushed forward to prevent a scene.

Antoine, however, as a prudent man, had told La Palferine that Madame la marquise was out.

When Beatrix heard from the old servant who had called and the answer he had given, she replied, "Very good," and returned to the salon, thinking: "I will escape into a convent; I will make myself a nun."

Calyste, meantime, had opened the window and seen his rival.

"Who came?" he said to Beatrix on her return.

"I don't know; Antoine is still below."

"It was La Palferine."

"Possibly."

"You love him, and that is why you are blaming and reproaching me; I saw him!"

"You saw him?"

"I opened the window."

Beatrix fell half fainting on the sofa. Then she negotiated in order to gain time; she asked to have the journey postponed for a week, under pretence of making preparations; inwardly resolving to turn Calyste off in a way that she could satisfy La Palferine,—for such are the wretched calculations and the fiery anguish concealed with these lives which have left the rails along which the great social train rolls on.

When Calyste had left her, Beatrix felt so wretched, so profoundly humiliated, that she went to bed; she was really ill; the violent struggle which wrung her heart seemed to reach a physical reaction, and she sent for the doctor; but at the same time she despatched to La Palferine the following letter, in which she revenged herself on Calyste with a sort of rage:—

To Monsieur le Comte de la Palferine.

My Friend,—Come and see me; I am in despair. Antoine sent you away when your arrival would have put an end to one of the most horrible nightmares of my life and delivered me from a man I hate, and whom I trust never to see again. I love you only in this world, and I can never again love any one but you, though I have the misfortune not to please you as I fain would—

She wrote four pages which, beginning thus, ended in an exaltation too poetic for typography, in which she compromised herself so completely that the letter closed with these words: "Am I sufficiently at your mercy? Ah! nothing will cost me anything if it only proves to you how much you are loved." And she signed the letter, a thing she had never done for Conti or Calyste.

The next day, at the hour when La Palferine called, Beatrix was in her bath, and Antoine begged him to wait. He, in his turn, saw Calyste sent away; for du Guenic, hungry for love, came early. La Palferine was standing at the window, watching his rival's departure, when Beatrix entered the salon.

"Ah! Charles," she cried, expecting what had happened, "you have ruined me!"

"I know it, madame," replied La Palferine, tranquilly. "You have sworn to love me alone; you have offered to give me a letter in which you will write your motives for destroying yourself, so that, in case of infidelity, I may poison you without fear of human justice,—as if superior men needed to have recourse to poison for revenge! You have written to me: 'Nothing will cost me anything if it only proves to you how much you are loved.' Well, after that, I find a contradiction between those words and your present remark that I have ruined you. I must know now if you have had the courage to break with du Guenic."

"Ah! you have your revenge upon him in advance," she cried, throwing her arms around his neck. "Henceforth, you and I are forever bound together."

"Madame," said the prince of Bohemia, coldly, "if you wish me for your friend, I consent; but on one condition only."

"Condition!" she exclaimed.

"Yes; the following condition. You must be reconciled to Monsieur de Rochefide; you must recover the honor of your position; you must return to your handsome house in the due d'Anjou and be once more one of the queens of Paris. You can do this by making Rochefide play a part in politics, and putting into your own conduct the persistency which Madame d'Espard has displayed. That is the situation necessary for the woman to whom I do the honor to give myself."

"But you forget that Monsieur de Rochefide's consent is necessary."

"Oh, my dear child," said La Palferine, "we have arranged all that; I have given my word of honor as a gentleman that you are worth all the Schontzes of the quartier Saint-Georges, and you must fulfil my pledge."

For the next week Calyste went every day to Madame de Rochefide's door, only to be refused by Antoine, who said with a studied face, "Madame is ill."

From there Calyste hurried to La Palferine's lodging, where the valet answered, "Monsieur le comte is away, hunting." Each time this happened the Breton baron left a letter for La Palferine.

On the ninth day Calyste received a line from La Palferine, making an appointment to receive him. He hurried to his lodgings and found the count, but in company with Maxime de Trailles, to whom the young *roue* no doubt wished to give proof of his *savoir-faire* by making him a witness of this scene.

"Monsieur le baron," began Charles-Edouard, tranquilly, "here are the six letters you have done me the honor to write to me. They are, as you see, safe and sound; they have not been unsealed. I knew in advance what they were likely to contain, having learned that you have been seeking me since the day when I looked at you from the window of a house from which you had looked at me on the previous day. I thought I had better ignore all mistaken provocations. Between ourselves, I am sure you have too much good taste to be angry with a woman for no longer loving you. It is always a bad means of recovering her to seek a quarrel with the one preferred. But, in the present case, your letters have a radical fault, a nullity, as the lawyers say. You have too much good sense, I am sure, to complain of a husband who takes back his wife. Monsieur de Rochefide has felt that the position of the marquise was undignified. You will, therefore, no longer find Madame de Rochefide in the rue de Chartres, but—six months hence, next winter—in the hotel de Rochefide. You flung yourself rather heedlessly into the midst of a reconciliation between husband and wife,—which you provoked yourself by not saving Madame de Rochefide from the humiliation to which she was subjected at the Opera. On coming away, the marquise, to whom I had already carried certain amicable proposals from her husband, took me up in her carriage, and her first words were, 'Bring Arthur back to me!'"

"Ah! yes," cried Calyste, "she was right; I was wanting in true devotion."

"Unhappily, monsieur, Rochefide was living with one of those atrocious women, Madame Schontz, who had long been expecting him to leave her. She had counted on Madame de Rochefide's failure in health, and expected some day to see herself marquise; finding her castles in the air thus scattered, she determined to revenge herself on husband and wife. Such women, monsieur, will put out one of their own eyes to put out two of their enemy. La Schontz, who has just left Paris, has put out six! If I had had the imprudence to love the marquise, Madame Schontz would have put out eight. You see now that you are in need of an oculist."

Maxime could not help smiling at the change that came over Calyste's face; which turned deadly pale as his eyes were opened to his situation.

"Would you believe, Monsieur le baron, that that unworthy woman has given her hand to the man who furnished the means for her revenge? Ah! these women! You can understand now why Arthur and his wife should have retired for a time to their delightful little country-house at Nogent-sur-Marne. They'll recover their eyesight there. During their stay in the country the hotel de Rochefide is to be renovated, and the marquise intends to display on her return a princely splendor. When a woman so noble, the victim of conjugal love, finds courage to return to her duty, the part of a man who adores her as you do, and admires her as I admire her, is to remain her friend although we can do nothing more. You will excuse me, I know, for having made Monsieur le Comte de Trailles a witness of this explanation; but I have been most anxious to make myself perfectly clear throughout. As for my own sentiments, I am, above all, desirous to say to you, that although I admire Madame de Rochefide for her intellect, she is supremely displeasing to me as a woman."

"And so end our noblest dreams, our celestial loves!" said Calyste, dumfounded by so many revelations and disillusionments.

"Yes, in the serpent's tail," said Maxime, "or, worse still, in the vial of an apothecary. I never knew a first love that did not end foolishly. Ah! Monsieur le baron, all that man has of the divine within him finds its food in heaven only. That is what justifies the lives of us *roues*. For myself, I have pondered this question deeply; and, as you know, I was married yesterday. I shall be faithful to my wife, and I advise you to return to Madame du Guenic,—but not for three months. Don't regret Beatrix; she is the model of a vain and empty nature, without strength, coquettish for self-glorification only, a Madame d'Espard without her profound political capacity, a woman without heart and without head, floundering in evil. Madame de Rochefide loves Madame de Rochefide only. She would have parted you from Madame du Guenic without the possibility of return, and then she would have left you in the lurch without remorse. In short, that woman is as incomplete for vice as she is for virtue."

"I don't agree with you, Maxime," said La Palferine. "I think she will make the most delightful mistress of a salon in all Paris."

Calyste went away, after shaking hands with Charles-Edouard and Maxime and thanking them for having pricked his illusions.

Three days later, the Duchesse de Grandlieu, who had not seen her daughter Sabine since the morning when this conference took place, went to the hotel du Guenic early in the day and found Calyste in his bath, with Sabine beside him working at some adornment for the future *layette*.

"What has happened to you, my children?" asked the excellent duchess.

"Nothing but good, dear mamma," replied Sabine, raising her eyes, radiant with happiness, to her mother; "we have been playing the fable of 'The Two Pigeons,' that is all."

Calyste held out his hand to his wife, and pressed hers so tenderly with a look so eloquent, that she said in a whisper to the duchess, —

"I am loved, mother, and forever!"

ADDENDUM

The following personages appear in other stories of the Human Comedy.

Ajuda-Pinto, Marquis Miguel d'
    Father Goriot
    Scenes from a Courtesan's Life
    The Secrets of a Princess

Bixiou, Jean-Jacques
    The Purse
    A Bachelor's Establishment
    The Government Clerks
    Modeste Mignon
    Scenes from a Courtesan's Life
    The Firm of Nucingen
    The Muse of the Department
    Cousin Betty
    The Member for Arcis
    A Man of Business
    Gaudissart II.
    The Unconscious Humorists
    Cousin Pons

Blondet (Judge)
    Jealousies of a Country Town

Brossette, Abbe
    The Peasantry

Cadine, Jenny
    Cousin Betty
    The Unconscious Humorists
    The Member for Arcis

Cambremer, Pierre
    A Seaside Tragedy

Canalis, Constant-Cyr-Melchior, Baron de
    Letters of Two Brides
    A Distinguished Provincial at Paris
    Modeste Mignon
    The Magic Skin
    Another Study of Woman

A Start in Life
The Unconscious Humorists
The Member for Arcis

Casteran, De
The Chouans
The Seamy Side of History
Jealousies of a Country Town
The Peasantry

Chocardelle, Mademoiselle
A Prince of Bohemia
A Man of Business
Cousin Betty
The Member for Arcis

Conti, Gennaro
Lost Illusions

Espard, Jeanne-Clementine-Athenais de Blamont-Chauvry, Marquise d'
The Commission in Lunacy
A Distinguished Provincial at Paris
Scenes from a Courtesan's Life
Letters of Two Brides
Another Study of Woman
The Gondreville Mystery
The Secrets of a Princess
A Daughter of Eve

Ferdinand
The Chouans

Gaillard, Theodore
A Distinguished Provincial at Paris
Scenes from a Courtesan's Life
The Unconscious Humorists

Gaillard, Madame Theodore
Jealousies of a Country Town
A Distinguished Provincial at Paris
A Bachelor's Establishment
Scenes from a Courtesan's Life
The Unconscious Humorists

Galathionne, Prince and Princess (both not in each story)
The Secrets of a Princess
The Middle Classes
Father Goriot
A Distinguished Provincial at Paris
A Daughter of Eve

Gerard, Francois-Pascal-Simon, Baron

A Daughter of Eve
The Muse of the Department
Cousin Betty
A Prince of Bohemia
A Man of Business
The Middle Classes
The Unconscious Humorists

Maufrigneuse, Georges de
The Secrets of a Princess
The Gondreville Mystery
The Member for Arcis

Maufrigneuse, Berthe de
The Gondreville Mystery
The Member for Arcis

Portenduere, Vicomte Savinien de
The Ball at Sceaux
Scenes from a Courtesan's Life
Ursule Mirouet

Portenduere, Vicomtesse Savinien de
Ursule Mirouet
Another Study of Woman

Rochefide, Marquis Arthur de
Cousin Betty

Rochefide, Marquise de
The Secrets of a Princess
A Daughter of Eve
Sarrasine
A Prince of Bohemia

Ronceret, Du
Jealousies of a Country Town

Ronceret, Fabien-Felicien du (or Duronceret)
Jealousies of a Country Town
Gaudissart II

Ronceret, Madame Fabien du
The Muse of the Department
Cousin Betty
The Unconscious Humorists

Simeuse, Admiral de
The Gondreville Mystery
Jealousies of a Country Town

Stidmann
Modeste Mignon

Lector House believes that a society develops through a two-fold approach of continuous learning and adaptation, which is derived from the study of classic literary works spread across the historic timeline of literature records. Therefore, we aim at reviving, repairing and redeveloping all those inaccessible or damaged but historically as well as culturally important literature across subjects so that the future generations may have an opportunity to study and learn from past works to embark upon a journey of creating a better future.

This book is a result of an effort made by Lector House towards making a contribution to the preservation and repair of original ancient works which might hold historical significance to the approach of continuous learning across subjects.

HAPPY READING & LEARNING!

LECTOR HOUSE LLP
E-MAIL: lectorpublishing@gmail.com